BLOODLINE

OF REDEMPTION

A THRILLER

BRIAN DICKINSON

FOCUSED
ASCENT

For Tony DiCenso

December 10, 1956 – February 16, 2018

and

Brian Gurr

June 1, 1963 – September 26, 1998

This story is shaped by your strength, your friendship, and your legacy.

Forever honored. Always remembered.

He reached down from on high and took hold of me; he drew me out of deep waters.

— Psalm 18:16 (NIV)

ALSO BY BRIAN DICKINSON

Blind Descent

Surviving Alone and Blind on Mount Everest

Calm in the Chaos

True Tales from Elite U.S. Navy Aviation Rescue Swimmers

PRAISE FOR BLOODLINE OF REDEMPTION

Few thrillers carry this much grit and authenticity. Dickinson writes with the authority of someone who has stared down impossible odds, and it shows in every chapter. Bloodline of Redemption is a bold, uncompromising story of loyalty, betrayal, and the fight to endure.

-Jack Carr, #1 New York Times Bestselling Author of Cry Havoc

Brian Dickinson has delivered a masterful thriller with Bloodline of Redemption. From the opening pages, you feel the tension of a Navy crew on the knife's edge of World War III—and then the story takes you deeper, far beyond the battlefield. This isn't just a novel about submarines and secret missions. It's a story about family, about the scars we inherit, and about the fight to overcome the demons of the past.

As someone who's lived through the brotherhood of special operations and knows the weight of carrying secrets, I can tell you this book captures both the adrenaline of the mission and the quiet battles that come after. If you want action, you'll find it here. If you want a generational story of resilience and redemption, you'll find that too. The bottom line—read this book. You won't be disappointed.

-Jason Redman, Former Navy SEAL (Ret.)
#1 NY Times Bestselling Author of The Trident and Overcome

Dickinson drops you into the cockpit and the kill zone, where split-second decisions and unflinching courage decide who lives, who dies, and who carries the weight of it forever.

-Brandon Webb, Former Navy SEAL
New York Times Bestselling Author

BLOODLINE

OF REDEMPTION

PROLOGUE

"Sonar contact, bearing zero-nine-three, range 1,600 yards. Contact increasing speed and altering course toward passive buoys," reported Antisubmarine Warfare Operator Petty Officer Second Class Brody Hayes, his voice taut with urgency as he relayed the information to his U.S. Navy SH-60F helicopter aircrew.

"Roger. Contact classification confidence level?" Lieutenant Commander (LCDR) Jerry Carter acknowledged, maintaining composure as he requested the details needed for relaying to the on standby Tactical Action Officer (TAO) waiting in the Anti-Submarine Warfare Module (ASMOD) on the aircraft carrier. These highly classified operations were part of the ship's Combat Information Center (CIC), which oversees the tactical picture based on the on scene ASW assets.

"High confidence, sir. Acoustic signatures match a Russian Oscar II nuclear submarine," Hayes shot back.

"I concur, Lieutenant Commander. This is a confirmed Russian sub," Chief Petty Officer (AWC) Phillip Bishop added with calm authority.

"Roger that. I'll inform the CIC and request instructions," Carter replied, his voice revealing slight unease.

A terse, minute-long conversation over a secure channel ensued between Captain William Boyd of the USS *Constellation* (CV-64) and Commander Carter. After confirming the data multiple times, Carter received his orders. A seasoned helicopter aircraft commander (HAC), he paused to absorb the weight of the moment before acknowledging the warship's captain. Pivoting slightly toward his co-pilot, he toggled the helicopter's internal communication system and relayed the command.

"Petty Officer Hayes, switch the sonar to passive mode. We're cleared to eliminate the target. Lieutenant Ellis, arm the Mark 46 torpedo and set the ceiling depth to 50 feet."

Hayes froze for an instant as the gravity of the order registered. "Roger that. Switching sonar to passive mode." He turned the acoustic sensor control knob counterclockwise to the *passive* setting. The sharp pings in his headset ceased, replaced by the soft hum of oceanic noise as the sonar dome began listening for underwater disturbances. The passive mode would now allow the team to monitor the torpedo's deployment and impact without interfering with the weapon's internal tracking and acquisition system.

"Mark 46 armed, ceiling depth set to 50 feet," confirmed Lieutenant Tayla Ellis, her hands trembling from a surge of adrenaline. She focused intensely on her task, steadying herself as she activated the weapon's arming system. An aircraft carrier's hull typically sits above 40 feet of depth, with other Navy ships operating even shallower due to their weight comparison. The depth setting was critical to avoid the torpedo mistaking a friendly ship for the target—a potentially catastrophic error.

"Dropping NOW, NOW, NOW!" Carter announced, his voice steady as he lifted the safety lever and pressed the ordnance release button. The BRU-14/A bomb rack released the Mark 46, and gravity took over. The torpedo plunged from 60 feet, its stabilizing parachute deploying before it entered the water at a precise 45-degree angle to prevent damage during deployment.

"Torpedo away! Splashdown confirmed," Bishop called out, peering through his night vision goggles (NVG). The Mark 46 entered the water flawlessly, ready to engage.

"I have sonar contact with the active torpedo. It's searching and acquiring the enemy sub!" Hayes reported, his voice steady despite the surge of adrenaline. It felt eerily like the training simulator back at NAS North Island, Coronado, California. The crew focused intensely on their roles: Hayes tracked the torpedo's progress, Bishop monitored tactical data on his multifunction display (MFD), Ellis held the hover, and Carter coordinated with the USS *Constellation* while plotting tactics.

"Sonar contact is increasing speed and turning hard to starboard. The sub is going evasive!" Hayes reported. "Contact bearing one-three-five, range 2,400 yards. Contact bearing one-four-zero, range 2,500 yards. Contact…" Hayes stopped abruptly, staring at his blank display. Frantic, he adjusted controls while Bishop mirrored his actions on the tactical display. They exchanged bewildered looks as Hayes shrugged.

"Hayes, what's going on?" Carter demanded; his usual calm tone sharpened by impatience. "I need an update for the captain!"

"Sir, we've lost sonar contact," Hayes admitted, his voice tight with disbelief. "The Russian sub is gone. So is the torpedo… but there's no impact. They just… vanished."

PART I

THE COVER UP

CHAPTER 1

July 7, 1997, 0200

USS Constellation CV-64 - U.S. Navy Aircraft Carrier

North Pacific Ocean

300 miles south of the Bering Sea

"NOW LAUNCH THE ALERT 30 HELO!" The air boss's order blared through the USS *Constellation*'s intercom, jolting awake half of the 5,000 sailors aboard the massive warship.

In the ship's classified Anti-Submarine Warfare Module (AS-MOD)—an intelligence hub coordinating antisubmarine operations—a senior officer was already on the phone with LTJG Bryan Winston, the officer on duty assigned to Carrier Air Wing 2's helicopter squadron, HS-2. Meanwhile, the officer gestured urgently to the enlisted duty petty officer, Petty Officer Benjamin Smith, signaling him to wake the alert crewmen.

"Hayes, get up! You and Chief Bishop are launching!" Smith shook Brody Hayes awake in his six-by-three-foot coffin of a bunk–cramped and unforgiving. Startled by the abrupt 0200 wake-up call, Hayes shot upright, only to smack his head on the underside of the top rack. The loud bang and ensuing string of F-bombs didn't even stir the snoring aircrewman in the bunk directly above.

The aircrew rescue swimmer berthing was tucked away near the edge of the carrier's angled deck, directly beneath the roaring end of the catapults. After five months of deployment, they had grown accustomed to sleeping through the thunderous roar of fighter jets launching at all hours with full afterburners just above their heads.

"What the hell?" Hayes muttered, disoriented as his consciousness slowly sharpened. Just moments ago, he had been deep in an REM dream state, relaxing with his family on Scripps Beach in La Jolla, California—thousands of miles from his actual location. Anger flared within him at the abrupt disturbance, but it quickly transformed into laser-focused determination. Hayes and his aircrew teammates were accustomed to being launched at all hours, often for false alarms on search-and-rescue missions. Yet, every launch was treated with the utmost seriousness, as any mission could be a matter of life and death.

As an Aviation Rescue Swimmer, Hayes had undergone over two years of intense training to prepare for water and land rescues, combat search and rescue, MEDEVACs, aerial gunnery, antisubmarine warfare, logistics, vertical replenishment, and virtually any mission the helicopter was called to support. They were the quintessential special operations "jacks of all trades," with no margin for complacency or error.

"I don't know what's going on, but you're launching now! The AOs are loading HUNTER 613, and the rest of the crew is heading to the PR shop!" Smith relayed the basic information, just enough to point Hayes in the right direction.

The parachute rigger (PR) shop was where pilots and aircrew stored and prepared their flight gear. It's also where they suited up before missions. The PRs are responsible for maintaining the flight and survival gear, ensuring that everything is available, functional, and mission ready.

Hayes rolled out of his rack and quickly pulled on his flight suit and boots, which he had staged neatly beside his bunk. Navigating the narrow aisle between rows of bunks stacked three high, he made his way to the berthing door. He pulled it open and crossed the five-foot-wide hallway bordered by four doors, one of which led to the ready room. The ready room, where crews typically gathered to brief and review the flight plan two hours before takeoff, was empty. Since they were on alert status, the team had already pre-briefed the night before. Hayes sprinted through the ready room, the freshly waxed blue floor reflecting the overhead lights, and exited through the back door. From there, he crossed into the PR shop.

The alert crew quickly transitioned from groggy to mission ready. Sporting intense bed hair and morning breath, they systematically moved to their individual cages to gather flight and survival gear, along with night vision goggles and extra battery packs. No one knew the exact reason for the zero-dark-thirty launch, but the assumption was either a man overboard or some other type of rescue mission.

LCDR Jerry Carter, the helicopter aircraft commander (HAC), was receiving a brief from LTJG Winston as he zipped and strapped on his SV-2 flight survival vest. Chief Petty Officer Phil Bishop, the designated crew chief, tried to catch the details of the briefing but only managed bits and pieces as he focused on gathering supplies to carry topside. Among the gear Bishop grabbed was a collapsed rescue litter encased in its distinctive orange fabric, designed with backpack straps to ease the transfer from below deck to the flight deck.

Carter and Bishop signaled they were heading up and made their way to the ship's pitch-black catwalk. Using right-angle flashlights attached to their SV-2 vests, they illuminated the narrow, non-skid pathway. The waves crashed against the carrier's side as they staggered slightly, struggling to maintain a straight line in the dark. A metal staircase led them to a catwalk just below the flight deck. From there, they climbed another set of steps to the waiting SH-60F helicopter. It was surrounded by the squadron's plane captain, maintenance crew, ordnance handlers, and safety personnel, all working with practiced urgency.

LT Tayla Ellis slid her arms through the SV-2 shoulder straps, zipped the front, and secured the leg webbing hooks to the front waist buckle. She retrieved a pair of NVGs from a bin, attaching the NVG battery pack to a Velcro strip on the back of her helmet.

Meanwhile, Aviation Warfare Systems Operator Second Class Petty Officer (AW2) Hayes unzipped his flight suit and let it drop to his waist, pulling on the sleeves of his shorty wetsuit top and zipping it up the front. He wrestled with the tangled webbing and stubborn Velcro closures of his rescue harness before zipping his flight suit back over the top layer of his gear. He then placed his SAR-1 flotation device over his neck and secured its webbing strap around his waist. Lieutenant Ellis grabbed her small flight bag, while Hayes shouldered his 50-pound SAR pack, flight bag, NVGs, and helmet as they headed out the door. They moved swiftly but safely toward the helicopter, which was chalked and chained to the flight deck's padeyes on Spot 4 near the waist catapults.

Commander Carter was already running through the pre-flight checklist, preparing the SH-60F helicopter for spin-up, when Lieutenant Ellis climbed into the co-pilot seat. Plugging her helmet cord into the internal communication system (ICS), she began her checklist with practiced precision, as she had done countless times over the past five and a half months of deployment. The pilots operated with unwavering focus and consistency, their procedures automatic and unaffected by the specifics of the mission they were about to undertake. Aviation safety protocols demanded strict adherence, and they executed them with the same discipline for every launch, no matter the mission set.

Hayes walked around the front of the SH-60F Seahawk helicopter, conducting a visual inspection of its critical components. Each aircrew member, along with the maintenance teams, meticulously checked and rechecked the systems and parts to ensure everything was cleared for operation. The engines roared to life, whining as they drew power from the connected external units and the pilots continued their checklists. As Hayes rounded the nose of the aircraft, something caught his eye. The Aviation Ordnance (AO) team, clad in their standard red safety vests, were mounting and arming a Mark 46 torpedo on the starboard weapons pylon. A jolt of adrenaline surged through him as the gravity of their mission shifted. This wasn't just another routine rescue—something far more serious was unfolding.

Aviation Warfare Systems Operator Chief Petty Officer Bishop was in the helicopter cabin, arming a mix of passive and active sonobuoys in the forward chutes. The process was decidedly old-school, requiring each buoy to be prepped manually, almost like setting a mousetrap. Bishop pinned down the deployment rod of each buoy with a retracting chute sleeve, readying it for action. Once deployed—either remotely by the pilots or manually by the aircrew—the sonobuoy would drop from the chute, releasing a small parachute to control its descent. Upon hitting the water, a saltwater-activated mechanism triggered, opening the bottom of the buoy to deploy hundreds of feet of hydrophones. These hydrophones transmitted acoustic data over a specific frequency via an erected antenna that extended from the buoy's surfaced portion. After a preset duration or manual command, the sonobuoys were scuttled, sinking into the depths and ending their mission.

Chief Bishop multitasked with precision, arming the sonobuoys, testing the rescue hoist operations, and managing his Tactical Systems Operations (TSO) gear—all while listening intently to the mission update coming through the internal communications channel with the pilots. Hayes tossed his SAR bag into the back corner near the AQS-13F dipping sonar system and climbed past Bishop to the Acoustic Systems Operator (ASO) seat. Securing himself with the 5-point harness, he plugged in his helmet's ICS cord, switched to communications channel one, and began listening to the mission details. As he performed tests and system checks on the ASO equipment and sonar, he was stunned by the information coming through the comms. He could hardly believe what he was hearing.

Chief Bishop noticed the confused look on Hayes's face and gestured by tapping his helmet and holding up two fingers. Hayes immediately understood and switched to communication channel two for a private conversation without interrupting the pilots.

"Chief, what the hell is going on?" Hayes asked, his voice tinged with dazed concern and confusion.

"Not exactly sure," Bishop replied calmly. "The Air Boss said we're investigating a suspected underwater threat. We'll get a full briefing once we're in the air. For now, focus on your sonar checklist and make sure everything's operational. I'll handle plotting the coordinates and sonobuoy pattern on the MFD." Chief Bishop's calm and confident tone made it seem like just another training flight, despite the growing tension.

After completing the pre-flight checklists and receiving confirmation from the tower, Carter released the rotor brake, bringing the main rotors to life. The blades began their slow, deliberate rotation, causing the aircraft to rock slightly while secured to the deck with chalks and chains. As the rotors gained momentum, the blades churned violently, shaking the helicopter in place, their ferocious spinning producing ear-piercing screams that blended with the deafening roar of the twin turboshaft engines, a sound destined to leave the crew with permanent hearing loss.

Just outside the deadly rotor arc, the plane captain stood with lit signal wands, directing the Aviation Ordnancemen (AO) to approach from the three o'clock position. The AOs removed the safety pins and covers from the 500-pound polymer-bonded explosive torpedo mounted on the starboard pylon. Once the torpedo was armed, the aircraft maintenance crew quickly removed the chalks and chains. The plane captain signaled with his wands that all personnel were clear, indicating readiness for takeoff.

Commander Carter pulled up on the collective control with his left hand, lifting the SH-60F into a controlled hover. He conducted a quick check of all gauges before pushing the cyclic control forward and left, transitioning the helicopter smoothly into forward flight. As the Seahawk climbed to 500 feet, turned left, veering to the port side of the carrier, Lieutenant Ellis entered the destination longitude and latitude coordinates provided by the Air Boss.

The SH-60F, optimized for night operations, was nearly invisible in the pitch-black, moonless sky. The crew wore NVGs, and only an occasional strobe from the tail rotor broke the darkness. On the flight deck, the crew watched the Seahawk vanish into the horizon, while the ship's Combat Information Center (CIC) and Anti-Submarine Warfare Module (ASMOD) tracked its progress via radar and radio communications. The flight deck, moments ago a storm of noise and motion, now stood eerily still as the ASW helicopter disappeared into the night, en route to investigate the looming threat.

CHAPTER 2

4 days prior

Kremlin Moscow, Russia

"Mr. President, we have an urgent situation developing. We need to brief you immediately."

Mikhail Popov, the Russian Chief of General Staff, burst into the office, interrupting President Boris Novikov as he reviewed a classified energy report at his polished mahogany desk, which overlooked the summer crowds in Red Square.

President Novikov barely looked up, unfazed by Popov's characteristic sense of urgency. He was well-acquainted with the General's habit of overdramatizing crises and had little patience for it. Still, replacing incompetent staff wasn't an option this close to the legislative elections.

Popov, however, was at the top of Novikov's list of officials to dismiss in the coming year, particularly after the recent military debacle that dominated major news outlets through December. The scandal, the largest data breach in the five years since the Soviet Union's dissolution in 1991, had been an embarrassment of historic proportions. President Novikov held Popov personally accountable for the disaster and intended to ensure he took the fall, just not until

Novikov himself was safely insulated from any political repercussions.

Novikov's irritation deepened as he wiped sweat from his weathered, pockmarked face. Moscow was in the grip of a relentless summer heat wave, bringing drought and unusually early forest fires. Dense smoke from the Saltykovsky Forest choked the capital, and to make matters worse, the Kremlin was battling issues with its air filtration and cooling systems.

"What's the issue, General?" Novikov asked sharply, his voice edged with frustration.

"We've lost contact with one of our Northern Fleet submarines," Popov replied, his voice unsteady as he avoided meeting the president's gaze.

"That's not uncommon," Novikov shot back, narrowing his eyes. "But I'm guessing there's more?" His patience, already worn thin by the oppressive heat and mounting problems, was quickly evaporating.

"The *Medved*—Project 949A Oscar II-class, commanded by Kapitan Yaroslav Vasiliev…."

"How did this happen? Full sitrep? And don't leave out any details!" President Novikov snapped, cutting Popov off mid-sentence. He had no patience for the General's slow, calculated drip of information.

Novikov had always been a straight-to-the-point leader, a trait that had propelled him to the top. He prided himself on transparency, even when it meant ending careers over bad decisions. More often than not, those poor choices stemmed from his own orders. That was precisely why Novikov kept a cadre of scapegoats close, ready to deflect blame and absorb accountability when needed. The Russian President had always governed with a blend of fear and militaristic authority. For those on his good side, the rewards included long and lucrative careers in politics. But crossing Novikov could end a career—or a life—in an instant.

"Of course, Mr. President. The *Medved* departed its base in Gremikha precisely ten days ago. Kapitan Vasiliev was authorized to operate in the Navarin Canyon with a minimal payload," Popov spewed out, his words spilling over each other in his effort to preempt another interruption.

"Authorized by whom? And what exactly is a minimal payload?" President Novikov barked, his face flushed and dripping with sweat. Spittle sprayed from the corner of his dry lips as his temper flared. He was enraged, searching for accountability, knowing this escalating situation would once again drag his motherland into the world's unforgiving spotlight under his leadership. He needed to contain the fallout, both in reality and in the press, and find someone or something to blame.

"The *Medved* is carrying ten ballistic missiles equipped with nuclear warheads," Popov answered, meeting Novikov's blazing glare. He knew what such news would provoke, and the weight of the revelation was unbearable. The General also knew too well what his ruthless leader was capable of as he had personally executed Novikov's orders to make people disappear for less. Now, as the messenger of disastrous news, Popov felt an overwhelming emptiness and dread.

"My God! And how long has the *Medved* been out of contact?" Novikov demanded, his eyes burning with fury as they bore into Popov's visibly shaken demeanor.

"Five days," the General croaked, his voice barely audible.

"And I'm just hearing about this now?!" Novikov erupted, springing from his leather desk chair with such force that it toppled backward, crashing against the wall. His fist slammed down on a scattered pile of papers littering his desk, the sound reverberating through the room. He stood there, chest heaving, sweat soaking through his dress shirt beneath his suit jacket.

He paused, drawing a long, deliberate breath to steady his pulse.

"I'll deal with you later, General," he said in a low, menacing tone. "Right now, I need to speak to the President of the United States. I don't know what Vasiliev is up to, but I'm not willing to risk the next world war over his—or *your*—incompetence!"

CHAPTER 3

U.S. Navy SH-60F Seahawk Helicopter

Callsign - HUNTER 613

North Pacific Ocean

"Lieutenant Ellis, set course zero-four-zero for fifteen miles. Petty Officer Hayes, a P-3 has already scattered a pattern of buoys ahead. Tune in to their frequencies ASAP and see if you can get a hit on the boomer. Chief Bishop, configure a passive buoy pattern as soon as you've got the system data," Commander Carter ordered, his tone calm but focused as the crew prepared for real-world antisubmarine warfare.

LCDR Reggie Watson from the USS *Constellation*'s ASMOD connected over a secure radio channel, his voice cutting crisply through the static as he briefed the crew en route to their target location. This mission carried weight, as orders came directly from the President of the United States, seated 4,000 miles away in the White House Situation Room alongside his national security team.

The President had been alerted to the rogue Russian submarine, the *Medved*, four days earlier. Intelligence teams had been mobilized to monitor the situation using every available asset. Satellite imagery had last captured the *Medved* ten days ago, departing its base in Gremikha. The submarine's captain, a seasoned veteran, had a reputation for evading detection. He and his 130-man crew—consisting of 44 officers and 68 enlisted sailors—knew the Navarin Canyon's intricate seabed and its layered waters better than most. Operating with precision, they skillfully exploited the region's unique acoustic environment to slip past the U.S. Navy's underwater hydrophone network, the Sound Surveillance System (SOSUS), deployed across the Pacific Ocean floor.

The senior officers of Carrier Air Wing 2 and the ASMOD (Anti-Submarine Warfare Module) had been briefed on the missing *Medved* days earlier by the White House, as the Pentagon scrambled to gather intelligence. While there was no credible evidence to suggest the Russian submarine posed an imminent threat to the United States, there was equally no reason to dismiss it as harmless. This delicate ambiguity demanded a careful balance—closely monitoring the situation without inciting widespread panic.

Two days prior, they had authorized a pair of P-3C Orions, stationed at NAS Whidbey Island in Washington State, to patrol the potential routes Kapitan Vasiliev might take if his submarine attempted to penetrate the western waters of Canada and the United States. The Orions deployed sonobuoys in tactical patterns across the region, methodically scouring the projected path with listening devices. Flying sweeping grids that spanned hundreds of miles, the aircraft relied heavily on their magnetic anomaly detection (MAD) systems. The MAD boom, mounted on the extended tail of the fixed-wing aircraft, was designed to detect magnetic distortions in the Earth's field—an indicator of a submarine's presence.

For hours, the crew meticulously analyzed data as they combed the vast expanse of open ocean. Yet, despite their efforts, finding a submarine in these conditions was akin to finding a needle in a haystack. Each sweep yielded nothing but silence. It wasn't until late on the second evening that an enlisted ASW crewman monitoring a passive sonobuoy pattern spotted something unusual. The sonogram displayed a faint but distinct sound signature—one that didn't belong in the natural underwater symphony. His pulse quickened as he flagged the data for verification, knowing it could be the first clue in the hunt for the *Medved*.

"Course zero-four-zero set. Hayes, any update on those P-3 sonobuoys? Chief Bishop, report on sonobuoy and pattern readiness," Lieutenant Ellis said, her voice tight with focus as she keyed coordinates into the communication control panel.

"Roger, sonobuoys are set in launchers one through six," Chief Bishop replied, his tone calm but efficient. "I've added a P2 passive pattern into my MFD. You should see it on your screen now." He double-checked the AN/SSQ-53 sonobuoys, each three feet long, ensuring they were secure in the sleeves of the launchers and physically staged for deployment.

The extreme vibrations of the SH-60F Seahawk helicopter in transit were notorious for causing the sleeves to shift, sometimes dislodging the metal rod that kept the parachute mechanism in place. The last thing anyone wanted was a sonobuoy's parachute deploying inside the cabin during a critical ASW mission. Chief Bishop's vigilance was born of experience, having learned this lesson the hard way on a flight earlier in his career.

Lieutenant Ellis validated the sonobuoy pattern on her multifunction display (MFD) unit, then selected SONO LAUNCH MODE: AUTO. A ready light illuminated, indicating the sonobuoys were programmed to deploy automatically, one by one, as the helicopter passed over the fly-to points entered in the MFD.

"Roger, P2 pattern confirmed," Ellis said, her voice steady over the comms. "Commander Carter, come two degrees left and prepare to drop the first buoy on my signal."

The SH-60F Seahawk adjusted its course slightly, the ferocious pounding of its rotors filling the cabin as the crew prepared for launch.

"Buoy deploying," Ellis called out. "NOW. NOW. NOW."

"Buoy away," Chief Bishop confirmed, his voice calm but focused. Through the green-tinted lens of his night vision goggles, he watched as the number one gravity-fed launcher released the 20-pound sonobuoy.

Flying at 100 feet and 100 knots, the SH-60F's launcher trapdoor opened, allowing the device to slide out into the pitch-black night. As soon as it cleared the helicopter, the mousetrap mechanism sprung open, deploying the parachute. The chute slowed the sonobuoy's descent and, more critically, stabilized its entry into the water. A sideways impact could easily damage the fragile omnidirectional microphones, sensors, and radios housed inside the tube, rendering the device useless.

"Roger that. Come left 20 degrees and prepare for the second buoy drop," Lieutenant Ellis instructed, her tone precise and steady. Systematically, she called out the pattern, confirming each sonobuoy deployment with the assistance of her aircrew.

Chief Bishop twisted the center buckle of his five-point harness, releasing himself from his seat. Securing a gunner's belt around his chest to allow freedom of movement while maintaining safety, he got to work. Moving efficiently in the dimly lit cabin, he began refilling the launchers with six more sonobuoys, ensuring the devices were properly seated, armed, and ready for the next phase of the mission.

Meanwhile, the P-3 Orion maintained its orbit at 20,000 feet, flying wide circles while monitoring a network of deployed sonobuoys. Constant communication with HUNTER 613 ensured that additional buoys were not inadvertently dropped in the path of the low-flying helicopter.

Chief Bishop adjusted the P2 passive pattern using data analytics relayed from the Orion overhead. Intermittent anomalies had been detected through the sonobuoys, prompting the continued deployment of additional buoys to maintain contact. HUNTER 613 positioned itself to create a passive acoustic trap, preparing to engage its active sonar to drive the Russian submarine toward the detection zone.

"Pilot, aft. I've got positive radios on our buoys. I'm also picking up the P-3 sonobuoys. No contacts," Hayes reported, his focus locked on the spinning clockwise dial of his graphical display as he monitored the frequencies, watching and listening for any potential response.

Commander Carter adjusted the helicopter into the wind, preparing for a hover. The front of the SH-60F flared slightly upward as the intense vibrations from the main rotors shook everything inside the cabin. Chief Bishop kept a sharp eye on the sonobuoy chutes while scanning the night horizon out the starboard door window through his NVGs. The frequent flashes of the helicopter's strobe light lit up his green-tinted view of the dark sky. Hayes, peering out his port-side window, performed a similar scan to avoid becoming disoriented with vertigo.

"Hover engaged. Sonar, down dome," Commander Carter commanded, signaling to Hayes that the helicopter was stable and sonar operations could begin.

"Roger, down dome," Hayes acknowledged, pressing the down toggle to deploy the sonar. He swiveled his head back and forth, monitoring both the acoustic sensor operator gauges and the physical sonar drum spinning rapidly as it paid out hundreds of feet of cable.

The AQS-13F dipping sonar descended into the black ocean, the cable unwinding from its spool at maximum speed. Hayes took an ocean temperature reading as the sonar reached its maximum depth, data that Chief Bishop immediately began analyzing on his systems. Bishop was working to identify the submarine's likely tactical operating areas while ensuring HUNTER 613 remained undetected. His calculations factored in how sound traveled through the ocean, influenced by variables like temperature, salinity, and pressure.

Petty Officer Hayes then raised the sonar dome back to the thermal layer—a thermocline separating the surface and mixed layers. He reached forward, his gloved hand gripping the sonar control knob, and switched from passive to active mode.

PING!

A faint green blip appeared on the top quadrant of his screen, drawing his attention immediately. "Sonar contact!" Hayes called out. "Bearing zero-nine-three at 1,600 yards!"

CHAPTER 4

Russian Navy K-151 Medved

Oscar-class Submarine

North Pacific Ocean

"Kapitan, we've detected a United States *Kitty Hawk*-class aircraft carrier at three-three-five degrees, distance ten kilometers," announced Boris Petrov, a wide-eyed sonar technician with greasy hair flattened beneath his audio headset. He turned to face Kapitan Yaroslav Vasiliev with a tense expression.

The Kapitan swiveled in his black leather chair, slightly elevated above the crew on the *Medved*'s bridge. Normally calm and confident, his steady demeanor had always made him an easy leader to follow into any military conflict. However, this deployment had brought a noticeable shift in his behavior. He seemed unusually eager, his temper sharper, his actions more abrupt. Rarely absent from the bridge, he showed clear signs of sleep deprivation and malnutrition. His uncharacteristic micromanagement of the crew added to the growing apprehension aboard the submarine.

"Roger that," Vasiliev replied, his voice clipped. "What about the American carrier battle group assets?"

"Yes, Kapitan. We're also tracking an *Arleigh Burke*-class destroyer at three-three-two, distance ten kilometers, and a *Ticonderoga-*

class guided missile cruiser at three-three-seven, distance twelve kilometers. All American warships have increased speed to 20 knots and are adjusting their heading due east," Petrov reported, his voice steady despite the beads of sweat running from his forehead, along his close-shaved chin, and dripping onto the faded keys of his analytics keyboard. His eyes remained locked on the circling graphic displayed on his sonar screen.

Every sailor aboard the *Medved* played a critical role in ensuring the safety and success of the clandestine mission, but Petrov felt an especially heavy weight of responsibility. Though he was a highly competent operator, he was keenly aware that even a single mistake on his part could mean the difference between life and death for every man confined within the submarine's steel hull.

Operating in darkness was part of life as a submariner, but this mission felt particularly opaque. The crew had been provided with limited information. What they did know was that Kapitan Vasiliev and his senior officers were executing direct orders in response to what was described as an imminent threat from the United States. Their mission was to navigate along the North American coast without detection, awaiting further instructions somewhere in the Pacific Northwest's coastal waters.

"What about American submarines?" Kapitan Vasiliev demanded, his voice sharp. "A United States aircraft carrier does not operate without at least one submarine present! Has the *Topeka* left Osaka?"

Though his intelligence was only hours old, Vasiliev insisted on constant SITREPs—situation reports—to ensure he had the most current and pertinent data. For a mission as critical and likely one-way as this, staying ahead of any potential threats was his only chance of success.

"Kapitan, the *Los Angeles*-class attack submarine *USS Topeka*, which pulled into Osaka two days ago with the battle group, still remains in port according to current satellite intelligence," the sonar technician reported. The information had just been relayed through Moscow via satellite, transmitted as encrypted electromagnetic wave feeds to the submerged *Medved*'s antennas.

Petrov, ever cautious, double-checked the data with other radio crewmembers to ensure their leader received the most accurate update. If anything were to go wrong, he was determined to make sure it wouldn't be his fault.

"Sir," Petrov continued, his voice tinged with unease, "the American P-3 Orions have been deploying additional sonobuoys and have increased their search patterns. We have evaded detection so far, but it appears they are aware of our presence near American waters."

"Excellent. Continue silent running on course," Kapitan Vasiliev ordered, his voice low and resolute. "Avoid any maneuvers that could expose us to the enemy's passive sonobuoys. The last thing we need is to be intercepted when we're this close." His grim expression, paired with the tension in his tar-stained teeth, suggested there was more to their situation than he had shared. The weight of unspoken information seemed to linger in his words, hinting at a secret he kept tightly guarded. The phrase "this close" stirred quiet curiosity among the crew. Glances were exchanged, questions unspoken, but the officers and enlisted men quickly returned to their respective tasks, suppressing their unease as they focused on their critical roles.

"Roger. Continuing silent running, course zero-one-five at 10 knots. Holding depth at 100 meters," the *Medved*'s helmsman confirmed. The Russian submarine glided silently through the thermal layer, heading steadily toward North America's west coast. Their course would allow the U.S. battlegroup to continue its trajectory at three-three-five toward Puget Sound, while the *Medved* edged north, slipping further out of detection range.

Thus far, Kapitan Vasiliev had successfully evaded SOSUS and the P-3 Orions' acoustic detection systems. To him, the Americans were proving to be even more incompetent than he had anticipated. With all their grandiose claims of being the world's dominant superpower, their failure to detect his submarine only fueled his determination. He clenched his jaw, his mind set on fulfilling his orders—orders that, if successful, would challenge the very perception of American supremacy on the world stage.

Vasiliev had been handpicked for the Special Access Program due to his proven ability to follow and execute questionable orders without hesitation or question. His methods were rarely conventional, but his loyalty and discretion had been tested time and again. While others faltered under the weight of state secrets, Vasiliev had carried his burdens to the grave—sometimes sending others there as well.

The seasoned Kapitan believed he was destined to make his motherland proud and secure a legacy for his wife and unborn child. This legacy, he envisioned, would catapult him into a lucrative political career, granting him wealth and power beyond imagination. This mission, concealed even from the Russian President, was set to define him. Every blemish on his military record, every bridge burned in his ruthless climb to command, would pale in comparison to his success here. Vasiliev's efficiency and cold precision would cement his name in history as the architect of the greatest preemptive strike against the United States—a feat his own father had failed to achieve during the height of the Cold War.

Sonar Technician Petrov's urgent voice shattered Kapitan Vasiliev's moment of triumphant reflection. "Kapitan! Helicopter rotors detected—closing in fast! Acoustic pattern matches an American Sikorsky SH-60 Seahawk with antisubmarine capabilities!"

CHAPTER 5

U.S. Navy SH-60F Seahawk Helicopter
Callsign HUNTER 613
North Pacific Ocean

Moments after HUNTER 613 lost sonar contact, Petty Officer Hayes and Chief Bishop stared intently at the Acoustic Sensor Operator's sonar screen, eyes frozen in anticipation, waiting for a blip—any sign of contact. An active MK-46 torpedo was in the water, hunting a Russian submarine, but the sonar had gone alarmingly silent.

Without hesitation, both men shifted into troubleshooting mode, their movements precise and automatic. Hayes quickly checked and reset the fuses before power cycling the sonar system, hands steady despite the mounting stress. Meanwhile, Chief Bishop conducted a visual inspection of the gear, ensuring everything was physically intact, before cycling his Tactical Sensor Operator systems. They worked with practiced efficiency, their focus unbroken by the mission's high stakes. But despite their efforts, the sonar screen remained blank. Neither the *Medved* nor the torpedo registered—leaving the crew in a chilling void of uncertainty.

"Hayes, what's going on? What's your status?" Commander Carter demanded impatiently, his voice cutting through the cabin's tension. He needed an update to relay to the ASMOD aboard the USS *Constellation*.

"Sir, we've lost sonar contact," Hayes admitted reluctantly, tone edged with frustration. "The sub is gone. The torpedo is gone. But we didn't hear an impact. They both just… vanished."

Hayes continued troubleshooting, fingers moving swiftly over the controls. He lowered and raised the sonar dome, testing different depths and sound responses through the ocean's stratified layers. Each attempt yielded the same result—nothing.

"No joy," he muttered under his breath, eyes fixed on the blank display, the weight of the mission pressing heavily on his shoulders.

"What do you mean you lost contact, Petty Officer Hayes?" Commander Carter pressed, his usual confidence faltering. Doubt crept into his voice as he repeated the question, this time with higher-pitched urgency. His eyes scanned the dark horizon through the green glow of his night vision goggles, searching for answers that weren't there.

Lieutenant Ellis remained silent, her hands fumbling with her multifunction display, as if sheer determination could resolve the situation. The mood in the cabin was palpable.

"Sir," Hayes replied, voice tight with respectful frustration, "the sonar isn't picking up any sounds. Nothing from the Russian submarine or the MK-46 torpedo."

"I concur, sir. Everything went silent," Chief Bishop added, backing up his junior crewman.

Commander Carter trusted the chief's judgment, but the lack of answers gnawed at him. His career wasn't his primary concern anymore; what weighed heavily was the possibility that they had just lost track of a Russian nuclear submarine south of the Aleutians.

They had dropped an active torpedo to neutralize the threat. The submarine had gone evasive—and now, complete silence. The questions burned in his mind.

Had they provoked Russia into retaliating? Could this be the spark that ignited World War III?

"Did you hear an explosion or anything to indicate a torpedo hit?" Carter asked, though he already knew the answer. Still, he needed reassurance—confirmation of what his sweat-slick helmet earphones were telling him.

"Nothing, sir," Hayes replied, steady under pressure. "I recommend we reposition the sonar." His gloved finger hovered over the control toggle. It was textbook SOP: raise the dome, reposition the aircraft near last known contact, and reacquire.

Chief Bishop and Lieutenant Ellis were already in sync, plotting the *Medved's* plausible course based on last-known speed and heading. Bishop marked a waypoint, which Ellis confirmed. Carter paused, considering Hayes's suggestion—just as his earphones filled with garbled static, slicing through the cabin like a knife.

"Hold. A radio call from the ASMOD is coming through," Carter said, switching to a secure channel. A flicker of confusion crossed his face as he nodded and exchanged clipped words with the senior officer aboard the carrier.

Ellis glanced over, waiting for an update, fingers poised over the multifunction display. Carter stared straight ahead, grip firm on the cyclic and collective, holding the Seahawk steady in its 60-foot hover. The airframe vibrated under the relentless whine of its high-pitched engines, cutting through the black night above the North Pacific.

After a few tense seconds, Carter switched back to internal comms. His tone was clipped and firm. "Petty Officer Hayes, raise the sonar dome. We've been ordered to return to the carrier immediately."

"I don't understand, Commander Carter! There's an active Russian nuclear submarine near the U.S. west coast!" Hayes exclaimed, tone filled with frustration and confusion. He knew he wouldn't get a straight answer, but protocol demanded he voice his concern. The aircraft's mission tape was recording everything—ensuring accountability.

Carter glanced at his co-pilot, aware she shared his confusion. "Hayes, raise and secure the sonar," he ordered, voice even. "We're heading back. I think we just got out-classified. We no longer have a 'need to know.' Our orders are to land and report directly to the ASMOD."

The cabin fell silent, save for the engines' drone as the SH-60F shifted course. Each crew member processed the unsettling truth: whatever was happening was now far above their clearance.

The 20-minute flight back to the USS *Constellation* passed in uneasy silence. The usual crew banter was absent, replaced by an oppressive quiet. The adrenaline high of near-lethal action gave way to exhaustion and introspection.

Hayes shifted uncomfortably, the weight of his night vision goggles pulling at his spine. He twisted his neck side to side, trying to ease the tension. As he nodded forward, his ICS cord snagged on the NVG battery pack Velcroed to his helmet, pulling it from the plug above. Swearing under his breath, Hayes quickly reconnected—just in time to hear the carrier's Air Boss break the silence.

"HUNTER 613, cleared to land on spot four," the voice crackled.

The landing gear compressed under the weight of the 7-ton helicopter as its wheels touched the dimly lit flight deck. Chock-and-chain crews rushed out with heavy securing gear, tethering the aircraft to the padeyes.

In the cockpit, LCDR Carter and LT Ellis methodically shut down the engines and engaged the rotor brakes. The high-pitched whine faded, replaced by the muted hum of carrier life. The aircrew powered down systems and began gathering their flight gear for the PR shop.

Chief Bishop unbuckled and slid open the cabin door—then froze. Standing just outside were four senior ASMOD officers flanked by ship security personnel armed with AR-15s and holstered sidearms. Their presence sent a chill through the cabin.

"Please remain in your seat, Chief Bishop!" barked a towering security officer, his tone as commanding as his frame. The order sliced through the lingering silence.

Bishop froze, hand resting on his harness buckle. The sharp tone drew the pilots' attention—they turned, helmets in hand. Another officer raised his palm, signaling them to stay put.

The ASMOD officers, familiar faces the crew had worked alongside for months, entered the cabin without acknowledgment. Cold, efficient, and unreadable.

LCDR Huntington leaned in, ejecting the VHS tape from the Tactical Sensor Operator (TSO) console. LT Cooper, clipboard in hand, inventoried the interior—armament, equipment, conversations. LT Brown recorded everything with a Sony handheld camcorder. The crew exchanged uneasy glances as their routine was swallowed by secrecy.

They were ordered to leave their flight gear and follow the officers to a secure area. Deflated and drained, the four-person aircrew complied, trailing the armed security team. Down ladders, through tight hatches, they were led deep into the carrier's bowels.

Upon arrival, the crew signed in and entered a dimly lit operations room. Plexiglass screens displayed current war zones and ASW assets, marked with glowing annotations. Familiar shipmates sat at stations, avoiding eye contact. Orders had clearly gone out: *no one speak to the aircrew.*

Finally, they were ushered into a small conference room in the far corner of ASMOD. The heavy door closed behind them. Armed guards remained outside.

Inside, silence reigned.

LCDR Huntington began the debrief. The other officers documented every word. No new information was shared—just a firm reminder that their role had been critical. All mission recordings had been confiscated and were now classified above their clearance. Any personal notes or related material were collected. The aircrew was left with nothing but questions.

Then came the final order: silence.

"You are not to discuss any aspect of this operation with anyone—not among yourselves, not with other crew, no one," Huntington said firmly. "Any breach of this directive will result in immediate consequences: loss of clearance, military termination, prison time, and substantial fines."

The weight of the command settled over them. They had been part of something they couldn't comprehend, and now they were being asked to bury it—perhaps forever. They knew too little to grasp the whole picture, but too much to be allowed to question it.

CHAPTER 6

U.S. Navy USS Santa Fe SSN-763
Los Angeles-Class Submarine
North Pacific Ocean

The Los Angeles-class attack submarine *USS Santa Fe*, commanded by CMDR Ronald Casey, had spent the past few months of its maiden voyage silently shadowing the *USS Constellation* in the Persian Gulf. Devoid of foreign port calls, the *Santa Fe* maintained strict radio silence, patrolling the contentious waters north off the coasts of Iran and Iraq. The *Constellation* battle group had been operating in the Persian Gulf for three months as part of Operation Southern Watch, enforcing no-fly zones and conducting surveillance. Its mission came to an end with the arrival of the *USS Kitty Hawk* (CV-63) battle group, which assumed operational control in the region.

In mid-August, under the cover of darkness, the line of warships cautiously steamed through the Strait of Hormuz, navigating from the Persian Gulf into the Gulf of Oman. The narrow channel, just 30 miles wide, curves sharply around the Omani Musandam Peninsula to the south and Iran to the north, making it one of the most precarious maritime chokepoints in the world. With tensions high, the full complement of attack aircraft and shipboard weapons systems stood at the ready—primed to launch within minutes if an incident arose during their vulnerable transit. Every radar sweep, sonar ping, and radio transmission was scrutinized as the battle group passed through volatile waters, where any misstep could ignite conflict.

Around the same time, U.S. reconnaissance satellites detected the Russian K-151 *Medved* departing its base at Gremikha. The *Santa Fe* received an encrypted message during a scheduled nighttime radio antenna deployment after clearing the dangers of the Strait of Hormuz. The message detailed the *Medved*'s departure and ordered the U.S. attack submarine to move ahead of the battle group to intercept the Russian sub in the North Pacific Ocean, near the Bering Sea. Meanwhile, the *USS Constellation* (CV-64), *USS Merrill* (DD-976), *USS John Paul Jones* (DDG-53), *USS Chosin* (CG-65), *USS Lake Erie* (CG-70), *USS Cimarron* (AO-177), *USS Mount Hood* (AE-29), and *USS Topeka* (SSN-754) prepared for well-deserved port calls in various host cities across the South China Sea. From there, the battle group would begin its return to home ports scattered across Pearl Harbor, HI; Everett, WA; and San Diego, CA.

The *Constellation*'s final port call was scheduled for Everett, WA. There, the carrier would offload a significant portion of ship and squadron personnel to make room for sailors' families. These families would then have the unique opportunity to ride aboard the aircraft carrier down the U.S. west coast, participating in what was known as the Tiger Cruise. For many civilian family members, this was a once-in-a-lifetime experience—offering a rare glimpse into the operational life aboard a naval vessel. However, growing concerns from the Pentagon cast a shadow over the planned transit. The timing of the *Medved*'s departure from Gremikha coincided with the carrier's route, raising the possibility of a dangerous interception near the Aleutian Islands during its journey toward the Puget Sound. In response, the *Santa Fe*, fully armed with 10 MK-48 Advanced Capability (ADCAP) torpedoes as well as Tomahawk and Harpoon anti-surface missiles, was ordered to expedite its course. Its mission: to investigate and intercept the rogue Russian submarine before it could pose a threat to the *Constellation* or its battle group.

* * *

3-days prior
The West Wing of the White House
Washington D.C.

"Mr. President, Russian President Novikov is on line one." A tall, slender West Wing staffer, dressed impeccably in a fitted navy-blue power suit, knocked twice before swinging open the oversized, bulletproof door. The interruption cut into President Clarence Palmer's ongoing situation report with Reggie Gladwell, the Secretary of Defense. Gladwell paused mid-sentence as Palmer lowered his reading glasses, his sharp gaze focusing on the staffer. He hesitated briefly, an annoyed smirk tugging at the corner of his mouth—not at the staffer, but at how long it had taken Russian President Novikov to finally make contact.

The United States was already well aware of the unfolding situation with the missing K-151 *Medved*, thanks to its intelligence sources. Reconnaissance satellites had tracked the *Medved* leaving port over a week ago, and since then, the Russian Navy had been conducting a sweeping search. An unprecedented number of vessels and aircraft had launched from their eastern bases, spanning from Gremikha in the north to Fokino in the south, scouring the Bering Sea and Northern Pacific. President Palmer sighed, the weight of the moment pressing down as he prepared to address his Russian counterpart.

At DEFCON 3, Palmer had already ordered the readiness and deployment of several armed U.S. Navy assets in response to the Russian search. It was a calculated move—a passive nod to President Novikov in a high-stakes game of brinkmanship. Palmer wanted the Russian president to know that the United States was fully aware the Russian Federation was up to something. The timing of U.S. deployments was no coincidence, and Palmer knew the Russians would notice. Their Molniya spy satellites would undoubtedly track the sudden activity: the mobilization of multiple naval ships and aircraft strategically positioned near the Pacific theater. But Palmer couldn't openly acknowledge or expose the sensitive intelligence driving his actions. Doing so would invite scrutiny and risk revealing critical ISR (Intelligence, Surveillance, and Reconnaissance) capabilities. Instead, he opted for a defensive posture, letting the U.S. military's movements speak for themselves. As the Kremlin scrambled to locate their missing submarine, Palmer waited—hoping Novikov would break the silence first.

The U.S. National Security Cabinet had been briefed that the *USS Santa Fe* had identified the *Medved* three days earlier just south of Attu Island in the Aleutian chain. The Russian submarine had been moving through the Aleutian Trench, a staggering 26,600 feet deep. In mountaineering terms, that depth was akin to the death zone—where only a third of the air is breathable. Reversed, it represented nearly 12,000 pounds per square inch of crushing pressure—far beyond survivability. While the *Medved*'s maximum dive depth was 830 meters (2,723 feet), far short of the trench's full depth, its operational depth of 500 meters (1,640 feet) gave it room to maneuver within the massive undersea crevasse. That terrain also offered ideal conditions for the *Santa Fe* to shadow the Russian vessel undetected. Coated in sound-absorbing anechoic tiles, the U.S. submarine maintained its distance in tactical stealth mode, silently observing the *Medved*'s every move.

For days, the *Santa Fe* trailed the Russian sub, documenting every maneuver. The *Medved* remained consistent in its behavior—until the arrival of U.S. P-3 Orions. Once passive sonobuoys were deployed across the area, the Russian submarine's behavior shifted. It reduced speed, dropped to the thermal layer, and went silent in an effort to evade detection. Despite the tactics, the *Santa Fe* maintained contact, tracking the sub with unwavering precision.

"I'll take the call in my office. Mr. Secretary, please gather the NSC members," Palmer instructed firmly, locking eyes with the Secretary of Defense. His tone left no room for delay. Palmer wanted as many National Security Council members present as possible. As the Secretary departed, Palmer allowed himself a beat of patience. Letting Novikov sit on hold a few extra minutes wouldn't hurt—if anything, it might provide a subtle psychological edge.

Straightening his tie, he prepared mentally for what he expected to be a tense exchange.

Every presidential call with a foreign leader was witnessed and transcribed by NSC staff. This one would be no different. Palmer stepped into his office and pressed the Conference 1 button.

"President Novikov, to what do I owe this pleasure?" he asked, voice calm and laced with subtle sarcasm.

The Russian president fumbled over his words, struggling to explain the situation without igniting panic. But the reality was clear: a fully armed Russian nuclear submarine was likely near the U.S. west coast, and Moscow hadn't authorized its mission. Palmer didn't hold back. He laid into Novikov—not because the man was vulnerable, but because he had failed to notify the United States sooner. Palmer's voice was firm, his tone edged. He made it clear that the U.S. would take every precaution necessary to avoid incident, but that the safety of the American people came first. After a tense exchange, both leaders agreed to maintain open lines of communication, ensuring neither side acted in ignorance.

As the call ended, Palmer turned to his cabinet, eyes steeled with resolve.

"Move us to DEFCON 2. Check what other ASW assets are near the *Santa Fe*. Get a lock on that Russian sub—and eliminate it. We have high reason to believe it poses an imminent threat to the United States of America."

* * *

U.S. Navy USS Santa Fe SSN-763
Los Angeles-Class Submarine
North Pacific Ocean

"MK-46 deployed from ASW helo. Target acquired, sir. Russian K-151 *Medved* is increasing speed and turning five degrees starboard," reported Sonar Technician Submarine First Class Malcolm Williams. His voice was steady, but his right knee bounced with nervous energy, tapping against the deck as he sat at his station.

Commander Casey stood at the tactical display, processing the update with calm intensity. He noticed Williams's restlessness but said nothing. The young sonar tech wasn't alone in feeling pressure.

Submariners enjoyed a unique comfort while underway: rubber-soled tennis shoes. Williams's worn Nike Air Max muffled his steps, an essential detail in stealth operations. But casual wear did not mean casual attitude. Every man aboard understood the gravity of the moment.

"Neutralize the torpedo and set a plot to silently engage the *Medved*," Casey ordered, his voice resolute.

For days, they had shadowed the Russian sub. What once felt like routine training had become a live op. This was no drill. Every sailor trained for this—few faced it. Now, the *Santa Fe*'s 100-person crew was about to be tested.

"Roger that. Matching MK-46 torpedo frequency and sending squelch. NOW. NOW. NOW," Williams called out, focused.

Through his headset, he filtered underwater noise, eyes fixed on real-time frequencies.

He reached up, adjusting the rotary dial to the torpedo's frequency. With his other hand, he pressed the override button, sending an inaudible squelch—a form of legacy cyberwarfare. The torpedo's lock broke. It slowed, executed fail-safe protocols, and shut down, sinking inert into the trench.

"Torpedo neutralized, sir," Williams reported, hands returning to rest.

"Excellent work, Williams. Status of the *Medved?*"

"Sir, they launched countermeasures—noisemakers—then cut engines. They're descending silently into the trench. ASW helo is pinging to reacquire."

Casey nodded. Classic tactics. But the Russian captain had altered the playbook—dropping noise decoys, then relying on gravity to disappear into the depths. Clever. And risky.

"Hold steady. They'll be called back to the carrier shortly. The helo gave us what we need," Casey said.

They had triangulated the *Medved*—passive sonobuoy hits, sonar confirmation from both helo and *Santa Fe*, and three days of surveillance. The picture was clear. Now came execution.

"Commander, the helo is retracting its sonar dome. Departing toward the *Connie*. Should I scuttle their passive buoys?" Williams asked.

"Hold tight. Let them scuttle their own. We don't want the Russians knowing we're here," Casey replied, voice firm.

He knew what the *Medved*'s captain was likely thinking. The torpedo disappeared. The helo returned. He'd be analyzing every detail—likely suspecting a shadow in the water.

Casey's tone hardened.

"Maintain stealth mode. Plot a firing solution. Prepare to engage the *Medved*!"

CHAPTER 7

Russian Navy K-151 Medved

Oscar-class Submarine

North Pacific Ocean

"Release countermeasures and come full starboard!" Kapitan Vasiliev's voice was unnervingly steady—his calm deepening as the situation grew more intense.

Sonar Tech Petrov obeyed instantly, his hands moving on instinct even as his mind struggled to process the transformation he was witnessing. Their commanding officer seemed to thrive in chaos, exuding a composed authority that only magnified Petrov's own unraveling. What Petrov couldn't know was that Vasiliev's calm wasn't a calculated trait—it was unconscious, the residue of a fractured past. Raised by an abusive alcoholic father and emotionally scarred by the Cold War, Vasiliev had spent his formative years in an environment defined by volatility. Chaos, whether it found him or he subconsciously created it, was the only place he truly felt at home. Pandemonium wasn't something he endured—it was where he thrived.

Spanning decades of service from the Cold War's end to the present, Kapitan Vasiliev had seamlessly taken up where his father left off. His mission in life had been hardwired since childhood—

shaped by the anger and violence learned from Vasiliev Sr. and reinforced by relentless state propaganda drilled into his developing mind through school and military doctrine. He was a student of war. And his war was against the United States.

Vasiliev's personal life bore the scars of that upbringing. A trail of failed relationships in Russia revealed his inability to escape the abusive behaviors he had inherited. Only recently had he found a partner who matched his dysfunction: Mila, a woman molded by her own broken father. She remained behind in their stifling, unair-conditioned one-bedroom home in Gremikha, pregnant with their first child and entering her third trimester. Her discomfort, her dependency—none of it had entered Vasiliev's mind when he accepted deployment orders. In fact, neither Mila nor their unborn child had crossed his mind since the *Medved* left port.

Vasiliev possessed a chilling, narcissistic ability to flip a switch—to become the Kapitan that Mother Russia demanded. His abusive tendencies—both mental and physical—weren't liabilities. They were the very foundation of his leadership style. His crew didn't like him. But they respected him. Vasiliev's ability to remain composed where others faltered—especially in the unpredictable theater of submarine warfare—was both curse and asset. When failure meant annihilation, his ruthlessness became a shield.

"Kapitan, the United States torpedo has gone silent! Stupid American weapons failed!" Petrov blurted, his voice brimming with a sudden, overwhelming surge of enthusiasm. Just moments earlier he'd been on the edge of despair, convinced death was imminent. Now, the shift in tone sparked adrenaline through his veins.

Cold sweat streamed down both sides of his face, soaking the rubber ear covers of his headset. The oppressive heat of the *Medved*, combined with the tension of near-death, had drenched him. A chill rippled across his back, triggering a myoclonic jerk—a sharp, involuntary twitch, like the kind people experience as they fall asleep. The relief felt jarring, unnatural, and it collided with the eerie silence now flooding the sonar room.

Petrov's hands hovered over the controls, trembling slightly as he waited for the Kapitan's response. For all his excitement, a quiet unease lingered. This wasn't over.

"Hold tight. Cut all engines and listen for further weapons deployment. Ensure the American torpedo doesn't reacquire," Vasiliev ordered, his tone calm yet commanding. He wasn't convinced the torpedo had simply failed—whether due to countermeasures, evasive maneuvers, or both.

As a meticulous student of U.S. naval warfare, Vasiliev knew more about their systems than some of the sailors who operated them. He understood that the antisubmarine helicopters circling above likely carried one of two weapons: the MK-46 or the newer MK-50. The MK-46 lightweight aerial torpedo—the NATO stand-ard—was the more likely threat, as the MK-50 had yet to see wide-spread use among U.S. ASW units.

The stakes were stark. Operating at depth, the *Medved*'s Os-car II-class double hull reduced but did not eliminate its vulnerabil-ity. The MK-46 was no ordinary weapon. It was designed to deto-nate *beneath* a submarine, creating a massive air void. That sudden absence of pressure would cause the hull to flex and rupture catastrophically. If the torpedo had functioned as designed, they would already be dead—engulfed in freezing black seawater, crushed by thousands of pounds per square inch.

Vasiliev had unshakeable confidence in his ship and crew—but he also knew how thin the line was between survival and death.

"Aye aye, Kapitan. The United States ASW helicopter has broken hover and is returning to the aircraft carrier," Petrov reported, his voice steady despite the emotional churn underneath. He listened closely to the fading rhythm of the Seahawk's rotors, the vibrations fading into the night sky above the Pacific.

The *Medved* remained in silent running, slowly drifting deeper into the Aleutian Trench. Through his headset, Petrov picked up the faint songs of migrating gray whales, their distant calls echoing across the sea floor. The low hum of U.S. surface ships grew quieter with every passing second. Beyond the biological and mechanical whispers, the ocean had gone unnaturally still.

Too still.

The Americans *knew* they were there. But how long had they known? Why had they fired—and then backed off?

The silence pressed in like a phantom weight, amplifying the questions Petrov dared not speak aloud.

After several long minutes, Vasiliev finally broke the silence, his voice cool but laced with contempt.

"Hmm. Why would they disengage? To prevent a war? Typical weak Americans… they'll do anything to avoid conflict, even when provoked on their own soil."

The weight of his classified orders bore down on him. Vasiliev had been warned: this mission might be one-way. His briefers had predicted the American response with chilling accuracy. He'd been told not to hesitate, not to falter—not even if the enemy appeared to back down. His mission was clear. His loyalty to Mother Russia was absolute.

"Hold depth. Change course to zero-one-eight," he said, his peppered brows knitting into a sharp V, gray eyes fixed forward with steel resolve.

Then came the final command.

"Plot a target package for the American cities of Seattle and Portland. Prepare the forward missile tubes for 3M-51 Alfa launch."

His voice, though steady, now carried the unmistakable weight of purpose.

"Let's finish what we came to accomplish."

CHAPTER 8

U.S. Navy USS Santa Fe SSN-763
Los Angeles-Class Submarine
North Pacific Ocean

The USS *Santa Fe* idled at a safe distance, acoustically mapping the *Medved*'s every move. The Russian submarine had successfully evaded the MK-46 torpedo, slipping past an arsenal of bubble-making countermeasures before falling completely silent. Its descent into the depths of the Aleutian Trench left only faint traces for the U.S. attack submarine to track. If Sonar Technician Williams hadn't sent the squelch frequency to disrupt and shut down the torpedo's pursuit, the MK-46 would have likely reacquired its target and eliminated the *Medved*. The Oscar II-class submarine had been seconds from annihilation, its fate narrowly spared—not by its crew's skill alone but by decisions made far above the frigid waters. Back in the Situation Room in Washington D.C., U.S. officials had opted to hold fire, their focus shifting from destruction to understanding. The *Medved*'s motives remained unclear, and for the moment, that uncertainty had bought the Russian crew precious time.

Were the Russians conducting a close target reconnaissance, or had the Medved defected to pose an imminent threat to the United States?

For decades, the U.S. and Russian militaries had engaged in dangerous games of cat and mouse, a precarious balance of deterrence and provocation. In the skies over Alaska, jets were regularly scrambled to intercept Russian reconnaissance, bomber, and fighter planes—actions mirrored by Russia from the east. At sea, ships and submarines routinely skirted the edges of national security, forcing escorts out of contested waters and testing the boundaries of international law. On rare but significant occasions, these encounters escalated. Aircraft and vessels had sustained damage, and military personnel on both sides had been injured in close calls. Yet, the media often amplified these incidents, taking fragments of information from embedded sources to spin a narrative that fed fear into their eager, addicted audience. The buzz of speculation and dramatized headlines further obscured the truth, making it even harder to discern whether this latest confrontation with the *Medved* was merely another act in the ongoing geopolitical theater—or the prelude to something far more dangerous.

Acting on the advice of his National Security Council, President Palmer issued a direct order to the USS *Constellation*'s Commanding Officer: launch the SH-60F ASW alert helicopter to the projected location of the *Medved*, confirm contact, and engage with a torpedo if necessary. Onboard the aircraft carrier, the levels of security clearance and *need-to-know* classification varied widely. Personnel in the ASMOD, the flight deck, and the helicopter's aircrew were briefed only to the extent necessary for their specific roles. Some knew the mission involved a Russian submarine; others were aware of the broader implications of a potential threat to U.S. shores. Few, if any, understood the full scope of the White House's intended response to the rogue submarine's advance. As the USS *Constellation* prepared to execute the president's orders, every team operated with precision, each step bringing them closer to a response that could determine the fate of a tense international standoff.

Commander Casey of the USS *Santa Fe* had been briefed days earlier through an encrypted message transmitted via extremely low frequency (ELF) radio. The orders outlined the anticipated tactics of the P-3 Orion, the carrier's ASW helicopter launch, and the subsequent deployment of weapons. As events unfolded, Casey couldn't help but feel a sense of admiration for how seamlessly the plan was executed and the competence displayed by all U.S. assets involved. Now, the USS *Santa Fe* was perfectly positioned to observe whether the carefully coordinated strategy would expose what the Russians seemed so intent on hiding. The pieces were falling into place, but Casey knew this was far from over. Every move was calculated, every counter measured, yet the uncertainty of the *Medved*'s true intentions kept the volatility razor-sharp.

"Commander Casey, Bora-class Corvette quickly approaching from the northwest. Contact bearing one-four-eight, 53 nautical miles, speed over 30 knots," reported Williams, his voice steady as he relayed the critical update. Through his sonar headset, he identified the distinct thrashing of the Russian navy surface ship's dual three-bladed propellers cutting just below the ocean surface.

Williams's skill in classifying water vessels based on the unique frequencies emitted by their screws—or other distinct acoustic signatures—was unmatched among his peers. His accuracy had earned him the crew's unwavering confidence, but as was standard practice, his findings were always double-checked. In this instance, no corrections were needed. The data aligned perfectly with the secure intelligence he had recently downloaded. The situation was escalating. The presence of the Bora-class Corvette confirmed earlier suspicions: the Russians were mobilizing a suspicious fleet of ships and ASW-capable aircraft toward the area. The pieces of their strategy were beginning to reveal themselves, and Casey knew the stakes were rising.

"Roger that, Williams. Keep me updated on the Corvette and the *Medved*'s response. If we can hear them, you know they can hear them," Commander Casey replied, his tone calm but deliberate. His approach was methodical, carefully mapping out the situation while staying within the clandestine parameters of his mission.

The SH-60F's active sonar and MK-46 attack served a dual purpose: to provoke the Russian nuclear submarine into action and, in doing so, reveal its true intentions. Whether the *Medved* chose to evade, counter, or retaliate, its response would determine the next move. The USS *Santa Fe* remained ready, a silent predator in the depths, waiting for the moment to act. Casey knew the stakes: their response had to be precise, not only to neutralize any threat but also to avoid escalating a delicate international situation into open conflict.

It was Kapitan Vasiliev's move. With the P-3 sonobuoys overhead, the ASW helicopter circling, and Russian ships en route, he knew his location was compromised. The provocation of the airborne torpedo had forced his hand, leaving him with two choices:

retreat to international waters or retaliate in a desperate engagement with the United States. Commander Casey prayed for the former, knowing that a retreat would defuse the situation—at least temporarily. But deep down, he suspected the Russian Kapitan's orders left no room for negotiation and demanded escalation.

"Sir, the *Medved* has turned on their engines and is altering course to zero-one-eight," Williams reported, his voice steady but edged with anxiety. Casey's jaw tightened as he processed the new information. The *Medved* wasn't retreating. The Russian submarine had chosen its path, and the stakes had just risen to a perilous new level.

With a tight-lipped sigh through his nose and a subtle nod, Commander Casey gave the order to commence their silent pursuit. He understood the gravity of the moment and knew his immediate crew needed to be brought into the fold. Their need-to-know status had just been elevated. Casey pressed the intercom, his voice steady but charged with authority. "Crew, I am informing you of orders I've received directly from the Commander in Chief, President Palmer. We are entering uncharted waters on a Top-Secret mission. This mission is classified as Sensitive Compartmented Information (SCI) and will remain so for an indefinite period. What I'm about to share is on a strict need-to-know basis."

He paused briefly, letting the weight of his words settle before continuing. "The President and his National Security Council believe the *Medved*, commanded by Kapitan Vasiliev, is heading toward the west coast of the United States with hostile intent. Intelligence strongly suggests they are carrying multiple nuclear-tipped

3M-51 Alfa missiles." Casey's tone sharpened, his words cutting through the hostility. "Gentlemen, we are now at DEFCON 2. Our orders are clear: track and eliminate the *Medved* if they come within firing range and depth of any U.S. city. This is not a drill. Stay focused and execute your duties with precision. The safety of millions depends on it." He released the button, letting the hum of the intercom fade. Around him, the crew exchanged determined glances, their faces set with the resolve that came with knowing their mission could change the course of history.

A heavy silence settled over the already subdued crew of the American submarine as they processed the new information. They had operated with a sense of foreboding, each member harboring their suspicions about the nature of the mission. But confirmation changed everything. The shift from assumption to certainty sharpened their focus and fixed their minds in a more intense, unyielding state. This was no drill. The gravity of their orders now weighed heavily on them. They weren't just operating as professionals; they were engaged in the grim reality of sub hunting. It was exactly what they had trained for, drilled into muscle memory through countless exercises. But this wasn't practice. This was real.

As the USS *Santa Fe* continued its silent shadowing of the *Medved*, new orders from the White House Situation Room were securely delivered to the USS *Constellation* Battle Group. The aircraft carrier, along with most of its supporting surface ships, was directed to change course and steam southwest toward Pearl Harbor, HI. The U.S. attack submarine, USS *Topeka*, cutting short its liberty port call in Osaka, Japan, departed a day early to provide escort for the battle group's journey to Hawaii. Meanwhile, the guided missile destroyers USS *John Paul Jones* and USS *Chosin* received a different directive: intercept the Russian *Bora*-class warship and other vessels reportedly joining the clandestine search for the *Medved.* As pressure mounted in the North Pacific, the destroyers patrolled the waters, ensuring that Russian ships stayed outside U.S. territorial boundaries. Above them, U.S. aircraft maintained constant patrols, vigilantly guarding the airspace. The coordinated effort underscored the gravity of the situation—an escalating chess match between two nuclear-capable adversaries, with the stakes higher than ever.

For the next 48 hours, the USS *Santa Fe* shadowed the K-151 *Medved* with unwavering silence, tracking its route toward Vancouver Island, British Columbia. Rather than staying within the depths of the Aleutian Trench and hugging the outer rim of Alaska and British Columbia as expected, Kapitan Vasiliev took a more direct course toward the 12,400-square-mile island situated just outside the Puget Sound.

Aboard the USS *Santa Fe*, the crew operated with relentless exactitude, maintaining their covert posture while working grueling 18-hour days. Rotating six-hour shifts ensured round-the-clock vigilance, with each watch team laser-focused on keeping the submarine invisible to the Russian sub's sensors. Every decision, every adjustment in course or depth, was carefully planned to remain undetected. The discord was intense. The USS *Santa Fe*'s crew knew they were trailing a nuclear-armed adversary capable of striking U.S. soil. Their mission demanded nothing short of perfection—and the slightest mistake could tip the balance in a deadly game of underwater hide and seek.

The intensity of the situation began to feel routine to the crew of the USS *Santa Fe* as they patiently shadowed the *Medved*, matching its speed and maneuvers while maintaining a cautious distance. Each turn, adjustment, and subtle move was executed with the precision of a silent predator stalking its prey across the vast Pacific Ocean.

Early on the third day, Kapitan Vasiliev brought the K-151 *Medved* to a slower pace as they neared the northern entrance of the Strait of Juan de Fuca. Flanked by Vancouver Island to the north and the Olympic Peninsula of Washington State to the south, the Strait served as the gateway to the Emerald City of Seattle. The *Medved* came to a hover 120 miles west of Cape Flattery, its nuclear payload lurking beneath the waves. Vasiliev's expression hardened with resolve as he prepared to unleash devastation in a way that would reverberate through history. His plan promised to etch his name into Russian history books for centuries—cementing his legacy, no matter the cost.

Nearly six months ago, Kapitan Vasiliev had been approached in secret by two stern officials from Moscow's shadowy Special Access Program (SAP). Now, he could scarcely believe he was mere minutes away from honorably completing what had been described as an almost impossible mission for Mother Russia. When they first approached him, the officials had carefully played to his pride, feeding him a litany of reasons he had been chosen. They painted him as the perfect candidate—a patriot, a proven leader, a man whose legacy would endure for centuries. Many of these reasons were blatant fabrications, crafted to inflate his ego and secure his cooperation. But the truth was, Vasiliev had never really had a choice. He had been so caught up in the grandeur of the opportunity, in the promise of glory and historical significance, that he failed to see the coercion beneath the surface. Refusal wasn't an option. Had he declined, he would have almost certainly "disappeared," another casualty of SAP's ruthlessly efficient methods. Loose ends were unacceptable in an operation of this magnitude. Vasiliev's resolve hardened as he prepared to see the mission through, oblivious—or perhaps willfully blind—to the cost of the path he had chosen, or the one that had been chosen for him.

The Cold War spanned 45 tense years between the United States and the Soviet Union, marked by a persistent ideological and geopolitical struggle. One of its most perilous moments came during the Cuban Missile Crisis of 1962, when both nations placed nuclear missiles within striking distance of each other's territories, bringing the world to the brink of catastrophe. Tensions remained high for decades, even as efforts toward resolution emerged. In 1986, President Ronald Reagan and General Secretary Mikhail Gorbachev of the Communist Party of the Soviet Union made significant strides during the Reykjavik Summit in Iceland, paving the way for arms reduction agreements. The symbolic fall of the Berlin Wall in 1989 and the dissolution of the Soviet Union into independent republics in 1991 brought an official end to the Cold War. The Iron Curtain, which had divided East and West for decades, was abruptly lifted. But while the public narrative framed the Cold War's conclusion as definitive, its shadows lingered beneath the surface. The rivalry between the two superpowers may have shifted in appearance, but its echoes still shaped international relations, strategies, and covert operations well into the future.

New generations of leaders were elected with grand ideals of progress and diplomacy, but the persistent distractions of global conflicts and proxy wars continually delayed meaningful change. Meanwhile, older generations, pushed out of traditional political influence, quietly shifted to the shadows, assuming roles in clandestine organizations like the Special Access Program (SAP). While the allure of dropping a nuclear weapon on Washington D.C. or Manhattan had its appeal, the devastating short- and long-term consequences of economic chaos, global political fallout, and the immediate death of millions made it an impractical strategy. SAP's ambitions were far more insidious. Instead of a single destructive blow, they sought a subtler, more devastating form of warfare. Employing U.S.-based seismologists, geologists, and environmentalists under the guise of legitimate research, SAP explored unconventional methods to destabilize their enemy. Their goal wasn't just to reduce population numbers but to orchestrate a cascading collapse of economic ruin, environmental uncertainty, and widespread chaos that would shatter the foundations of the so-called Great Nation.

The SAP-contracted scientists had spent over a decade gathering research and data to support their ominous hypothesis: a catastrophic natural disaster was lying in wait, ready to be triggered under the right conditions. The North American tectonic plate, spanning the continent from east to west, intersects with the Juan de Fuca oceanic plate in a critical subduction zone stretching from Seattle to southern Oregon. Here, the oceanic plate slides beneath the continental plate—a geological collision prone to seismic activity and overdue for a cataclysmic event. This vulnerable fault line, known for its normal seismic rumblings, has been dormant for centuries, but geologists warn that it is overdue for a major rupture. Compounding the danger is the *Ring of Fire*, an 800-mile volcanic chain running just east of the coast, containing 13 active volcanoes capable of explosive eruptions. Seismologists predict that an earthquake measuring 8.0 or greater on the Richter scale in this region could unleash one of the most devastating natural disasters in human history. The destruction wouldn't end with the quake; the resulting tsunami and volcanic chain reactions could mirror the ruinous Chicxulub event, which wiped out the dinosaurs 65 million years ago. Such an event would not only result in unprecedented loss of life but could also cripple the infrastructure and economy of an entire nation.

Targeting two major cities—Seattle and Portland—perched atop the volatile Cascadia Faultline with multiple 3M-51 Alfa cruise missiles, each carrying 150-kiloton nuclear warheads, was the perfect trigger to cripple the United States of America. The devastating dual strikes wouldn't just annihilate urban centers; they would unleash a chain reaction of tragic events.

Would the U.S. retaliate with its own nuclear strike, or would it be paralyzed by the magnitude of its losses?

The Russian government had meticulously studied the American psyche and response patterns, predicting that even a superpower would falter under such unimaginable devastation. While the Americans might eventually respond, the initial aftermath would be overwhelming. The cascading effects of the attack would plunge the Pacific Coast into chaos. The immediate detonations would likely trigger secondary and tertiary disasters—erupting volcanoes along the *Ring of Fire*, towering tidal waves swallowing entire coastal areas, relentless aftershock earthquakes, and the spread of deadly radiation carried inland by the prevailing Westerlies. The United States would be consumed by survival efforts, struggling to navigate the unprecedented chaos. Meanwhile, Mother Russia would be ready. Anticipating any form of retaliation, the Kremlin would position itself to strike again or defend against weakened U.S. forces. With America at its most vulnerable, the stage would be set for Russia to rewrite the global balance of power.

"Sir, the *Medved* is at 10 meters and opening the doors to their forward vertical launch tubes!" Petty Officer Williams' high-pitched voice cracked with urgency before he quickly cleared his throat, steadying himself to deliver the critical update.

"Roger that," Commander Casey responded, his voice firm despite the weight of the moment. "Check final bearing and shoot. Fire one and two!" The order, precise and deliberate, echoed through the submarine's control room. It was a command Casey had hoped he would never have to give. His hands gripped the edge of the console as he let out a long, controlled breath, calming his body as if preparing to take a sniper's shot. "Lord," he murmured under his breath, barely audible amidst the tense atmosphere, "have mercy on us all."

"Set. Fire one and two!" The Torpedo Fire Control team simultaneously launched the MK-48 Advanced Capability (ADCAP) torpedoes from the number one and number two forward tubes. With a thunderous hiss, the swashplate piston engines roared to life, propelling the 19-foot, 2.5-ton torpedoes from their tubes and into the black depths. The crew held their breath, the hum of the submarine's systems the only sound in the suffocating silence. Every second felt like an eternity as they awaited the results of an action that could alter the course of history.

Once clear of their housings, the torpedoes activated their preprogrammed acoustic transducers, emitting sharp, methodical sonar pings toward the Russian target. The reflected sound waves locked onto the *Medved*, guiding the lethal payloads with exactitude. As the torpedoes closed the distance, their warheads armed in transit, ready to deliver a disastrous blow. Kapitan Vasiliev barely had time to react. His sharp commands to deploy countermeasures and initiate an evasive turn echoed through the cramped confines of the *Medved*. The crew scrambled in a desperate bid to save their submarine, but the torpedoes were too fast and too precise. The seconds ticked down, and the Russian sub was caught in an inescapable web of sound and steel.

The first MK-48 torpedo locked onto the slow-moving target, its propulsor assembly accelerating to 50 knots as it closed the gap. Ignoring the *Medved*'s desperate last-ditch decoys, the torpedo homed in on the keel, detecting the submarine's magnetic signature. Within seconds, the 600-pound warhead, packed with high-explosive Trinitrotoluene (TNT), detonated with devastating force. The explosion was compounded as the second MK-48 arrived at nearly the same location, triggering its warhead in a fierce tandem strike. The dual detonations created a massive air pocket beneath the *Medved*, violently lifting the 18,000-ton steel leviathan out of the water. The sheer force of the blast ripped the submarine's hull in half, exposing its interior to the crushing pressures of the Pacific. The shockwave tore through the *Medved*, obliterating systems and killing most of the crew instantly. Those who survived the initial impact were rendered unconscious by the concussive force, only to drown moments later as the shattered halves of the K-151 *Medved* plunged thousands of feet to the ocean floor. As the submarine disappeared into the abyss, the waters above churned with debris and bubbles, marking the violent end of the once-mighty vessel and its ill-fated mission.

Petty Officer Williams confirmed the kill to Commander Casey. Cheers erupted in the control room as the crew celebrated their success, but the jubilation was short-lived. A heavy, unspoken sadness began to creep in as the reality of what they had done settled over them. They had performed an honorable duty for their country, but the psychological toll of that day would linger, haunting many of them in the years to come. For some, the weight of their actions became an unshakable burden. Decades later, members of the crew would struggle with post-traumatic stress, their experiences compounded by the inability to discuss the classified mission with anyone, even loved ones. Without proper psychological resources for veterans, some would tragically succumb to their inner battles, their lives cut short by the echoes of that fateful day.

Williams, in particular, bore the heaviest scars. His exceptional skill as a sonar technician made him indispensable during the mission, but it also meant he heard every detail of the *Medved*'s destruction. As the wreck sank into the crushing depths, the haunting sounds of the submarine's implosion, groaning steel, rushing water, and the final, shuddering collapse etched themselves into his mind. The *Medved*'s death knell became his own. Years later, those same horrific sounds would resurface, relentless and unyielding. They followed him into civilian life, where their presence grew louder in the silence of sleepless nights. Less than a decade after the mission, unable to escape the torment, Williams placed the barrel of a SIG Sauer P226 9mm in his mouth and pulled the trigger, ending a life consumed by the weight of a duty no one could understand.

CHAPTER 9

Gremikha Bay Naval Base
Kola Peninsula, Russia

"Yaroslav?" Mila Vasiliev gasped, jerking awake from an uneasy, sweat-drenched sleep. Her chest heaved as she struggled to steady her breathing, her body trembling as if seized by an unseen force. Disoriented, it took her a moment to ground herself in the dim stillness of the room. She lay on her back, her swollen, third-trimester belly rising and falling as she tried to calm the storm within. The sheets beneath her were damp with sweat, clinging to her skin. With effort, she tilted her weight to the side and reached for the bedside lamp, her bony fingers fumbling to pull down the string toggle before flooding the room with a soft, yellow glow. The light revealed the unpredictability of her emotions. She wasn't sure if it was the hormonal surge from her pregnancy, a premonition, or something more profound. But a deep, unshakable sadness had taken hold. Tears began to stream down her cheeks as she buried her face in her hands, muffling the sobs that erupted from her chest.

How could he leave me here? I need him. I need my husband more than ever right now.

Her hands slipped from her face, and she stared blankly at the wall, her tear-streaked expression a mix of despair and longing.

The silence of the room felt oppressive, as if mocking her helplessness. The ache of abandonment gnawed at her, and the uncertainty of Yaroslav's fate made it all the more agonizing.

Unusually hot and dry weather plagued much of the Northern Hemisphere. A winter with below-average snowfall had created the perfect conditions for forest fires to ignite and spread uncontrollably. In Eastern Russia and Siberia, hundreds of active fires raged across the vast landscapes, fanned by persistent high winds. These smaller blazes merged into an inferno of biblical proportions, consuming everything in their path. The skies were choked with smoke, turning daylight into an eerie twilight. Most of Russia faced dangerously poor air quality, the atmosphere saturated with pollutants from both the raging fires and the industrial output of major cities.

Mila was trapped in this inhospitable landscape, confined to the upper northeast of the largest country on Earth. The Gremikha Naval Base, officially decommissioned a year earlier according to the tightly controlled Russian media, was far from abandoned. The base still operated in secrecy, housing multiple active submarines as they prepared for a phased relocation to Fokino in Primorsky Krai, scheduled to be completed by the end of 1998. The isolation of Gremikha, coupled with the congesting smoke and oppressive heat, made life unbearable for Mila. The naval base, with its skeletal staff and air of abandonment, felt more like a prison than a home. Her swollen belly and the relentless discomfort of her pregnancy only deepened her sense of despair. The idea of surviving another day in this forgotten corner of the world seemed as daunting as the fires ravaging the countryside.

Gremikha's weather rarely deviated from its cold, inhospitable norm. Temperatures hovered between cold and freezing year-round, with thermometers seldom climbing above 50 degrees Fahrenheit in July. Air conditioning or central air filtration was considered a needless luxury in this remote naval outpost, as there simply wasn't enough heat to justify the expense. But this summer broke all the rules. For weeks, temperatures lingered above 70 degrees, a stark anomaly that even the staunchest climate change skeptics would struggle to dismiss. The heat itself was manageable, but when paired with the harsh, smoke-filled skies, it created dangerous conditions—especially for someone carrying a child.

Mila struggled to adapt. The insistent haze made every breath feel labored, and she worried constantly about the impact on her unborn baby. To protect herself and the child growing inside her, she often wore a surgical mask she had discreetly taken during a recent on-base doctor's appointment. It offered little relief, but it was better than nothing. Her greatest fear wasn't just the quantity of oxygen her baby received; it was the quality. Every inhale seemed heavy with toxins, and the thought of her child's first breath being tainted by this poisoned air kept her awake at night. The heat, the smoke, and the isolation bore down on her, making the final weeks of her pregnancy feel like an endurance test. Mila tried to remind herself that this was temporary, but as the cruel summer dragged on, hope felt like a distant luxury.

Mila was 20 years younger than her husband, Kapitan Yaroslav Vasiliev. They had met just a year earlier at a military picnic on the peninsula. The sun was shining, vodka flowed freely, and

Yaroslav's sharp gray eyes lingered on the daughter of a close friend in the Russian Navy. Mila, young and impressionable, was captivated by the Kapitan's status and charm. His commanding presence and silver-tongued flattery swept her into a whirlwind romance. Her father, however, harbored reservations. The significant age gap was one thing, but Yaroslav's reputation for boldness—both in and out of uniform—left him uneasy. Still, he recognized the security and respect that came with having a son-in-law of such high rank. Reluctantly, he gave his blessing when Vasiliev formally asked for Mila's hand in marriage.

Now, a year later, Mila carried their first child—a pregnancy that tied her future to the Kapitan's legacy in ways she hadn't fully grasped. It was her first child, but far from his. Yaroslav had fathered several daughters during his long military career, fleeting reminders of past relationships left in his wake. But this baby was different. This would be his first son—a fact he took great pride in. For Vasiliev, this child wasn't just a new addition to his family; it was the heir to his name, the carrier of his legacy. Mila understood how much this meant to him, even as she struggled to reconcile her feelings about the life they were building together. Alone, with Yaroslav deployed on some shadowy mission, she wrestled with the weight of her new reality—a reality she wasn't entirely sure she had chosen for herself.

Knock! Knock! Knock!

Once again, Mila jolted awake, her body tangled in the stale, damp embrace of faded white sheets. Her heart raced as she struggled to steady her shallow breaths, the lingering haze of sleep blurring the line between dream and reality. Gradually, her senses adjusted, and she became aware of the soft morning light filtering through the hallway window, casting faint beams into the bedroom through the open doorway. The restless night had left her exhausted, her swollen body unable to find comfort no matter how she turned. She hadn't realized she had drifted off again, her fitful sleep offering no reprieve from the weight of her worries. For a moment, she lay still, the silence of the room pressing down on her, her thoughts already shifting to another day of solitude and uncertainty.

Knock! Knock! Knock!

"Da?" Mila called out as she flung the door open, her unsteady frame swaying in her unbalanced stupor. Her blurry vision struggled to adjust, and when it finally cleared, she saw them—two mid-sized, finely dressed military men standing rigidly at attention on the other side of her dusty screen door. She didn't need an explanation. The air left her lungs in a sharp, silent gasp as her knees buckled. Collapsing to the floor, she lay on her side, emotionally paralyzed. No sound escaped her lips. No tears streamed down her cheeks. The numbness enveloped her completely, a void where panic, grief, or anger should have been.

The men began to speak, their words formal and sedated, but their voices blurred into a hollow drone. She couldn't focus. She couldn't understand. It didn't matter. She already knew. Yaroslav was gone. And now she was left alone. Alone with a child she wasn't sure she could bear to bring into this world, in a place that felt more isolating than ever. She was abandoned. Utterly abandoned.

Time stood still. Mila barely registered the hands that helped her to her feet and guided her to the worn linen couch inside. Her body moved, but her mind remained frozen, trapped in the disbelief of what she had just heard. She sat stiffly, her gaze unfocused, her hands trembling in her lap. Shock wrapped around her like a suffocating fog, delaying the crushing reality that her husband was truly gone. But Mila didn't want time to process. She didn't want their words, their formal condolences, or their carefully chosen explanations. She wanted Yaroslav. She wanted her husband, whole and alive, walking through the door to hold her in his arms.

The Russian military officers stood before her, their postures stiff, their voices measured as they expressed their deepest condolences. They answered her questions as best they could, though their words felt hollow. They explained that the *Medved* had experienced technical issues and had sunk in the North Pacific Ocean. The entire crew was lost. The men were deemed heroes, their sacrifices lauded as honorable and necessary.

Mila stared at them, her chest tightening with a rage she could barely contain. Their empathy felt patronizing, their words meaningless. She didn't want their grief or their empty reassurances. She refused to believe them. Her husband couldn't be gone—not Yaroslav. Her hands clenched into fists as she silently rejected their story. The *Medved* might have sunk, but Yaroslav had survived. He had to. He would come home to her, just in time to hold her hand and welcome the birth of their son. He had promised, and she clung to that promise with every ounce of her being.

One of the men gently placed a hand on her exposed knee, his voice low and empathetic as he offered words of comfort. He was doing what he thought was best in a moment of unspeakable grief. But his touch ignited a spark of fury in Mila. Her body stiffened, and with a sudden burst of energy, she rose to her feet. Her trembling hands pushed against the ribbons and medals adorning his chest, a symbolic strike against the uniform that represented the source of her anguish. The force of her movement, however, betrayed her fragile state. The abrupt rise triggered postural hypotension—her blood pressure plummeted as her body failed to adjust.

Her vision blurred, her head spun, and within seconds, darkness enveloped her. Mila collapsed forward, unable to catch herself, her body crumpling toward the coffee table. The glass top shattered with a deafening crash as her forehead struck it, followed by the sickening crunch of her nasal cartilage. Crimson streaks spread across the jagged shards as she lay motionless, her limp form draped across the bloodied remnants of the table. The two men froze, their training no match for the sheer unpredictability of the moment. Their instincts kicked in a beat too late as they rushed to her side, shouting for help. The room, filled with grief moments earlier, now echoed with chaos and fear.

* * *

Gremikha Naval Medical Center, Emergency Room

Strobe lights pierced the darkness behind Mila's closed eyelids, while a cacophony of urgent beeping filled the room, relaying critical updates on her faltering vitals. The sterile air was heavy with tension as Russian Navy medical technicians worked in frantic precision. Mila tried desperately to open her eyes, to fight her way back to consciousness, but her eyelids felt impossibly heavy, as if glued shut. Each feeble attempt was met with a wave of darkness, pulling her back into the depths of a temporary coma. The potent opioid coursing through her IV dulled her pain but kept her trapped in a twilight state, her mind hovering between awareness and oblivion.

The surgical team surrounded her, their methods quick and deliberate. A commanding surgeon stood over her, scalpel in hand, his voice barking orders in clipped Russian as he made a decisive incision across her swollen abdomen. Blood pooled beneath her as he worked to retrieve the 7-month-old fetus from her womb. Every second counted, but Mila's body had reached its limit. The monitors blared in protest as her vitals flatlined. The doctors fought to stabilize her, their voices rising in urgency, but the hemorrhaging was unyielding. Despite their best efforts, Mila's life slipped away on the operating table, her body unable to withstand the trauma. Her newborn son, tiny and fragile, was rushed to intensive care. The surgical team turned their focus to him, their faces shadowed by a mix of determination and sorrow. He was alive—for now—but his fight for survival had only just begun.

His fragile life was preserved in an incubator for three months before he was quietly transferred to a top-secret government program in Moscow known as Komitet Gosudarstvennogo Razvitiya (KGR)—the Committee for State Development. On paper, the program didn't exist. In reality, it was a breeding ground for orphans and trafficked infants, designed to forge a new generation of expendable operatives for a covert division of the Russian Foreign Intelligence Service (Sluzhba Vneshney Razvedki or SVR).

Formerly known as the KGB, the SVR was tasked with intelligence gathering and espionage operations beyond Russian borders. But KGR agents weren't just spies; they were weapons. Hidden deep within the Caucasus Mountains, a thousand miles south of Moscow, the KGR compound was an isolated and fortified facility. There, operatives grew up in a world devoid of outside influence. They learned basic life skills to function within society, but their primary education revolved around military strategy, espionage, and special operations. Their sole purpose: to serve and defend Mother Russia at any cost.

Among them was KGR6695, later known as Aleksandr Vasiliev. From the beginning, Aleksandr exhibited an unrelenting drive that set him apart. Something innate in his blood propelled him to success, creating a zero-tolerance attitude toward failure. Second place was never an option, even if it required bending rules or altering tactics. Aleksandr was a born leader, commanding respect and fear among his peers and instructors alike. But more than that, he was a born killer—efficient, detached, and devoid of remorse. For him, the concept of morality was irrelevant; his focus was singular and absolute. In the isolated world of KGR, where failure equated to erasure, Aleksandr thrived. He didn't just survive the program— he mastered it, becoming the crown jewel of Russia's most secret and sinister project.

CHAPTER 10

U.S. Naval Station Pearl Harbor

Pearl Harbor, Hawaii

A few days after the Russian Oscar II submarine settled as a mangled heap of steel on the Pacific Ocean floor, the USS *Constellation* and its accompanying warships made their way into Naval Station Pearl Harbor, Hawaii, in a solemn, single-file procession. The massive carrier, its imposing 1,088-foot frame cutting through the waters, was met by a fleet of tugboats just outside the harbor. The smaller vessels carefully guided the 40,000-ton ship toward the Berthing Wharf, located northwest of Ford Island. On the flight deck, sailors stood shoulder-to-shoulder in their crisp white uniforms, performing the time-honored naval tradition of manning the rails, a sign of respect for the port. Above, two HH-60H helicopters maintained a vigilant channel guard, flying patrol routes around the colossal ship to ensure safety and respond swiftly to any potential threats or mishaps.

Despite the carrier's grandeur, its arrival was subdued. A small gathering of families and curious civilians stood onshore, many already visiting the nearby USS *Arizona* Memorial. For the most part, the USS *Constellation* slipped into port unnoticed by the broader public, its presence unpublicized, its mission still cloaked in secrecy. Though the USS *Constellation's* crew carried out their ceremonial duties, many sailors couldn't shake the weight of the recent mission, nor the secrets they were sworn to keep.

The battle group was originally scheduled to dock in Everett, Washington, but unforeseen circumstances forced a diversion to Pearl Harbor. Onboard the ships, rumors ran rampant, ranging from reports of bad weather to speculation about facility issues in the Emerald City. No one had definitive answers, but the abrupt change left many sailors and their families scrambling. The families who had planned to travel to Everett to board the USS *Constellation* for the much-anticipated Tiger Cruise down to San Diego were notified of the last-minute adjustment. They were offered the opportunity to meet the ship in Hawaii instead, but less than half were able to rearrange their accommodations on such short notice. The disappointment and frustration among families were substantial, as months of planning and excitement were upended in an instant.

Still, the military's priorities were clear, and this was always communicated to the families as a potential risk. Schedules and objectives could shift without warning, a reality of life in service to the U.S. Navy. For the sailors, it was just another reminder of the sacrifices their loved ones made to support their mission. For the families left behind, it was a bitter pill to swallow, one that underscored the unpredictable nature of life in the armed forces.

The 5,000 personnel aboard the USS *Constellation* weren't overly disappointed by the unexpected detour to Pearl Harbor, especially after a grueling six-month deployment. Spending a few days in Waikiki before heading east to their home port in southern California wasn't much of a hardship. Any U.S. port would have sufficed, but between Pearl Harbor and Everett, there was little debate. Not that the crew had a say in the matter. What they didn't know, and wouldn't be told, was the full extent of the Russian incident that had unfolded a thousand miles to the north. Beyond the Commanding Officer, Executive Officer, and a select few personnel from the ASMOD with top-secret clearances, no one had the "need-to-know" clearance to understand what had transpired.

Keeping the crew in the dark wasn't just protocol; it was a calculated necessity. Sharing even the faintest hint of classified information could lead to curiosity, and curiosity could lead to prying where it didn't belong. For national security, it was safer if the majority of the sailors remained oblivious. Fortunately, the Navy controlled all channels of communication with an iron grip. E-mail was still in its infancy, tightly monitored by information technology and security teams. Social media and cell phones—the modern engines of rumors and misinformation—were still years away from becoming everyday staples. In an era where information traveled at a more controlled pace, the risk of leaks or speculation was far easier to manage. For the sailors, ignorance was bliss. For their commanders, it was a necessity.

LCDR Carter, LT Ellis, AWC Bishop, and AW2 Hayes left the ASMOD briefing room that fateful night, each retreating to their separate berthing quarters. Sworn to secrecy, they were bound by duty to remain silent, forced to carry the weight of a fabricated story. Officially, the mission was recorded as a routine dipping sonar operation marred by the "accidental" loss of armament—a narrative carefully crafted to conceal the truth.

The events of the night were meticulously documented in their NATOPS records as a mishap, triggering an investigation. But the inquiry was nothing more than a formality. A select group of handpicked personnel managed the process to ensure the predetermined outcome: a clean cover-up that absolved the crew of misconduct while keeping the operation buried under layers of classified obfuscation. For the team, this was just another day in the life of special operations. Yet the nature of this mission, like so many others, carried a unique burden. These were the assignments no one spoke of beyond the immediate crew. Not in passing, not in camaraderie, and certainly not outside the confines of their unit. The stakes were too high; leaked information could easily fall into the wrong hands, jeopardizing national security.

Being part of an elite team was both a blessing and a curse. In the moment, it felt exhilarating—a chance to live out the kinds of experiences most only see in the most gripping fictional movies. But with time, the cost became evident. The adrenaline faded, and the unresolved emotions crept in. The silence meant there was no outlet for the memories that lingered, for the questions and the guilt that festered in the shadows of their minds. The curse of the elite wasn't the missions themselves. It was the aftermath—the moments alone, long after the fact, when the experiences resurfaced to wreak havoc on the soul.

* * *

The White House Situation Room

Washington D.C.

"Mr. President, Russian President Novikov is on line one," a staff member announced, stepping into the room where the U.S. President sat surrounded by his National Security Council. President Palmer leaned forward in his chair at the head of the conference table, strewn with documents from a binder marked "Sensitive Compartmented Information." He closed his eyes briefly, drawing in a deliberate four-second breath through his crooked nose—a relic of a decade-old deviated septum. As he exhaled forcefully through dry, pursed lips, he noted the faint sting of chapped skin— a reminder of the long hours spent under the glare of the West Wing's lights. Steadying himself, he reached out and pressed the speaker button on the phone. The room tensed as the voice of Russian President Boris Novikov broke the silence. It was subdued, tinged with weariness and a faint note of surrender.

"Mr. President," Novikov began, his voice measured yet strained, "it appears we have a... complicated situation on our hands."

President Palmer straightened in his chair, his expression calm but his eyes sharp as they scanned the faces of his Security Council. "A complicated situation?" he replied, his tone carrying a subtle edge. "Please, President Novikov, tell us how we may assist."

He locked eyes with his team, a silent display of confidence and authority that filled the room. Despite the hostility humming in the air, Palmer's demeanor projected unwavering control—a deliberate reminder to all present, both allies and adversaries, that the

United States would approach this matter from a position of strength.

"Yes, well, I'm not sure if I should be thanking you for preventing a third world war or furious with you for destroying a $100 million submarine—along with its weapons and personnel," President Novikov retorted, his tone laced with thinly veiled irritation. "Either way, we now have a mess to clean up before conspiracy theories start spiraling out of control." President Palmer's posture shifted slightly, his tone softening in a rehearsed display of diplomacy. "In this case, Mr. President, the theories wouldn't be too far from reality. But let me say this—I'm grateful you reached out before it was too late." He offered a thin veneer of grace, though he and his team had known about the defecting submarine days before the Kremlin's official acknowledgment.

Palmer leaned back in his chair, allowing a beat of silence to emphasize his next point. "I assume we'll agree to call this a training accident. Of course, the actual location will need to be altered and classified."

Novikov's expression darkened, though Palmer couldn't see it through the secure line. "A training accident? That doesn't exactly bode well for our multi-billion-dollar submarine program," he replied, his sarcasm sharp. "And frankly, I doubt the media will buy it."

"All due respect, Mr. President, I couldn't care less what the media buys!" President Palmer's voice rose with restrained fury, his frustration cutting through the room like a blade. "You lost a nuclear submarine carrying nuclear warheads on your watch—a direct threat to the safety of the United States of America! And let's not pretend this is an isolated incident. Add this 'training accident' to your growing list of failures: K-8, K-219, K-278, K-429!"

Palmer's piercing words echoed in the tense silence that followed. Without waiting for a response, he pressed the speaker button with finality, abruptly ending the international call. The room remained frozen, the weight of the President's fiery rebuke settling over the Security Council like a heavy fog.

* * *

20 Nautical Miles west of San Diego, CA

The HUNTER 613 aircrew sat in the HS-2 ready room alongside five other combat crews, brimming with anticipation for their final flight after a grueling six-month WestPac deployment. Passengers, equally eager, mingled quietly while the briefing officer detailed the mission plan. The squadron's four SH-60F and two HH-60H helicopters would depart the USS *Constellation* approximately 10 nautical miles west of Point Loma, flying in tight formation to their destination: Naval Air Station North Island.

The plan was seamless. Upon landing, the helicopters would taxi along the winding runways to the HS-2 hangar flight line, where the final phase of their journey awaited. Coordinated over the radio by the squadron's Commanding Officer, all helicopter pilots would perform a synchronized shutdown of their rotors and engines. The moment the aircraft settled and the rotors stilled, the aircrew would exit their helicopters, stepping into the arms of their loved ones who had gathered at the hangar. After six months away, it wasn't just another homecoming—it was a moment that held the promise of reunions, relief, and celebration. For the weary crew, the mission wasn't just about delivering their aircraft safely to the ground. It was about delivering themselves back to the people who had been waiting for them, counting the days, hours, and minutes until this very moment.

Returning from a six-month deployment was an emotional event on many levels, each crewmember carrying their unique weight of experience. Some had endured the heartbreak of losing a loved one during their time away, while others had missed monumental life events like the birth of a child. A few returned to the sting of Dear John letters, knowing there would be no one waiting for them on the tarmac. Yet for the majority, the moment of reunion with family and children was a long-anticipated milestone—a beacon of hope that sustained them through the endless days at sea.

That moment of arrival felt surreal, almost dreamlike. It was an overwhelming blend of emotions: nervousness, excitement, shyness, and even lingering sadness. For some, it was the joyous culmination of months of longing; for others, it was a bittersweet reminder of what they had missed. Each crewmember processed the experience in their way, placing their emotions on a temporary back burner, focusing instead on navigating the delicate balance of returning to a world that had moved on without them. The homecoming was not just a return to port—it was a return to life, filled with joy, adjustment, and, for many, healing.

Anxious sailors, dressed in their impeccably pressed dress white uniforms, gathered in a growing mass near the superstructure of the USS *Constellation.* They waited eagerly as the last of the aircraft prepared to depart, anticipation buzzing in the salty sea air. Soon, they would take their positions along the outer edges of the flight deck to man the rails, signaling their much-anticipated return to their home port in Coronado.

On the flight deck, six Seahawk helicopters roared to life, their main rotors spinning with ferocious energy as the aircrew completed their final pre-flight checks. The powerful downdraft whipped across the deck, kicking up the last remnants of deployment grit. One by one, the helicopters lifted gracefully from the Connie, banking northeast toward their final destination. Inside the aircraft cabins, excitement radiated through the cramped spaces. The aircrew, brimming with nervous energy, chatted eagerly about their loved ones and detailed plans to make up for lost time. Laughter mixed with snippets of stories as they leaned into the joy of what awaited them. Each mile flown brought them closer to the reunions they had dreamed of for six long months.

"HUNTER 613, please divert to San Clemente to pick up high-value PAX." The voice of the USS *Constellation's* Air Boss crackled over the radio, delivering the deflating orders.

Commander Carter's jaw tightened as he keyed the mic. "Roger, HUNTER 613 diverting to San Clemente." His tone carried reluctant professionalism, masking the frustration that hung heavily in the cabin.

The aircrew exchanged glances but said nothing, the weight of their heavy thoughts filling the confined space. After everything they'd endured, after months at sea and the unease of their recent mission, this felt like one final gut punch. The chance to finally head home, to embrace their families, was delayed yet again.

As the helicopter banked toward San Clemente, the crew shifted in their seats, resigned to the detour. They were all desperate for the escape—a break from the monotony and the secrecy that had defined their deployment. The change of scenery and the chance to return to normalcy seemed just out of reach for a little while longer.

The SH-60F Seahawk touched down on a helicopter pad at the north end of the Naval Auxiliary Landing Field, its spinning rotors slicing through the morning air as the rising sun began to burn off the fog lingering across the 57-square-mile island. The low-hanging mist swirled and dissipated under the force of the rotors as the helicopter taxied toward the nearby Special Warfare training facility flight line. In the aft cabin, Chief Bishop and Petty Officer Hayes prepared for the high-value PAX (passenger) transfer. They secured the troop seats near the sonar dome, ensuring the cabin was ready for their unexpected guest. Bishop, always mindful of his crew and passengers, chose to occupy the less comfortable seat, leaving the more padded and ergonomic TSO seat for the incoming VIP. At the controls, Commander Carter carefully followed the painted taxiway markings, guiding the aircraft to a designated stopping point. Once in position, he applied the brakes and brought the helicopter to a steady halt. The crew sat in relative silence, waiting for the arrival of their mysterious passenger, the deafening sound of the rotors the only thing breaking the stillness of the moment.

They sat in the vibrating helo, its rotors pounding the tarmac with rhythmic force, for what felt like an eternity. In reality, only 10 minutes had passed, but each second dragged as they silently wondered who was so important that they had to divert from the aircraft carrier to pick them up. The decision made little sense—there were plenty of other U.S. Navy helicopter assets in the area that could have handled this task without sending them 50 miles in the opposite direction.

No one spoke, but the frustration was unmistakable. Each crewmember sat with their thoughts, bitterly imagining the other helicopters already on the ground, their engines shut down. By now, those aircrews would be embracing their loved ones, soaking in the joy of long-awaited reunions. Meanwhile, they were stuck here, tethered to duty, waiting for an unnamed passenger who had stolen their moment. The cabin felt heavy—not from the weight of their gear, but from the unspoken jealousy and longing that hung in the air like the relentless drone of the rotors above.

The crew expected to see a senior officer in khakis, wearing a deflated orange PAX life vest secured around their neck and waist. Instead, their attention was drawn to two burly, clean-cut men approaching from the three o'clock position. They wore matching gray suits and charcoal Ray-Ban sunglasses, their presence immediately exuding authority. As they neared, one of the men flipped open a black leather wallet, revealing a Central Intelligence Agency badge behind a clear plastic display. The second agent did the same, their movements crisp and deliberate. Without hesitation, one of them politely but firmly addressed Commander Carter.

"Commander, we need you to shut down the helicopter," he shouted in an even tone that carried no room for negotiation.

Carter exchanged a glance with his crew but complied, toggling the switches. The rotors whined as the brakes engaged, gradually slowing their violent spinning to a steady halt. The deafening roar faded into silence, leaving only the rhythmic hum of cooling engines as the men in suits stood waiting, their stoic expressions betraying nothing of the purpose that had diverted the crew's flight.

Chief Bishop and Petty Officer Hayes exchanged a quick glance, their confusion mirrored in their eyes. Silently, Hayes mouthed, "What the hell does the CIA want with us?"

One of the agents stepped forward, his tone polite but firm. "Gentlemen, please come with us."

Bishop raised a hand, his voice steady but laced with suspicion. "What's this about?"

Before the agent could respond, Commander Carter, standing tall outside the cabin doorway, gave a subtle downward motion with his hand, signaling his crew to stand down and follow orders.

The agent softened slightly, his voice calm and measured. "I apologize for the inconvenience. I understand you're all eager to get home to your families, and I assure you this shouldn't take long. We'll explain everything inside. We can't discuss the details out here." The crew hesitated for a beat, the weight of the moment sinking in, before nodding in reluctant agreement. Without another word, the agents gestured for them to follow, their brisk, measured steps leading the way toward whatever answers and questions awaited inside.

The four were escorted in a military Humvee to a secure safehouse just a few miles from their helicopter. The unassuming facility was typically used for Navy SEAL advanced interrogation tactics training, situated near the infamous BUD/S Phase III "Kill House," a site dedicated to close-quarters battle (CQB) exercises. Its stark, utilitarian exterior only heightened the aircrew's unease.

Upon arrival, they were subjected to an exhaustive frisk by the agents, who methodically stripped them of any possible recording devices or electronic gear. The process was thorough, bordering on invasive, and only served to amplify the frustration simmering beneath their professional demeanor. After completing the search, one of the agents offered yet another measured apology. "We're sorry for the inconvenience, truly. We understand this isn't how you expected to spend your day, but rest assured, you'll be back with your loved ones as soon as possible."

The reassurance fell flat. The aircrew exchanged silent glances, their skepticism growing with every passing minute. Whatever was going on, it wasn't standard protocol, and their mission's unexpected detour now felt like the opening act of something far more complex.

"First off, thank you all for your service," the CIA agent began, his voice calm yet devoid of warmth. "What we discuss today is classified as Top Secret. Since you hold Secret clearances, we are required to brief you on the circumstances surrounding your involvement."

The agent's gaze swept across the room, meeting each crew member's eyes with a piercing intensity. "You were instrumental in locating and identifying the Russian asset in the Aleutians Trench. Your diligence was imperative to the safety of this great nation. In fact, the President of the United States is fully aware of your contributions and commends your actions." He paused, letting the weight of the statement settle before continuing, his tone sharpening. "However, this is not a mission that will be awarded, acknowledged, or discussed in any way. The mission was pre-classified beyond your need to know and resulted in what we'll call an unfavorable outcome for the Russian navy.

"In the next few days, you'll see reports in the media about what happened. Whatever narrative you hear is how we'll keep it. You are not to discuss what you saw, heard, or did with anyone— not even with each other." The agent's face remained stone-cold, his expression cutting through the tension in the room like a scalpel. "Failure to comply will result in immediate court-martial under UCMJ Article 92, for violating general orders and regulations. The consequences of such actions include imprisonment, dishonorable discharge, and fines. Do you understand and agree with what I'm telling you?"

Silence hung in the air, heavy and oppressive, as the crew members processed the gravity of the agent's words. Each nodded slowly, knowing there was no room for misunderstanding—or error.

The verbal agreements were recorded by a small device sitting ominously in the center of the table, surrounded by uncomfortably hard plastic chairs. The aircrew leaned in, tense but composed, as each gave their quiet affirmation. Following the recording, they were presented with an official document stamped with the Pentagon's embossed seal at the header. Despite their exhaustion, none of them signed immediately. Each read the document twice, meticulously parsing every word. Whether official or not, this was a contract that would define the rest of their lives. Only when they were certain of its implications did they finally put pen to paper.

In silence, they returned to their helicopter, the weight of the moment pressing down on them. The rotors whined as HUNTER 613 spun up and lifted off from San Clemente Island, setting a direct path to Naval Air Station North Island. The cabin was heavy with deep thoughts, a somber mood blanketing the crew. Though they had done nothing wrong—in fact, they may have prevented a world war—an inexplicable feeling of guilt and shame clung to them, as if the burden of what they knew was too much to bear.

The lonely SH-60F Seahawk touched down on the HS-2 flight line, a stark contrast to the usual buzz of activity. The flight line was eerily quiet, devoid of the other crews who had already long since reunited with their loved ones. But in the distance, through the glass of the double hangars, they saw them—their families, waiting patiently.

* * *

As the engines powered down and the rotors slowed to a halt, the crew quietly disembarked. For a moment, their compartmentalized training kept them restrained, their emotions locked away. Then, one by one, LCDR Carter, LT Ellis, AWC Bishop, and AW2 Hayes broke into a run. Years of rigorous discipline and secret missions melted away in the arms of the people who mattered most. Though they returned to their day-to-day lives, the weight of that historic night in the North Pacific remained. Not a word of what transpired was ever disclosed. True to their orders, they carried the secret—buried deep in their hearts—to the grave.

Weeks earlier, a 3.7-magnitude undersea earthquake had been detected off the coast of Washington. The tremor, while noticeable to seismologists, didn't trigger any tsunami warnings or raise alarms. Minor quakes were common along the tectonic plates running up and down the Pacific Northwest, and this one was quickly dismissed as routine. It had been over three decades since any significant seismic event had caused widespread damage in the region. The last major natural disaster was the 1980 eruption of Mount St. Helens, which claimed 57 lives, reshaped the landscape, and blanketed ash across states as far away as Wisconsin and the Dakotas. The disastrous eruption left a lasting psychological impact, shifting public concern toward volcanic activity and leaving earthquake fears in its shadow. The recent tremor, centered just west of Cape Flattery, didn't even warrant a passing mention in major news outlets. It was covered only in the local Makah Tribal News, where it was briefly noted and quickly forgotten—a small blip in the constant hum of natural activity along the Cascadia Subduction Zone.

The morning after the USS *Constellation* returned home, CNN broke the story, their bold headline dominating the screen: RUSSIAN NUCLEAR SUBMARINE RESCUE IN PROGRESS.

Within hours, FOX News, NPR, and other media outlets followed suit, branding the event as the world's top story. News anchors speculated on the details. According to reports, a Russian submarine had been conducting a routine surveillance mission in international waters in the North Pacific Ocean when it suffered a catastrophic main reactor failure. The sub had reportedly sunk somewhere within a 100-mile radius of the Bering Sea, sparking an urgent joint rescue operation between U.S. and Russian forces.

Journalists emphasized the stakes, highlighting the limited time the crew had for survival. While nuclear submarines can theoretically remain submerged for years, producing their own oxygen, the crew's food and water supplies would eventually be depleted. Worse, concerns grew over the possibility that the submarine had sunk to crushing depths, where the immense water pressure could breach the hull and flood the vessel, dooming those trapped inside. The ticking clock of survival gripped viewers worldwide. Experts debated the risks of radiation leaks, international cooperation, and what the rescue efforts might mean for the strained relationship between the two superpowers. The narrative spun a harrowing tale of diplomacy, technology, and human endurance—while those truly in the know stayed silent, aware that the real story lay far beneath the surface. The United States government allowed the Russian government to take the lead in a carefully orchestrated false investigation, feeding misinformation to the global media. This strategic move absolved the U.S. from direct accountability for the incident while providing valuable intelligence on Russia's ability to craft and disseminate deceptive narratives to the public.

News outlets worldwide ran with the empathetic angle provided by Russia, showing pictures of the *Medved's* crew, their faces solemn and heroic. These carefully curated images aired hourly, paired with repeated updates about the supposed rescue effort, creating a poignant human-interest story. The tactic successfully deflected anger and potential calls for revenge that might have arisen if the truth—an American torpedo sinking the Russian sub—had been revealed. The narrative painted the tragedy as an unfortunate technical failure rather than an act of war, quelling the conflict between two global superpowers while keeping the true events buried deep beneath the waves, both literally and figuratively.

For over two weeks, false updates of hope and survival dominated the airwaves, carefully fed from Moscow to news outlets worldwide. Civilians in both Russia and the United States held candlelit vigils in public squares, their handwritten signs bearing messages of love, hope, and solidarity. In an unexpected irony, the tragedy seemed to unite the two nations in a rare moment of harmony. When the unfortunate deaths of all 44 crew members were officially confirmed, the heartbreak reverberated globally. Thousands mourned, shedding tears for sailors and families they had never met but felt a deep compassion for. The incident had offered many a cause larger than themselves, a fleeting sense of connection in an often-divided world.

But as is the nature of public attention, the grief was short-lived. Just weeks later, the tragic and unexpected death of Princess Diana captured headlines, drawing focus away from the loss of the Russian submarine's crew. The vigils, protests, and cries of solidarity faded into the background, overtaken by new waves of collective mourning.

Time moved on, for both nations and for those directly involved. The true story of the *Medved* and its demise remained locked away, classified to this day, a secret buried as deeply as the submarine itself.

PART II

THE REDEMPTION

CHAPTER 11

High above in the rugged North Cascade Range with icy peaks dominating the Pacific Northwest horizon, Brody Hayes yelled over the howling wind to the struggling Drew Washburn below him, "Focus on your breathing! Purse your lips and push out from your lower abdomen! We're close to the pinnacle! We'll rest there!"

The Navy corpsman from NAS Whidbey Island, tethered below Hayes by a sturdy 9.8 mm climbing rope, nodded in acknowledgment, catching most of the words through the wind gusts. He turned to relay the message down the line to the other climbers, Chief Conrad Jacobia and Petty Officer Mike Tofino, who were staggered at 30-foot intervals connected to the rope, their positions carefully spaced for safe and efficient glacial travel. Each step tested their endurance as their crampons crunched into the ice, the rope swaying slightly between them as the wind tried to pull them off balance. The cold air burned their lungs, and the vast expanse of the glacier below seemed to stretch endlessly. Hayes pressed forward, the spike of his ice axe biting into the taxing terrain with each determined step.

Mountaineering is the ultimate test of patience, technique, fitness, and decision-making under constant distress. In the unforgiving alpine world, where every choice carries weight, Brody Hayes was the one you wanted on the sharp end of the rope when disaster struck. While many physically trained individuals can manage the climb, few possess the ability to think critically and act selflessly when confronted with the harsh realities of high-altitude survival. At elevations where oxygen is scarce, energy is drained, and resources are limited, mother nature's unpredictable wrath becomes the greatest adversary. It's in these moments—when the elements conspire against you—that true heroes emerge. Time and again, Hayes had proven himself to be one of those rare individuals. Calm under pressure, decisive in chaos, and unyielding in his pursuit of safety for his team, he exemplified the grit and resilience demanded by the mountains.

Brody Hayes was honorably discharged from the U.S. Navy in February 2002. His extensive training and experiences as an aviation rescue swimmer allowed him to seamlessly transition into the private sector as a mountain guide in his home state of Washington. He primarily led clients through the rugged Cascade Range, but his expertise often took him eastward for seasonal climbs in the Himalayas. With seven successful expeditions on Mount Everest under his belt, Hayes was more than qualified to help others achieve their dreams at high altitude.

Unlike many in the mountaineering world, Hayes wasn't driven by ego or a desire to pad his resume with impressive stats. He loved the outdoors with a passion that was almost instinctual, fueled by an insatiable thirst for adventure. It was a mindset instilled in him by his grandfather, his childhood role model, who often advised, "Find a career you love, and you'll never work a day in your life." Hayes clung to those words after his grandfather lost a vicious battle to cancer a decade earlier, carrying his legacy and wisdom with him to every summit.

As he gazed out at the picturesque layers of snow-capped peaks stretching endlessly toward the horizon, Hayes couldn't help but feel a profound sense of gratitude. His life wasn't without its challenges, but it was fulfilling in ways few could understand. Surrounded by the beauty and unpredictability of nature, he wouldn't trade it for anything.

"One step in front of the other! Nice and slow, it's not a race! Focus on that next step!" The seasoned guide called out, his voice steady and empathetic as he encouraged his three friends to keep climbing. They followed his advice, pressure breathing and utilizing the rest step to combat the demands of the ascent toward the summit of Mount Shuksan.

Pressure breathing is a technique used to counter the effects of decreasing atmospheric pressure at higher altitudes. It involves forcing an exhale while engaging in belly breathing. Since the lower portion of the lungs has greater capacity than the upper, maximizing the use of this area improves oxygen exchange. The forced breath increases pressure in the lungs, optimizing gas exchange in the alveoli, and helping to mitigate altitude-related oxygen deprivation. The rest step is an essential climbing gait for steep ascents. With each step, the climber pauses briefly to shift the burden of their body weight and heavy pack to the rear outstretched leg, allowing the forward leg to bend and rest. The duration of the pause depends on the altitude and the angle of the slope, ranging from a quick moment to an extended hold. When combined, pressure breathing and the rest step create an efficient and effective method for mountaineering, preserving strength and stamina while reducing fatigue. Teaching these techniques, ingrained in the guide's expertise, allowed the group to focus on the basics while pushing through the unrelenting climb.

The climbing team had left their basecamp at the mosquito-infested Lake Ann around 3 a.m., stepping into the darkness with a line of headlamps bobbing like fireflies in the night. Their route took them through the intricate Fisher Chimneys, a challenging section featuring a series of 4th-class rope-assisted rock climbs. The steep granite scramble required careful focus. As they reached the top, the early morning light began to transform the pitch-black landscape, revealing the majestic North Cascades in hues of pink and orange. The team took a short break, breathing in the crisp mountain air as they prepared for the next phase of their climb. Crampons were secured to mountaineering boots, and ice axes replaced trekking poles as they transitioned onto the snowy expanse of the Upper Curtis Glacier and Sulphide Glacier. The glacier route was a complex, frozen maze dotted with yawning crevasses and towering seracs.

At the front of the rope team, Hayes led with confidence, teaching the Navy climbers the essential skills to safely navigate the hazards of high-altitude glacier travel. He demonstrated how to assess avalanche risks and identify unstable snow bridges that could collapse underfoot. Throughout the climb, they practiced proper rope travel, maintaining safe distances and clear communication. Occasionally, a misstep would send a climber tumbling. Hayes would shout commands as the team instinctively dropped to their ice axes, driving the picks into the snow to arrest the fall and secure the line. Despite the physical toll and technical challenges, the team pressed on, their progress a testament to their resilience and Hayes's leadership. The mountain was an arduous teacher, but under Hayes's watchful eye, they were prepared for every challenge it threw their way.

Mountaineering was a natural transition from military special operations for Hayes, as it mirrored many aspects of his former life. Each day presented a new mission, sharp decision-making, physical endurance, and a focus on survival. The specialized gear, strategic tactics, and sense of camaraderie felt familiar, though nothing could fully replicate the intensity of his military career. The trauma Hayes endured during his time in the Navy was unconsciously channeled into the challenges of the arduous mountains. The suffering inherent in climbing, from harsh weather to physical exhaustion, served as a subtle balm for wounds he had yet to confront. Though he meticulously avoided unnecessary risks and hazards to ensure his clients' safety, Hayes found fulfillment in the rare moments when his training allowed him to save lives. It was a deeply ingrained part of who he was, forged through years of preparation and hard-earned experience.

* * *

As his climbing team ascended higher, each deliberate step accompanied by the distinct sound of crampons biting into frozen snow and the howl of wind gusts, Hayes's mind wandered to his 2005 Everest expedition. It had been his second attempt on the world's tallest peak, a climb that had tested every ounce of his resolve. A freak storm, carrying 80 mph winds, had hammered their high camp at 26,000 feet, forcing his team to hunker down and fight through the night. The tents, though built for extreme conditions, were no match for the storm's fury. Guy lines were fastened around heavy rocks to anchor the shelters, but the persistent wind bent poles, collapsed fabric, and dragged the tents—rock anchors and all—across the exposed expanse of the South Col.

Hayes, bundled in his Eddie Bauer down suit, braved the chaos outside. Shielding his face from ice shards propelled by the gale, he crawled through the screaming wind to reinforce the tents with ice screw anchors. One by one, he twisted the aluminum screws deep into the rock-hard ice, securing them to the tent's corner webbing with locking carabiners. His efforts anchored the tents in place, but without the protective barrier of a snow wall, the gusts continued to batter them mercilessly. Inside, the thin fabric walls amplified the cacophony—the constant flapping of nylon sounded like thunder trapped in a confined space. The mountaineering team could do nothing but huddle in their sleeping bags, praying the seams would hold until morning. For Hayes, it was a night seared into memory, a reminder of both the mountain's unforgiving nature and his own resilience in the face of it.

Hayes monitored the open radio frequencies on his Motorola handheld, the static punctuated by fragmented calls for updates and assistance. Among the voices, a grim situation emerged: a team of four Climbing Sherpa paired with four Chinese clients had become pinned down at an area known as the Balcony, roughly 27,500 feet above sea level. The group had been making their summit push through the frigid night when the storm suddenly swept in with brutal force, obliterating visibility and turning the mountain into a hostile battlefield. Cut off from any safe route, either upward toward the summit or back down to the relative safety of Camp IV, they made the difficult, desperate decision to hunker down and wait out the storm. Hayes felt a knot tighten in his chest as he listened. The Balcony, with its limited space and exposure to the elements, was no place to ride out extreme weather. At that altitude, the human body was already in a state of deterioration, and every minute spent waiting in the thin, freezing air brought them closer to exhaustion, frostbite, or worse. He tightened his grip on the radio, fully aware that the clock was ticking against them.

Survival in the death zone—altitudes above 26,000 feet or 8,000 meters—is nearly impossible for extended periods. At this height, the atmosphere contains only about a third of the oxygen found at sea level, and the human body begins to shut down, cell by cell. Even with weeks of preparation, climbers must carefully manage their exposure to this extreme environment. Prior to entering the death zone, climbers spend weeks acclimatizing, ascending to higher camps and then returning to lower ones to allow their bodies to adapt. This process, often referred to as "climbing high and sleeping low," encourages the production of additional red blood cells, which carry oxygen more efficiently throughout the body. After three to four weeks of this grueling routine, most climbers are as physiologically prepared as possible for their summit attempt. However, no amount of preparation can fully counteract the effects of the death zone. At this altitude, the body is in a state of gradual deterioration, with essential systems straining to function. The goal is to move swiftly to the summit and descend to safer elevations without lingering. Time is the enemy; every moment spent above 26,000 feet pushes climbers closer to the brink of hypoxia, frostbite, or fatal exhaustion. It's a brutal reality that makes each decision on the mountain a matter of life and death.

As the Chinese team huddled together on the precarious Balcony, bracing against the relentless storm, Hayes and his Climbing Sherpa partner, Pasang, scoured the storm-battered South Col high camp, desperate to find willing guides to assist in a rescue. Despite their pleas, none of the other climbers or guides agreed to join the effort. The situation felt like a death trap, not just for the eight mountaineers stranded above, but for anyone attempting to reach them. A handful of Climbing Sherpa from other teams expressed willingness to help, but their western guides swiftly intervened, insisting they remain at camp or risk forfeiting their pay. Hayes's frustration grew as he listened to the Chinese team's increasingly desperate calls for assistance over the radio. The pleas painted a vivid picture of their plight but fell on the deaf ears of climbers below, many of whom were singularly focused on their own survival. Everyone on the mountain understood the stakes. The inherent risks of climbing at such altitudes were no secret. You lived or died by the decisions you made with the information available to you at the time. But there were moments when the mountain threw something at you so far beyond control or prediction that survival depended on finding strength and courage buried in reserves you didn't know existed. Hayes knew this was one of those moments.

Hayes was no stranger to risking life and limb. His years in the military had deep-rooted a calm acceptance of danger and a willingness to act when others hesitated. As he weighed the risks of attempting a rescue, the alternative of doing nothing became unbearable. He couldn't live with himself if the stranded climbers lost their lives while he sat idly below, knowing he hadn't even tried. He pulled Pasang aside for a heart-to-heart. Hayes laid out the risks in stark detail, making sure his Sherpa partner understood the gravity of what they were about to undertake. It was a gamble with slim odds of success and a high probability of a fatality. Pasang didn't hesitate. His determination was immediate and unwavering. "I go, with or without you," he said firmly, his voice carrying the weight of personal stakes. One of the Sherpa stranded at the Balcony was Pasang's cousin, and nothing short of death would stop him from trying to save him. Hayes nodded, finding reassurance in Pasang's resolve. If they were going to attempt the impossible, they would do it together, bound by a shared sense of duty and an unshakable refusal to leave anyone behind.

Hayes and Pasang prepared meticulously for the grueling rescue ahead. They loaded their packs with extra oxygen bottles, thermoses filled with warm drinks, and the essentials needed to fight the brutal conditions. Switching on their headlamps, they pushed forward into the 80 mph winds that whipped across the desolate South Col, each step a battle against the stinging snow and ice that propelled painfully against their faces. The ascent was a slow, torturous crawl, but by 3 a.m., the two rescuers reached the Balcony. The dim glow of their headlamps cut through the darkness, and the stranded team could hardly believe their eyes. Eight weary climbers, on the brink of despair, stared in disbelief as their rescuers appeared from the storm. Pasang moved quickly, offering warm tea to the frostbitten climbers while Hayes replaced their depleted oxygen bottles with fresh ones, leaving a small cache on a nearby rock outcrop. With words of encouragement, Hayes rallied the team, organizing them into a slow-moving assembly line for the descent. They drunkenly staggered down the treacherous ice and rock path, leaning into gravity's assistance while Hayes and Pasang kept them moving. Each step was agonizing, their bodies teetering on the edge of collapse, but after two harrowing hours, they finally stumbled into high camp.

The sight of the bright orange, wind-beaten tents brought a flicker of relief. Hayes and Pasang worked swiftly to re-erect the collapsed shelters, anchoring them securely with ice screws and rocks. The rescued climbers, barely able to remove their crampons, crawled inside the tents to thaw their frozen bodies and snatch a few hours of desperately needed rest. By sunrise, the storm had subsided. Over the next two days, the Chinese team, under the watchful guidance of

Hayes and Pasang, descended safely to base camp. Half of the team bore the lasting scars of their ordeal, losing fingers and toes to frostbite. But they were alive. They would return home to their families within a week and, for some, live to climb another day where others decided to find new, less threatening hobbies. Hayes and Pasang, though physically spent, felt the profound reward of knowing their efforts had defied the odds and saved lives.

At the time, Hayes and Pasang's actions were celebrated as one of the most remarkable rescues in Everest's storied climbing history. The daring effort brought a flood of media attention, much of it unwelcome for Hayes. He had never sought recognition or accolades, feeling that the real reward was simply being in the right place at the right time to help those in need. For Hayes, the survival of all eight members of the stranded team was more than enough. He viewed the rescue as a testament to teamwork, grit, and the human spirit, rather than a personal achievement. While the world lauded his heroics, Hayes quietly retreated to the mountains, seeking the solace of their quiet peaks and rugged trails over the noise of fame.

* * *

"Nice job, everyone!" Hayes called out, his voice carrying over the brisk mountain air as the team reached the final major obstacle before summiting Mount Shuksan. The Sulphide Glacier leveled off, leading to the imposing granite summit pyramid that towered 600 feet above them.

Hayes stomped out a small, flat platform in the snow, signaling the team to take a break. "Hydrate and grab a snack," he advised as he unpacked the group's rock-climbing gear. Each climber peeled off their packs, sipping water and catching their breath while taking in the stunning, snow-covered peaks surrounding them. The thin air and hours of exertion had begun to take their toll, but the group's excitement was palpable. The mountain guide explained their next steps, outlining the customized class-5 route they would take up the pyramid. This wasn't just about reaching the summit; it was a training opportunity. Hayes planned to lead the climb, placing protection and securing the route as they ascended. His goal was to teach the Whidbey SAR group new climbing techniques and instill the confidence needed for their real-world rescues during their demanding day jobs.

"This is where the fun begins," Hayes said with a grin, securing his harness and double-checking his equipment. The team exchanged excited but nervous glances as they geared up, eager to push their limits and take on the challenge ahead.

No matter the clientele, capability, or experience levels, lessons were taught from the moment they left the parking lot to the moment they returned to the car. For Brody Hayes, complacency had no place on a climb, as disasters rarely come with warnings. As the saying goes, "The summit is only halfway," because the descent can be even more dangerous. Statistics showed that a staggering 80 percent of mountaineering accidents occur on the way down—a sobering reality Hayes never overlooked. Fatigue, overconfidence, the rush to descend, and the changing conditions of warmer afternoon temperatures were just a few reasons behind the high accident rate. Hayes was acutely aware of these risks, and it shaped his approach to guiding. His style emphasized constant vigilance—continually assessing the climbers, monitoring the route conditions, and remaining sharp. For him, a climb wasn't complete until everyone was safe, back at the trailhead, and swapping stories over a well-earned IPA at a local tavern.

Every climb reinforced his philosophy that the mountain doesn't care about skill or preparation. The lessons it teaches are often brutal, and only those who respect its power and remain cautious make it back to tell the tale.

CHAPTER 12

Two months prior
British Columbia, Canada

The Earth continued its obstinate rotation at an average speed of 1,000 mph, its northern hemisphere subtly tilting further away from the sun. Deep within the valleys of British Columbia, bigleaf maple and paper birch trees strained toward the diminishing light, their leaves undergoing their annual chlorophyll breakdown. The vibrant shift in color signaled the arrival of autumn, delighting tourists and locals alike, who eagerly anticipated the first heavy snowfall to herald the coming ski season. For others, however, the changing leaves were less a spectacle and more a harbinger. To them, it was a reminder of the long, cold months ahead—a season that demanded relentless preparation and steadfast resolve to ensure survival.

Six Russian operatives, all in their mid-20s, paid no attention to the picturesque surroundings outside, buried instead in the dim confines of their local asset's basement. The air was heavy with the scent of mildew and damp cement, so dense it seemed almost visible. Dust-coated bins and haphazard stacks of old books leaned against the walls, reducing the sense of space in the already cramped room. Their focus remained on preparing their newly acquired outdoor gear, hastily purchased from a nearby Canadian Tire superstore. A faded, threadbare rug, rolled out by the house owner, offered minimal insulation against the cold cement floor, but served its purpose as a makeshift workspace. The men moved in deliberate silence, organizing their supplies, their expressions set in stone as the gravity of their mission loomed over them.

Over the past week, the operatives punctiliously staggered their 12-hour flights from Moscow to Vancouver, utilizing different airlines, terminals, and days to avoid detection by customs surveillance systems. For transportation to the rendezvous point, they relied on ride-share services booked under fake aliases and paid for with one-use gift credit cards. Their orders directed them to a non-disclosed meeting site 32 kilometers east of the city, in an area just outside of Coquitlam. It was here they first encountered their local contact, a man simply known as Jack. Jack served as the logistics coordinator and intelligence officer for a decentralized Russian cell that had been embedded across western Canada for over a decade. His appearance was strikingly stereotypical, like a Russian undercover agent straight out of a Hollywood spy thriller. Standing at an unassuming 5'10" with a sturdy build of 185 pounds, he was clean-cut except for a perfectly kept brown beard flecked with gray. His piercing blue eyes sat in a pale, pasty face that gave away his years of operating in the shadows. Jack's demeanor was as sharp as his appearance, and the operatives quickly understood they were under the guidance of a seasoned professional.

Jack was a man of few words, shaped by a life built on secrets and lies. His reserved demeanor mirrored the cautious, intensive personalities of the operatives he picked up each day. Jack used an unremarkable vehicle and chose routes free of predictable patterns or heavy surveillance. He drove them back to his apartment on the city's outskirts, pulling into an underground parking lot where the surveillance cameras had long been rendered nonfunctional. Once inside, the operatives were directed to the basement—a stark, windowless space beneath Jack's unit. The room served as a temporary hideout, a secure place for the men to regroup as the final arrivals trickled in. Its sparse furnishings and utilitarian design felt more like a dungeon than living quarters, but none of the men voiced complaints. They were hardened professionals, well-acquainted with much harsher conditions from years of rigorous training and covert operations. Despite its grim appearance, the basement provided the essentials: a space to acclimate to the local time zone, review their strategy, and finalize the details of their infiltration plan across the U.S. border. It was a holding cell for preparation, each day bringing them closer to their mission's execution while ensuring any loose ends from their travel could be identified and neutralized. The air was thick with quiet focus as each operative methodically checked and rechecked their gear, their minds already in the field.

* * *

The six Russian orphans first met a decade earlier within the confines of the ruthless Komitet Gosudarstvennogo Razvitiya (KGR) program. Tucked away in an isolated pocket of the Caucasus Range, north of the Georgian border, the program operated in complete secrecy. The harsh terrain served as both a physical and psychological barrier, ensuring that no outsider stumbled upon the compound where the children were being molded into operatives. The orphans were raised by hand-selected former KGB families, individuals willing to abandon their former lives for the clandestine mission. These families committed fully to the program, erasing all traces of their civilian identities. Officially, they ceased to exist—scrubbed from government and civilian databases, with falsified death certificates issued to close the book on their previous lives. Family and friends mourned their supposed losses, often comforted by generous financial compensations that ensured no further questions would be asked. Over time, these former operatives assumed new identities—numerical designations within the top-secret system. For the families, the transition into anonymity was seamless. Their past lives as KGB agents had already conditioned them for the isolation and secrecy required. Within weeks, their memories of civilian attachments faded, replaced by the all-encompassing mission to train the next generation. The children under their care were not seen as dependents, but as assets—future operatives destined to serve the Russian state at all costs.

In the contentious lead-up to the 1986 meeting between Mikhail Gorbachev and Ronald Reagan in Reykjavik, the KGB worked feverishly to create a clandestine organization capable of safeguarding Russian interests. With the potential for Western treaties to erode the Soviet Union's global influence, the KGR was born. Initially funded through a KGB-controlled slush fund, the operation expanded with covert financial support from a cadre of disillusioned oligarchs. These powerful figures opposed the liberalization efforts of Gorbachev and sought to maintain Russia's dominance through unconventional means. Material and weaponry were easily acquired within the tightly controlled communist state, where oversight and accountability were practically nonexistent. This unmonitored access to resources enabled the fledgling organization to stockpile tools of covert warfare without raising suspicion. As the years passed and the Soviet Union collapsed, the advent of the Internet and the rise of the Dark Web transformed KGR's operational capabilities. Anonymous digital transactions made it nearly impossible to trace funding sources or destinations, enabling the program to thrive without detection. By leveraging this evolving technological landscape, KGR secured the resources it needed to build a network of operatives capable of executing high-stakes missions. Their ultimate goal: ensuring that the Russian establishment remained untouchable, regardless of political agreements or international scrutiny.

Students KGR6695 (Aleksandr Vasiliev), KGR6773 (Sergey Baranov), KGR6688 (Oleg Gusev), KGR6775 (Viktor Sokolov), and brothers KGR6822 (Pavel Kuznetsov) and KGR6823 (Andrei Kuznetsov) were introduced into the KGR program as orphans or trafficked infants in the late 1990s. Isolated from the world, they were molded into elite operators, their identities erased and replaced with their KGR designations. Their daily lives revolved solely around intense training and indoctrination with no view of the outside world.

Days and nights blurred together in a relentless cycle of military and covert training, sharpening their skills in all aspects of clandestine warfare. They became proficient in land and water survival, interrogation methods—both applying and resisting—and a wide array of weaponry and marksmanship techniques. Their hand-to-hand combat expertise was honed through rigorous training in Sambo and Krav Maga, creating dominance in close quarters fighting. Occasionally, they were blindfolded and transported to remote alpine lakes for SCUBA diving and aquatic tactics, expanding their versatility in hostile environments.

KGR recruits rarely ventured beyond the confines of their secluded mountain training grounds, ensuring their complete focus on the program's objectives. Love and loyalty for Mother Russia were deeply ingrained in their psyches through a steady diet of Russian propaganda and revisionist history. With no knowledge of their biological families or the outside world, their loyalty belonged entirely to their instructors and the state. Religion and global awareness were deliberately kept from them. Their education centered exclusively on Russian achievements, military history, and a fabricated narrative of victimization and superiority, fueling an intense hatred for opposing nations. By the time they reached adulthood, these operatives were not just skilled agents but living weapons, trained to operate without question in service to their country's ethereal objectives.

A staggering 80 percent of KGR students successfully graduated as covert Russian agents by their eighteenth birthday. Those who failed to meet the program's rigorous standards vanished without a trace, their remains lost in the remote southern mountains. Decades later, a Slovakian mountaineering expedition would accidentally stumble upon a shallow graveyard of children and teens, a chilling testament to the program's brutality. The graduates who survived this grueling existence transitioned to the next phase of their training in a concealed interurban cell within Moscow's Khamovniki District. Here, they were taught to seamlessly blend into civilian life amid the bustling scenes of Moscow's Central Administrative District. During a year of immersive urban warfare training, they mastered the art of navigating city environments and perfecting social tactics to blend into the chaotic rhythm of unsuspecting civilians. This phase solidified their ability to operate unnoticed, setting the foundation for their future missions.

When the students flawlessly demonstrated their abilities in controlled scenarios, they were issued genuine capture and kill assignments on a small scale to test their readiness. As they excelled in these missions, the complexity of their orders increased. Eventually, they were relocated to a secured compound outside Moscow to live, train, and await directives transmitted through a top-secret channel managed by the Russian Foreign Intelligence Service (SVR). The KGR agents executed operations both individually and as members of small, specialized teams, carrying out assignments on domestic and international soil. During the United States' prolonged war in Afghanistan, all six agents were deployed to participate in covert missions. Their tasks included training high-value Taliban leaders in advanced tactics designed to counter and undermine American forces. The intelligence they shared provided the insurgents with strategic advantages over their adversaries. This surreptitious collaboration served as a calculated act of reciprocity for the support the United

States had offered to the Afghan Mujahideen during the Soviet-Afghan War in the 1980s—a long-remembered humiliation for Russia.

KGR6695 had just concluded an arduous two-month deployment to Afghanistan's Panjshir Province when he received what was described as sealed intelligence from a KGR instructor rumored to be defecting after 22 years of service. The recruits of the KGR program were pedantically conditioned to suppress emotions and reject any curiosity about their origins. Their heritage was deemed irrelevant to their present purpose and future assignments—a concept deeply ingrained in their psyches. However, Olga Chernoff, a senior instructor who had served as a mother figure to many of the recruits, managed to breach this psychological barrier. Chernoff, whose presence commanded a rare blend of authority and compassion, shared classified personnel records with KGR6695. These records, deliberately concealed by the program's leadership, contained fragments of information about his lineage. For a young man trained to discard emotional attachments, the revelation was destabilizing. The covert disclosure was Chernoff's premeditated gamble, intended to spark a sense of identity in her top student. Her motives remained ambiguous—whether driven by guilt, loyalty, or a desire to dismantle the program's dehumanizing grip. What was clear, however, was that the information she provided threatened to unravel the tightly controlled narrative KGR had instilled in its agents.

KGR6695 had never known familial love or warmth, but Olga Chernoff came the closest to embodying such a figure in his life. The envelope she had slipped under his Khamovniki flat's front door was cryptic yet precise. It contained instructions to meet her at sunrise by the entrance pillars of Gorky Central Park of Culture and Leisure. For an operative like him, trained in vigilance and skepticism, the message immediately aroused suspicion, but curiosity won over caution. Arriving an hour early, KGR6695 methodically surveyed the area. His demeanor was composed, blending with the wary habits of other Muscovites who walked the city streets with an ingrained sense of distrust. His eyes scanned for inconsistencies—lingering figures, poorly concealed observations, or anything out of place. Finding nothing to indicate a setup, he positioned himself near the agreed-upon location.

The park's beauty unfolded as the sun rose, illuminating flowerbeds and paths with a soft golden glow. Morning joggers, walkers, and bikers filled the park, their movements choreographed by routine. But Olga was nowhere to be found. After 30 minutes of waiting, KGR6695 decided to abandon the scene. As he moved south along the Moskva River, keeping his pace steady and unhurried, his finely tuned instincts detected motion on his left. A jogger overtook him, seamlessly sliding a manila folder into his awaiting arm. Without breaking stride or acknowledging the exchange, the jogger disappeared into the throng of park-goers, their identity obscured by the sea of bobbing heads and colorful tracksuits. KGR6695 continued walking, his expression unchanging, the folder blending into his casual hold as though it had been with him all along. Reaching the pedestrian crossing at Novoandreyevsky Bridge, he adjusted his course slightly to avoid lingering too long in open spaces. His mind raced, calculating the risks and rewards of opening the folder's contents, knowing that whatever was inside had the potential to alter the carefully controlled trajectory of his life.

KGR6695 walked back to his flat with composure, betraying no hint of hesitation or unease. To any observer, he was just another unremarkable white male going about his day, giving no indication that he carried stolen classified documents from one of Russia's most secretive agencies. Once inside, he locked the door, slid the deadbolt into place, and settled at the small four-person dining table in the center of the room. Under the dim light, he opened the folder marked Особой важности—Top Secret—in bold red letters. The papers inside chronicled the lives of over 20 KGR operatives, each document detailing their family origins. Some included parents' names and histories, if known; others recounted abductions and the reasoning behind their selection for the program. The reverse side of each document carried decades' worth of evaluations and notes, coldly cataloging the operatives' progress and conditioning over 20 years. He hesitated briefly before pulling out his own file. The name on it was foreign, a fragment of a life which had been erased. With a deep breath, he opened the file, apprehensively confronting the story of a past he had never known.

The room seemed to close in around him, the edges of his vision blurring as his eyes scanned the pages, struggling to process the inconceivable information. His instinct, deeply ingrained through years of training and conditioning, was to reject it outright. This couldn't be true—his entire existence, his identity, was built on the foundation of carefully constructed lies. But there it was, in stark black ink: his name. Aleksandr Vasiliev. For the first time in his life, he had a name beyond a number. He wasn't just KGR6695. He had parents. A history. His hands trembled slightly as he read on. His father had been a Russian Navy submarine commander, now deceased. His mother had died giving birth to him. The weight of the revelation bore down on him, a mixture of shock, anger, and an unfamiliar ache in his chest. Aleksandr Vasiliev. A name that felt both alien and eerily familiar, like the ghost of a life he was never meant to know.

Why would they hold this information from me?

He quickly skimmed through the other files, glancing at the origins of his fellow KGR operatives, but his focus kept returning to his own. Aleksandr reread the same few paragraphs repeatedly, desperate to extract every possible detail from the limited information. The revelation consumed him, but he knew he couldn't keep it to himself forever. He needed to share the files with the others—but not yet. He needed time to process, to think, and to plan his next move.

Was he now in danger for having this knowledge? What happened to Olga? Why would she risk her life to provide these?

Aleksandr would probably never know Olga's fate. She might have succeeded in her defection or met a grim end. Either way, it was irrelevant to the KGR authorities; to them, she had been officially dead for over 20 years. Killing her again, in the shadows of their secrecy, wouldn't change a thing. But Aleksandr couldn't dwell on her now. In his mind, she was just another actor in the elaborate fiction that had been his life. His right knee bounced anxiously under the table, a reflexive response as he stared out the dining room window. The line of government buildings and museums across the skyline blurred in his peripheral vision, an ironic backdrop for the revelations of truth he now held in his hands.

Abruptly, his head snapped to the side, breaking the trance. Aleksandr reached for his encrypted Xiaomi mobile phone, his fingers moving with accurate speed as he composed a message. The contents were short and direct, a command disguised in casual brevity. He sent it simultaneously to KGR6773, KGR6688, KGR6775, and the Kuznetsov brothers, KGR6822 and KGR6823. The summons was clear: it was time for a meeting. Time to decide what to do with the truth.

* * *

Cough. Cough.

Sergey broke the rhythmic silence with a raspy cough, the musty, damp air of the basement finally settling into his tobacco-stained lungs. The sound drew fleeting glances from the others, who briefly acknowledged the oppressive environment before lowering their heads back to their tasks. The air felt heavy, a stale reminder of the isolation they had been confined to for days. Each operative meticulously sorted through their gear. They had rehearsed the mission countless times back in Russia, every detail etched into their minds.

Yet, being on foreign soil always added an unpredictable layer to the plan, making these final reviews essential. The first objective loomed large in their minds: crossing the Canadian–United States border undetected. The so-called "invisible line" between the two countries was anything but intangible to these men. It was a high-stakes threshold, guarded by surveillance technology and watchful eyes. To succeed, they would need to be both invisible and perfect in their execution.

Sergey exhaled, breaking the fragile stillness once more, and muttered under his breath, "Let's hope the plan holds." His voice carried a weight that the others silently understood, but no one replied. They simply continued, each lost in the quiet rhythm of preparation.

The United States had long been preoccupied with securing its southern border, pouring billions into surveillance, patrols, and even constructing a controversial partial wall to deter illegal migration from Mexico. This intense focus, however, served as a convenient political distraction, leaving vulnerabilities along the northern border largely overlooked. With the longest international boundary in the world—stretching over 5,500 miles—the northern frontier was a quiet sieve for those with the resources and cunning to exploit it. For the Russians, the Pacific Northwest presented the perfect opportunity. Its sprawling wilderness, dense forests, rugged mountains, and intricate network of waterways created a labyrinth of concealment. Thousands of miles of unguarded terrain offered countless discrete entry and exit points, an infiltrator's dream. Here, they could move like ghosts, crossing undetected to carry out their operation.

They would be in and out before anyone even knew they had been there. The land itself was their greatest ally, masking their presence and providing the cover they needed to execute their plan.

CHAPTER 13

Skagit Valley Provincial Park
British Columbia, Canada

Soon after turning off from Canadian Highway 3, Jack brought his Toyota Highlander to a stop. He climbed out without a word, the chill of the mountain air brushing against him as he popped the hood. Moving quickly but methodically, he pulled the brake light fuses. The last thing they needed was the glow of bright red taillights betraying their position to a patrolling border service agency. When Jack slid back into the driver's seat, the journey resumed without ceremony, the constant hum of the tires the only sound as they ventured deeper into the night.

The dusty, primer-black vehicle crept along the crushed gravel road; a narrow 40-mile stretch carved through monstrous Douglas firs. The pitch-dark path twisted through the dense forest of Skagit Valley Provincial Park, leading toward the remote northern banks of Ross Lake. Inside, Jack's compact SUV groaned under the weight of its occupants and their cargo. Six oversized operatives crammed into the vehicle, their broad shoulders brushing against each other as they jostled for space. Duffel bags packed with camping and survival gear were wedged tightly from floor to ceiling. More bags spilled over into the laps of the KGR agents, pinning them in place like sardines in a can. The rear windows were rolled halfway down, letting in the crisp mountain air. It mixed with the humid tang of sweat and the chemical bite of new gear, dispersing the stagnant odor that hung in the cabin. The cool air also kept the windshield from fogging, a small blessing as heavy breaths filled the tense moment. No one spoke. Each soldier stared into the dark forest beyond the glass, anticipating the illegal border crossing ahead.

The off-road drive stretched over an hour, the SUV crawling along at a deliberate, near-silent pace. The 31-inch all-terrain tires worked tirelessly, absorbing the rugged, winding path through the wilderness. Jack leaned forward in his seat; his focus absolute as he guided the vehicle using a head-mounted AGM monocular night vision device. The green-hued world illuminated through the lens rendered headlights unnecessary—and dangerous. The men inside the vehicle remained quiet, their breaths visible in the frosty night air. There was no chatter, no idle speculation—only the weight of their collective mission, looming ahead like the dense shadows of the forest. Each man carried an acute awareness of the task before them. The first phase of their plan had to unfold perfectly, or there would be no second chance.

* * *

Aleksandr sat in the passenger seat, staring into the darkness ahead. His thoughts drifted to six months earlier, to a clandestine meeting with his comrades in Khamovniki. They had gathered to review sensitive documents Aleksandr had secretly obtained. Unbeknownst to them, the KGR had compromised their so-called "encrypted phones" and was tracking their every move. The operatives had barely begun skimming the first few paragraphs of their individual files when the front door was violently breached. Within moments, all six were subdued. Zip-tied, gagged, and with hoods thrust over their heads, they were marched down to the basement garage and thrown into the back of a waiting van. The drive was disorienting, a 30-minute journey filled with sharp turns and the muffled drone of the engine. When the van finally came to a stop, they were dragged out and unmasked inside a dimly lit KGR safehouse west of the city. The cold, sterile air and unyielding stares of their captors confirmed the grim reality: their mission had been halted before it even began.

"KGR6688, 6695, 6773, 6775, 6822, and 6823," the senior KGR official began, his tone carefully measured, as though reading from a prepared script. "You are all in violation of possessing KGR top-secret documents. We are fully aware of Olga Chernoff's unauthorized removal of these materials and her subsequent attempt to defect from the program." The man's voice was calm but carried an undercurrent of authority that silenced the room. The bound agents exchanged uneasy glances, their restrained bodies tense as he continued.

"You will each be individually briefed on the information you accessed," he stated, his cold eyes scanning the group. "During this time, you will have the opportunity to ask questions. Understand this: your identities, as well as those of your families, have been classified to ensure your protection within the KGR program." He paused, letting the weight of his words sink in before delivering his final statement. "The reasoning behind these actions—and your ultimate purpose—will become clear soon enough."

Two KGR instructors, familiar faces from their years of punishing training at the Caucasus Camp, methodically cut the plastic bindings from their wrists and removed the gags from their mouths. The six operatives sat in hard plastic chairs arranged on a cold cement floor, the room around them stark and featureless—a basement, by all appearances.

One by one, they were escorted up a narrow wooden staircase to a windowless room. There, each was presented with unsettling revelations about their existence. KGR6695, who already knew his name to be Aleksandr Vasiliev, learned that his father had been a decorated nuclear submarine commander. He was told his father had died at the hands of the Americans during a critical mission. His mother, unable to cope with the news, had succumbed to a fatal heart attack shortly after.

Each agent was fed a similar tale, linking their heritage to the infamous 1997 disappearance of the K-151 *Medved* in the North Pacific Ocean. For Aleksandr, the story aligned with fragments of his past, as did the account given to KGR6688—Oleg Gusev—the son of one of the *Medved*'s fire control technicians. For the others, however, the narratives were more dubious. KGR6773, now identified as Sergey Baranov, and KGR6675, Viktor Sokolov, were given histories they couldn't verify. The final two, brothers KGR6822 and KGR6823, were told they were Pavel and Andrei Kuznetsov, the sons of another high-ranking crew member of the *Medved*. The stories, while meticulously crafted, felt like veils drawn over a deeper truth. For Aleksandr and Oleg, fragments of legitimacy clung to their identities. For the others, uncertainty hovered ominously, as though their entire existence had been rewritten by the KGR's hand.

The instructors, along with the nameless senior KGR official, fielded the operatives' questions with carefully rehearsed responses, ensuring their explanations remained consistent with the narrative they intended to convey. They recounted the last piece of satellite intelligence received during the decades-old incident: the deployment of an American anti-submarine warfare (ASW) helicopter from the aircraft carrier USS *Constellation*. Russian intelligence had spent years identifying and tracking the aircrew involved. Though a chain of command ultimately led up to the President of the United States, the KGR had resolved that those directly responsible for the attack would pay the price. It was framed as a matter of justice—for Russia, and for the families left in ruin.

For Aleksandr and the team, the revelation that they were orphans because of an American military attack ignited a visceral hatred toward the United States. The realization that their families had been taken from them—families they hadn't even known existed until 12 hours earlier—stoked a fiery need for retribution. The KGR authorities seized on that anger, expertly channeling it into a mission for vengeance. It was the culmination of years of planning, a response designed to turn the operatives' fresh rage into a weapon aimed at avenging Russia's losses.

The KGR received top-secret orders through the Special Access Program (SAP), bypassing standard government communication channels and procedures. This deliberate measure ensured complete deniability from the Kremlin, shielding it from any potential fallout. The failed mission to decimate the United States' western coast, coupled with the devastating loss of their flagship nuclear submarine and its full complement of nuclear armaments, was a wound Russia had neither forgotten nor forgiven. The sting of that failure lingered, fueling a decades-long thirst for revenge. When the leaked bios of the six KGR agents surfaced, it was as if the opportunity for vengeance had presented itself on a silver platter. The timing was perfect, the circumstances undeniable. For the KGR, it was a chance to settle old scores and reclaim lost pride.

For the next six months, the KGR operatives immersed themselves in intensive studies of American geography, culture, language, and intelligence. Leveraging public resources like Google Maps and Meta Oculus virtual reality, they could virtually explore and familiarize themselves with any location on Earth without ever leaving their base. This technology proved invaluable for preparing them to operate undetected in foreign territory. Their training was tailored to the regions where they would be deployed, with tactics refined for maximum efficiency. And tracking the current whereabouts of the U.S. Navy aircrew responsible for the *Medved* incident didn't require a cybersecurity expert. However, the KGR had access to some of the world's most skilled hackers, ensuring no stone was left unturned.

The SAP facilitated the coordination of embedded Russian contacts across North America, along with the provision of necessary equipment and weapons. Every detail of the mission was painstakingly constructed, studied, approved, and rehearsed. The result was a well-designed, coordinated assassination plot on American soil. It would be more than a strike; it would be a declaration. A clear message to the United States that Russia neither forgave nor forgot acts of aggression against its military.

***

As they approached the sandy shoreline of the lake, Jack shifted the Highlander into neutral, letting it coast to a gentle stop. He twisted the key counterclockwise, cutting the engine, and pulled it from the ignition. Darkness enveloped the group as they sat in the calm, their eyes scanning the surroundings for any signs of park rangers or authorities who might be monitoring this secluded backdoor entrance into the U.S. The stillness was profound, broken only by the occasional rustle of 5 mph wind gusts brushing through the treetops. The forecast had predicted unseasonably warm autumn winds with a 30 percent chance of rain, but so far, the weather had cooperated. Jack hadn't needed the wipers during their drive, except to clear the occasional bug splatter, which left streaks of smeared guts across the windshield. For the Russians, the weather was a minor concern compared to the threat of discovery. A chance encounter with a border service agent could be handled—they had the training and the means to overwhelm, eliminate, and dispose of anyone who stood in their way. But it would cost them precious time, an asset they couldn't afford to waste. Fortunately, the area was deserted, abandoned for the off-season. They remained still for a moment longer, letting the silence confirm their solitude before taking the next step in their mission.

The men exited the vehicle, quickly unloading duffels and beginning to assemble their supplies and transportation. Their equipment included two four-person rafts, each equipped with 12V battery-powered outboard trolling motors, with oars packed as backups. The Kuznetsov brothers pulled the deflated rubber rafts to the side and began inflating the chambers manually using handheld pumps. Meanwhile, Viktor organized the camping essentials: two four-season tents, six sleeping bags, two Jetboil cooking stoves, four 450g fuel canisters, and a case of Mountain House freeze-dried meals. Sergey and Oleg carefully loaded the refilled expedition duffels into the inflated rafts, ensuring the weight was evenly distributed. On the far side of the SUV, Aleksandr and Jack stood huddled together, deep in conversation about U.S. contact protocols and finalizing communication plans. The scene was one of quiet efficiency, each man focused on his role as the cool night air settled around them, the tension of their impending mission palpable.

Their Canadian contact handed the KGR leader a SPOT satellite communication device, instructing him to power it on and activate the preset beacon once they reached the far side of the lake. The Russian Special Access Program had embedded a resource in Winthrop, WA, who was waiting for the KGR operatives' SPOT signal. The SPOT device, a common tool for outdoor adventurers, operated on the 1611.25 MHz frequency, which was routinely monitored by authorities. However, its widespread use—and frequent misuse—meant that first responders often ignored false-positive alerts. The device had become a staple for climbers, backpackers, and weekend warriors, many of whom were only allowed to venture into the wilderness because their worried spouses insisted on 24/7 trackability. Local REI stores often sold out of SPOT devices, further normalizing their presence in remote areas.

Aleksandr planned to transmit the signal as a brief burst, just long enough for their preset contact to pinpoint their location. This would minimize the risk of drawing attention from emergency responders. Upon receiving the alert, the contact would drive the 40-mile North Cascade Scenic Highway to extract the KGR team. From there, the route was carefully planned: they would travel east across the northern stretch of Washington State before turning south into Idaho's panhandle. Their final destination was a Russian Federal Counterintelligence Service (FSK) safehouse in Coeur d'Alene, where they would briefly regroup and prepare for the next phase of their operation.

The black Toyota Highlander receded into the dense forest, retracing its path, now empty of all passengers except the driver. Aleksandr and his team had split into two groups, three men to a raft. Carrying the loaded rafts to the water's edge, they moved with practiced efficiency. Once at the shoreline, each group settled into position: one man seated aft to handle the motor, and two positioned on either side in the middle, ready to paddle. With a forceful push, they launched the rafts into the water, their oars pressing against the rocky lakebed to propel them out to deeper waters. As soon as the rafts cleared the shallows, the aft crewmen lowered the propellers into place. Moments later, both rafts came to life, their quiet electric motors slicing through the still water. Without a word, the operatives vanished into the inky blackness, heading south across the lake and disappearing into the night.

With their eyes fully adjusted to the darkness, the stealthy Russians glided across the glassy waters, the rafts enveloped by the towering western red cedars that lined the shoreline. Hugging the eastern coast, the KGR members remained vigilant, their senses attuned to any sights or sounds that could indicate a potential threat. At this time of year, the lake was expected to be nearly, if not completely, deserted, as the long and brutal winter loomed on the horizon. Still, the possibility of encountering hunters or mountaineering enthusiasts couldn't be ruled out. It was unlikely, but their training had instilled in them the importance of never assuming or letting their guard down.

Ross Lake, stretching 23 miles long, barely extended into British Columbia; the majority of its waters lay within the United States. Within the first half-hour of their journey, the operatives uneventfully crossed the invisible international border, their passage marked only by the faint hum of the trolling motors and the rhythmic sound of water lapping against the rafts. Using a topographic map, they identified a remote area between Hozomeen and Boundary Bay as their ideal location to establish camp. The spot was chosen to minimize the risk of running into anyone, ensuring they could remain undetected as they prepared for the next night's task.

Sergey moved to the front of the leading raft, assuming the role of navigator. Using precise hand signals, he guided Andrei, who sat at the rear, manually steering the rudder. At Sergey's signal, Andrei adjusted to port as they passed a distinct rock outcropping—a key landmark marking their approach to the night's destination. The trailing raft followed closely, matching their every movement. Both rafts idled as they neared the shore, their progress slowing until the hulls dragged to a stop on the shallow lakebed. One by one, the crew disembarked, their boots crunching softly on the rocky shoreline. Working together, they hauled the rafts onto dry land and into the cover of the surrounding woods. Once concealed, they covered the inflatables with branches, leaves, and other downed foliage, ensuring nothing was left visible to prying eyes. With the boats hidden and the team regrouped, they turned their attention to setting up camp, remaining cautious and inaudible under the dark canopy of the forest. Without a word, each man went to work. Some erected tents, others boiled water, secured the perimeter, or stood watch. They worked efficiently and synchronized—a clear testament to their experience working together. Yet, this mission felt different. Though the terrain was no different from the mountains and forests they had trained in before, being in the enemy's backyard added an unmistakable tension. This was their first operation on U.S. soil.

Once the campsite was established, the team settled into their tents for some much-needed rest, adhering to alternating hourly watch shifts. They maintained their vigilance throughout the night, the stillness broken only by the soft sounds of the wilderness around them. A few hours later, the sun crept over the horizon, its brilliant hues reflecting across the glacier-blue surface of the lake, transforming the dark expanse into a dazzling panorama. It was a brief moment of serenity, a stark contrast to the mission they were executing. With daylight now in full force, the KGR agents moved to camouflage their campsite and rafts deeper within the forest. They carefully concealed any trace of their presence to avoid detection from aerial surveillance or wandering eyes. As the fall season brought shorter days, the group used the remaining daylight hours to eat, rest, and prepare for the next leg of their journey. Their plans depended on the cover of darkness, and when night fell once more, they would return to the lake, resuming their silent advance into enemy territory.

By midnight, the campsite was torn down, every trace packed neatly into their duffel bags and loaded back onto the rafts. The operatives left no sign of their presence on the shore before setting out on the lake once more. The conditions had changed drastically. Wind gusts from the north reached 20 mph, churning the water into rough waves. The trolling motors struggled against the increased resistance, forcing the Russians to supplement their efforts with oars. The crews worked in unison, their muscles straining as they fought to keep the rafts steady in the face of each whitecap. Glacial freshwater sprayed over the gear and crew with every rise and fall of the rafts. The relentless pitching and battering waves tested their endurance, but they pressed on, cutting through the turbulent waters with determination. Hours passed as they paddled with intensity, the wind seemingly intent on driving them backward.

As the first rays of dawn broke through the coniferous canopy, Sergey consulted his map, comparing it to the geography now visible before them. Satisfied, he signaled to the crews to veer toward an opening on their port side. Both rafts pushed toward the shore, beaching just north of Rainbow Point Campground. As expected, the campground was deserted, the off-season leaving the area devoid of campers. Exhausted but focused, the Russians prepared for the next step of their mission.

"Strong work, comrades! Get some food and water. Hide the gear. We move out in 30 minutes," Aleksandr barked, his voice cutting through the crisp morning air.

Andrei and Pavel immediately set to work, opening the three air chambers of each raft to deflate them. They rolled the flattened rubber vessels tightly, compacting them to fit neatly back into their duffels. Meanwhile, Viktor and Oleg scouted the forest for a suitable hiding spot. About 500 yards from the shore, they found an ideal location near a cluster of massive granite boulders cloaked in thick, green moss, evidence of years of undisturbed growth. The team worked quickly, each operative carrying a full duffel to the designated spot. Using the natural forest resources—fallen branches, leaves, and moss—they carefully concealed the gear. Once satisfied, they stepped back to take a mental snapshot of the area, memorizing key landscape markers to ensure they could locate the cache when needed. The plan was simple but critical: retrieve the gear and reverse their path back to Canada in a month, after the successful execution of their mission—*Operation Bloodline Redemption.*

With one last look over his shoulder, Sergey turned and led the six-man team south along the East Bank Trail. Clad in forest camouflage jackets and pants with black beanies, the operatives moved in hushed disciplined. The towering, snowcapped Jack Mountain loomed above them, its 9,000-foot peak casting long shadows that shielded them for the first half of their journey. Only when the sun climbed above the mountain's massive presence did the light break through, dappling the trail in patches of gold. After hiking eight miles through the rugged terrain, they neared their destination. With just one mile remaining before reaching the East Bank Trailhead, Aleksandr powered up the SPOT emergency device and pressed the beacon.

Forty miles east, Susan Forsythe, a broad-shouldered, middle-aged woman in a wool-lined blue and green flannel jacket, sat at an outdoor table at Sheri's Sweet Shoppe. She had just settled down with a steaming *Caffè D'Arte* espresso and a freshly baked apple fritter when her iPhone app pinged with the awaited signal. Without hesitation, Susan grabbed her breakfast to go, crumpling the paper bag in one hand as she headed for her oversized white Ford Expedition parked nearby. She climbed in, started the engine, and drove west, her destination clear in her mind.

CHAPTER 14

"Tonight's training op will take place in AUSTIN 2 MOA, just east of Bunker Hill," Commander Ellis began, her voice steady and authoritative as she addressed the aircrew. "DASH ONE and DASH TWO will launch from NAS Fallon at 2200. My crew in DASH ONE will execute the first SEAL Team fast-rope insertion while DASH TWO provides overwatch. Once DASH ONE completes the insertion, we'll transition to overwatch and provide weapons support as DASH TWO moves in for its insertion. After the SEALs are boots on the ground, both DASH ONE and DASH TWO will return to base to refuel. Both birds will remain spinning on base until 0030, at which point we'll launch to the extraction point. DASH ONE will take lead, with DASH TWO in the overwatch position." Commander Ellis's tone left no room for doubt, her confidence resonating in the room. The aircrews and pilots were at full attention, absorbing every detail of the plan. Their focused expressions and firm nods reflected both respect and readiness, mirroring the professionalism she exuded in every word.

Commander Tayla Ellis sat in the designated Helicopter Aircraft Commander (HAC) chair in the flight operations ready room at Naval Air Station (NAS) Fallon, Nevada. With her characteristic poise and authority, she briefed her aircrew and NSW passengers on the training mission, outlining timelines, objectives, and safety procedures for the night's flight. With over 20 years of service, Ellis had a distinguished career that included multiple wartime deployments and high-stakes missions downrange. Now, as the commanding officer of Helicopter Sea Combat Squadron-12 (HSC-12)—the U.S. Navy's oldest rotary-wing squadron—she was preparing for the final chapter of her career. Ellis planned to retire in a year, closing out her journey in the very squadron where it began. The squadron, which changed its designation from HS-2 in 2009, held deep significance for Ellis. It was here, decades earlier, that she co-piloted the infamous flight that helped locate—and likely eliminate—a Russian nuclear submarine with ill intent. A mission so covert it was never to be discussed again, not even among the combat crew who executed the flight that "never occurred." As Ellis finished her briefing and prepared for the night's mission, the weight of her past accomplishments and secrets hung silently in the background, a testament to a career defined by skill, sacrifice, and unwavering service.

It felt surreal to brief her aircrew, just as she had done hundreds of times over her 20-year career. What seemed like a lifetime ago at times also felt like yesterday. With her career winding down and only a few months remaining until retirement, Commander Tayla Ellis found her final flights growing more significant, each one a moment of rumination on the path she had traveled. Yet, the anticipation of retirement didn't bring the peace she had expected. Instead, it introduced an unfamiliar slowness—a pause that gave space for reflection and analysis of her life. Some might call it a mid-life crisis, but to Ellis, it felt more like a mid-life analysis. It was an analysis of everything: the good, the bad, the lessons learned, and the trauma endured. It was a reckoning with the lives lost under her command and the ones saved through her actions. It was a careful inventory of the moments that had shaped her, for better or worse, and a contemplation of the roadmap to her future—a future still uncertain, despite her scrupulous planning.

The ordnance teams armed DASH ONE and DASH TWO with port and starboard-mounted GAU-21 .50 caliber machine guns, attaching belts of ammo. Chaff and flare dispensers were also loaded, providing defensive countermeasures against surface-to-air threats as part of the training scenario. Commander Tayla Ellis conducted her pre-flight inspection with thorough attention to detail, shining her flashlight on various components of the helicopter. She methodically checked off items from her list, ensuring everything met the Navy's high standards before opening the starboard-side pilot door and climbing into her seat.

Around her, the rest of the crew worked diligently, each member performing their checks with determined focus under the radiance of the full moon. Despite the familiarity of the process, there was no hint of complacency. By 2200, both MH-60S helicopters were spinning, their rotors slicing through the cool night air. Ground crew members moved with experienced efficiency, removing the chalks and signaling with their lit wands for the aircraft's departure.

Senior Chief Robert Long, the Crew Chief for DASH ONE, sat in the aft jump seat near the starboard cabin door and the hoist operations control panel. Keyed into his radio headset, he relayed the status of his equipment test, "Pilot, aft. FRIES rigged for deployment. Crew secured. Cabin checklist complete." Long was referring to the Fast Rope Insertion Extraction System (FRIES), a mechanical rig mounted to the helicopter's cabin to facilitate rapid infiltration (INFIL) and exfiltration (EXFIL) in hot zones. Its presence underscored the high-stakes nature of the night's training mission.

Aboard DASH ONE, six operators from SEAL Team Three were secured with gunner's belts, each equipped with a full complement of weapons, communications gear, safety equipment, and night vision devices. DASH TWO, flying in tandem, mirrored DASH ONE in armament, configuration, and personnel. Its crew was equally prepared for their role in the operation. Both helicopters were set to infiltrate the northeast corner of AUSTIN 2 MOA, a designated special use airspace reserved exclusively for military operations. As the rotors continued their relentless spin, the aircrews and SEALs braced for the mission ahead.

"Roger that, Senior Chief," Commander Ellis acknowledged over the internal comms before switching to radio. "TANGO ONE, DASH ONE and DASH TWO request permission to launch."

"DASH ONE and DASH TWO, this is TANGO ONE. Permission granted. Have a good training mission, Sir," came the crisp reply from the NAS Fallon control tower.

TANGO ONE personnel double-checked their radar and communication systems, ensuring the flight path was clear for the

Combat Search and Rescue (CSAR) helicopters. With the all-clear received, the rotors of DASH ONE and DASH TWO thundered steadily against the cool desert night air as the helicopters lifted into the sky.

* * *

One week prior
Coeur D'Alene, Idaho

Susan picked up the rank-smelling KGR agents from the trailhead at the southern end of Ross Lake. To anyone watching, they appeared like ordinary day hikers enjoying the last accessible weeks of the North Cascade Range before winter set in. The trailhead parking lot was packed with cars, with several vehicles ticketed for illegally parking along the highway. Aleksandr and his team had passed a handful of hikers on the trail, but not nearly enough to account for the number of abandoned vehicles. They reasoned that the majority of hikers must have been exploring other trails in the vast spiderweb of interconnected paths typical of the Pacific Northwest. Inside Susan's white Ford Expedition, bags of snacks and bottles of water she had picked up from a local market in preparation for the extraction, were waiting for them. The team climbed into the vehicle quickly, wasting no time. Once everyone was onboard, Susan spun the Expedition around and headed back the way she had come, seamlessly integrating into the traffic of weekend adventurers.

They spent the next five hours driving in near silence, the miles stretching between them and the trailhead at Ross Lake. They arrived at a single-car garage of a modest three-bedroom rambler on the north side of Coeur d'Alene. The air in Idaho was noticeably warmer, feeling more like late summer than fall. The lingering haze from forest fires near Glacier National Park in Montana added a faint, acrid scent to the breeze, intensifying the unseasonal warmth. Susan wouldn't be staying at the safehouse. Like everyone involved, she had been given specific orders and knew only her part of the mission—nothing more. After the KGR agents exited her oversized vehicle, she backed out of the driveway without a word. As Susan's SUV disappeared down the street, a white Subaru Crosstrek pulled into the garage, its headlights cutting briefly through the smoky air. The garage door closed behind it, sealing the operatives into their next phase of secrecy and preparation.

"Welcome to the United States, comrades!" Jonathan Bradfield—a stocky, 5-foot-four, forty-something-year-old man—kicked open the driver's door and introduced himself. The six men turned with no emotion and gave a subtle nod. They had been conditioned since birth to trust no one, keep their guard up, and always assume the worst. They would proceed with caution, even posting an hourly watch while in the safehouse. "Grab those bins on your way in. Bring them to the living room—straight down the hall, through that door."

A large stack of unlabeled black Costco 27-gallon bins with yellow lids sat neatly in the far corner of the garage. The KGR team made multiple trips to transport the bins into the living room. Inside the house, all the window shades were drawn, sealing off the interior from prying eyes. The layout was simple: three bedrooms, each furnished with two beds, two small bathrooms, a functional kitchen, and a sparsely furnished living room where the bins were being re-stacked. Unlike the stable cement floor in the garage, the bins now wobbled precariously on the uneven, brown shag carpet that looked original to the house and clung to decades of cigarette smoke. The six special agents stood silently around the stacked containers, their postures rigid, their expressions unreadable. Their piercing gazes seemed to cut through the air, a reminder of the discipline and intensity drilled into them since childhood. Despite the mundane surroundings, their concentration never wavered. This was no safehouse to them—it was merely another staging ground in enemy territory.

"Please, sit. You can relax here. It's safe," Jonathan said, his tone upbeat as he attempted to ease the tangible stiffness in the room.

Aleksandr and his team didn't flinch. To them, Jonathan's words were not reassuring but a confirmation of their suspicions: time spent in the United States had softened him. Every attempt at small talk or comfort only chipped away further at his credibility. Jonathan sighed, shifting awkwardly under their cold, unyielding stares. "Fine, stand. I'm sure you've been sitting for hours on your drive anyway," he muttered, the edge in his voice betraying his frustration. The KGR operatives remained motionless, their stoic demeanor unbroken. For them, trust was not freely given—it was earned through action, not words. Jonathan's attempts at camaraderie fell flat, meeting a wall of silence that spoke louder than any response.

"Where is our identification? And the vehicles?" Aleksandr asked, his voice steady but sharp as he took the lead. The question was more of a demand than a query, his piercing gaze fixed on Jonathan.

"I have your identification in a safe in the hall closet, hidden beneath the carpet," Jonathan replied, his tone measured as he gestured toward the hallway. "I'll retrieve them in a moment. As for your cars, they're like the one I arrived in—parked a couple of blocks away on different suburban streets. We'll stagger the pickups to avoid drawing attention. Once you've gathered your supplies and are ready to depart, you'll head out separately in pairs. All vehicles are fueled and ready."

"Very good," Aleksandr replied, his eyes flicked briefly toward the bins before meeting Jonathan's gaze again. "I'm assuming these bins have everything we requested?"

Their contact nodded and left the room to retrieve the counterfeit U.S. passport IDs from the hallway closet safe. Meanwhile, the operatives began pulling down the bins, opening each one to inventory their mission supplies. Idaho's loose gun laws had made Jonathan's preparation relatively straightforward from a legal standpoint, but he still took precautions. He spread his purchases across multiple stores and spaced them out over time to avoid raising suspicion. Each operative was equipped with a fully automatic and silenced AR-15, paired with multiple .223 Remington 30-round magazines. In addition, Jonathan had acquired a SIG Sauer P365 9mm pistol for each agent, compact yet reliable for close-quarters situations. Two of the bins were noticeably heavier than the others—

filled with boxes of ammunition for both weapon models and extra magazines. The weight explained the effort it had taken to haul them into the house. As they unpacked and inspected the weapons and gear, their movements were methodical, ensuring everything met the exacting standards of their operation.

Some of the bins contained civilian clothing to help the Russians pass unnoticed among the local population. Another was packed with LBT 6094 modular plate carrier vests, designed for any tactical assaults that might arise during their "vacation" in America. One container held a rugged, high-quality drone equipped with a virtual reality headset for reconnaissance. Yet another bin contained seemingly innocuous over-the-counter household items, all carefully selected for constructing a highly effective improvised explosive device (IED). The Russians moved with exactitude, gathering their assigned weapons, ammunition, clothing, and equipment. They organized their supplies into personal gear sets, dividing the living room into individual quadrants to ensure nothing was overlooked. Once their gear was prepped, they reviewed the operation's plan and timelines, meticulously going over every detail. The weight of their tasks loomed over the room, yet their discipline never budged. Afterward, they shared a quiet dinner and prepared for rest. Early the next morning, the team would split up, leaving in pairs with two operatives assigned to each vehicle. Their departure marked the next phase of their covert mission, one step closer to achieving their objective.

Aleksandr and Viktor were assigned to drive 740 miles south to central Nevada. Sergey and Oleg had a longer route ahead, covering 1,300 miles down to southern California. Meanwhile, Pavel and

Andrei faced the longest journey of all—2,700 miles straight east along Interstate 90 to Massachusetts. Each pair had a specific task to complete, critical to the success of the overall mission. After two weeks of executing their assignments, they would reconvene in Washington State to finalize their operation. From there, the plan was to vanish, slipping back across the Canadian border and returning to Mother Russia without a trace.

CHAPTER 15

AUSTIN 2 MOA, NAS Fallon
Fallon, Nevada

"DASH TWO on overwatch, DASH ONE proceeding to INFIL. Senior Chief, rig for insertion. Coming right," Commander Ellis announced, her tone steady and authoritative over the comms. She pulled the cyclic control to starboard, adjusting the mechanical pitch of the main rotors to guide the helicopter smoothly to the right. The MH-60S responded with accuracy, banking toward the designated insertion point as the crew inside prepared for the next phase of the operation.

"Clear right," Senior Chief Long called out, swiveling his helmet-mounted night vision goggles toward the starboard side of the cabin door. He scanned carefully, ensuring the aircraft maintained a safe distance from any terrain or nearby air traffic. "Rigging for insertion," he added, his hands already moving to prepare the fast rope system for deployment. Meanwhile, the door gunners remained vigilant, manning the mounted .50 caliber machine guns on either side of the helicopter. Their eyes scanned the darkness, searching for any potential threats that could compromise the mission. Each crewmember fixated on their role as the MH-60S continued its steady approach toward the insertion point.

The Crew Chief secured the fast rope's eye-top termination to the FRIES Bar assembly and stood ready with the bag of coiled 44 mm rope in hand. He then signaled the SEAL team to prepare for insertion as the MH-60S flared into a hover above a high-point opening in the desert mountain range. The Crew Chief called out directional and speed adjustments as the helicopter steadied into position. Once the hover was confirmed stable, he received permission from the HAC and kicked out the 60 feet of rope, ensuring it was taut before signaling the SEALs to exit the aircraft. The special operators moved with practiced professionalism, sliding down the rope in rapid succession. Within seconds, the team was on the ground, forming a swift and synchronized defensive perimeter with their M4s at the ready. As the last SEAL cleared the rope, Senior Chief Long disengaged the fast rope from the FRIES Bar. With the team safely deployed, Commander Ellis wasted no time, maneuvering the MH-60S out of the landing zone (LZ) and departing into the night.

"DASH ONE moving to overwatch. DASH TWO, proceed to INFIL," Commander Ellis relayed over a secure channel, her voice calm and authoritative.

The two Navy helicopters executed a seamless maneuver, essentially swapping positions to allow DASH TWO to insert the remaining SEAL team members. DASH ONE pulled back from the LZ, maintaining a steady hover at a safe distance. With weapons at the ready, the crew scanned the terrain. Their helmet-mounted night vision goggles (NVGs) cast an eerie green glow, augmenting their visibility in the dark desert expanse. Simultaneously, the helicopter's Forward-Looking Infrared (FLIR) system provided thermal imaging to detect any potential threats lurking in the shadows. DASH ONE held its position, vigilant and prepared to provide immediate support if needed, while DASH TWO moved in to execute the next phase of the operation.

"Pilot, aft. Large object spotted—possibly a bird—at 9 o'clock, 300 yards and closing," the portside aircrewman manning the machine gun reported, his voice calm but firm as he alerted the crew to the potential hazard.

"Roger, I see it on FLIR. Keep an eye on it, and I'll do the same," the co-pilot acknowledged. While he didn't seem overly concerned, the report was taken seriously. The crew maintained their vigilance, each member ready to react if the situation escalated. The aircraft's systems and the crew's sharp eyes ensured that even minor anomalies would not go unchecked, a testament to their professionalism and preparedness.

"Holy shit! Break right!" the crewman shouted, his voice urgent and barely ahead of the rapidly closing object.

Commander Ellis reacted instantly, pulling up the collective control and slamming the cyclic hard to the right. The MH-60S responded with the ferocity of a machine pushed to its limits. The dual turboshaft engines roared at maximum power, their scream cutting through the night as the main rotors arced sharply, biting into the dense air in a desperate maneuver. The g-forces pressed hard against the crew, straining both man and machine in a coordinated attempt to evade. But even the sharp reflexes and honed instincts of the experienced naval aviators weren't enough to avoid the inevitable. Tragedy struck, and the night erupted into chaos.

Viktor's eyes remained locked on the infrared feed displayed in his VR goggles, the live visual representation transmitted from the aerial drone via the 2.4 GHz antenna. He and Aleksandr had hiked six miles from the east the previous evening to establish a camouflaged staging area just outside the perimeter of the military operating area. It was there that the KGR operatives assembled the necessary components—ordinary household items that, when improperly combined, became a highly toxic and destructive mixture. Using a simple burner phone rigged for remote detonation, they had created an improvised explosive device (IED) capable of delivering a blast force equivalent to a pound of C4 plastic explosive. Aleksandr worked with care, attaching the pipe bomb to the drone's undercarriage. He powered up the burner phone, ensuring the detonation mechanism was active before stepping back to oversee the final preparations for launch.

The two U.S. Navy combat helicopters flew through the valley right on schedule, just as predicted by the intel the KGR agents had received a day earlier. The Russian Special Access Program had embedded a local contact in the area, someone who made quick work of acquiring the flight training schedules for the combat training center. The U.S. military's reputation for overworked and underpaid service members made this infiltration all too easy. It hadn't taken much—just the right financial incentives and a carefully crafted cover story—to extract the necessary details. With this critical information in hand, the Russians had judiciously planned their operation to eliminate Commander Ellis, one of the U.S. Navy's most experienced rotary aviators.

Aleksandr used a pair of high-powered infrared binoculars, not to guide a sniper with an M91 rifle firing .300 Win Mag rounds, but to act as a spotter for Viktor's unconventional weapon: a DJI Phantom drone packed with explosives. As soon as the distinct thumping of helicopter rotors echoed from the north, Viktor launched the drone into the air. Its small, silent frame blended seamlessly into the darkened landscape. Aleksandr tracked the aircraft through his binoculars, observing the infiltration operation unfolding on the opposite side of the valley.

"DASH ONE has taken overwatch," Aleksandr relayed, his voice calm and precise. "You're clear to attack."

With that confirmation, Viktor leaned forward, fully immersed in the VR goggles that gave him a pilot's perspective from the drone. The high-definition infrared camera fed him a live view, making it feel as if he were inside, flying the drone himself. As the Phantom approached the hovering DASH ONE, Viktor guided it toward the open portside door. Through the lens, he caught a glimpse of the crew's panicked faces, their expressions illuminated in infrared.

Viktor didn't hesitate. "NOW!" he signaled to Aleksandr. With the push of a button, the drone detonated.

What felt like slow motion, the three DASH ONE aircrewmen turned their NVG-covered eyes toward the center of the cabin. In barely a fraction of a second, their brains struggled to process the sight before them. Up in the cockpit, both pilots remained locked forward, their green-tinted lenses scanning the terrain as the helicopter banked to the right. Oblivious to the danger closing in behind them, they had no indication of what was about to strike. The small drone's four propellers fought against the powerful rotor wash of the MH-60S, momentarily losing altitude before regaining balance. The drone's forward momentum carried it through the open cabin door, its approach silent and unnoticed. Then it happened. The taped-down burner phone attached to the drone's payload lit up, its green LED signaling activation. The phone sent an electrical pulse to the initiator, triggering the dirty bomb's main charge. The detonation was instantaneous.

The tightly packed pipe bomb erupted with the initial detonation, shattering and releasing hundreds of galvanized roofing nails. The shrapnel, propelled at 3,000 feet per second, tore through the drone and filled the cabin in a deadly storm. The razor-sharp fragments ripped through the crewmen and the thin aluminum skin of the helicopter with ease, slicing into the cockpit and fatally wounding the pilots as if the walls weren't even there. Senior Chief Long was torn from his gunner's belt by the force of the blast, his protective gear offering no defense against the inferno. His lifeless body was ejected from the open cabin door, falling more than 100 feet to the rugged terrain below. The rearward concussion of the explosion hurled Commander Ellis violently forward, snapping the cyclic control in her hands. Her NVGs were driven deep through her face as her helmet struck the dashboard controls with devastating force.

The explosion radiated upward, ballooning the cabin ceiling and inflicting catastrophic damage to the main rotor assembly. Even if the pilots had survived or remained conscious after the IED detonation, the helicopter was far beyond operable—any chance of an autorotation attempt was rendered impossible. The MH-60S maintained its steep angle of bank, its systems completely unresponsive as gravity took control. The aircraft plummeted like a stone, spiraling toward the desert mountain below. The main rotors, spinning freely at over 700 feet per second, shattered on impact with the rocky terrain a split second before the 20,000-pound combat helicopter crushed itself under its own weight.

At the same moment, DASH TWO hovered over the LZ, fast roping the remaining SEAL team into position. Their portside gunner, scanning the terrain, caught sight of a fireball at his 8 o'clock. His heart sank as the unmistakable glow illuminated the night. Moments later, the radio crackled to life with the chilling tone of an Emergency Locator Transmitter (ELT) beacon transmitting on 406 MHz—the automated signal from a downed aircraft.

"DASH ONE is down," the co-pilot of DASH TWO confirmed grimly into the radio.

DASH ONE was down. No survivors.

CHAPTER 16

Snoqualmie, Washington

"Control your breathing! Stay calm and don't panic!" Brody instructed his teenage children, his voice steady as he treaded water in the 10-foot-deep member pool at the Club at Snoqualmie Ridge. Maddy and Mitch floated nearby, their faces tense but focused on his commands.

A thick layer of steam rose from the water's surface, a result of the warm pool contrasting with the crisp early morning air. The mist obscured the usually breathtaking view of Mount Si and the Cascade Range, though the telltale signs of fall were undeniable—the vibrant hues of changing foliage, the briskness of the mornings, and the earthy smells of the season. Pumpkin spice's inescapable presence had already infiltrated every coffee shop in town, a signal that cozy holidays were just around the corner. But for Brody, the changing season meant something else: fewer people were willing to brave the effort of swimming outdoors. This seasonal shift provided a rare opportunity—peace and privacy, perfect for tactical water training without interruptions.

The Hayes teenagers began their session with drown-proofing as a warm-up before moving on to pool weights, swimming laps, and practicing lifesaving techniques. With their ankles and wrists bound, they exhaled fully, releasing the air from their lungs and allowing themselves to sink slowly to the bottom of the pool. At the bottom, they bent their knees and pushed off hard, propelling themselves to the surface for a quick gasp of air. They repeated this cycle for 10 minutes, finding a rhythm that turned the exercise into a meditative practice. Drown-proofing taught them to remain calm under constraint, even in situations that could trigger panic. Their father had emphasized the importance of staying calm in stressful situations, particularly in oxygen-deprived scenarios in the water. Brody Hayes had learned this lesson himself during his training as a U.S. Navy Aviation Rescue Swimmer. Having saved several lives during his career, he understood how most people lacked comfort and confidence in water. He was determined that his children wouldn't be among them. As a father, Brody didn't care if his kids became the fastest swimmers in the pool. His priority was that they become confident and strong swimmers, equipped to handle emergencies with steady resolve.

* * *

Brody's mind drifted back ten years to the same pool, on a scorching Pacific Northwest summer day. The water had been alive with the joyful splashing of kids, while every lounge chair was occupied by parents sipping their poolside punches. In the deep end, pre-teen Maddy and Mitch were drown-proofing under his watchful eye. Their focused practice stood in stark contrast to the carefree chaos around them. The scene, however, took a sudden turn when a young lifeguard blew her whistle, the sharp sound cutting through the warm air. Brody remembered the confused concern in her eyes, a mix of panic at what appeared to be drowning children and hesitation over whether she was witnessing abusive parenting. Her whistleblowing was the result of her basic lifeguard training, which hadn't prepared her for a situation like this. Brody had chuckled at the time, shaking his head as he glanced around the pool. The irony wasn't lost on him: while intoxicated parents ignored their children in the shallows, he was actively teaching his kids vital survival and life skills. Her whistle may have startled the moment, but to him, it underscored just how out of sync others' priorities could be.

Trained as one of the best lifeguards in the world—jumping from helicopters into high sea-states to rescue panicked downed military pilots—Brody now found himself face-to-face with a high school student equipped with a rubber floaty and a whistle. Despite the stark difference in their training and experience, the unworried father responded with calm respect. He acknowledged her concerns, explained his intentions, and even extended an invitation for her to join them in the water to better understand the exercise. She politely declined, her whistle still clutched tightly in her hand, opting to keep her distance from the unconventional father-daughter-son training session.

* * *

During the fall months, with kids back in school, the pool was rarely occupied—especially in the early mornings, when it was almost guaranteed to be empty. After their warm-up, Maddy and Mitch took a short water break before transitioning to lifesaving tactical training. Their father had gone through the rigorous military training program in the early 1990s. Back then, lifesaving techniques were largely conducted underwater. It was common for panicked victims, whether drowning or stranded, to instinctively grab at their rescuer, often treating them as flotation. This behavior posed significant risks, which led to specific training to regain control of the situation and save the victim's life. The procedures were straightforward but demanding: if a rescuer was grabbed from the front or back, they were taught to take the victim underwater. The sudden submersion typically induced a reflexive panic in the victim, causing them to release their grip. From there, a series of pressure points and turns were used to gain control and bring the survivor to safety.

In recent years, however, techniques have evolved. Modern training emphasized staying on the surface while employing similar methods to subdue and control a panicked survivor, minimizing risk to both parties. Brody taught his kids both the older and newer methods, believing there was value in mastering multiple approaches. "It's essentially mixed martial arts in the water," he explained to them. Rescue Swimmer instructors often referred to the process as water Jiu Jitsu—a name that perfectly captured the skill, discipline, and physicality required for the life-saving craft.

From a young age, both Maddy and Mitch had demonstrated the effectiveness of staying calm and applying proper techniques in the water. Brody often put their skills to the test, ambushing them during playtime in the pool to see how they would respond under pressure. He even recruited adult friends to challenge the kids, playfully pitting them against his ten-year-olds in the water. While the adults could rely on sheer strength to overpower the children, they were frequently caught off guard by the kids' fluid techniques, purposeful distractions, precise pain application, and unshakable composure. The experience often left the challengers impressed—and occasionally nursing their bruised egos. It was no surprise when the Club offered both Maddy and Mitch lifeguard positions as soon as they came of age. They accepted, drawn by the money and the convenient location, but found the job mind-numbingly dull. Instead of engaging in high-stakes situations, they spent their days watching over splashing kids and, more often than not, inattentive adults.

"Great work, Mitch! Your technique is looking solid," Brody called out, encouraging his youngest as he pulled himself out of the pool. Water dripped from his arms as he reached for a towel draped over a nearby chair. On the metal mesh table beside him, his iPhone buzzed atop a copy of the latest Jack Carr novel. Brody paused, glancing at the screen to see the caller ID: Phillip Bishop.

A smile crept across his face as he answered. "Master Chief! It's been a while. How's it going?" Brody hadn't heard from Master Chief Phillip Bishop in a few years. The familiar voice on the other end of the line brought back a flood of memories, and it felt good to reconnect with his old mentor and friend.

"Hayes, did you see the news?" Bishop's tone was grim, cutting straight to the point. Brody furrowed his brow as he glanced at his phone, noticing for the first time the over 20 unread text notifications cluttering his screen. Bishop continued before Brody could respond. "Commander Ellis' helo went down in Fallon. I just got off the phone with Franklin. He was on DASH TWO during a SEAL training INFIL when DASH ONE crashed. That's all he knows—or all he's saying for now. You know how it is. Normal investigative protocol BS comes first." Bishop paused, his voice heavy. "Sucks. She was legit. And she was close to retiring."

Brody stood frozen, the weight of the news settling over him like a lead blanket. "Everything okay, Dad?" Maddy's voice cut through his thoughts. She had stopped grappling with Mitch, her focus shifting to her father. Brody's expression, a mixture of shock and sadness, was enough to make her pause mid-step.

Flashes of thoughts and memories overwhelmed Brody's mind, as often happens after hearing tragic news. He hadn't thought of his past junior combat pilot, Commander Ellis, in quite some time—both of their lives swept up in the demands of busy seasons. Sadness washed over him like a tide, leaving his face flushed, his breathing slowed, and an ache growing deep in his chest. The weight of loss bore down on him, silent but heavy. Maddy's question snapped him out of his emotionless stare. Blinking, Brody turned toward his children, his eyes refocusing on Maddy and Mitch. He gave a subtle shake of his head, a quiet but clear gesture that something terrible had happened.

CHAPTER 17

La Jolla, California

Captain Jerry Carter, retired U.S. Navy, sat on the small balcony of his La Jolla home, the morning sun casting a golden glow over the glassy waters of the Cove. The serene view offered a stark contrast to the weight he carried after the call he'd received the evening before—a colleague informing him of his former co-pilot's tragic and untimely death. The news had hit hard. That night, Carter had poured himself a couple of generous neat servings of Johnnie Walker Blue Label, sharing the sorrow and memories in a long, heartfelt conversation with his wife, Annie. Eventually, the exhaustion of grief pulled him to bed, where he hoped sleep would offer some reprieve. But Carter was always an early riser. Before the sun crept over the horizon, he was awake. For a moment, he thought the news had been a cruel dream. Then reality settled in, heavy and unrelenting. Moving quietly so as not to wake Annie, he rolled out of bed and padded into the kitchen, brewing a fresh pot of coffee. The aroma filled the air as he prepared for a day that promised no solace, only reflection on a loss that had become all too real.

Carter sat alone on the balcony, the weight of shock and sadness pressing down on him as he recalled years of memories with Tayla Ellis. The details of her death were still scarce; all he knew was that there were no survivors and that an investigation was underway. He understood all too well how long such investigations could take—weeks, even months—as every angle was scrutinized. Ground and maintenance crews would be interviewed, and their routines dissected for any anomalies. Every piece of aerial footage, from base cameras to satellite images (if available), would be analyzed. The process was exhaustive and emotionally taxing. Carter's thoughts turned to the personnel involved in the investigation. He knew how traumatic it would be for them, reliving the tragedy over and over as they were interrogated. They would be forced to recount every detail, big or small, while simultaneously grappling with the loss of their colleagues and friends. It was an unforgiving process—necessary but brutal—and one he wouldn't wish on anyone. Carter took a sip of his coffee, staring out at the tranquil Cove, the beauty of the morning a cruel contrast to the devastation that lingered in his mind.

Thoughts collided faster than Carter could process them. He couldn't sit still any longer. Rising abruptly, he threw on a pair of Under Armour shorts and a sweat-wicking running shirt, lacing up his size 11 ASICS running shoes. A quick stretch—just a couple of toe touches to ease the tension in his aging hamstrings—and he was out the door, jogging east on Nautilus Street. For the captain, there were only two ways to clear his head: flying or getting outside to exercise. With flying out of the question, the crisp morning air and the rhythmic motion of his feet hitting the pavement would have to do. As he picked up his pace, the La Jolla streets gradually came to life around him. But Carter barely noticed, his focus turned inward, searching for clarity amid the chaos in his mind.

Super fit from years of daily jogs and open ocean swims, Carter maintained a steady 9-minute pace for the first two miles as the road began its ascent. Another half mile along La Jolla Scenic Drive, the 58-year-old gradually slowed to a brisk walk, allowing himself to take in the sweeping, panoramic views above La Jolla. Though he'd run this route hundreds of times, the breathtaking vistas never grew old. From the mountains to the sea, the scenery from the Mt. Soledad National Veterans Memorial was as majestic as ever. Reaching the steps leading to the iconic towering 43-foot cross, Carter paused to stretch his burning calves with each deliberate step. At the summit, he found an open park bench and sank onto it, facing west toward the endless Pacific. The hypnotic crashing of the waves far below seemed to echo through him, and he fell into a trance. His mind, overwhelmed by grief and confusion just minutes earlier, now drifted into a deep, detached thoughtfulness—focused on nothing yet encompassing everything.

Carter, a man of faith, closed his eyes and bowed his head, silently praying for his co-pilot friend, the fallen aircrew, and their grieving families. He asked God for answers, for understanding, for some glimmer of clarity amidst the tragedy. But no response came. The silence only deepened, a familiar reminder of life's unanswerable questions. Carter sighed, his heart heavy yet steady. He knew there were things in this world he would never understand, no matter how hard he tried. His only solace was in trusting his heavenly Father's plan—a plan far greater than his limited mind could ever begin to grasp.

* * *

As Carter prayed, a gentle breeze swept over him, cooling his sweaty face and causing his closed eyelids to spasm slightly. His thoughts began to drift, pivoting from his conversation with his maker to memories of one of his final flights with Tayla Ellis nearly two decades earlier. It had been their fourth deployment to the Persian Gulf, aboard the nuclear aircraft carrier USS Abraham Lincoln (CVN-72). The region was a tinderbox of intense conflict in the wake of 9/11. With the twin towers reduced to rubble, America was consumed with grief, anger, and the need for retribution. The U.S. Navy delivered that retaliation in force. Day and night, aircraft launched in relentless sorties, dropping payload after payload on strategic targets to set the stage for the eventual ground invasion of Iraq. The mission: an all-out search for weapons of mass destruction. For Carter and Ellis, those days were a blur of high-stakes operations, adrenaline-fueled flights, and a sense of duty that outweighed fear. But now, sitting alone on the bench overlooking the vast Pacific, those memories felt distant yet painfully vivid, stirring emotions he had long tried to bury.

Ellis and Carter were forward deployed to a Kuwait outpost near the Iraqi border for a detachment assignment in support of Special Operations. Their combat crew consisted of two Combat Search and Rescue (CSAR) operators and a Navy Corpsman. Alongside their HH-60H Seahawk helicopter, the detachment included an additional Seahawk, its aircrew, and a small team of maintenance personnel to keep the aircraft mission-ready. The Helicopter Sea

Combat Squadron's primary objectives were to provide insertion, extraction, and aerial support for SEALs and Explosive Ordnance Disposal (EOD) teams operating in the region. To maintain peak readiness, the CSAR helicopter crews conducted nightly training exercises. These training missions served dual purposes. Not only did they sharpen the team's skills and boost their confidence for impending operations, but they also served as a strategic tool to confound Iraqi intelligence. Each U.S. military launch prompted enemy radar systems to light up and local forces to spin into action, exposing valuable patterns and weaknesses for U.S. and allied intelligence to analyze. Through meticulous planning and relentless execution, the squadron played a pivotal role in both preparing for missions and gathering critical data on their adversaries—an invisible but essential front in the larger conflict.

The blazing heat of the desert seemed to vanish the moment the sun dipped below the horizon, replaced by a rapidly cooling chill that crept across the arid landscape. The main rotors of two Navy gray helicopters roared to life, their powerful blades slicing through the cool night air as the aircrews completed their pre-launch checklists. Inside the cockpits, both Helicopter Aircraft Commanders (HACs) of DASH ONE and DASH TWO—standard callsigns for CSAR rotary assets—confirmed that all systems were green.

"DESERT BASE, DASH ONE and DASH TWO requesting permission to launch," one of the pilots radioed, the steady hum of their engines vibrating through the cabins.

"Permission granted," came the reply, clear and authoritative. Dropping their night vision goggles into position, the pilots adjusted their focus to the glowing green hues of the darkened desert. Slowly and precisely, the helicopters taxied forward across the sandy runway, their powerful rotors kicking up faint clouds of dust as they prepared to lift into the night sky.

With DASH ONE in the lead, Commander Carter pulled up on the collective control and pushed the cyclic forward, smoothly transitioning the helicopter into forward flight. The powerful rotors roared as the HH-60H climbed into the night sky, leaving the sandy base behind.

"DESERT BASE, DASH ONE is feet wet," Carter radioed, his voice steady and confident. The confirmation marked their transition over water—a critical phase in their mission—and signaled the beginning of another perilous operation under the cover of darkness.

"DESERT BASE, DASH TWO…" Lieutenant Commander Ellis began to report, following Commander Carter's aircraft closely. Suddenly, she pulled back on the controls and banked hard to starboard to avoid an erupting fireball.

"DESERT BASE, DASH ONE is down!" Ellis shouted into the radio, her voice sharp with urgency.

A fiery explosion of sparks tore through the night as DASH ONE's main rotor assembly failed catastrophically, briefly blinding both DASH TWO pilots with a "whiteout" effect through their night vision goggles. For what felt like an eternity but was only a second, their vision was rendered useless, the green glow overwhelmed by the intense flash. Ellis fought to regain control, her hands steady as the NVG display cleared. She banked the HH-60H to avoid the chaos in front of her, narrowly steering DASH TWO away from disaster. As they came around, all they could do was watch in helpless horror as DASH ONE spun violently out of control, descending rapidly toward the northern Kuwaiti shoreline. The aircraft's lights flickered before disappearing into the darkness, leaving behind only the fiery trail of its descent.

"AUTO! AUTO! AUTO!" Commander Carter shouted, his voice cutting through the chaos as he dropped the collective, initiating an autorotation maneuver. With the unworkable main rotor assembly, Carter knew the only chance for survival was to crash on his terms. Inside the aircraft, the aircrew and passengers braced for impact, gripping whatever they could as the HH-60H spiraled downward. The cataclysmic failure had been caused by an undetected hydraulic line leak, which triggered severe vibrations in the main rotor. The imbalance had grown rapidly, culminating in an explosion that rendered the rotor system completely inoperable. With no other options, Carter focused solely on putting the aircraft down as safely as possible. The descent was incredibly violent, the cabin shaking as the Seahawk plunged toward the ground. Carter's hands remained steady on the controls, his mind racing to calculate every adjustment needed to give his crew even a sliver of a chance.

The low surf absorbed the initial impact of the HH-60H, but the sheer weight and velocity of the fall drove the aircraft deep enough to strike the ocean floor, just four feet below the surface. The force of the crash shattered the struts, which broke upward and punctured through the cabin floor. Simultaneously, the remaining rotation of the main rotor caused the helicopter to lurch violently off balance. With violent intensity, the rotors tore into the water and detonated, hurling deadly shards of debris in every direction. The aircraft pitched uncontrollably and rolled hard to the port side, the shattered remnants of the main rotor blades slicing into the water with terrifying power. Inside the cabin, the pilots and aircrew endured broken limbs, minor lacerations, and the relentless chaos of the crash. Despite the injuries, they remained strapped into their seats, bracing as the helicopter finally settled upside down in the shallow water. The engines screamed at an unnaturally high pitch, their intakes choked by water as they continued to spin uselessly, now embedded in the sandy ocean floor. The once-mighty Seahawk was battered and broken, its frame twisted and submerged, as the crew struggled to process the violence of the crash and their next move.

DASH TWO hovered at a helpless distance, its crew watching in grim silence as DASH ONE rolled over in the shallow surf. The bottom of the wrecked aircraft was barely above the waterline, its exposed frame illuminated by the pale moonlight. From their vantage point, the pilots could see waves washing over the wreck, but no sign of anyone exiting. With their crew already rigged for rescue and an Air Force Pararescue Pave Hawk preparing to launch from base, Commander Ellis made the call to move closer. Hovering forward toward the crash site, she assessed the situation. The awkward depth of the site posed a unique challenge: the water wasn't deep enough to lower the Rescue Swimmer using fins, yet it was also too submerged to safely land the helicopter on dry ground. The Crew Chief quickly suggested an alternative. "We need a low hover," he said over the comms. "We can jump the swimmer, corpsman, and

EOD members to assist with the rescue or recovery." Ellis nodded, understanding the urgency. The team needed to act fast if there was any chance of saving the crew of DASH ONE. She steadied the Seahawk in a low hover, preparing for the team to deploy and enter the crash site.

Commander Ellis hovered the HH-60H just above the surf near DASH ONE, the powerful rotor wash creating a hurricane-like force over the downed aircraft. The rescue team leapt from the helicopter, landing in the turbulent water as Ellis skillfully lifted the Seahawk up and back, providing the Special Operations crew the space they needed to operate. By the time the rescue team reached the wreckage, most of the aircrew and EOD members had already egressed from the overturned helicopter. The first EOD member on site assisted the co-pilot, who was crawling through her shattered window, visibly dazed but determined to escape. Rescue Swimmer, Megan Whitehurst, quickly assessed the situation, mentally accounting for personnel, but her sharp eyes couldn't locate Commander Carter. Without hesitation, she submerged into the dark, inverted cabin, maneuvering through debris and water. She quickly located the HAC still buckled in his seat, unconscious. Whitehurst twisted the center buckle release, freeing him from the webbing. With steady focus, she righted his limp body and carefully guided him through the fragments of a broken window, surfacing into the moonlit pandemonium. An EOD operator was waiting to help, grabbing hold of Carter as Whitehurst struggled to steady him in the waves. Together, they carried the Commander to the shadowed shoreline, where Whitehurst and the DASH TWO Corpsman immediately began

CPR, their focus unshaken despite the overwhelming scene around them.

* * *

Jerry Carter gazed out at the Pacific Ocean, its vast expanse shimmering in the morning light. Its beauty felt almost cruel, a serene backdrop to the turmoil in his heart. He still couldn't believe Tayla Ellis was gone. Carter had lost his fair share of military friends throughout his long career. It was never easy, but this loss hit differently—deeper. He owed his life to Tayla. If she and her crew hadn't responded so quickly that terrifying night in Kuwait, he surely wouldn't have survived the crash. And now, she was gone.

The questions swirled in his mind. How had it happened? Why? Something about it didn't feel right. The thought gnawed at him, a weight in his chest that refused to ease. Carter sighed heavily. He clenched his fists, unable to shake the feeling that there was more to the tragedy than he'd been told.

CHAPTER 18

La Jolla, California

The dream of retiring from a long military career often conjures thoughts of peace and relaxation. It's a time when you can finally let your guard down, stop operating at 100 miles per hour, and focus on making up for the moments lost during years of forward deployments. Compared to the countless second- and third-world warzones scattered across the globe, the United States offers a profound sense of safety and security. It's a place where most veterans can settle into the next chapter of their lives without worry, ready to enjoy the stability they fought to protect. Captain Carter had every reason to believe he was no different. As a retired officer, his life should have been about reconnecting with family, pursuing passions, and relishing the slower pace of civilian life. But even as he tried to embrace the transition, something gnawed at him—a faint unease he couldn't quite identify, a fog cast over what should have been a bright new beginning.

Carter began his day with his cherished morning ritual: a steaming mug of Peet's Major Dickason's Blend coffee and a fresh print copy of *The New York Times*. He savored both from the luxurious comfort of his balcony, overlooking the serene beauty of La Jolla Cove. After taking care of business with what he proudly considered a glorious morning success in the restroom, he laced up his running shoes for his usual five-mile round-trip route to Mount Soledad. The run offered the perfect balance—a punishing uphill climb rewarded by a downhill return. The descent was hard on his aging knees, but gravity always felt like a welcome reprieve after the initial effort. Back home, Carter made a quick pitstop to rehydrate and change into swimming shorts and a rash guard. He didn't linger long, knowing his muscles would tighten if he delayed—unless, of course, his wife had other plans for a different kind of morning workout. His starting point for his daily one-mile open ocean swim was a mere two blocks from his front door, an easy stroll that allowed him to mentally prepare for the cool Pacific waters. The swim was invigorating, another box checked in his disciplined daily routine. The rest of his day was blissfully unstructured. Whether it was diving into a good book or simply doing whatever he pleased, Carter truly felt like he was living the dream. Life, for once, was his to enjoy.

Unaware of the danger lurking in his shadow, Carter went about his daily routine with ease. What he didn't know was that for the past week, he had been under the close observation of KGR operatives Sergey Baranov and Oleg Gusev. Tasked with learning the retired captain's schedule, the operatives meticulously studied his every move, seeking a clandestine means to dispose of him. Breaking into his 1970s-built single-story home and staging it as a robbery gone wrong would have been simple enough. But that kind of attention—from local police or federal authorities—was precisely what they had been trained to avoid. Any trace of their existence or intentions would be unacceptable, especially while they operated on U.S.

soil. Their mission was clear: no evidence, no loose ends, and no ties that could connect the premeditated murders of decorated military personnel back to their motherland. The operation demanded precision, subtlety, and absolute deniability. Carter, oblivious to the sinister plans unfolding around him, remained the target of their relentless focus.

Lacking suitable jogging gear, Oleg drove their borrowed Subaru Crosstrek to a Big 5 Sporting Goods on Rosecrans Street. The bright, overly patriotic designs of the American clothing disgusted him, but he begrudgingly selected items that would allow him to blend into the local environment. It was a necessary inconvenience. Carter's morning run provided Oleg with the perfect opportunity for reconnaissance. He used the time to study the route, observe the environment, and assess the human population. Jogging at a distance, he remained undetected, using the winding roads and dense eucalyptus-lined streets for cover. Carter, though impressively fit for his age, was completely oblivious to being followed. His focus was on his run, not his surroundings. Oleg, on the other hand, stayed hyper-alert, scanning for potential threats or unexpected interactions. He quickly realized there was no need to hide—not once. The retired captain moved through his routine without suspicion, making Oleg's task far easier than he had anticipated.

Carter found an open space on a bench at the base of the controversial Mount Soledad Cross. He sat, catching his breath, and gazed out at the panoramic views, his thoughts drifting as the morning sun illuminated the National Veterans Memorial. Oleg, having slowed his pace to a casual jog, merged naturally with the crowd of tourists milling about the site. He moved to the far side of the cross, carefully scanning the surrounding area for potential body disposal locations. The high point, perched at 823 feet above sea level, was a popular destination. Tourists with cameras and smartphones bustled around, vying for the perfect selfie with the breathtaking ocean backdrop. It was far too crowded for any covert operation, a reality that irritated Oleg as he surveyed the cluttered scene. Snatching Carter on the ascent was a potential option, but the numerous houses and early risers walking the neighborhood made it a risky proposition. He needed more time, more certainty, and perhaps a better plan altogether. Later, he would meet up with Sergey to compare notes and brainstorm alternatives. Oleg hoped his comrade's observations would yield more promising options; the mounting challenges of the task were beginning to test his patience.

While Oleg was out tracking their objective, Sergey took the Crosstrek south a few miles to Garnet Avenue, heading for La Jolla Watersports. At the Idaho safehouse, Jonathan had provided each of the six operatives with a stack of meticulously crafted documents: a fake passport, a Texas state driver's license, an insurance card, a license to carry, and even a PADI open water diving card. Sergey walked into the store armed with confidence, knowing exactly what he needed and what he'd be leaving with. Inside, he spent no more than 30 minutes selecting his gear. After paying in cash, Sergey exited the store with a 5 mm Spearpro Coastal Camo wetsuit, booties, mask, fins, weight belt, and a DiveLink underwater communication device. The white Crosstrek left the parking lot, heading east for a quick detour at the southern California phenomenon, In-N-Out

Burger. Sergey, curious to try the famed fast food, left unimpressed. The hype, he thought, was clearly overstated. Continuing north, Sergey made his next stop at House of Scuba, where he rented a scuba regulator and two Nitrox diving tanks for the week. With his purchases complete, he plotted a course back to their Airbnb rental near La Jolla Cove. The plan was taking shape, but Sergey's mind remained focused. Every piece of gear had its purpose, and every move he made was part of a much larger design.

Carter was just returning to his house to change for his morning swim as Sergey settled into the warming sands of a small beach called Children's Pool in La Jolla. A picturesque spot popular with tourists was dotted with sunbathers—and crowded with harbor seals basking lazily in the sun. Sergey slipped into his brand-new wetsuit, the 5 mm Spearpro Coastal Camo snug against his frame and conducted a thorough pre-dive safety check of his regulator and Nitrox tank. Methodical as always, he double-checked each connection and tested his airflow, ensuring nothing was left to chance. With his booties and fins secured, he eased into the water, moving with deliberate care to avoid drawing attention. Cradling backward into the salty embrace of the Pacific, Sergey let the waves carry him out until he was far enough to turn and submerge. The Russian operative disappeared beneath the surface, submerging quietly within a distributed crowd of over 50 other scuba divers exploring the Cove's marine wildlife. Among the kelp forests and schools of fish, Sergey's presence was indistinguishable—a silhouette with a mission, hidden in plain sight.

"STOLI ONE, radio check," Sergey said, his voice steady as he activated the DiveLink underwater communicator.

"STOLI TWO, read you loud and clear," Oleg replied. Earlier, he had stopped by their rental to retrieve the preconfigured DiveLink wireless surface-to-diver communication system, which Sergey preset to their designated frequency.

Leaving the Airbnb behind, Oleg jogged down to the cliffs above La Jolla Cove. The morning sun cast long shadows over the rocky terrain as he settled into a green gazebo overlooking the ocean. From his elevated vantage point, he could see the shimmering water below, dotted with swimmers and divers enjoying the calm Pacific. Oleg positioned himself discreetly, blending in with the other early risers enjoying the view. His focus, however, remained razor-sharp as he waited for their target, Captain Carter, to arrive at his predictable water entry point. The stage was set, the equipment ready, and the plan in motion. Now, it was only a matter of time.

"Affirmative. Status of package?" Sergey asked, his tone steady over the DiveLink.

"Package has not arrived," Oleg replied from his perch above the Cove. "Keep channel open for further communication."

Sergey continued his dive, weaving through the intricate underwater rock formations as he studied the topology and currents. A school of leopard sharks glided gracefully below him, indifferent to the presence of the scuba diver. Nearby, bright orange Garibaldi—the California state fish—gathered in small schools, nibbling at floating patches of kelp. Sergey's movements were gauged as he made his way toward a group of what appeared to be an organized scuba tour.

He kept a safe distance, mirroring their path as they explored natural artifacts along the ocean floor. Positioning himself within the group gave him an inconspicuous vantage point while he awaited further instructions.

Moments later, Oleg's voice came through the communicator. "STOLI TWO, package has arrived and is entering the water. Package is wearing black shorts and a black shirt." Sergey acknowledged the message silently, his focus sharpening as he adjusted his position and prepared to act. The plan was now in motion.

"Affirmative, STOLI ONE. Moving in," Sergey replied, his voice calm and controlled.

With a powerful kick of his fins, Sergey propelled himself through the water, heading toward the narrow inlet connecting the Cove to the open sea. Reaching the bottom, he settled into a concealed position within a bed of kelp, letting the swaying brown and red vegetation obscure him from view. As he waited, a young harbor seal poked its head through the moving kelp, its large, curious eyes fixed on the intruder. Sergey impatiently pushed its head to the side, startling the creature, which darted away in a playful flash. Moments later, Carter glided out from the small beach Cove, his rhythmic strokes propelling him smoothly through the water. As the retired captain swam directly overhead, Sergey left his concealed position, emerging from the kelp to pursue his target. Keeping a slow, comfortable pace, Sergey maintained a safe distance behind Carter, staying deeper in the water but not so much that he risked losing sight in the 20-foot visibility. His KGR combat dive training ensured he remained undetected as he closed in on his unsuspecting prey.

The antsy operative felt a surge of temptation to eliminate the target immediately, but Sergey stayed disciplined, reminding himself of the mission's broader objectives. This dive was strictly for reconnaissance. He needed to tail his target, assess his routine, and later reconvene with Oleg to finalize a detailed plan of attack. Carter's swim was straightforward—a one-mile route to a buoy and back to shore. However, the area was teeming with activity. Divers, paddleboarders, and kayakers filled the water, adding layers of complexity to any potential operation. Sergey knew the crowds provided both challenges and opportunities. As he glided silently beneath the surface, Sergey took note of the possibilities the environment offered. After carefully studying the currents, underwater terrain, and patterns of activity, he began to piece together a plan—one that would end Carter's life in a gruesome yet undetectable manner. Sergey's eyes squinted behind his mask as bubbles rose from his steady exhale. A sinister grin crept across his face, barely visible behind the tight grip of his regulator. The pieces of the puzzle were falling into place, and he relished the satisfying thought of executing his plan.

CHAPTER 19

La Jolla, California

The following day dawned predictably calm, another serene southern California morning. The 1–2-foot swells gently rolled in, barely lapping against the smooth rocks along the La Jolla Cove shoreline. Carter made a quick pitstop at his house, just a couple of blocks from the water, to change into his Lululemon swim trunks—a gift from his wife of 30 years, Annie, for his recent birthday. While he didn't usually see the value in name-brand clothing, he had to admit they fit well and spared him the inner thigh rash that his old Navy Exchange models often caused. He grabbed a lemon-lime Gatorade from the fridge and pounded it in a few gulps, careful not to overdo it. He still had a one-mile swim ahead of him, an essential part of his morning routine. Decades of experience had taught him how to manage his body's nutritional needs and avoid the debilitating ocean cramps that could ruin even the calmest swim. Feeling prepared, Carter grabbed his gear and stepped out into the crisp morning air, the smell of saltwater faint but familiar on the breeze.

The death of Tayla Ellis still weighed heavily on Carter's mind as he slipped on a worn pair of Quiksilver flip-flops and headed for the door. The memories and unanswered questions lingered, a fog he couldn't quite shake. "Have a nice swim, honey!"

Annie's cheerful voice called out, surprising him from the upstairs balcony.

Carter looked up, a faint smile crossing his face. "Thanks, Annie," he replied, his tone softer than usual. Her presence was a small comfort, a grounding force against the storm of thoughts swirling in his mind. With a quick wave, he stepped outside, the morning sun casting long shadows on the quiet La Jolla Street as he made his way toward the Cove.

Carter glanced back and gave her a thumbs-up, but then did a double take, unable to resist admiring Annie's timeless beauty. She stood on the balcony in her flowing nightgown, a steaming latte cradled in her hands, her expression a mix of admiration, empathy, and unwavering compassion for her forever soul mate. Annie had been by his side through countless hardships during his military service, weathering every storm with grace and resilience. She knew him better than anyone and understood that he needed this time to find peace and make sense of the loss that still clouded his mind. Though part of her was tempted to pry, to offer words of comfort, she held back. She knew her husband too well. Carter needed space to process his emotions, and Annie trusted him to come to her when he was ready. For now, she simply stood, offering him silent support as he headed out to confront another day.

The retired captain carefully descended the sand-covered, rusted metal stairs below the lifeguard station just south of La Jolla Cove. The small, secluded beach was a haven for sunbathing harbor seals, their rounded bodies scattered across the shoreline like lazy sentinels of the sand. From above, an on-duty lifeguard yelled into a megaphone at a pair of teenage snorkelers. "Hey! Stop harassing the seal!" he barked, directing his ire toward the kids who had cornered an adolescent seal attempting to waddle onto dry sand. Carter paid them little attention as he kicked off his flip-flops near the rear rock cliff wall, where the crumbling southern California seawall curved unevenly into the sand, its jagged edges shaped by years of storms and saltwater erosion. With a deep breath, he turned and waded into the 68-degree water, passing the guilty teens on his way out. The cool water was a refreshing contrast to the warm morning air, but it shocked his muscles, causing them to tighten as his body adjusted to the sudden drop in temperature. Blood shifted instinctively to his core, a natural response to the cold. Allowing himself time to acclimate, Carter began with a slow, modified freestyle stroke, carefully navigating past clusters of sea life and dense vegetation in the narrow inlet. As the Cove opened into a broader expanse of ocean, he stretched into a fluid tempo. He adjusted his course, aiming for an anchored buoy about half a mile north. The buoy marked his halfway point, parallel to the rocky shoreline that framed the pristine waters of La Jolla Cove. This was his sanctuary, a place where the pattern of the ocean waves could wash away his thoughts, if only for a while.

"STOLI TWO, package has entered the water," Oleg reported into the communicator. "He's wearing black shorts, black shirt, and goggles. With ocean currents, he should be on top of you in 15 minutes."

Oleg had positioned himself among the morning tourists strolling along Coast Boulevard, which offered stunning views of the southern California ocean cliffs. Blending seamlessly into the crowd, he appeared to be just another casual observer enjoying the striking scenery. The wireless underwater communication headset he wore was inconspicuous, easily mistaken for a pair of sleek Bose headphones. To complete the act, Oleg held a cellphone in front of his face like countless others, giving the impression he was entranced by social media posts or a video call. His practiced indifference rendered him invisible, a ghost in plain sight, as he kept watch over their target's predictable routine.

"STOLI ONE, copy 15 minutes. Moving to secondary position," Sergey responded, his voice calm and precise despite being 10 meters underwater.

He spoke through the state-of-the-art DiveLink communication device, which allowed him to remain fully submerged while maintaining contact with Oleg on the shore. The cutting-edge technology gave the KGR operatives a tactical edge, enabling real-time coordination between land and sea without drawing any attention. Sergey adjusted his position, kicking his fins gently to conserve energy as he navigated the cool, clear waters. His training and equipment ensured he remained undetectable beneath the surface, a silent predator waiting for the right moment to strike.

"STOLI TWO, moving to secondary position," Oleg confirmed, rising from the uncomfortably hard cement bench where he'd been sitting.

He set off at a medium pace, walking north along the sidewalk while keeping visual contact with their target. His steps were casual, ensuring that no one—whether tourists, locals, or anyone potentially watching—would suspect he was shadowing Carter. Oleg also kept track of his distance from Sergey, mindful of the 500-meter range limitation of their underwater radio. The sunny path along the cliffs provided plenty of cover, blending him into the morning crowd of joggers, walkers, and selfie-takers. At precise five-minute intervals, Oleg relayed updates to Sergey. "Package is 200 meters out, approximately 10 minutes," he murmured. As he moved, Oleg's focus remained razor-sharp, the operation unfolding exactly as planned.

Carter stretched his six-foot-one frame, his wingspan matching his height as he glided through the glassy morning ocean with practiced ease, propelling him through the calm waters of La Jolla Cove. As he approached a dense kelp bed, Carter adjusted his course, staying on the surface to avoid getting tangled in the shifting seaweed. The kelp seemed to change daily, its floating tendrils a familiar but unpredictable obstacle. Once past the seaweed nest and back in open water, he glanced downward and spotted a pair of leopard sharks 15 feet below. Leopard sharks were a common sight in the Cove, their graceful motion a staple of the underwater ecosystem. They rarely posed any threat to humans, but the smooth, side-to-side motion of a shark's dorsal fin never failed to trigger a surge of primal panic in Carter. His fight, flight, or freeze response kicked in for a split second before his rational mind took over, calming his nerves. No matter how many times he encountered the harmless creatures, they still sent chills through his body. Watching *Jaws* at a young age had left an indelible mark on his psyche, one he couldn't completely shake, even in his years of open ocean swimming experience. Carter exhaled deeply, pushing the lingering unease aside as he refocused on his swim, his steady strokes carrying him toward the buoy in the distance.

Breathe, stroke, kick.

Breathe, stroke, kick.

The former helicopter pilot settled into his rhythm, his strokes smooth and deliberate as he glided through the cool water. In that moment, Carter found a fleeting sense of peace, temporarily releasing the sadness and pain that had weighed on him since Tayla Ellis's death. Every couple of strokes, he raised his head to ensure he maintained his line of sight to the buoy. Though rip currents were rare in the Cove, they were still a possibility, and Carter wasn't one to take chances. He knew all too well how many lives had been lost to the unpredictable power of Mother Nature. As he lifted his head once more, he saw the large red buoy 20 feet ahead. The mossy chain anchoring it to the ocean floor swayed gently in the current, its weathered links laced with seaweed. Beneath it, far below, the chain disappeared into the depths, secured to a cement block buried in the sandy bottom. The familiar sight gave Carter a small sense of reassurance. The buoy marked the halfway point of his swim, a steady constant in the ever-changing ocean.

"STOLI ONE, initiating attack," Sergey said flatly through the DiveLink, his tone cold and focused.

Carter, oblivious to the danger behind him, remained fixated on the oversized chain links and kelp as they disappeared into the black depths of the Pacific. He never saw the diver in a full-body camouflage wetsuit approach, moving with the silent precision of a great white shark. Sergey struck without hesitation. Unsheathing an

EVO Titanium Dive Knife, he drove it into Carter's kidney with brutal efficiency. The retired captain froze as a searing pain ripped through his side, the shock and surprise overwhelming his senses. His mind raced to make sense of the attack, a wave of heat flooding his body as panic took hold. His first thought was a shark attack, and he instinctively began to struggle, pulling desperately toward the surface for air. But Sergey wasn't about to let him escape. He locked Carter into a controlled cross-chest carry, expertly securing him as he dove deeper. Kicking with relentless power, Sergey dragged Carter downward, 10 feet, 20 feet, 30 feet into the cold, dark void. The retired pilot's struggles weakened with each passing second, his oxygen-deprived body succumbing to Sergey's vicious assault. The silence of the underwater world was deafening, broken only by the faint sound of bubbles escaping as Sergey descended, his mission methodical and merciless.

Carter gasped involuntarily as the knife pierced just below his right ribcage, allowing a mouthful of saltwater to flood in. His body convulsed against the automatic gag reflex, his lungs aching as he thrashed frantically, trying to break free. The pressure in his head intensified, like a vice tightening around his skull, as Sergey dragged him deeper into the cold depths. The pulsing pounding of his heart echoed in his ears, a primal reminder of his dwindling time. His mind reeled, struggling to process the surreal shift—from the calm serenity of his morning swim to the lancing pain of an unknown assailant and the unstoppable plunge toward certain death. But Carter's instincts kicked in. He was no stranger to dire situations, and even as his body screamed for oxygen and his brain begged for clarity, one thought cut through the chaos: Not without a fight! With whatever strength he could muster, Carter prepared to resist, his survival instincts igniting a desperate final effort.

Carter had spent most of his military career alongside Aviation Rescue Swimmers, regularly training in the base pool or open ocean. Though he hadn't endured the grueling Rescue Swimmer program himself, he had picked up a few tricks over the years. As his vision flickered in and out of blackness, Carter dug deep, summoning a final surge of adrenaline. His hands clawed upward, finding Sergey's arm and wrenching it free with a desperate burst of strength. The sudden release brought a fleeting sense of relief as he floated free in the water, but it was short-lived. Pushing through the excruciating pain radiating from his stabbed side, Carter forced his legs into a powerful frog kick. The motion sent a searing jolt through his injured body, but he had no time to care. Survival trumped discomfort. Ignoring the agony, he thrust his arms forward, pulling into a downward stroke to propel himself toward the surface. The bubbles escaping from his lips served as his guide—a fragile trail of air that marked the only way to salvation. Every fiber of his being screamed for oxygen, but Carter's determination burned brighter. He would not succumb—not like this, not here.

Jerry Carter expelled the last remaining air from his collapsing lungs as he felt the killer's sharp blade slice horizontally across his abdomen. A burning pain radiated through his core as his liver, stomach, and intestines began to slip free, snaking their way out through the gaping wound. Instinct took over one final time, forcing Carter to draw a desperate half-breath, but the water rushing into his esophagus sealed his fate. His body convulsed in a series of intense spasms before falling still, his soul departing into the dark abyss to join his co-pilot in the afterlife.

"STOLI ONE, package delivered," Sergey reported coldly through the DiveLink.

"STOLI TWO, package delivery acknowledged," came Oleg's calm response from the shoreline. The ocean returned to its serene regularity, the waves lapping gently against the rocky shore, masking the horrific act that had just transpired below the surface.

Sergey sheathed his knife with cold proficiency and took control of the corpse. Carter's lifeless body leaked warm, heavy blood into the surrounding water—a potential problem for the KGR operative. Remaining calm, Sergey paused to survey his surroundings. His eyes scanned the 360-degree, 20-foot visibility range, methodically searching for any human witnesses. He checked level and downward for telltale bubbles that might indicate nearby scuba divers. Then, tilting his gaze upward, he searched for swimmers, snorkelers, kayakers, boaters, or paddleboarders. Satisfied that no one was in the vicinity, Sergey grabbed the retired pilot's body and began towing it toward the ocean floor, heading west into deeper waters. He cautiously dragged the corpse further from the Cove to give it time to bleed out. The constant motion helped dissipate the blood into the seawater, reducing the risk of forming a noticeable red cloud that could draw unwanted attention from the surface. Sergey's focus remained sharp; every stroke of his fins was purposeful, ensuring the mission would remain undetected.

After 10 minutes of towing the body through the open ocean with no signs of detection, Sergey began searching for a natural tomb to stash the cadaver. La Jolla Cove was renowned for its intricate network of underwater caves, some of the most extravagant along the California coast. Navigating through the deep, kelp-infested waters, Sergey's sharp eyes quickly identified a coral-covered cavern 100 feet below the surface. He maneuvered into the cave, its dark, vegetation-draped walls offering an ideal hiding spot. The Russian diver secured the retired pilot's ankle with a heavy-duty zip tie, attaching it to a loop he'd prepared in advance. He threaded the loop through a sturdy opening in the rocks, ensuring the body would remain anchored even as currents shifted. Before leaving, Sergey double-checked his work, tugging firmly on the binding to ensure it was secure. The corpse blended into the vegetation-covered surroundings of the sea cave, its concealment almost perfect. Satisfied, Sergey turned and began his ascent, carefully retracing his path back toward the shore.

Captain Carter's remains wouldn't be discovered for weeks, delivering both the crushing blow of loss and the faint relief of closure to his heartbroken wife, Annie. Even then, only a partial left foot was found, washed ashore by the tide and discovered by an early morning metal detectorist searching for hidden treasures along the beach. Authorities ran DNA tests, confirming the foot belonged to the missing local swimmer. The rest of Carter's body was never recovered. The blood in the water had attracted a frenzy of marine life, starting with adult leopard sharks. Their feeding was short-lived, however, as an 8-foot great white shark patrolling the area claimed dominance, tearing Carter's torso apart in a violent feeding frenzy. The massive predator ripped the appendages clean from the body, scattering fragments of flesh and bone across the ocean floor. What remained of Carter's ravaged corpse became a gruesome buffet for the ocean's opportunistic scavengers. Giant Sheep Crabs, California Spiny Crabs, and mussels descended on the remains, joined even by the seemingly innocent Garibaldi, nibbling at what was left. Jellyfish drifted lazily in the aftermath, their delicate forms a stark contrast to the brutal feast. By the time the waters settled, all that remained in the sea cave was an empty zip tie, swaying gently with the currents, still attached to a rock beneath the kelp beds—a silent witness to the horrifying event.

CHAPTER 20

Newburyport, Massachusetts

Bish, have time to talk? Brody Hayes texted his former Master Chief SAR brother.

Give me 10, Phil Bishop replied, setting down his empty bourbon glass.

With a groan, Bishop pushed himself off the couch, his right knee emitting a crunching sound that had become all too familiar. Years of wear and tear during his military career had left him with mounds of scar tissue in both knees and his right shoulder—a permanent reminder of decades spent pushing his body to the limit. He shuffled into the kitchen, his gait uneven, and opened the doors of a custom oak aging barrel cabinet. Inside sat a collection of half-empty whiskey bottles, their amber hues catching the dim light. Reaching for a bottle of Elijah Craig Small Batch, he poured two fingers over a half-melted block ice cube, the rich aroma rising to meet him. Drink in hand, Bishop staggered back to the couch and sank into its worn cushions. He stared at the screen for a moment, then clicked on Hayes' name in his contacts. With a heavy exhale, he pressed *Call.*

"What the hell is going on, Hayes?" Bishop skipped any formalities, diving straight to the issue.

"No clue, man," Brody replied, his voice heavy with concern. "I spoke to Annie earlier this morning. She's understandably hysterical—and frustrated. She said the police aren't doing much since he's only been missing for a few days. I didn't know what to say, Bish. I just listened while she poured her heart out."

"There has to be a connection!" Bishop snapped, his words tinged with both anger and disbelief. "First Ellis, and now Carter? I don't believe in coincidences!"

The slurred edges of his voice betrayed his growing intoxication, but the passion in his tone was unmistakable. "Two of the best we know, gone? Something's not right, Hayes. This stinks, man, and you know it!" Brody remained silent for a moment, his mind turning over Bishop's words. Deep down, he couldn't shake the same unsettling feeling.

"I don't know, man," Brody said with a sigh. "I'm just trying to process all of this right now. I'll catch up with you in a few days and let you know if I hear anything else. Take care of yourself, brother." The cellphone emitted a sequence of beeps as the call disconnected. Bishop lowered it from his ear, staring at the screen for a moment before tossing it onto the IKEA LACK coffee table in front of him. The table's lower shelf was cluttered with stacks of magazines—military, sports, and outdoor issues he hadn't gotten around to organizing. As Bishop leaned forward to grab his glass of bourbon, the current issue of *Rotor Review* caught his eye. *Rotor Review*, a U.S. Navy helicopter magazine, released quarterly editions covering squadron changes of command, rescue operations, mishaps, and other notable stories from the rotary wing community.

Bishop hesitated, his fingers hovering over the glossy cover. The bourbon could wait. Something about the magazine pulled his focus, stirring a sense of unease in his gut.

During his time in service, Bishop had been featured in multiple *Rotor Review* articles highlighting mission sets and mishaps he had been involved in. The magazine often served as a small window into the U.S. Navy's rotary wing community, capturing moments that resonated with those who had lived them. The current issue sat on the tabletop, its cover showcasing an MH-60R Seahawk holding a hover while dipping the AN/AQS-22 ALFS sonar during an anti-submarine warfare (ASW) training mission. Bishop stared at the image, noting the subtle ambiguity: was the helicopter lifting or lowering the sonar dome? It didn't matter. He knew the truth behind most cover shots—they were usually moments of pure chance. The photographer, likely in another aircraft nearby, would spot an angle or light they liked and snap away. It wasn't about a pivotal mission or a defining moment; it was just another day of training captured in a way that looked compelling. The pilots probably hadn't even thought twice about the image, but the photographer had convinced them to hover nearby for their personal collection. Bishop smirked faintly at the memory of similar scenarios he'd been part of. He took a sip of bourbon and leaned back, the unease in his gut stirring again. Something about this issue, this moment, felt different.

* * *

Bishop stared at the magazine cover, the image pulling him into vivid memories of that fateful night south of the Aleutian Islands in the unforgiving North Pacific. The Russian submarine mission—one sworn to secrecy—surfaced in his mind like a long-buried specter. Neurons fired in rapid succession as his mind pieced together fragments of that high-stakes operation. He tipped his glass back until the large block of ice slammed against his lips, sending a cold shock that snapped him further into the memory. Frustrated, he slammed the glass down on the table and snatched the magazine. In an instant, he was back, transported into the cramped Tactical Sensor Operator seat of the SH-60F HUNTER 613. The constant screaming roar of the main rotors and twin turboshaft engines consumed the cabin, vibrations rattling his bones. Despite the discomfort, Bishop had channeled all his focus into the mission, filtering every piece of incoming data through the haze of noise and adrenaline. The stakes were monumental. Waves of impending doom coursed through his thoughts as they worked to confirm the enemy contact. Every detail mattered—the criticality of an accurate classification, the immense weight of deciding whether to eliminate a potential threat to prevent what could become World War III. And then Commander Carter's calm, deliberate words broke through the chaos, each slow syllable electrifying Bishop's nerves like a live wire.

"Stand by for positive ID." The memory surged, sharp and unrelenting, as Bishop gripped the magazine tightly, his pulse quickening with the ghost of a moment that still haunted him.

"Dropping NOW! NOW! NOW!"

"TORPEDO AWAY!"

Bishop's body was safe in his New England home, but his mind was far from it. He was back in the cramped cabin of the SH-60F, reliving the mission that had permanently etched itself into his soul. The gray walls of the helicopter seemed to close in around him, pressing tighter with every heartbeat. The deafening roar of the main rotors filled his ears, but even above the cacophony, he could hear his racing pulse pounding through his headset. His breathing quickened, shallow and panicked. His mouth felt parched, desperate for water, but his Camelback hydration system was out of reach, his body pinned by the locked safety harness. The pilots were frozen, powerless to control the aircraft as it plummeted toward the ocean below. The SH-60F hit terminal velocity before smashing into the dark, turbulent seas. Bishop squeezed his eyes shut, and every muscle in his body tensed. He screamed at the top of his lungs, but no sound escaped. His trembling lips parted in silent agony as the memory overwhelmed him.

And then it was over. He opened his eyes to find himself back on his living room couch, drenched in a pool of sweat, his body visibly shaking. The adrenaline still coursed through him, but the world around him was eerily silent. The ghost of the past receded, leaving only a hollow ache in its wake.

CHAPTER 21

Newburyport, Massachusetts

"Hey, Bish! Want your usual?" Samantha, the friendly mid-40s bartender, called out with a smile. Her blonde hair was tied back in a loose ponytail, and she wore yoga pants paired with a low-cut white shirt that caught the attention of the college boys she was serving a pitcher of local IPA.

"Hey, Sam," Bishop replied, raising a thumbs-up in response. Samantha nodded, grabbing a bottle of Basil Hayden Bourbon from the shelf. She poured him two generous fingers over a sphere of ice and slid the glass onto a square napkin in front of his usual seat at the Port Tavern.

"Here you go," she said with a flirty wink before moving on to another table to take an order. Bishop lifted the glass, giving it a small swirl as he watched the ice glisten under the warm tavern lights. He took a slow sip, savoring the smooth burn of the bourbon, letting the familiar setting and Samantha's effortless charm momentarily ease his restless mind.

Bishop had become a fixture at the Port Tavern in the quaint New England town of Newburyport, frequenting the cozy establishment after retiring from a 25-year career in the U.S. Navy. With a steady pension and an abundance of free time following his second divorce, the tavern had become his refuge. His military career had been one of relentless dedication. Multiple deployments during both war and peacetime had demanded everything he had to give. Over the years, he had toggled between duty as an instructor and a squadron leader, his expertise pivotal in shaping the U.S. Navy Aviation Rescue Swimmer program to meet evolving threats. Bishop was one of the most decorated and respected aircrewmen in Navy history, his name synonymous with excellence and commitment. He had given his best years to his country, sacrificing family, personal relationships, and parts of himself he could never reclaim. Now, with all those sacrifices behind him, he found himself an empty shell of his former self. The sharp focus and clear purpose that had once defined his life were gone, replaced by the dull monotony of retired life. Bishop drifted aimlessly, searching for meaning in a world that seemed to have moved on without him. The Port Tavern, with its familiar faces and predictable comforts, was a small solace—but not the answer he sought.

The U.S. military has long faced criticism for its short-term focus on developing elite warriors to defend the nation against foreign and domestic threats. Its training methods encourage the compartmentalization of emotions, channeling those feelings to intensify an individual's ability to operate effectively in the chaos of war. While undeniably effective for mission success, this approach often comes at a steep human cost. Over time, the cracks begin to show. The staggering rates of suicide and PTSD diagnoses among veterans paint a grim picture of the long-term effects. The military's personnel transition programs—from defenders of the nation to civilians—

have been a persistent issue for generations. Veterans are left grappling with an overwhelming sense of lost purpose, unresolved trauma, and the inability to connect with those who have never shared their experiences. Bishop exemplified that struggle. Sitting alone at the far end of the bar, he numbed the pain of more than twenty years of trauma with familiar, nightly rituals. The Port Tavern offered no answers but provided a brief reprieve from the memories that haunted him. Focused on his self-imposed mission, he methodically reached his nightly state of anesthetized intoxication—a state where the pain dulled and the past became a little easier to bear, if only for a few hours.

"Hey hero, need another hit?" Sam asked, locking eyes with the fading former Rescue Swimmer. Her warm, authentic smile pierced through his drunken haze, delivering a fleeting bump of joy to his otherwise dismal mood. Bishop sat slumped at the bar, drowning in a self-reflection that stung as much as the bourbon in his glass. Failed relationships, a hopeless future, and the recent, mysterious loss of his combat crew members swirled together in his mind like a storm he couldn't escape. He wondered, at his burnt-out age, if he would ever love again. Confidence was hard to muster with the weight he'd gained since retiring and the motivation he lacked to climb out of the downward spiral that seemed to define his life. The twenty-five years he had spent serving his country—building an identity as one of the best—felt more like a distant dream. Now, he lived a nightmare. Praise and respect from others for his service only deepened his unease. It felt hollow, undeserved. Bishop felt like an imposter, trapped between the person he once was and the broken man he had become.

"Yeah, Sam," he said after a moment, sliding his glass toward her with a faint nod. "Actually, it's getting late," Bishop started, hesitating as though weighing his options. But then he shrugged, forcing a faint smirk. "But then again, you only live once. Sure, one more!" Sam didn't pry, offering only a knowing look before pouring him another two fingers of bourbon.

A flicker of pride warmed him for almost answering responsibly, but it was quickly swallowed by the familiar pull of self-loathing. Vulnerability gnawed at him—the unshakable fear of appearing less than a man. That front had been ingrained in him long before his years of military service. His abusive stepfather, a Vietnam War veteran, had been his first and harshest teacher. The man had taught him what it meant to be "a man" in the same broken way he had been taught—through violence, ridicule, and the relentless cycle of generational trauma. Bishop had learned to harden himself young, hiding his pain behind a mask of toughness and resilience. The military only reinforced what his childhood had instilled: feelings were a weakness, and weakness was unacceptable. And so, he buried everything deep, letting it fester beneath the surface. Now, as he slid his glass back toward Sam, that weight felt heavier than ever.

* * *

Brothers Pavel and Andrei Kuznetsov arrived on the East Coast a week prior, their mission clear and their methods flexible to their reconnaissance findings. They spent their days shadowing Bishop, observing his daily and nightly routines to develop a thorough understanding of his patterns and behaviors. Like the other members of the HUNTER 613 crew, Bishop was a marked target. The KGR operatives had been tasked with eliminating him in a way that would arouse no suspicion beyond the unfortunate coincidence of timing. Even those connections, tenuous as they were, wouldn't be drawn until all six operatives were safely back in their motherland. The Kuznetsov brothers assumed Bishop would be the easiest target. His descent into alcoholism and depression made him a predictable mark. He was isolated, emotionally vulnerable, and fit the perfect profile for another tragic veteran suicide. It was a chilling calculation, cold and clinical. The Russians moved with the precision of men trained to complete their mission without error. Bishop, unaware of the hunters trailing him, continued with his days, his pain making him an unwitting accomplice in the illusion of his own demise.

Around 10 p.m., Pavel flagged down a Toyota Prius driven by a Lyft driver who had just dropped off three liquored-up college girls eager to continue their party at the Port Tavern. Approaching the driver with calm confidence, Pavel offered him $5,000 in cash to borrow the vehicle for the next hour.

"I'm writing a documentary," Pavel explained smoothly. "I want to experience life as a Lyft driver firsthand."

The driver hesitated for only a moment. Strapped for cash and calculating that $5,000 was more than a month's pay, he quickly decided the risk was worth it. Without further questions, he handed over the key fob. Pavel slid into the driver's seat, adjusting it and the mirrors to his preference before pressing the *Available* button on the dash-mounted iPhone running the Lyft app. He rolled the silent Prius out of its spot, gliding into the quiet streets of Newburyport's downtown. Circling the area, Pavel declined all incoming ride requests, patiently waiting for one specific name to appear on the screen: Phillip Bishop. This was his nightly routine at this time, and Pavel knew it wouldn't be long before the drunken ex-Navy man summoned a ride home. Pavel's quiet demeanor belied the callous intention behind the act. The plan was set, and now it was only a matter of time.

Andrei sat in the white Subaru Crosstrek parked adjacent to the Port Tavern, his patience growing thin as he watched the weak, drunken Americans stumble in and out of the bar. He grimaced at the sight of college students tripping over their own feet, their laughter grating on his nerves. The historic district's ancient red, black, and sand-colored bricks only added to the chaos. The uneven diagonal patterns and warped elevation caused by subsurface tree roots turned the streets into a minefield for the inebriated. Every other staggering idiot seemed to trip on their bar-hopping journey, eliciting laughter from their companions. Andrei's disdain for everything the United States represented festered with each passing moment. He despised their frivolity, their excess, their arrogance. The thought of causing even a small element of destruction filled him with grim satisfaction. The mission couldn't end soon enough; he was eager to return to Mother Russia, far from this land he loathed. Still, he had to remain disciplined. His orders were precise: eliminate the former Navy helicopter crew responsible for his country's humiliation when he was just an infant. It felt like an insignificant task to Andrei, a mission beneath the skills of a trained KGR operative. He wished the orders had been more destructive, more impactful. But he also understood the bigger picture. Success here would prove their competence and loyalty, leading to larger, more devastating assignments in the future. For now, Andrei channeled his frustration into focus, his steely resolve pushing him forward.

A sudden commotion snapped Andrei's attention back to the tavern as a group of men in suits pulled open the rustic wooden doors. One of them yanked the heavy iron door handle just as Bishop, unsteady on his feet, pushed the door open from inside. The sudden absence of support sent the intoxicated Navy veteran stumbling forward, straight into the arms of the businessmen trying to enter. Bishop, already off balance, tripped over the uneven bricks beneath him, forcing two of the men to catch him before he could hit the ground.

"Whoa there, buddy!" one of the men exclaimed, steadying him with a firm grip. "I hope you're not driving tonight."

The men exchanged awkward glances before gently helping Bishop regain his footing. His slurred attempt at gratitude was almost drowned out by the chuckles of passersby who had stopped to watch the scene unfold. From the Crosstrek, Andrei watched intently, a flicker of disgust crossing his face. He leaned forward slightly, his eyes narrowing as the scene played out, waiting for the moment when Bishop would inevitably stumble out into the street, ripe for the taking.

Bishop caught his balance and shuffled past the suited men, fumbling to pull his phone from his front pocket. He raised it in front of his face, unlocking the screen with the iPhone's built-in biometrics. His thumb swiped down to initiate the search feature, quickly displaying the Lyft app from a previous use. With two DUI arrests behind him, Bishop was now a professional at securing safe rides home. He tapped his preset home address and hit send, the process so routine it barely registered in his alcohol-addled mind.

"Target in sight. He's on his cellphone," Andrei said into his two-way radio, watching from the Crosstrek as Bishop swayed under the dim streetlights.

"Affirmative. Target in sight. Accepting his request now," Pavel responded, the borrowed Toyota Prius idling nearby. He swiftly accepted the incoming ride request on his Lyft app, beating out any other local drivers poised to snatch up the fare.

Moments later, the Prius rolled to the curb in front of Bishop. Oblivious to anything but the ride confirmation on his phone, Bishop staggered forward and pulled open the rear door. He dropped heavily into the back seat, blissfully unaware that this was more than just another shared ride—it was his final one. Pavel glanced at the rearview mirror, a cold smirk flickering across his face as he shifted the Prius into drive.

CHAPTER 22

Newburyport, Massachusetts

"Phillip?" the imposter Lyft driver spoke to his rearview mirror's reflection of his new passenger.

"Yep, that's me," Bishop slurred, fumbling to right himself from his not-so-graceful entry into the backseat.

Six generously poured glasses of bourbon coursed through his system, amplifying his intoxication. His world spun violently when he closed his eyes, but spun and blurred even worse when he opened them. He couldn't decide which was more unbearable, but he knew that closing his eyes meant risking unconsciousness—a battle he wasn't ready to lose just yet. His commute was short, just a couple of miles, and all Bishop wanted was to collapse into bed for the night. The idea of checking the driver's identity against the photo on the Lyft app didn't even occur to him. Even if it had, he doubted he could focus long enough to match the blurry image to reality. Pavel eased the Prius away from the curb, its electric engine barely audible over the soft hum of the tires on the brick-lined streets. He continued down State Street for a short block before flipping on the left turn signal and making a turn onto Prospect Street. The 1700s-era historic town, with its charming brick buildings and towering church steeples, passed unnoticed by both occupants of the car.

Bishop faded in and out of his inebriated stupor, slouched against the seatback, too drunk to care about his surroundings. He made no attempt at conversation, simply grateful not to be behind the wheel.

The Prius emitted a faint, unpleasant whistling noise as its engine droned through the peaceful streets, crawling past rows of pastel-colored, colonial-style houses. The sleepy neighborhood exuded the kind of peace one would expect from a small New England town late at night. Up ahead, two blocks to the right, a pair of streetlights were out, leaving an intentional patch of darkness. To the untrained eye, it would appear as just another minor infrastructure oversight—hardly worth noticing. But Pavel knew better. As they approached the dimly lit section of Federal Street, he slowed the car and pulled it to the right curb. The darkness enveloped the Prius as it came to a stop, the faint glow of a distant streetlamp barely brushing the edges of the scene. Pavel's gaze flicked to the rearview mirror, his sharp eyes locking on Bishop's hazy reflection.

"This isn't my…" Bishop began to protest, his drunken slur trailing off as his door swung open.

Before he could finish, he was violently yanked from the car by Andrei and thrown hard onto the uneven cement sidewalk. The impact jarred his senses, but years of military conditioning and survival instincts kicked in, overriding his intoxicated state. As Andrei dragged him further onto the sidewalk by his shoulders, Bishop instinctively fought back. Twisting his body, he rolled onto his back and lashed out with his legs, locking them around the Russian's arms. With a surge of aggression fueled by years of pent-up frustration and muscle memory, he broke free from Andrei's grip. Andrei stumbled, momentarily caught off guard, and Bishop didn't waste the opportunity. Pushing himself to his feet, he transitioned smoothly from one foot to the other and swept the Russian's legs out from under him. The bulky young operative hit the cement with a resounding thud, the impact knocking the wind from his lungs. Andrei gasped for air, stunned and momentarily incapacitated. He hadn't anticipated such a fierce and immediate retaliation from the American, especially one who appeared so incapacitated moments earlier. But Bishop had quickly reclaimed the element of surprise, evening the battlefield in an instant. The retired aircrewman, still unsteady but laser-focused, knew he couldn't afford to hesitate.

Now back on his feet, Bishop's bloodshot eyes burned with unbridled rage as he charged toward the attacker sprawled on the ground. In that moment, he had no reservations about beating the man into unconsciousness—or to death. Self-defense was a justification he was more than willing to lean on. But just as his powerful legs propelled him forward, his momentum came to an abrupt and excruciating halt. Fifty thousand volts of electricity ripped through his back, searing his veins like liquid fire. His muscles seized instantly, locking his body in paralyzed agony. The 200-pound sailor collapsed hard onto the uneven sidewalk, the impact violently dislocating his left shoulder. Pain radiated through his body, but the overwhelming current left him unable to scream or resist. Pavel stood a few feet away, his finger firmly on the trigger of the taser. He didn't release the charge until Bishop's convulsions subsided, and his consciousness faded under the relentless onslaught of pain. Andrei, now back on his feet and gasping for air, rolled the limp, electrically shocked American onto his stomach. Dropping to one knee, he pinned Bishop down with his weight while expertly binding his wrists and ankles with heavy-duty zip ties.

"Stay down," Andrei muttered under his breath, his pride stung by the unexpected retaliation. Pavel stepped closer, ensuring their target was fully subdued, his icy gaze scanning for any signs of witnesses in the darkened street. The brothers worked quickly. Time was not on their side, and leaving no trace was paramount.

The Kuznetsov brothers moved swiftly, lifting Bishop's dead weight and hauling him into the hatchback of their Subaru Crosstrek. They worked efficiently, ensuring no witnesses were present in the darkened neighborhood. Pavel returned to the Toyota Prius, methodically wiping down every surface he had touched with disinfecting wet wipes he had picked up earlier from Market Basket. He took care to leave no evidence, wiping the steering wheel, door handles, and even the seatbelt latch. Satisfied, Pavel abandoned the vehicle a few blocks away, leaving it parked inconspicuously on a side street. The legitimate Lyft driver would eventually find his deserted car, but Pavel doubted he would report it to the authorities. Doing so would mean admitting he had willingly handed over his work vehicle for a quick $5,000—a blatant violation of company policy that could cost him his job and credibility. With their tracks covered, the brothers regrouped at the Crosstrek. Andrei adjusted the comatose Bishop's position, ensuring he was securely concealed in the back, and slid into the driver's seat. Pavel joined him, the two of them exchanging curt eye contact before the vehicle pulled away into the night.

Andrei kept the white Crosstrek steady, carefully staying within the speed limit as he turned left onto Federal Street. The road, lined with various shades of white and gray clapboard houses and cedar shake roofs, felt frozen in time. Streetlights cast soft halos over the historic homes, their wooden siding weathered by years of salty air from the nearby coast. The road followed the gentle curve of the Merrimack River to the left, where the moonlight reflected off the dark, rippling water. As Federal Street transitioned into Water Street, Andrei adjusted his grip on the wheel, his focus unwavering. The road eventually merged into Plum Island Turnpike, slicing through the expansive Newbury Salt Marsh. The marshland, part of the 17,000-acre "Great Marsh" stretching from Cape Ann into New Hampshire, was alive with the pungent smell of sulfur from the tidal ebb and flow. The odor clung to the air, a byproduct of the thriving marine life hidden in the muddy trenches and dense saltmarsh grasses. Andrei's eyes darted between the dark road ahead and the dimly lit dashboard. The stillness of the marsh was unnerving but provided the isolation they needed. Pavel sat quietly in the passenger seat, his eyes scanning the rearview mirror for any signs of pursuit. The brothers moved with precision, their course set, their assignment far from complete.

The car vibrated as its tires rolled over the metal grates of the Donald A. Wilkinson Bridge, the dull buzz of the graded surface reverberating through the cabin. The bridge, a vital connection to Plum Island, stretched over the Merrimack River, its skeletal structure illuminated by sparse streetlights. Pavel glanced into the backseat to check on their bound prisoner. The rhythmic shaking of the car had done little more than lull Bishop deeper into unconsciousness, his body slumped awkwardly against the hatchback's interior. The bridge's namesake, Donald A. Wilkinson, was a somber tribute to the town's only casualty of the Vietnam War. Wilkinson, along with 22 other servicemen, had perished in a tragic transport plane crash into Dong Nhut Mountain, obscured by dense ground fog. There were no survivors. Pavel's gaze lingered on their captive for a moment longer before turning back to the road ahead. The irony of the bridge's history—a memorial to fallen service members—was not lost on him as they drove toward the island.

After a cautious 7-mile drive, both brothers kept their heads on a swivel, scanning for any sign of law enforcement. They finally arrived at the southern edge of Newbury Beach. The Subaru rolled to a stop in the small public beach parking lot, its tires crunching softly over windblown sand that had drifted across the asphalt. Pavel stepped out of the passenger side, closing the door with careful silence. He straightened his jacket, doing his best to appear casual in case they had been followed. His movements were measured as he began a methodical recon of their surroundings. He strolled toward the trail entrance that led to the beach, his boots leaving faint impressions in the loose sand. Once there, he stopped and made a slow, horizontal scan of the area, his sharp eyes peering through the darkness. The beach was deserted. He strained his ears, listening for anything unusual, but all he could hear were the distant crashes of waves against the shore, partially masked by the gusting wind. A clanking sound drew his attention. An attached rope, missing its flag, whipped wildly against a chipped white flagpole, its metallic cadence adding an eerie undertone to the night. Satisfied that no one was nearby, Pavel turned and gave Andrei a subtle nod. The operation would proceed.

The beach entrance was flanked by weathered fences made of wooden slats woven into rusted metal wire strands. Commonly used to assist in dune creation and maintenance, these sand fences were designed to reduce wind speeds and trap sand. However, this particular fence seemed to have long since given up on either task, its warped slats barely clinging to the shifting dunes. Pavel stood at the edge of the wooden barrier, the steady northern wind stinging his exposed face. His sharp eyes scanned the horizon, the dim outline of the shore stretching before him. The beach appeared deserted, its only occupants the relentless waves and whispering gusts.

"Area is clear," Pavel announced, turning to his brother, who was now standing outside the Subaru, his silhouette framed by the faint light of the parking lot.

Andrei gestured toward the car. "Go get the boat, and I'll meet you on the shore. I'll signal with three flashes from my penlight when it's time." Pavel acknowledged the directive before heading back to the vehicle. Andrei remained at the beach entrance, his back to the wind, his eyes scanning the dark expanse. The crashing sound of the waves seemed to grow louder as they prepared for the next stage of their operation.

Pavel acknowledged silently before vanishing into the darkness, heading toward the firmer sand near the shoreline. Earlier that day, he had dry-docked a 16-foot aluminum boat with a 25 hp Mercury outboard motor just north of their current position. Every detail had been meticulously planned. They had researched the tide schedules to ensure the boat would neither become swamped by the rising waters nor buried too deeply in the sand by the time they arrived. The boat was their primary means of executing the next phase of their mission. If it were compromised, they had a secondary plan in place to eliminate the crewman. Failure wasn't an option. Pavel moved cautiously, his boots sinking slightly into the sand as he approached the vessel. His sharp eyes darted left and right, scanning for anything out of the ordinary—shadows that didn't belong, movements in the distance, or the faint glow of an unfortunate witness's flashlight. The beach was eerily still. The only sound was the trancing murmur of waves gently rising and falling against the shore. The faint breeze carried a salty tang, but otherwise, the air was still, heavy with anticipation. Reaching the boat, Pavel crouched low, running a gloved hand along its surface to check for tampering. Satisfied that everything was as they had left it, he began preparing the vessel for its grim task.

The boat was buried slightly deeper in the sand than Pavel had anticipated. He planted his feet firmly and rocked it back and forth with a series of forceful jerks, loosening it from the wet sand. Each wrenching motion shot tension through his arms, but he persisted, adrenaline from the earlier abduction fueling his efforts. Once the boat was free, Pavel untied the rope anchored to a weathered log further up the shore. He gripped the stern and began pushing it toward the ocean, timing his efforts with the incoming waves. With each surge, the water helped lift the aluminum craft, allowing him to push it a few feet farther. The cold ocean spray stung his face as he waded deeper, the water rising past his knees. When he was in deep enough, Pavel lowered the engine into position and gave the starter a crank. The small outboard sputtered for a moment before roaring to life, its purr blending with the recurrent crash of waves behind him. Slightly winded from the manual labor and the fading high of adrenaline, Pavel let out a deep, controlled breath as he maneuvered the boat eastward, away from the shoreline. He drove out to gain enough depth, then turned south, idling in place as he scanned the dark horizon. Now all he could do was wait for Andrei's flashing light signal to begin the next stage.

Andrei hoisted the unconscious American over his shoulder in a fireman's carry, his muscles straining under the awkward, heavy load. Bishop was completely out, a cocktail of intoxication, adrenaline letdown, and the lingering effects of his recent electrocution rendering him limp and unresponsive. The KGR operative trudged through the coarse sand, each step deliberate as he ensured his boots gained full purchase to support the weight on his back. The effort was grueling, but Andrei's focus remained unwavering. As he reached the wetter, firmer sand near the water's edge, he unceremoniously dropped Bishop from his shoulder. The American hit the ground with a dull thud, a faint groan escaping his lips as his body splashed into a retreating wave. Andrei knelt briefly to catch his breath before pulling a small penlight from his pocket. Clicking it on, he signaled three short flashes toward the open water. The faint, steady purr of the Mercury outboard grew louder in response. The boat shifted its course, turning directly toward Andrei's position on the shore. He stood, his eyes scanning the surrounding darkness one final time for any sign of unwanted witnesses. The only disturbance was the regular crash of waves and the glint of moonlight reflecting off the rippling surface of the ocean. The mission was proceeding as planned.

Bishop stirred awake as the freezing Atlantic waters lapped against his body, splashing over his face and limbs. He tried to cry out, but the gag stuffed into his mouth muffled any sound. Each attempt to draw a full breath was a struggle. Bound at both the wrists and ankles, he was immobilized, disoriented, and powerless. The cold jolted his mind into survival mode, transporting him back to U.S. Navy SERE (Survival, Evasion, Resistance, and Escape) training. He had spent two brutal weeks immersed in scenarios designed to break him. Bound, tortured, and even waterboarded, he had endured relentless drills meant to push his body and mind to their absolute limits. Those experiences had taught him how to confront fear, pain, and the suffocating sense of hopelessness. Lying there in the wet sand, the icy waves soaking his clothes, panic clawed at the edges of his mind, threatening to take hold. His heart pounded, each beat reminding him how precarious his situation was. But Bishop clung tightly to what he had learned during SERE: control the fear. Panic was the enemy—it would paralyze him, cloud his judgment, and seal his fate. He forced his focus inward, calming his breathing as much as the gag would allow. His mind began to work, searching for a resolution, any opportunity to escape or resist. He had no idea who these men were or why they had taken him, but one thing was certain: he would not give up. Not here. Not like this.

If he was still breathing, then he still had a hope of survival.

Pavel cut the engine as the boat glided smoothly toward the shore, its momentum carrying it the last few feet. Andrei stepped forward, grabbing the bow to bring the boat to a halt. Without hesitation, he turned back to Bishop, gripping him by the collar and dragging him from the shallow water to the boat's side. The brothers worked efficiently together to hoist their bound hostage onboard. Bishop landed hard against the aluminum deck, coughing and groaning, the cold air biting at his soaked clothes. Pavel turned the engine over again, the Mercury outboard sputtering before roaring to life. He steered the boat due east, cutting through the black waters of the Atlantic. The coastline disappeared behind them as they drove farther into open ocean. Bishop lay on his side, shivering, his mind racing despite the lingering fog of intoxication and shock. He strained against the bindings on his wrists and ankles, testing for any give, but the zip ties held firm. He considered his options, futile as they seemed. Rolling off the side of the boat crossed his mind, but he dismissed it almost immediately. The freezing water temperatures, the depth, and the currents made survival highly unlikely. And with his limbs bound, swimming to safety wasn't just improbable—it was impossible. His best chance, he decided, was to wait. He clung to the faint hope that this was a kidnapping for ransom. If that were the case, they might keep him alive. For now, he had no choice but to endure, watching and waiting for the moment when a real opportunity to act might present itself.

If they were going to kill me, I'd already be dead.

Pavel hit the kill switch on the Mercury outboard, and the motor fell silent. The lapping waves broke against the bow, sending a mist of cold spray over the passengers as the boat gradually slowed to a stop. An eerie silence settled over the open water, broken only by the gentle swaying of the sea. The KGR agents didn't speak. They didn't need to. The plan was set, and both men were ready to execute it. With a synchronous nod, they rose from their seats, the boat rocking slightly under their shifting weight. Bishop lay helpless, his bound body tilted awkwardly on the aluminum deck. His bloodshot eyes darted between the two Russians, his heart pounding as he tried to anticipate their next move.

In one fluid motion, Andrei reached down and clipped a carabiner to Bishop's zip-tied ankles. The other end of the rope was tied to a 30-pound anchor lying on the floor of the boat. The realization of their grim intent struck Bishop like a thunderclap. His eyes widened in panic as he made a desperate, last-ditch effort to lunge at Andrei. His frantic action was clumsy, fueled by adrenaline and hopeless determination. But before he could reach his target, Pavel stepped in, shoving him forcefully over the side of the boat. Bishop hit the freezing water with a splash, gasping as the cold enveloped him. Andrei waited for him to resurface before hefting the anchor and tossing it overboard a few feet to Bishop's right. The heavy weight plunged into the water, the rope pulling taut almost instantly.

The brothers expected a panicked struggle, desperate cries for mercy, or perhaps an attempt to break free. Instead, what they got was something they hadn't anticipated. Bishop floated briefly, his eyes locking with theirs in a steady, daggered gaze. His expression was tranquil, almost defiant, as if daring them to watch. With meditative control, he took a deep breath and allowed himself to sink beneath the surface, the anchor's weight pulling him into the dark abyss. For a moment, neither man moved. Andrei and Pavel stood frozen, transfixed by the image of their victim's final act of composure. They didn't speak of it, but that gaze—a piercing look of calm resolve—would haunt them for the rest of their lives.

CHAPTER 23

Snoqualmie, Washington

"What's the forecast through Sunday?" Brody Hayes' seventeen-year-old daughter, Maddy, asked.

"Sun breaks on Sunday but snowing mostly throughout the weekend. Looks heaviest when we'll head in on Friday," Brody replied, glancing out the window as gray clouds rolled over the nearby ridgeline.

"Perfect! Sounds like a great weekend to get off the grid!" Maddy exclaimed, her voice carrying the excitement that came with their annual winter mountaineering trip. Despite being slightly earlier in the season than usual, the family decided to take advantage of the heavy snowfall that blanketed the Cascade Range. For Maddy, it was the highlight of her year; a chance to escape the noise of the world and embrace the stark beauty of nature.

This year's trip was extra special. Brody, a professional mountain guide, had plans to lead expeditions in Argentina—where summer peaks during North America's winter—making this weekend one of the last chances for the family to venture out together before his departure. Though their backpacks were always packed for regular camping and hiking trips, the winter excursions held a unique magic of pristine snowfields, frozen peaks, and quality time of playing card games in a thin nylon tent in the icy wilderness, miles away from other humans. It was the kind of adventure most would shy away from, but for the Hayes family, it was a cherished tradition.

"Agreed! Looking forward to our annual winter mountaineering trip, Dad," chimed in Mitch, Brody's fifteen-year-old son.

Standing tall for his age, Mitch was starting to fill out his once-slender build. It was hard for Brody not to see himself in his son, as Mitch had his determination and a natural sense of adventure. This year, Brody intended to increase his son's leadership role during the trip, guiding him through the responsibilities of planning routes, managing gear, and ensuring safety. The timing was perfect. Mitch's mom and he were leaving a day later to meet up with Brody and Maddy, allowing Mitch to lead his part of the trip. It was a chance for growth and bonding, something Brody had been looking forward to for months. As they prepared their gear and checked off the list of essentials, Brody felt a quiet pride in watching his son step into the role he'd been gently training him for over the years.

"Yep, sounds perfect..." Bridget, Brody's wife of twenty-two years, added with a touch of sarcasm. Though she appreciated the unique adventures Brody planned for their family, Bridget wouldn't have minded swapping snow caves and freezing winds for warm sand and Mai Tais in Hawaii. Still, she never let her personal preferences hold back their trips. She encouraged these experiences, knowing they fostered resilience, grit, and memories that would last far longer than a week at a luxury resort. In truth, Brody loved the idea of a tropical beach getaway too, but he found unmatched fulfillment in the mountains. There, surrounded by rugged beauty and the raw challenge of the outdoors, he felt at peace. Away from the noise and entitlement of crowded human spaces, these trips offered something deeper: a connection to his family, to nature, and the work of survival and self-reliance. It was a sense of purpose that no ocean breeze or sandy shoreline could ever replicate.

Brody carried an awkwardly heavy storage bin labeled "Mountaineering Crap" from the garage, holding the door open with his foot as he pivoted his way inside. The weight of the bin was nothing compared to the load clouding his mind. The past week had been a whirlwind of death and uncertainty. Two of his former U.S. Navy combat aircrew pilots had met eerily untimely ends—one confirmed dead, the other missing in what were described as unrelated freak incidents. Brody couldn't shake the feeling that something was off. He didn't believe in coincidences, and the timing of these tragedies gnawed at his instincts, which were sharpened by years of life-or-death decision-making. Yet, no concrete evidence of foul play had surfaced—just gut feelings and lingering doubt. On top of that, the sudden losses dredged up the post-traumatic stress he'd spent years managing, a darkness that never fully disappeared but had, until now, stayed mostly at bay. He'd considered canceling the family's annual adventure, tempted to bury himself in investigating what little he could about his former teammates' fates. But deep down, he knew better. The mountains had always been his refuge, a place where the chaos of the outside world faded into insignificance. If there was anything that could help clear his mind and restore a sense of peace, it was the silence of the wild, the challenge of the climb, and the grounding presence of his family.

The hardest part was always getting there, but he was always glad he did.

"Everybody, be sure to pack extra layers," Brody instructed, his tone steady but firm. "I'll pull out the shared gear, and we'll divvy it up. Maddy and I will carry the bulk of it since we're heading up Friday. Mitch, you can take some extra fuel and food when you and Mom join us later."

"Sounds good," Mitch replied nonchalantly, though a hint of disappointment lingered beneath his tone. He was bummed he wouldn't get to head out with them on Friday, but the important biology test looming that morning—one that made up a large portion of his grade—meant he had no choice. Trying to shift the focus, he asked, "How's the avvy danger?"

"According to ATMOS, it's low danger. Nothing like last year's trip!" Maddy chimed in, clearly excited about the forecast. "But with the expected snow dump on Thursday and Friday on top of last week's ice storm, who knows? I'm guessing it'll increase to moderate. Either way, we'll be cautious and steer clear of any avvy chutes on the way in."

Her confident tone reflected the preparation Brody instilled in her and Mitch over the years. He had always emphasized the importance of training for what you can control and researching and preparing for the things you can't. Weather was at the top of that list. The ATMOS site, a resource provided by the University of Washington, offered invaluable data. Its text-based reports detailed weather conditions, including temperature, wind, precipitation, and avalanche risks at varying altitudes and timeframes. For the Hayes family, it was an indispensable part of planning any local mountain-eering trip.

* * *

Brody paused, his mind drifting to the year prior as Maddy referenced their memorable adventure. It had been a season like no other, marked by the strange realities of the global pandemic. With much of the world on pause, the wilderness became an even greater refuge for the Hayes family. Already known among friends for their remarkable outdoor exploits, they seized the opportunity to deepen their connection with nature, embarking on a string of unforgettable adventures. That February, while many families flocked to warmer destinations during mid-winter break, the Hayes packed their gear and headed for a week of snow immersion on Mount Rainier, Washington's tallest peak. It had been a bold and ambitious undertaking, even by their standards, combining challenging conditions with the allure of pure isolation. It was a trip that tested their skills, strengthened their bonds, and cemented their reputation as a family deeply at home in the untamed beauty of the outdoors.

Mount Rainier, known as Tahoma to the indigenous peoples of the Pacific Northwest, is the tallest active volcano in the Cascade Range. Rising 14,411 feet above sea level and situated approximately 60 miles southeast of Seattle, it is the most glaciated peak in the contiguous United States. The mountain's striking prominence makes it a breathtaking feature of the Seattle skyline and a centerpiece of natural beauty. Although it can be climbed year-round, the safest and most popular season runs from May to September. During this time, thousands of visitors flock to Mount Rainier National Park to capture stunning photos and explore its numerous lower trails. Of the approximately 10,000 climbers who attempt to reach the summit each year, only about 50% succeed, underscoring the challenge and allure of this iconic peak.

The previous year's El Niño winter brought an unusually heavy snowfall to the Cascade Range, creating the ideal conditions for Brody Hayes to teach his family vital survival skills while making the experience enjoyable and memorable. Brody cautiously drove his 2011 Jeep Wrangler Rubicon along the freshly plowed road from Longmire to Paradise, the 33-inch BFGoodrich all-terrain tires gripping tightly to the fresh dusting of snow. The winding road to the 5,400-foot parking lot was both scenic and treacherous, with countless shaded patches of packed ice lurking as potential hazards. Brody took his time, his hands gripping the wheel in white-knuckle focus as the family chatted excitedly, oblivious to the tension of the drive.

After ten and a half miles of slow, careful navigation, the Hayes family arrived in Paradise. Appropriately named, Paradise sits on the southern slope of Mount Rainier, offering views that are nothing short of breathtaking. On a clear day, the towering snow-capped volcano dominates the landscape, framed by the rugged peaks of the Tatoosh Range. Wildlife thrives in this alpine haven, and it's not uncommon to spot Cascade red foxes, deer, black bears, and, more recently, elusive wolverines making their return to the region.

When the kids were younger, Brody would plan simple overnight trips where they would snowshoe a couple of miles into an isolated location, dig in for the night, and return the following afternoon. Over time, as Maddy and Mitch grew more adventurous, they began requesting multi-day trips with multiple locations. These excursions involved breaking down camp, relocating, and rebuilding their snow fortresses, adding an exciting element of challenge to their winter adventures.

The previous year on Rainier, Brody decided to push their limits with a unique experience inspired by the higher elevation climbs he had guided, which neither Bridget nor the kids had yet encountered. They loaded their heavy packs and trekked through the heavy snow 4 miles and 4,000 feet of elevation gain from Paradise to Anvil Rock. Upon arrival, they established a comprehensive basecamp, complete with sleeping tents, a cooking tent, and a carefully dug-out bathroom area resembling an igloo-like structure. Their basecamp served as a staging ground for several ambitious activities.

One day was dedicated to crevasse rescue training on the Cowlitz Glacier, where Brody taught his family how to use ropes, prusiks, and anchors to navigate the dangerous glacial terrain. Another day involved a short hike up to Camp Muir and Gibraltar Ledges, providing a glimpse into the demanding conditions of high-altitude mountaineering. For their final day, Brody planned a glaciated team climb to Ingraham Flats at 11,000 feet. Unfortunately, a massive lenticular cloud capped the icy volcano, signaling the presence of high upper winds and preventing a winter summit attempt.

The forecast predicted snow showers and moderate wind gusts, gradually increasing as the days progressed. Brody planned to assess the weather conditions each morning to decide the day's activities, fully prepared to hunker down at basecamp if necessary. Anvil Rock, situated on the Muir Snowfield, offered a relatively safe location free from crevasse hazards, making it an ideal basecamp. Despite its safety, the area between Paradise and Camp Muir was notorious for its unpredictable weather and the dangers it posed to ill-prepared hikers. Sudden whiteout snowstorms combined with freezing temperatures often caught climbers off guard, leading to hypothermia, frostbite, or worse. Brody, however, was no stranger to Rainier's volatile conditions, having faced similar and far harsher storms on mountains around the world. His experience and meticulous planning were key to ensuring his family's safety during their winter adventure.

The snow and wind arrived earlier and stronger than predicted by the ATMOS forecast, creating a situation that was both challenging and exciting, depending on perspective. The Hayes family had enough supplies to comfortably last a week, and even longer if they rationed carefully. Brody, ever the cautious planner, carried a Garmin GPS unit that could guide them back down to Paradise in case of an emergency. However, retreating wasn't on anyone's mind. The kids enthusiastically viewed the unexpected blizzard as an adventure—an opportunity to spend a few days in the storm's embrace, hunkered down in their snow fortress while playing endless rounds of Mitch's favorite card game, *President*. Bridget, less enthusiastic but equally resilient, approached the situation with cautious optimism. She appreciated the unique memories they would create, even if she preferred a cozy lodge to a snow-covered tent. With top-notch gear, ample supplies, and the skills to weather the storm, the Hayes family was well-prepared for the ordeal. Their primary tasks were maintaining the integrity of their tents and keeping their spirits high as they waited out the blizzard. For the Hayes, it was another chapter in their legacy of turning challenges into unforgettable family memories.

Lose your mind, Lose your life.

With two 4-season tents for sleeping and one dedicated cooking tent, the family took shifts clearing the heavy snow that accumulated on the sides. The weight of the snow posed a serious risk as it could collapse the tents, breaking the poles and potentially trapping the occupants inside. Additionally, excessive snow buildup could hinder proper ventilation through the tent's nylon walls, causing CO_2 levels to rise and increasing the risk of asphyxiation. Brody emphasized the importance of maintaining the tent structures and airflow, turning the task into a shared responsibility and a vital lesson in survival. Each family member dutifully took their turn braving the cold and wind, carefully brushing and knocking away the snow to ensure the tents remained stable and safe throughout the storm.

Inside the tents, the relentless high wind gusts roared and shook the fabric walls, making it feel as though the securely anchored shelters might be torn from the mountain. After two restless nights, the Hayes family decided to consolidate, all four piling into one tent for warmth and morale. Throughout the night, Brody woke up hourly to punch the roof of the tent from the inside, dislodging accumulating snow to prevent structural collapse.

By the third night, the exhaustion from fragmented sleep caught up with him. When his 4 a.m. Garmin watch alarm went off, he and the rest of the family slept through it, worn out by the unyielding storm. Meanwhile, the snowfall continued unabated, dumping over a foot of fresh powder on their already buried camp. The quiet crunching sound of metal under strain broke the early morning silence, followed by the sharp crack of a tent pole snapping. Maddy was the first to wake, jolted by the alarming noise. "Dad!" she cried out, her voice laced with panic.

Brody's eyes snapped open, his heart racing. The weight of the snow-filled nylon pressed down, pinning his legs and looming just inches from his face. Disoriented in the pitch-dark, he immediately understood the gravity of the situation. "Everyone, stay calm!" he called out, his voice steady despite the adrenaline surging through his body. He reached for his headlamp, fumbling to assess the collapse and figure out their next move.

"It's okay, honey," Brody reassured Maddy, his voice unnervingly calm despite the chaotic situation. His demeanor had always been his superpower in moments like this, a skill honed through years of training and experience. He punched the inside of the tent, sending chunks of snow flying off the roof and scattering into the powdery landscape outside. With each strike, the tension in the fabric eased, and the weight pressing down on them lightened. After clearing enough snow to restore some structure to the sagging tent, Brody pushed upward against the roof, forcing the remaining snow to slide off in cascading heaps. The damage was clear—one of the main tent poles had snapped, leaving a sagging section near their feet. Brody barely glanced at it, his focus on his frazzled daughter. Crawling over to her, he wrapped her in a warm, reassuring hug. "You did great, Maddy," he said softly. "Thanks for waking me up."

Bridget and Mitch stirred awake as Brody worked to stabilize the tent, blinking groggily at the muffled chaos. "What's going on?" Mitch mumbled, rubbing his eyes.

"Just some snow buildup," Brody replied nonchalantly, unwilling to escalate anyone else's nerves. "We're good now. Let's get some rest."

Bridget glanced at the sagging section of the tent, concern flashing across her face. "Is it safe?" she asked, sitting up slightly.

"It's fine for now," Brody assured her. "We'll reinforce it in the morning. Just try to get some more sleep."

The family lay back down, the adrenaline slowly fading as the wind howled outside. Maddy, still nestled in her father's comforting embrace, felt her heart rate settle. For all the stress and uncertainty, she knew they'd be okay. Her dad always made sure of that. They huddled together in the tent, the howling wind outside providing an ominous backdrop to their hushed conversation. Wrapped in layers of down and fleece, they took turns sharing their thoughts about the night's events, reflecting on lessons learned. Brody encouraged each family member to voice their observations and what they'd do differently in the future—a family tradition after challenging moments in the mountains.

The group later unanimously agreed to pack up and head down the mountain. The idea of hitting the first Starbucks they'd find on their drive home was a beacon of hope after the stormy ordeal. For now, they burrowed into their sleeping bags, drawing warmth from each other as they waited for the promise of daylight to signal the start of their descent back to civilization.

* * *

"Dad? Dad? Hello?" Maddy waved her hand in front of her father's distant, glassy-eyed stare.

Brody abruptly shook his head, blinking as if trying to reset himself. "The weather looks good. Should be a good one," he said, his voice steady but his expression slightly off. He struggled to remember where the conversation had left off, piecing together fragments as his mind wrestled with the flashback that had consumed him moments earlier.

Maddy tilted her head, concern etched across her face. "You okay, Dad?"

Brody forced a smile, the kind that meant to reassure. "Yeah, just got lost in my thoughts for a second." She didn't push further, sensing that whatever had momentarily taken him away wasn't something he was ready to share.

Brody Hayes had a rare gift for survival—a knack for maintaining unnerving calm in the most chaotic of situations. It had served him well in his years of military service and countless life-or-death scenarios in the mountains. But survival came at a cost. While he could face trauma head-on in the moment, it always found a way to haunt him later, creeping in through the cracks during moments of stillness or vulnerability. He didn't zone out often, but often enough.

CHAPTER 24

Snoqualmie, Washington

"Take a deep breath, Laura. Slow down," Brody Hayes tried unsuccessfully to calm Bishop's recent ex-wife over the phone.

"Something is wrong. I can feel it! He's never been gone this long!" Laura's voice was fraught with hysteria, her worry fueled by the fact that Phil had last been seen leaving the Port Tavern two nights ago. Despite the divorce, the Hayes family had maintained a close bond with Laura and her kids. They'd known her for years and had long harbored doubts about whether her and Phil's marriage could withstand the toxicity that had grown between them. Though their divorce wasn't shocking, it was still a somber reminder of two good people who simply weren't good together. Laura could be overly dramatic at times, but this—this felt different. Her profound anxiety felt justified.

"What do I do, Brody? What do I tell the kids?" she pleaded, her voice trembling.

"I'm not sure," Brody said gently. "But for now, we need to keep our hope alive. Worrying about things that haven't happened won't help. Phil has isolated himself before when he needed to clear his head. I'm praying that's all this is."

Over the phone, Brody joined Laura in prayer, his voice steady as he quoted Philippians 4:6:

Do not be anxious about anything, but in everything by prayer and petition, with thanksgiving, present your requests to God.

The verse brought Laura a fleeting moment of peace as she took a deep breath and tried to release her anxieties. But the calm didn't last, and soon her sobs resumed. After a quiet goodbye, Hayes pressed the end button on his cellphone and sat in stillness, the weight of the conversation heavy on his mind. Before hanging up, they had agreed to update each other the moment they had any news about Phil.

Hayes had last spoken to Bishop a few days earlier when they first heard about Carter's disappearance in La Jolla. Since then, Bishop himself had gone missing. The last confirmed sighting was by Samantha, a bartender at the Newburyport Port Tavern. She reported nothing out of the ordinary—Bishop, a regular, had his usual routine. He'd arrived using a ride share, already buzzed, and left the same way, noticeably drunk but responsible enough these days after his most recent DUI. Bishop lived alone and wasn't in regular contact with anyone, so it took a few days for his absence to raise alarms. Laura, hoping to let the kids spend time with him that Saturday, stopped by his house. Instead of finding Bishop, she found an empty home. An unwashed glass sat beside a half-full bottle of Elijah Craig on the counter. Her calls to his cellphone went straight to voicemail, leading her to assume the battery was dead, the phone turned off, or Bishop had gone off the grid. In reality, his phone was most likely still crammed into his pocket—now at the bottom of Scantum Basin,

600 feet below the Atlantic's surface. The iPhone would have long surpassed its crush depth, resting alongside Bishop's bloated body, tethered to a 30-pound anchor that settled on the ocean floor.

Hayes set his cellphone down on the end table beside the couch and stared out the bay window. A typical Pacific Northwest drizzle coated the glass, the low clouds painted in every imaginable shade of gray, obscuring the distant Cascade Range. The dreary morning mirrored his desolate mood, heavy with shock and confusion.

What in the hell is happening?

The thought gnawed at him. His U.S. Navy helicopter combat crew from over two decades ago—one by one, they were either dead or missing. This couldn't be a coincidence. The unease sat like a stone in his gut, leaving him with far more questions than answers.

Am I in danger? Am I next?

The chilling thought lingered as he continued to stare at the rain-streaked window, his reflection blending into the storm beyond. Brody was already in his workout clothes, stretching for a morning run around Snoqualmie Ridge, when Laura's call came through. Shaken by the latest news but knowing he couldn't let himself fall into a funk, he laced up his ASICS running shoes. He needed to clear his head before talking to Bridget, and the best way for him to gain clarity was through some much-needed outdoor therapy. Hayes was fortunate to regularly travel to mystically therapeutic destinations while guiding expeditions around the world. At home, he was equally spoiled, with endless options nestled within the breathtaking Mount Baker–Snoqualmie National Forest. The Hayes house was just three miles from one of Washington State's largest natural attractions, making the six-mile loop to Snoqualmie Falls and back the perfect route to reset his mind.

Most joggers seemed to wear earbuds, retreating into a virtual world shaped by podcasts or personal music playlists of memory-triggering genres. Brody, however, was different. He rarely listened to music, a habit rooted in his guiding work, where staying acutely aware of his clients and surroundings was essential. Even during recreational runs, he preferred the unfiltered experience of nature. The sounds of rustling leaves, distant bird calls, and the rhythm of his breath grounded him in the present. The sights, scents, and ambient noises of the outdoors transported him to a mental space that music or podcasts could never reach—a place of clarity and connection to the world around him.

After a quick climb up Douglas Avenue, the rest of the route to the Falls was a downhill stretch that paralleled the heavily trafficked Snoqualmie Parkway. As soon as Brody stepped out of his front door, his thoughts raced, consumed by the traumatic events unfolding with his former aircrew in Nevada, California, and Massachusetts. He launched into an almost sprint, shocking his legs into a lactic acid response. This intense effort deprived his muscles of oxygen, forcing them to break down glucose to create essential energy—a process he knew well from years of military training and high-altitude expeditions. The anaerobic burn left his legs screaming, but he embraced it, knowing the lactic acid response would soon fade. Once his muscles stopped rebelling and oxygen flow returned, Brody transitioned into a long, steady stride, his breathing falling into tempo. As his body found its pace, so did his mind. The blur of racing thoughts began to settle, shifting into focused clarity. Running had always been his way to untangle the chaos.

The Pacific Northwest autumn carried the unmistakable smells of crisp, cool air, fallen leaves, and the comforting smoke wafting from chimneys throughout the valley. It was a constant reminder of why Brody had chosen to live here. The weather was unpredictable, swinging wildly from record-breaking warm days to heavy rain or even ice storms, followed by heavy snowfall. While it made planning difficult, it also demanded flexibility and preparedness—traits he'd long since mastered. As he descended the parkway toward the Falls, the cloud layer began to lift, revealing the snow-dusted mountains for the first time in days. Their peaks had been hidden behind a dense shroud of storm clouds, and the sight felt like a quiet reward. Brody's thoughts began to shift from the unfolding events—those far beyond his control—to his upcoming family camping trip to Snow Lake. The weekend getaway, an adventure he could plan and manage, brought a sense of steadiness to his otherwise turbulent emotions, temporarily reining in his overarching sorrow.

At the bottom of the Parkway, Brody crossed the train tracks and took a sharp left. The flat stretch of road led to the historic steel green bridge spanning the Snoqualmie River. A short distance beyond lay the iconic Salish Lodge, where he slowed to a brisk walk, letting his heartbeat settle and stretching his legs as he approached the Falls' lookout. The 270-foot Snoqualmie Falls, first discovered by the Snoqualmie Tribe—a subgroup of the Coast Salish—had been a place of reverence for centuries before white settlers arrived. Brody always felt a profound sense of peace standing at the lookout among the scattered tourists. The sheer power of the unrelenting cascade had a way of mesmerizing him, putting him in a meditative trance. As he paused to take it in, he imagined the Native Americans centuries earlier, standing in the same awe he now felt. The majestic beauty of the falls demanded attention, making it nearly impossible to focus on anything else. For Brody, it was exactly the distraction he needed.

The mist from the raging water shifted with a cold breeze, sending a sharp chill through Brody's stiffening muscles. It was nature's way of reminding him it was time to head back, retracing his route—only this time, all uphill. Thirty minutes later, his legs burning from the climb, he opened the front door to the warm sight of his wife, Bridget. She was curled up on the couch, her face illuminated by the soft glow of her iPhone's YouVersion Bible app devotional, a steaming manuka honey latte cradled in her hands.

"How was your run?" she asked, glancing up with a smile. "It looks chilly out there."

"Felt good," Brody replied, a hint of calm in his voice. "I love the smells this time of year. The Falls are pretty raging right now, too." He paused, his expression darkening as reality pulled him back. "I talked to Laura this morning. Bishop's been missing for a few days."

"Bishop?" Bridget set her latte down, her brow furrowing. "What do you mean missing? Like not answering his phone again missing, or...?"

"Like Captain Carter missing," Brody said, his voice trembling. "Nobody can find him. What the hell is going on, Bridget?" His words cracked under the weight of his growing fear.

Bridget set her coffee cup on a marble coaster protecting the rustic wood of their Pottery Barn end table and stood. Without a word, she stepped into her husband's arms, and they silently embraced. Brody let out a long, slow breath, pulling her closer as though her presence alone could anchor him. Bridget held him tightly, her heart breaking for the man she loved. But despite her outward calm, thoughts of fear and terror crept into her mind. She knew there were truths about his military past that he couldn't share—things she had long accepted she would never fully understand.

Was something from that past resurfacing? Was their family in danger? Were they next?

She tightened her grip on Brody, refusing to let her fear show. Instead of voicing her concerns, she closed her eyes and prayed, silently releasing her worries to God. In that moment, her faith became the strength she knew Brody needed.

CHAPTER 25

Snoqualmie, Washington

The following day was much like the one before, only ten degrees colder. Pacific Northwest winters often blurred together—a patchwork of gray skies with persistent rain, the occasional sunbreak, and the rare chance of snow at lower elevations. Nothing about the morning felt unusual, apart from the lingering weight of recent events involving Ellis, Carter, and Bishop. As Brody prepared to head east with Maddy, he turned to Bridget with a look of unease. "I don't feel right leaving," he admitted, his voice low. "Not with Bishop and Carter still missing."

"I understand," Bridget replied empathetically, her tone steady despite the knot tightening in her stomach. "But there's nothing you can do right now. I'm sure they're fine. Plus, this is our annual trip. The kids are excited, and it'll do you some good to get out." She offered him a reassuring smile, though she was battling her own unease. Bridget had always trusted her sharp intuition—a sense she rarely ignored. But today, she pushed those instincts aside, convincing herself that the swirl of recent events and emotions were clouding her judgment. Still, the nagging feeling lingered, a weight she chose to bear silently for her husband's sake.

"I guess. I'm sure it'll be fine," Brody muttered, trying to convince himself as he stuffed his negative-20-degree North Face down sleeping bag into a compression sack. Around him, the living room was a controlled chaos of neatly exploded gear. He and the kids had their supplies meticulously organized, following a checklist that had been refined over years of lessons learned on past expeditions. Mitch sat cross-legged, diligently checking off items as they were pulled from the "Mountaineering Crap" bins. No matter how many trips Brody had been on—or guided—there was always a buzz of excitement in the packing and preparation. It reminded him of preflight prep with his aircrew before launching mission-sets around the globe. Each flight demanded an acute level of awareness and readiness for the unexpected—a mindset that mirrored his approach to every adventure. The kids shared in the excitement from their perspective, but they weren't oblivious. They sensed their dad was carrying a heavy sadness, rooted in a military past he rarely discussed. They didn't pry, knowing he'd share when he was ready. For now, they focused on the anticipation of the journey ahead, each piece of gear representing another step closer to their next great adventure.

"I wish I was going with you tomorrow. It's not fair. Why can't I just skip my test and take a sick day?" Mitch pleaded, though his tone carried a hint of resignation. He knew his dad wasn't opposed to pulling them out of school for trips—Brody valued education, but he also believed life experiences were just as important in shaping a well-rounded life.

"It's just one night, Mitch," Brody reassured him while tightening a compression strap on his pack. "You and Mom will meet us

Saturday morning. Besides, it'll be good for you to take the lead and help navigate through the fresh snowfall." Mitch's expression softened, the promise of responsibility brightening his disappointment. He'd learned from his dad that every trip offered an opportunity to grow—not just physically but mentally. He might have to wait a little longer to join the adventure, but at least he'd have an important role to play when he did.

Most years during their annual winter mountaineering trip, the Hayes family hiked in together, but this year was different. Mitch had an important biology final he couldn't afford to miss. Biology was his primary academic interest, and Brody placed high importance on ensuring Mitch stayed behind to focus on it. The final was a critical step toward Mitch's dream of attending the University of Washington, a goal inspired by his mom, who had earned her master's degree as a proud Husky. While the Hayes family was known for their unique blend of world travel and daring adventures, they were deeply rooted in a set of core values that always took precedence: faith, education, service, and discipline. These guiding principles shaped their decisions and kept them grounded, even in the face of their boundless spirit for exploration.

Maddy and Brody planned to set out early the next morning, snowshoeing five miles to Snow Lake from the Alpental Ski Area parking lot. Their route would take them cautiously through a couple of avalanche-prone areas before ascending a final steep ridge. From there, they'd take in the sweeping view of the frozen lake before descending to the icy shoreline to set up their basecamp. Bridget and Mitch would join them the following morning. While Bridget was fully capable of leading the hike, this year, Brody had decided to let Mitch take charge. It was a deliberate choice, offering their son an opportunity to experience leadership and responsibility. Guiding his mom through the snowy mountain trail would give Mitch a sense of ownership and excitement—a perfect chance to build confidence and refine his skills. For Brody, it was more than a hike; it was a parenting moment to nurture the leadership potential he saw growing in his son.

Brody methodically packed his Arc'Teryx Bora 65L expedition backpack, a routine he had perfected over hundreds of trips. He started with the heaviest items—his down sleeping bag and a stuff sack of extra clothes—stuffing them into the space near the small of his back for optimal weight distribution. Lighter items were layered on top, and he wedged the 4-season tent and fly into any remaining air pockets, creating a solid, balanced load. Years of hiking experiences, both good and bad, had taught him the importance of this precision. A fully packed backpack might feel manageable at the trailhead, but a poorly balanced 70-pound load could quickly translate into excruciating back and neck pain after just a few miles. Before finishing, Brody double-checked his daughter Maddy's pack, running his hands over the exterior to check for air pockets that could signal inefficiencies. Finding none, he smiled with quiet pride. It wasn't a surprise to see how thorough she had become, her expertise honed through years of shared mountaineering experiences.

High winds swept through the Snoqualmie Valley during the night, carrying a biting wind chill that paired with dropping temperatures to deliver an unexpected sideways dusting of snow. Brody had meant to take down the windchimes before bed and regretted his lapse as they clanged incessantly through the night. The Hayes family was up and moving before sunrise, their preparations moving along smoothly. Nobody had realized it had snowed at their lower elevation until Maddy flipped on the back deck light to let their dog, Sam, outside.

"Hey, Dad," she called, peering out into the white-coated yard. "It snowed last night! I hope the roads are plowed!"

"Oh, nice! I'm sure the roads are clear by now, but we'll check before we get on the 90," Brody replied to Maddy before turning to Bridget. "Honey, we're loaded up and about to head to the pass. I left a note on the kitchen island with details of our basecamp location and a topographic map. Mitch has my other Garmin GPS, and I added a waypoint for the basecamp. We should be easy enough to find, but cell service is spotty. If we don't see you by noon, we'll probably hike out to meet you."

"Okay, be careful," Bridget said, her voice warm but tinged with concern. "We'll finish packing tonight and plan to see you around noon tomorrow. I love you." She leaned in, pressing her soft lips to Brody's before turning to give Maddy a quick squeeze and a tight hug.

"Mitch, you feeling good? Ready for your test?" Brody asked, glancing at his son, who was spreading a thick layer of soy butter on his sandwich.

"Yep, I know the material," Mitch replied confidently. Then, with a slight edge of frustration, he added, "We'll see how it goes.

See you early tomorrow!" He emphasized *early* in a tone that made it clear he'd rather be joining them today, test or not.

"Love you guys!" both Brody and Maddy called out as they disappeared through the laundry room door that led to the garage.

"Oh, don't forget—Sam's still outside," Maddy said, popping her head back in to remind her mom with a mischievous grin.

CHAPTER 26

Snoqualmie, Washington

Brody carefully placed all the sharp objects onto the tire-treaded rubber mat in the rear storage area of the Jeep. Ice axes, crampons, snowshoes, a shovel, trekking poles, aluminum pickets, and harnesses with carabiners and ice screws attached—all meticulously arranged for the journey ahead. Maddy helped hoist the two heavy expedition packs on top, being cautious not to snag the fabric. She wedged both sets of mountaineering boots into the far-right corner, then slammed the tailgate shut with a satisfying click. Brody slid into the driver's seat and turned the key, bringing the 3.8L V6 engine to life. The deep roar of the MagnaFlow high-performance exhaust echoed through the still morning air. As they pulled out of the garage, he caught sight of Bridget in the rearview mirror, standing at the door with a warm smile as she pressed the button to close the garage door. Raising his right hand, Brody extended his thumb, index, and pinky fingers while folding down his ring and middle fingers—the American Sign Language gesture for *I Love You*. Maddy glanced back, caught the exchange, and turned to her dad with a smile.

The light dusting of snow blanketed Douglas Avenue, but with several tire tracks already carved into the surface, it made for an easy path to follow. Brody and Maddy took a backroad through old

Snoqualmie to avoid traffic as they made their way to the freeway. There was, however, one mandatory stop—eight miles away in North Bend. Huxdotter Coffee. No road trip could officially begin without a Twin Peaks latte, named after the iconic 1990s series, filmed in the charming town nestled at the base of the striking 4,167-foot Mount Si.

The father-daughter duo ordered their 16 oz Twin Peaks lattes, paired with hearty Lumberjack Breakfast Burritos, before jumping onto Interstate 90 heading east toward Spokane. The weather was predictably unpredictable for this time of year—low clouds obscuring the majestic scenery, 40 mph wind gusts rocking the road, and occasional snow flurries dusting the highway. Inside the Jeep, the warmth of their breakfast and conversation quickly fogged up the windows until the defroster begrudgingly kicked in to do its one job. The boxy shape of the vehicle seemed to catch every bit of wind, buffeting them from side to side. Brody gripped the steering wheel tightly, his knuckles whitening as he fought to keep the Jeep steady against the relentless gusts.

The black Jeep Wrangler cruised past the final North Bend exit, and Brody barely gave the flashing portable sign—*Chains or Traction Tires Required*—a second glance. The WSDOT snowplows were undoubtedly working around the clock, and his Jeep was more than capable of handling the current conditions. Still, as confident as he was in Bridget's SUV to manage the drive, a twinge of guilt surfaced at the thought of them braving the roads without him. Over the years, Brody had learned to lean on his faith during moments like this. As a Christian, he was reminded often to release his worries and trust that God was in control. Yet, he knew that was easier said than done. It required a constant effort—a practice of surrender through prayer, which he did silently in that moment, gripping the steering wheel as the Jeep pushed forward.

As expected, the drive was uneventful, and they pulled into the Alpental Ski Resort parking lot in just under half an hour. Maddy hopped out of the passenger side and leaned over to lift the windshield wipers, setting them straight out from the glass. After a weekend of heavy snow and ice, the last thing they wanted was to find the wipers frozen solid to the windshield. Wearing her tattered brown UGG boots, she stomped through the fresh powder to meet her dad at the back of the Jeep, where he was already unloading their gear. Together, they began the uncomfortable ritual of donning their cold, stiff La Sportiva mountaineering boots. The boots would warm up quickly once they started hiking, but there was always something inherently wrong about sliding warm feet into freezing boots. It was like jumping into a cold lake—no matter how much you reminded yourself the shock would pass—it didn't make it any easier. Still, they trusted their bodies to adjust, generating the natural heat they'd need to sustain them as they tackled the snowy trail ahead.

Snowflakes as large as Maddy's hand floated down, already accumulating on the parked Jeep and transforming its black exterior into a soft white canvas. Each warm breath escaped as a visible fog, hovering in the freezing air as Brody and Maddy worked to secure the sharp tools—ice axes, crampons, and shovels—onto the exterior webbing straps of their backpacks. Properly preparing an expedition pack was an art form, one that seasoned mountain guides like Brody deeply appreciated, especially when their clients got it just right. Before shouldering their heavy loads, they performed a final check of each other's gear, ensuring nothing was missed or improperly secured. Once satisfied, they set their well-worn MSR snowshoes traction-side down in the powder and slid their boots into the loose rubber straps. After torquing down the fasteners, Brody locked the Jeep and pulled on his rucksack. With a glance at each other and a shared sense of anticipation, they turned toward the snowy trailhead, ready to tackle the mountain.

On most multi-day adventures, it was common to feel like you were forgetting something. When you're carrying everything necessary for survival on your back, that nagging sense of doubt was worth paying attention to. But neither Brody nor Maddy felt that familiar twinge this morning. Maybe it was confidence in their preparation, or the fact that they were only hiking in four miles and could always head back if needed. Or perhaps, for Brody at least, the usual pre-trip jitters were overshadowed by an unsettling sense of impending doom. It wasn't new to him; the military veteran had lived with that recurring weight for years, a byproduct of the layers of trauma he'd experienced. He recognized the creeping darkness, though, and consciously tried to shrug it off as they left the parking lot behind, focusing instead on the snow compressing tempo of their steps in the snow.

"Think we'll get another warning note?" Maddy asked, a playful smile breaking through the silence and dissolving whatever grim thoughts had begun to take hold of her dad.

"I'm sure of it," Brody replied with a wink. Over the years, they'd received their fair share of warning notes from the ski resort officials, usually wedged into the rubber seal of the driver's window. Technically, leaving your vehicle unattended for the weekend wasn't allowed, but the Hayes family had perfected the art of playing the role of slow learners. Besides, most of the local staff knew Brody and his family from years of snowboarding and guiding expeditions at the pass. Their familiarity with the mountain community often softened the rules, and any notes left on their Jeep were more of a gentle reminder than an actual reprimand.

Brody pressed and held the Mark button on his Garmin handheld GPS, securely clipped to the carabiner on his right shoulder strap. A waypoint dropped, marking their starting location with an elevation reading just over 3,000 feet. Slowly, they began their ascent, the waffle-like pattern of their snowshoes crunching against the compacted trail. The path wound through a dense forest, its towering Spruce, Douglas Fir, Cedar, and Hemlock trees forming a natural canopy that shielded them from the heavier snowfall blanketing the exposed mountainside opposite them. As they worked their way upward, the trail switched back several times, quickly gaining altitude before turning northwest toward their destination. The quiet beauty of the snowy forest enveloping them in its serene stillness.

Like any significant shock to the body, the first 20 minutes of a hike often felt sluggish. Muscles moved awkwardly, restrained by lactic acid buildup that hadn't yet dissipated. Snowshoeing added an extra layer of challenge, altering the natural gait with their wide, awkward frames that demanded more effort and coordination. The initial stretch of the trek was critical, allowing the back, shoulders, and legs to adjust to the heavy pack and uneven trail conditions. Maddy and Brody, seasoned hikers, were well-acquainted with this adjustment period. They efficiently found their rhythm, settling into a steady pace as they breached the first opening to an exposed, snow-covered meadow. The snowflakes had grown heavier, falling fast enough to obscure the trail they'd been following, as well as their own steps behind them. Whiteout conditions like these would have deterred most weekend hikers, but not this pair. Further down the trail, Brody noticed movement—barely visible through the low cloud cover and swirling snow. It appeared to be a couple of ice climbers taking advantage of a frozen waterfall to the north. Though he couldn't see them clearly, the distinct sound of clinking metal gear carried through the crisp air. The early ice storm and snowfall were an unexpected gift for outdoor enthusiasts. Typically, conditions like these required traveling a couple hours further north or east or waiting another few months. But for those willing to embrace the elements, today was a rare treat.

The father and daughter took advantage of the gradual ascent to bond, with Maddy enthusiastically dominating the conversation. Brody chimed in only occasionally, mostly to point out potential hazards, like avalanche chutes and snow bridges concealing hidden creeks beneath their path. At the halfway point, they paused near a deep, snow-covered talus field to survey the area. Even with the heavy snowfall, the remnants of a recent avalanche were clearly visible—large ice blocks and displaced snow drifts had altered the trail. Brody noted that the slide was likely triggered by the collapse of an overhanging cornice above them to the right. A cornice is a wind-swept, hardened mass of snow and ice that forms along the edge of a mountain precipice. It builds over time from heavy snowfall, strong winds, and freezing temperatures. These formations can break off naturally or from external disturbances, sending chunks of snow and ice tumbling down the mountain's steep face and potentially triggering an avalanche. Maddy's eyes scanned the slope and chunky debris. It was a sobering reminder of the mountain's power and unpredictability, but it also deepened her respect for the environment they loved to explore together.

Avalanches can range from minor sluffs—small slides of loose snow—to fully destructive slab avalanches capable of uprooting mature trees and obliterating everything in their path. Most early mornings the Snoqualmie Pass Ski Patrol proactively triggered avalanches on the surrounding peaks to ensure the safety of motorists driving on the Interstate 90, plus the thousands of skiers and hikers attracted to the popular recreation area. As Maddy and Brody surveyed the aftermath of the slide, they refreshed their avalanche awareness knowledge, moving deliberately and with purpose. They maintained distance from one another as they crossed the area, a precaution to minimize risk and maximize their chances of responding effectively if trouble arose. Both wore active Backcountry Access Tracker avalanche transceivers, along with carrying probes and shovels—essential tools for survival and rescue in avalanche terrain. Years earlier, Brody had insisted his family attend a weekend avalanche safety course. They learned to identify hazardous snow conditions, recognize objective dangers, and practice survival and rescue techniques. It was a skillset he unfortunately had been forced to use multiple times over the years, both for rescues and, tragically, for body recoveries. Despite its importance, avalanche rescue was a skill he hoped they'd never have to use. Avoidance was always the priority, and he drilled this principle into his clients and family. Respecting the mountain and recognizing the warning signs were the most effective ways to stay safe.

Safely on the other side of the avalanche chute—commonly called an *avvy chute*—the trail straightened out. Maddy and Brody alternated leading, breaking through the deep, fresh snowfall in a process known as post-holing. The snow was so thick that they almost missed the buried two-mile marker, but a quick check of Brody's GPS map ensured they stayed on course and avoided veering into the popular backcountry ski area on Chair Peak. They marveled at the unusually heavy snowfall for this time of year, feeling fortunate to experience such a delight so close to home. Still, they knew to savor it while it lasted—early snow in Washington often signaled a potential lack of it later in the season.

At the base of a 500-foot hill, the two dropped their packs to prepare for the climb. The route would require a series of switchbacks to reach the top, but the conditions warranted extra precautions. Brody instructed Maddy to put on her harness, deciding it was safest to rope up. Although they weren't traveling on a glacier, where crevasse falls were a major concern, the mountain still held plenty of objective hazards. Last week's ice storm, coupled with the fresh snowfall, had created layered risks of avalanches, unstable snow bridges, and the possibility of uncontrollably slipping down the steep terrain. By roping up, they increased their safety margin. Tethered together, they could assist each other in case of a fall or an emergency. The rope also allowed Brody to set anchored protection at particularly hazardous crossings, further reducing the risks as they climbed.

With her dad leading—at the *sharp end* of the rope—Maddy waited for the line to nearly grow taut before stepping forward. Climbing while roped up requires finesse; the key is to maintain just enough slack to avoid pulling or being pulled unintentionally unless signaling the other members of the rope team. In its most graceful form, the rope between climbers creates a gentle smile, offering enough slack for natural movement while preventing trips caused by snagging crampon spikes. Maddy and Brody moved fluidly through the steep, snow-laden switchbacks, their coordination evident in the way they communicated and maintained their progression. The father-daughter duo made good time, efficiently navigating the climb with teamwork and an unspoken trust built from years of shared adventures.

CRACK!

Both climbers froze, instinctively leaning toward the uphill side of the mountain and bracing for impact. Silence followed. Maddy and Brody scanned the blinding white snowfall, their hearts pounding as they searched for the source of the eerie, gut-wrenching sound. From what they could gather, it sounded like a cornice had broken off a ridge on the far side of the valley. Moments later, the roar of a distant avalanche reverberated through the air, the sound bouncing off the sheer walls of the surrounding Cascade peaks. The powerful tremor carried an unsettling potential—it could trigger secondary avalanches on other slopes in the valley. Though they were in a relatively safe section of their ascent, the two remained still, waiting with bated breath for any signs of further activity. But none came. The mountain returned to an uncanny silence, as if nothing had happened, leaving only the echo of the avalanche's roar lingering in their minds.

"That's the worst!" Maddy called out to her dad, her voice carrying through the tether that linked them 30 feet apart.

"Yep," Brody replied, his tone steady but resigned. "There'll be more of that. Let's swap out gear." He paused, scanning their surroundings. They were in a relatively protected spot, making it a good place to transition. The terrain ahead was becoming too steep for snowshoes, as each step forward seemed to slide him frustratingly backward. It was counterproductive to the effort his body was exerting, and he knew they'd move more efficiently with crampons and ice axes. Maddy caught up, and together they worked quickly, shedding their snowshoes and strapping on crampons. Brody retrieved their Black Diamond ice axes from his pack, passing one to Maddy. The sharp, metal spikes and sturdy picks would provide the traction and stability they needed for the steeper, icy ascent ahead.

After securing their Cascade Mountain Tech trekking poles to the outside of their packs, they attached the axe leashes to carabiners on their harnesses for quick accessibility and safety. The ice axe is one of the most versatile tools in a mountaineer's arsenal. It serves countless purposes: providing balance, arresting a fall, aiding in crevasse rescue, creating anchors, cutting through ice, hammering, digging in snow, and more. Brody even recalled a time when he taught a client to use the adze—the flat, blade-like feature near the handle—as a spoon after she lost her utensil mid-expedition. He chuckled at the memory, sharing it with Maddy as they prepared to ascend. "I might write a book someday," he mused, "*101 Ways to Use an Ice Axe.*" Maddy smiled, shaking her head at her dad's humor, but she had to admit—if anyone could fill the pages with practical uses, it was him.

Step by slow, deliberate step, Maddy and Brody ascended the steep snowbank. If someone else planned to visit Snow Lake that day—a slim possibility given the conditions—they could thank the Hayes for carving out the path. Not that it would last; the relentless snowfall would likely cover their tracks within the hour. After navigating the final switchback, they paused briefly at a ridge overlooking what should have been a jaw-dropping view of the valley. Instead, a wall of white from the heavy snow masked the landscape, reducing it to a shadowy outline of peaks. Turning to their right, they continued toward the saddle above the lake. Most hikers typically stopped here, drawn by the spectacular vista of the surrounding mountains and the brilliant blue waters of Snow Lake below. An outcropping of rocks offered a postcard-perfect spot for a picnic or a rest before heading back down. But for Brody and Maddy, this was just a waypoint on their journey, the lake itself calling them further into its winter embrace.

Brody and Maddy weren't in any rush; with the entire day ahead of them, they had plenty of time to reach their destination and set up camp. While they preferred to finish before sundown, they were well-prepared with headlamps in case they needed to work in the dark. Still, it was only late morning, and losing daylight wasn't a concern yet. They unshouldered their packs and dropped them into the fresh snow, using them as makeshift seats while they snacked and rehydrated. Snowflakes quickly collected on their Gore-Tex jackets, but a quick shake sent the clumps scattering. Maddy pulled out her iPhone, hoping to snap a few Instagram-worthy shots. The snowfall was so heavy, though, that the images were almost entirely washed out by the whiteout conditions. The flash stubbornly illuminated the massive flakes mere inches from the lens, creating an effect that made her laugh but wasn't up to her social media standards. Disabling the flash didn't help much either; the photos still lacked the clarity she wanted.

"Guess I'll try again on the way out," she muttered. She figured the conditions would likely improve in a few days, offering a better chance to capture the pristine winter landscape. "Dad, I have a signal…barely," Maddy informed her father, holding up her phone as the faint bars flickered on the screen.

"Cool. Can you text Mom and Mitch about the conditions? Specifically, the avalanche danger at the talus field," Brody instructed. He trusted Bridget's caution but also knew Mitch's teenage brain could sometimes lead to impulsive decisions. Better to give them a heads-up. Not wanting to linger and risk getting cold or letting their muscles stiffen, they quickly tucked their snack wrappers into an empty Ziplock bag. After stowing their trash and adjusting their packs, they began moving again, making their way through the descending snowy forest. Maddy glanced at her phone and saw her message had delivered. Satisfied, she slipped it into the front pocket of her snow pants without waiting for a reply. Seconds into their descent toward the lake, the faint signal disappeared entirely, leaving them once again disconnected from AT&T's network.

With gravity on their side, Maddy and Brody quickly descended the half-mile trail and 400-foot elevation drop to the frozen lake. Brody led the way, post-holing through the fresh powder toward the right, where the trail eventually opened into a clearing. On a clear day, they would have been greeted by the breathtaking view of Snow Lake's icy expanse, framed by the towering 5,835-foot Roosevelt Peak. Today, however, the view was obscured by dense clouds and heavy snowfall. An old cabin's weathered remains marked the spot where they would set up their weekend basecamp. Without needing to discuss it, they both sprang into action. Swapping their crampons back for snowshoes, they stomped out a large area in the deep snow, compacting it into a firm perimeter for their campsite. Working like a well-oiled machine, they quickly erected their sleeping tent and a separate cooking and dining shelter. Within an hour, the ultimate winter basecamp stood proudly against the snow-laden backdrop. Brody stepped back, taking it all in, then pulled his daughter into a big, warm hug. Maddy grinned, her eyes drifting across the frozen lake and the serene, snowy wonderland that surrounded them.

"It doesn't get any better than this," she murmured, her voice filled with quiet contentment.

CHAPTER 27

Snoqualmie, Washington

"Wh…wha…" Mitch stammered, snapping out of a deep REM state, his heart pounding as he struggled to focus on the loud disturbance that had jolted him awake.

BOOM! BOOM! BOOM!

Three rapid gunshots shattered the silence, followed by a muffled discharge. Mitch's pupils dilated with panic as adrenaline surged through his system. Without hesitation, he ripped off his covers and sprang toward the bedroom door, his mind racing to make sense of the commotion.

* * *

30-minutes Prior

Two identical white Subaru Crosstreks rolled into the idyllic town of Snoqualmie, WA—a place that seemed plucked straight from a postcard. Here, the average family had 2.5 kids, a golden doodle, two SUVs (one almost always a white Subaru Crosstrek), and a million-dollar mortgage for a home worth half that. Unless, of course, you got in early like the Hayes, who paid on a $500,000 mortgage for what had now doubled in value. Sergey drove Aleksandr and Oleg in the lead Subaru, keeping well within the speed limit, while Viktor followed in the second vehicle with Pavel and Andrei. It was after 0200 as they descended the freshly plowed Snoqualmie Parkway, the stillness of the night broken only by the hum of their engines. At Douglas Avenue, they turned left and continued for 1.5 miles to its end, where the road curved left up the hilly Burke Street. Viktor pulled over beneath a burnt-out streetlamp, his headlights dimmed. The lead Subaru continued slowly past a modern three-story Cam-West home perched on the edge of a greenbelt high above the valley. Sergey drove past the target's house, its windows dark like every other home lining the quiet street. Reaching the top of the hill, he turned onto Cochrane Street, looping back to park a few car lengths behind Viktor. The engines fell silent, leaving the night heavy with anticipation.

Three days earlier, Aleksandr and Viktor had returned from their trip to Fallon, Nevada, to set up surveillance on Brody Hayes. Disguised as "dirtbag" hikers—a common sight in the Pacific Northwest—they blended seamlessly into the fabric of the out-doorsy town. They spent days conducting reconnaissance, exploring the hidden wildlife trails that wound behind the Hayes neighbor-hood. From the dense concealment of the thick trees, they silently observed, studying the family's routines and habits. Viktor, a cyber-security expert with advanced KGR technical training, had already identified the vulnerabilities in the home's weak security system. Jamming it wouldn't require much effort. The pair had ample op-portunity to eliminate Brody and his family, even the neighbors, dur-ing their stakeout. But they remained patient, disciplined, and loyal to the plan. This was no impulsive hit; they needed the entire KGR team to execute the final assassination. Once the mission was complete, they planned to retreat north, using Ross Lake to cross the border. It was the same path they had used to enter unnoticed. There was some concern about the highway closures caused by the heavy snowfall, but they had already identified alternative routes further east to circumvent any environmental challenges.

During their days of intelligence gathering, Aleksandr and Viktor confirmed that the Hayes family was planning a weekend getaway. Observing their recent packing activities, it was evident they intended to leave in the morning. This made tonight the ideal time to eliminate them while they slept. The Hayes family, like many privileged Americans, owned an oversized black Lincoln Navigator XL, typically parked in the driveway beside a black 4-door Jeep Wrangler Unlimited. Aleksandr had noted that Brody alternated between parking the Jeep in the driveway and the garage over the past few days. As Sergey drove past the Hayes' house that night, they observed that the Lincoln Navigator was alone in the driveway. This led them to conclude that the Jeep was parked in the garage, further confirming their assumptions about the family's plans and habits.

Both operative vehicles sat in obscurity, with all internal and external lights turned off. Aleksandr and Viktor quietly exited their car, each grabbing a duffle bag of equipment. Sergey, the driver, pulled away, retracing his route down the hill and heading toward their extraction point eight miles away in Fall City. Meanwhile, Viktor and his passengers—Pavel and Andrei—stepped out of their parked vehicle with their own duffle bags and regrouped with

Aleksandr and Oleg near a stormwater pond hidden behind the houses. The team's plan was meticulous: split the extraction between two vehicles departing from different locations. This strategy minimized the chances of raising suspicion from neighbors, local authorities, or surveillance cameras. Viktor, Pavel, and Andrei would leave directly from the house, while Aleksandr and Oleg would hike through the forest to the Preston-Snoqualmie Trail and rendezvous with Sergey. Both cars were to meet within the hour at a predetermined location in Redmond. There, they would change clothes and continue their journey north toward the border, vanishing into the night.

Viktor powered up and activated a portable wireless jammer, a device he had constructed from basic electronic components purchased at a Best Buy in the nearby town of Issaquah. The Hayes family relied on Amazon Blink WLAN cameras to monitor all the entrances to their house, but Viktor's jammer rendered them useless. By emitting a 2.4 GHz interference signal, it disrupted the cameras' connection to the Netgear WLAN router located in the corner of the downstairs office. The homemade device wasn't particularly sophisticated but was highly effective. In addition to jamming the Hayes' security system, it inadvertently disrupted the wireless routers in several neighboring houses on Burke Street. Viktor considered this a minor risk. It was the middle of the night, and frequent high winds in the Snoqualmie Valley often led to power outages, making such disruptions a common occurrence. Confident in the device's capabilities, Viktor pocketed the jammer, knowing it had given them the edge they needed to proceed undetected.

The five KGR operatives moved quickly and silently, filing single file from their drop-off point over a guardrail and vanishing into the inky blackness of the forest. They advanced in short bursts, pausing frequently to look and listen, ensuring they weren't being followed. The woods seemed alive with sound—distant cracks of branches echoing below hinted at unseen movement in the darkness. The forest and its ponds were home to deer, elk, black bears, bobcats, cougars, and beavers, any of which could be the source of the noises. High winds howled through the towering conifers, bending their massive trunks and threatening to uproot them from the earth. The cacophony of nature and the muffling effect of fresh snowfall worked to the Russians' advantage, masking their heavy breathing and the crunch of their footsteps. Windchimes rang frantically from the back porches of neighboring houses, adding another layer of cover for their covert approach. Every sound served as both a veil and a reminder of the precarious environment they navigated.

Each duffle bag was unzipped and quickly emptied of its contents. The KGR operatives methodically donned their tactical body armor vests, equipped with press-to-talk radio headsets, hip-holstered SIG Sauer P365s, Spyderco serrated tactical knives, and AR-15 rifles fitted with SilencerCo Omega 300 suppressors. The magazine pouches on their vests were fully loaded with 9 mm and .223 Remington rounds. Following a strict routine, the team conducted a radio check, then performed press checks on their weapons to ensure rounds were chambered and ready. With silent signals exchanged, Aleksandr, positioned at the front, indicated they were ready to proceed.

Moving with precision, Aleksandr led the group in hand-signal-directed bursts. They crossed from the cover of the woods two at a time, quickly reaching a cluster of trees on the back hill overlooking the neighborhood's cookie-cutter fences—mandated by the homeowner's association. Oleg reached over one of the fences, slowly unlatching the gate. The rusty hinges emitted a faint squeak, swallowed by the howling wind. He held the gate open as the others slipped through, carefully navigating around an oval Springfree trampoline in the backyard. Once the last operative had passed, Oleg silently closed and latched the gate, then rejoined the team beneath the second-story deck. The space below offered access to the finished basement, shielded from the view of prying eyes.

Pavel got to work on the sliding glass door, deftly picking the metal clip lock in seconds. However, the Hayes had smartly wedged a stick in the track to prevent it from sliding. Anticipating this obstacle, the team easily lifted the door off its track and carefully set it aside before stepping inside. With their eye pupils already adapted to the dark, the five Russians moved silently into the house. Two stories above, Bridget and Mitch Hayes slept, completely unaware of the imminent danger creeping through their home. Viktor and Oleg quickly cleared the basement while Aleksandr, Pavel, and Andrei followed closely behind. Once the basement was secure, the team ascended to the main floor. They moved cautiously but with confidence, not expecting resistance on the lower floors, as the family bedrooms were located on the third story. Each operative moved swiftly, their diligence heightened by the need to avoid any noise—especially anything that might wake the family dog. Even a creak in the floor or a whisper of a door hinge could compromise their mission. After ensuring the second floor was clear, they prepared to ascend the final set of stairs. Weapons ready, they covered all angles as they moved with deliberate care. Oleg stayed behind on the second floor, both to stand watch and to begin rigging a failsafe cover-up.

Viktor continued as point position up the winding staircase, the operatives trailing behind him spaced a couple of feet apart. As his head breached the top of the tan carpeted stairs, he came face-to-face with the family's golden doodle. The dog wagged its tail excitedly, oblivious to the danger.

Without hesitation, Viktor leveled his AR-15 and fired a single suppressed round, dropping the dog in the hallway. The thud of its falling body broke the silence as blood pooled beneath the motionless form. Viktor relayed hand signals to the team, warning them to step carefully to avoid tripping over the warm carcass.

He stepped over the deceased canine and moved through the open double doorway into the master bedroom. The king-sized bed loomed before him. Viktor swiveled to his right, aiming his weapon at the figure on the right side of the bed, while Andrei moved to his left, training his weapon on the opposite side.

BOOM! BOOM! BOOM!

The ear rattling shots shattered the silent tension. The sudden muzzle flash seared through the darkness, momentarily blinding the KGR operatives. Andrei bore the brunt of it, taking two hollow-point .45 caliber rounds squarely to his chest plate. Before the impact could knock him backward, a third round found its mark—striking the center of his face. The hollow-point bullet expanded violently upon impact, its fragmented core severing Andrei's brain from his spinal cord. The contents of his cranium erupted out the back of his head at nearly 600 mph, painting the dresser and flatscreen behind him with a gruesome splatter of O-positive and shredded gray matter. Viktor froze in the chaos, momentarily stunned by the sudden and lethal resistance. This was not the silent execution he had envisioned—it was a fight for survival, and they hadn't expected the unknowing Hayes to fight back.

Moments earlier, Bridget Hayes was startled awake by a sound from downstairs. As her mind cleared, she registered the noise—a sudden thud that sounded like their 9-year-old dog, Sam, hitting the floor. Alarm bells rang in her head. Unbeknownst to the intruders, they had already lost their element of surprise. Acting on instinct, Bridget pulled open the top drawer of her nightstand and retrieved her Smith & Wesson M&P Shield. Her heart pounded as she pulled back the slide to chamber a round, flipping the safety off with practiced ease. Growing up in Montana, Bridget had been around firearms her entire life and was extremely proficient. Her husband, a U.S. Navy Combat Search and Rescue veteran, had only sharpened those skills. Together, they had spent countless hours with their children shooting paper targets and practicing tactical drills, including the Mozambique Drill—two shots to the chest, followed by one to the head. But firing at wooden targets in a controlled environment was one thing. Facing armed intruders in the dead of night was entirely different. As she raised her weapon, adrenaline surged through her veins, overtaking any indecision. Her reaction felt almost automatic, as if driven by muscle memory and primal protective instinct. Years of training coalesced in this moment, enabling her to act swiftly and decisively against the unknown threat that had invaded her home.

Without hesitation, Bridget swung her smoking barrel toward Viktor and double-tapped the trigger. Two hollow-point rounds slammed into his chest armor, the force knocking him backward. His heels caught on Andrei's still-convulsing body, sending Viktor sprawling onto the blood-soaked carpet. Gasping for air, he struggled to recover as pain and shock overwhelmed him. In one fluid motion, Aleksandr slid into the room, his semi-automatic suppressed AR-15 raised and ready. He unleashed a volley of .223 Remington 55-grain slugs, zeroing in on the muzzle flash from the bed. The rounds tore into Bridget's chest and neck, shattering bone and shredding vital organs. The devastating trauma left her dead before her body hit the floor. Aleksandr and Pavel swiftly swept the room, their weapons trained on every corner. But as they scanned the chaotic scene, one glaring absence became evident—there was no sign of Brody Hayes.

Pavel lowered his weapon, his hands trembling as he dropped to his knees beside his fallen brother. The sight of Andrei's unresponsive body stopped him cold. In disbelief, he frantically pressed his fingers against Andrei's carotid artery, desperate to find a pulse. There was none. Andrei was gone, but the reality of it was too overwhelming to register. The brothers had endured hell together, forged in the brutal crucible of the KGR program since infancy. They had survived countless missions in the unforgiving Afghan mountains and across the harsh expanse of Mother Russia.

Through it all, Andrei had been his constant—his only blood relative, his tether to humanity. And now, in a single, devastating moment, he was gone. Pavel's mind raced, trying to comprehend what had just happened. How had a suburban housewife—a *housewife*—ended his brother's life? The thought burned like acid, mingling grief with confusion and rage.

The stages of grief churned chaotically in Pavel's mind, skipping from denial to blinding anger. With a guttural roar, he grabbed his AR-15 and unleashed a succession of vengeful rounds into Bridget Hayes' contorted corpse. Each shot reverberated with the raw fury and heartbreak of losing his only brother. Tears streaked down his unshaven cheeks, mingling with the blood splattered across his face. Forcing himself to compartmentalize his emotions, Pavel turned to assess Viktor's condition. Viktor, drenched in Andrei's blood, groaned weakly as Pavel helped him to his feet. Thanks to his body armor and Aleksandr's timely intervention, Viktor was still breathing. He would be bruised and in serious pain for the next week, but he would live to fight another day. Andrei, however, hadn't been so lucky. His lifeless body lay sprawled on the floor, a grim reminder of how quickly even the most seasoned operatives could fall.

"STOLI TWO, STOLI ONE. Confirm extraction point," Aleksandr barked into his radio, seeking reassurance that Sergey had reached their exfil location. Sergey responded promptly with two sharp clicks, signaling his position.

The ear-splitting sound of unsuppressed .45 caliber shots had surely disturbed the quiet neighborhood and risked drawing unwanted attention. Time was no longer on their side. Moving with urgency, Aleksandr and his team systematically began clearing the remaining rooms on the third floor, their suppressed weapons trained on every shadow and doorway. But their target—Brody Hayes—was nowhere to be found. Exchanging tense glances, the operatives regrouped, their frustration mounting as they prepared to reassess the situation.

Where was Brody Hayes?!

In a startled daze, Mitch opened his bedroom door and stepped into the pitch-black hallway, his bare feet shuffling forward toward his parents' room. His foot caught on something, sending him off balance. He stumbled, falling forward onto a warm, still mass of bloody fur. Panic surged through him as he scrambled to push himself up, his hand fumbling for the hallway light switch on the wall. The instant the light flicked on, his breath caught in his throat. Standing before him was an armored man holding a rifle. The brightness disoriented the KGR operative, momentarily robbing him of his night vision. Mitch, fueled by a surge of inexplicable adrenaline, didn't hesitate. He lunged at the intruder, his hands desperately grabbing for the AR-15. With all his weight, he slammed the man into the wall behind him. The impact shattered a dozen framed family photos, sending shards of glass raining to the floor. The operative, twice Mitch's size and far more experienced, quickly regained control. Unsheathing a Spyderco knife with ruthless efficiency, he drove the blade into Mitch's abdomen up to the handle. Pain radiated through Mitch's body, but the fight wasn't over—not yet.

Hearing the commotion, Pavel emerged from Maddy's empty room, his weapon raised. He aimed at the struggling figures in the hallway and fired a tight burst of .223 Remington rounds into Mitch's back. The force of the impact drove the youngest Hayes child forward, slamming him into Aleksandr and driving the buried knife deeper into his stomach. Mitch crumpled to the floor, motionless, his inert body bleeding out next to his loyal dog. Pavel lowered his weapon with cold precision, his face devoid of emotion. Yet deep within, he felt a fleeting surge of grim satisfaction—a hollow retribution for the loss of his brother, Andrei.

"STOLI ONE, STOLI FOUR," Oleg's voice crackled over the radio from downstairs. He had stumbled upon new information while rigging the house to detonate, ensuring no evidence would survive the night.

"STOLI FOUR, STOLI ONE," Aleksandr responded hastily, his voice clipped with urgency. Warm blood from Mitch's exit wounds coated the front of him, smeared into a single gruesome brush stroke as the boy's lifeless body slid down and crumpled at his feet. Without a flicker of emotion, Aleksandr turned toward the final upstairs room, his weapon sweeping the space as he continued the radio exchange.

"You'll want to see this," Oleg said, his tone carrying a mix of surprise and frustration. "Target and daughter aren't here. The Jeep isn't in the garage... and I found a note."

"Viktor, are you okay? Let's go downstairs. Pavel, clean this up and say your goodbyes. Meet us downstairs in five minutes,"

Aleksandr commanded, his voice cold and devoid of empathy as he directed the remaining members of his execution team.

Viktor, still catching his breath and wincing in pain, limped toward the stairway, stepping past the still boy and dog bodies strewn in the hallway. Aleksandr followed close behind, reaching for the hallway light switch and flipping it off. They had already risked enough exposure with the gunfire upstairs. While they hoped the deafening wind gusts pounding the neighborhood had masked the sounds, Aleksandr knew they couldn't rely on luck. They needed to be prepared for any further unexpected disturbances. The task was far from over.

The two descended the stairs, disappearing into the dimly lit main floor, where Aleksandr relayed the situation report to Oleg. Without a word, Oleg handed his leader a folded note left by Brody Hayes. His expression remained unreadable, betraying no hint of emotion. If he was processing the loss of his comrade, there was no outward sign. Oleg had heard the gunshots echo through the house but had remained at his post, trusting his team to handle the situation. He hadn't anticipated losing anyone on this operation, but he was no stranger to death. To him, human life was expendable, a price to be paid for the greater cause. Losing Andrei was a blow, but Oleg found solace in one cold belief: to die fighting for what was right was an honor.

Upstairs, Pavel reluctantly turned back toward his brother's unresponsive body. In that moment, the emotionally hardened KGR agent made a deliberate choice: Andrei was no longer his brother. He was just another nameless soldier lost in battle—a casualty of war. It was easier this way, especially with Andrei's face rendered unrecognizable, completely obliterated by the .45 caliber impact. Pavel stripped Andrei of his tactical gear, weapons, and radio, his actions mechanical and detached. He collected the scattered shell casings from the bedroom and hallway floors, then carefully placed Bridget's M&P Shield back into the partially opened nightstand drawer. With the extra gear slung over his shoulder, Pavel made his way downstairs, refusing to glance back at the scene of carnage. He refused to say goodbye. But deep within, a raw and unfamiliar hurt festered, triggering an anger unlike anything he had ever experienced. It was a fury that burned hot and unrelenting, igniting a singular, vengeful purpose: to find Brody Hayes and put him in the ground.

Aleksandr stood in the dimly lit room, reading the note Brody Hayes had left for his wife and son. When he spotted Pavel descending the stairs, he raised the small piece of paper with a grim smile. "Comrade, we have everything we need right here to avenge Andrei," Aleksandr said, his voice cold but charged with purpose. "You may have the honor of killing Brody Hayes."

The note contained the exact location of Brody and his daughter's campsite at Snow Lake near Snoqualmie Pass. It even detailed their estimated arrival timeframe the following morning. The foolish American had unknowingly provided a map to his and his daughter's demise. Aleksandr folded the note and slid it into the blood-stained pocket of his cargo pants. Pavel said nothing, but the fire in his eyes was unmistakable. He and Viktor moved to the basement, dragging their blood-soaked boots across the carpet as they descended. They exited the same way they had entered, slipping silently into the night and making their way to the edge of the forest. There, they held their position, taking up guard while waiting for the others to regroup. Any blood left on the soles of their boots imprinted a trail in the fresh snow, but the relentless flurries quickly erased the evidence, blanketing the valley in an eerie silence once again.

Earlier, as the team moved upstairs to eliminate the targets on the third floor, Oleg had been tasked with rigging the house to destroy all evidence. Working with cold efficiency, he crumpled a handful of aluminum foil and placed it inside the mounted JennAir microwave oven. After muting the microwave's audible beeps through the front control panel, he set a delayed start timer for 30 minutes. With Pavel and Viktor gone, Aleksandr moved swiftly to the adjacent stove and wrenched open the main natural gas line beneath it. The sharp hiss of escaping gas filled the air, mixing with the tension of their orderly retreat. Oleg checked his watch, then pressed the microwave's start button, which would be initiated in exactly 30 minutes. Exiting through the back gate, they disappeared into the snow-covered night, leaving the deadly trap to do its work.

Viktor and Pavel retraced their earlier path, carefully navigating through the forest and returning to the parked Subaru on Douglas Avenue. The vehicle's all-wheel drive handled the fresh snow with ease as they made their way toward Snoqualmie Parkway. They planned to take the back route along Highway 202 to the rendezvous point in Redmond, where the five remaining KGR operatives would regroup and discuss the next steps. Adrenaline coursed through their veins as they sat in the vehicle, bloodstained and reeking of gunpowder—a blunt reminder of the carnage they had left behind. Every turn of the wheel was deliberate, the weight of their situation pressing down on them. Keeping strictly within the speed limit, they were acutely aware of the risks of being pulled over. Any encounter with law enforcement would leave them with no choice but to eliminate the authorities, a scenario they desperately wanted to avoid. Eyes straight ahead, they watched the snow dance hypnotically in the low-beam headlights, the entrancing deflection on the windshield offering a momentary distraction from the gravity of their operation. The quiet tension in the car was matched only by the eerie stillness of the snow-covered landscape surrounding them.

Behind the Hayes' crime scene, Aleksandr and Oleg disappeared into the dark forest, their path softened by the blanket of snow illuminating the shadows. The intense winds howled through the trees, causing branches to creak and snap, some crashing to the ground around them. Nature's unpredictable fury often felt more dangerous than human conflict, a constant reminder of the perilous environment they navigated. Moving swiftly, they wove through the dense bushes and towering trees, following a faint animal trail that led them down the incline. The path eventually leveled out, merging with the Preston–Snoqualmie Trail. Turning left, they followed the flat trail toward their extraction point. Sergey waited nearby, concealed in the trees, his weapon at the ready. Fifty yards away, the white Subaru sat parked, blending into the snowy backdrop. As Aleksandr and Oleg emerged from the trail, Sergey stepped out of the shadows to reveal himself.

BOOM!

Right on cue, 30 minutes later, an earth-shaking explosion rocked the Snoqualmie Valley. The KGR operatives, though expecting it, were still startled by the deafening sound and the forceful tremor. The JennAir microwave's delayed timer had brought it to life, spinning the crumpled ball of aluminum foil on its glass turntable. By then, the house was saturated with invisible, odorless natural gas. The gas alone would have been lethal, silently replacing the oxygen in the Hayes family's red blood cells with carbon monoxide, choking their bodies of life-sustaining elements. But the microwave ensured there would be no survivors or evidence. Electric fields coursed through the foil, igniting it in a chaotic flurry of sparks. The combustion caused an explosive increase in pressure, as the fuel-rich air in the kitchen detonated with violent force.

The once-peaceful Snoqualmie neighborhood erupted into pandemonium as the house transformed into a war-like bomb. The fiery explosion obliterated the structure, blowing out windows in nearby homes and setting off car alarms for miles. Any remains inside were instantly incinerated, leaving nothing but ash and rubble. Authorities would spend months piecing together the incident, likely concluding it to be a tragic gas leak. Even if they suspected foul play, the five remaining KGR operatives would be safely back in Mother Russia long before any answers were uncovered.

CHAPTER 28

Snow Lake

Snoqualmie Pass, Washington

The night was brutal. Brody found himself wondering if the sun would ever rise as he endured the freezing temperatures, howling winds, and heavy snowfall. Meanwhile, Maddy rested peacefully in her down sleeping bag, oblivious to the storm raging outside. Wind gusts reaching 60 mph roared through the tree line high above them, each one sounding like a falling limb could crush them at any moment. Still, Brody took solace in knowing they had built their shelter in a protected area near the lake, minimizing the risk. Inside the thin nylon walls of their tent, every sound was amplified, each gust collapsing the fabric inward before snapping it back taut. The constant flapping and roaring of the storm tested his nerves. A night like this was a trial of endurance, both mental and physical. The claustrophobic confines of the tent, coupled with the unyielding battering of the elements, pushed even the most seasoned outdoorsmen to their limits. Yet Brody stayed alert, battling his fears to ensure his daughter remained safe through the storm.

Their North Face 4-season tent was securely anchored using snow stakes and a series of deadman anchors. This reliable technique involved digging horizontal trenches in the snow using the adze of an ice axe or a shovel. Pickets or snow anchors, attached to the tent's stake webbing or guy lines, were placed into the trenches, which were then packed tightly with snow. As the temperature dropped overnight, the snow froze solid, reinforcing the anchors and creating a virtually unbreakable tie-down capable of withstanding even tornado-strength winds. The deadman anchors easily held the base of the tent in place, keeping it stable against the relentless gusts. However, the ferocious winds still penetrated the sides, causing the nylon walls to cave inward with every mighty blow. The flapping and pressure tested the limits of the shelter, but the Hayes' careful preparation ensured it remained steadfast against the storm's fury.

* * *

The suffocating sound and unrelenting force of the wind rattling the tent walls triggered memories of past traumas Brody had endured, both in the military and on the mountains. One incident in particular came rushing back: a solo summit attempt on Aconcagua, the tallest peak in the southern hemisphere. Rising to 23,831 feet in the Andes Mountain range along the Argentina-Chile border, the climb had been one of Brody's greatest challenges. Ascending without clients allowed Brody to move efficiently, and he reached the summit with ease. However, as he descended to high camp, a forecast of 100 mph winds forced him to push further to a lower camp. Exhausted from a demanding summit day and carrying 90 pounds of gear an additional five miles, he set up his tent amid a violent windstorm. Using large rock walls as windbreaks and anchor points, Brody secured his shelter as best he could. Yet as the night wore on, the wind escalated to a terrifying fury. He sat with his back braced against the tent wall, absorbing the constant gusts. Despite his precautions, most of the tent poles snapped under the strain, and the nylon collapsed around his hunched form. The heavy rocks meant to secure the tent were no match for Mother Nature, as the wind dragged the tent—rocks, stakes, and Brody—inch by inch, across the snow. Brody survived the night, barely. Tragically, some mountaineers who had remained at high camp weren't as fortunate. The harrowing experience etched itself into his psyche, another scar in a long series of traumatic memories that would resurface later as PTSD. Now, as the winds raged around his family's mountain shelter, those memories clawed at the edges of his mind, reminding him of how close he had come to losing it all.

* * *

Brody woke up hourly, his heart racing and breath heavy as the memories of past storms scraped at the edges of his mind. Each time, he worked through mindfulness techniques to regain control.

Breathe. Focus. Breathe.

Slowly, his body calmed, and his mind sharpened. After steadying himself, Brody would assess their living space, carefully checking their supplies and making minor adjustments to their shelter as needed. Each time he stirred, he listened to Maddy's deep, steady breathing. He couldn't help but feel a swell of pride at his teen daughter's ability to sleep through conditions that felt like a hurricane outside. However, his greater concern was the snow accumulation. The ruthless Pacific Northwest storm system had already dumped over three feet of snow that night. The high winds drove the snowfall in all directions, piling it around the tent and creating an igloo-like effect that could become lethal if unchecked. Brody repeatedly punched the tent walls and roof from the inside, knocking the clinging snow free. He knew the risks all too well. The weight of the snow could collapse the tent, crushing them beneath its mass. Worse still, the accumulation could create an airtight barrier, entombing them inside. If that happened, the lack of ventilation could lead to a silent killer—carbon monoxide poisoning. With each clearing, Brody ensured their safety while battling the gnawing fear that every gust, every drift, brought a new threat.

The morning gifted a welcome calm after the storm, with patches of blue sky breaking through the fast-moving nimbostratus clouds. Maddy stirred in her sleeping bag, inch-worming her way out into the crisp air of the tent. She slipped into her 800-fill down pants and jacket before quietly unzipping the tent's front opening leading into the vestibule, mindful not to wake her dad, who was sound asleep. She paused, glancing back at him with puffy eyes and a hint of curiosity.

Did he get as good a night's rest as I did?

Reaching for her down booties, still toasty warm from her sleeping bag, she tugged them on and unzipped the vestibule's fly. Pulling on her gloves, she shook loose the frozen snow shovel they had stuck vertically outside. Her first glimpse of the camp revealed a fresh wall of snow blocking the exit. Maddy poked her head out of the top of the vestibule, her breath visible in the frigid air. The camp was completely buried. Without hesitation, she grabbed the shovel and began digging a path to the cooking tent. She worked methodically, clearing snow toward a spot behind the trees to serve as a makeshift restroom. The morning air was biting, but the satisfaction of moving with purpose kept her warm. Maddy didn't need prompting—this was second nature, learned from years of outdoor adventures with her dad.

By the time Brody woke, the camp had been transformed into a cozy winter village. The welcoming scent of instant coffee and Mountain House freeze-dried bacon and egg scramble wafted through the crisp morning air. After taking care of a behind-the-trees morning ritual and giving his hands a quick squirt of antibacterial wash, Brody joined Maddy at the cooking tent for breakfast.

"How'd you sleep?" he asked, his words carried on a cloud of fog from his warm breath meeting the icy morning air. He already knew the answer.

"Best night ever! How about you?" Maddy replied with energetic enthusiasm, her smile wide.

"Best night ever," Brody echoed, his grin spreading as he settled in beside her, savoring the quiet joy of the moment.

The two sat on their closed-cell Therm-A-Rest sleeping pads in the cooking tent, casually discussing their plan for the day. The previous evening, they had set up this dedicated space for cooking, eating, and socializing—a welcome comfort after the harsh conditions of the storm. They had dug out a circular area a few feet deep, leaving a central block of snow intact to support a single tent pole.

The teepee-style tent draped over the pole and was anchored tightly with multiple deadman snow stakes surrounding the structure. Maddy had meticulously crafted steps leading down from the tent's doorway fly and packed the snow along the sides, creating a functional cooking shelf and a seating area. The sleeping pads provided cushioning, dryness, and warmth—perfect for long meals or relaxed conversations. While a cooking tent might not be practical at higher, more exposed altitudes, it was a luxurious addition at their lower elevation, transforming their camp into a winter haven.

"Mom and Mitch won't be here for a few hours," Maddy said with a grin. "I thought we could check out the lake to see how thick the ice is, and then maybe hike up to the saddle to wait for them. I know Mom will appreciate us taking her pack for the descent." She giggled at the thought, clearly amused.

"Sounds good. Today's an easy day," Brody replied, stretching his legs out in front of him. "I was thinking about traversing around the lake and climbing Kaleetan, but the conditions don't look great. We can reassess later today to decide if we want an early start tomorrow—or just skip it this trip. The mountain will always be here. Better to play it safe with the avalanche conditions." He was referring to Kaleetan Peak, the prominent 6,259-foot summit west of their camp, across the ridge. They had climbed it several times in the past, so missing it this time wasn't a huge loss. While bagging a peak always added a sense of accomplishment to their cold-weather adventures, Brody was firm in his priorities. It was always better to return alive than to risk everything for the fleeting reward of standing on top.

Snow Lake certainly lived up to its name, its vast surface resembling a pristine snowfield after the night's fresh snowfall blanketed the thick ice below. Maddy cautiously stepped one boot onto the edge where the trees met the shore, testing the surface with a mix of curiosity and caution. It was hard to believe how different the lake looked now compared to just a few months ago. During the summer, their family had hiked here for the day, stripping down to their swimsuits before diving into the frigid waters. The lake, fed by its high-altitude location and shaded by towering peaks, never truly warmed up. But there was something invigorating about a Cascade polar plunge after a long, hot summer hike—a ritual that left them both refreshed and laughing.

CRACK!

The sharp sound echoed across the lake, cutting through Maddy's thoughts and jolting her to attention. Her breath caught as she froze in place, staring at the snow-covered surface beneath her feet. Maddy quickly recoiled, stepping back and removing her weighted mountaineering boot from the frozen lake's edge. The sharp crack had startled her, sending her heart racing, but she responded instinctively, retreating before breaking through.

"I guess it's not as thick as I thought," she said, glancing back at her dad, who had been watching her carefully.

"It's pretty thick," Brody reassured her, "but I doubt anyone's stepped on it since the snowfall. Probably just settled a bit when you put your weight on it." He gave her a reassuring wink. "Let's avoid it either way." Maddy nodded, the tension easing as they both shared a knowing smile. The lake, beautiful but unpredictable, was better admired from the shore.

Brody and Maddy alternated the exhausting task of post-holing through the deep snow, retracing their path from the day before as they ascended toward the saddle. Breaking trail in the wintery conditions was hard work, made even more challenging as heavy flurries resumed, swirling around them in icy bursts. Brody was no stranger to leading groups through similar conditions, often at much higher altitudes. But having Maddy there to willingly share the workload was a welcome change—one he gratefully accepted. With no pressing time constraints, they took their time, pacing themselves as they worked their way steadily toward the top. The hope was to gain enough elevation to pick up an AT&T signal and track Bridget and Mitch's location. Brody knew, however, that the freezing temperatures would affect their chances. Cold slows the battery's chemical reactions, reducing its ability to operate or power up the device. In preparation, Maddy had tucked her iPhone into the front pocket of her jacket, keeping it warm against her body as they climbed. The small act was just another example of her growing mountain savvy, a reflection of the years she had spent learning from her dad.

"No signal yet," Maddy announced, switching her iPhone out of Airplane Mode as soon as they reached the top of the saddle.

"You could try climbing up there for a better line of sight to the cell tower," Brody suggested, nodding toward a ridge about 100 feet to their right. Without a second thought, his eager daughter began hustling up the steep snow-covered slope, using her hands and feet for traction. While she was genuinely curious about tracking her mom and brother's location, she was also eager to check her Instagram feed. Brody chuckled to himself and made no move to follow her. He was perfectly content staying where he was, enjoying the hypnotic view of the blizzard swirling around them. The snow danced in chaotic patterns, a mesmerizing display of nature's power and beauty that seemed to quiet his restless mind.

Maddy disappeared into the trees as she crawled up the steep, snow-covered embankment with determined effort. Nearing what she thought was the summit, her progress was interrupted by a sudden vibration in her right front pocket. She stopped, catching her breath, and pulled out her iPhone. The screen lit up with a flurry of activity. The iCloud queue struggled to unload a backlog of stored text messages, missed calls, and voicemails. The AT&T signal was overwhelmed by the flood of inbound data, leaving her unable to open social media even if she wanted to.

"DADDY!" Maddy's scream pierced the silence as she dropped to her knees, clutching the phone in trembling hands.

Brody's heart surged with adrenaline at the sound of Maddy's blood-curdling scream. Without hesitation, he sprinted toward her voice, scrambling up the snowy embankment in a frantic bear crawl. Scenarios raced through his mind, each one sharpening his focus on her safety.

Was Maddy injured? Had she taken a fall? Did she stumble upon a dead body? What made her scream? And why was she now silent?

His thoughts moved faster than his legs could keep up as he slipped and clawed his way higher, the icy terrain working against him. Determination fueled his every movement, his fatherly instincts driving him to close the distance as quickly as possible.

Relief flooded through Brody when he spotted Maddy sitting in the snow. But as he drew closer, that relief quickly turned to dread. Something was very wrong. She was frozen in place, gasping for air, her body trembling in a state of shock.

"Breathe, honey," he urged, kneeling beside her. "Calm down. Take a slow breath in…"

With uncontrollable shaking, Maddy lifted her phone and extended it toward her father. As soon as he took it, she buried herself into his chest, gripping him in a tight embrace as she broke into hysterical sobs. Confused and alarmed, Brody wrapped his left arm around his daughter, holding her close as he glanced at the phone in his hand. His world instantly shattered. The words on the screen stole the air from his lungs, his soul collapsing under the weight of the unimaginable truth. It was the kind of news that altered everything, leaving a scar that would never heal.

Bridget and Mitch were dead.

CHAPTER 29

Fall City, Washington

"What the hell happened in there, comrades?" Sergey demanded as the tense and hurried Aleksandr and Oleg climbed into the getaway car.

"Shut your mouth and drive!" Aleksandr snapped, his frustration and anger boiling over.

Oleg silently handed Sergey the note Brody had left, detailing their snow camping location. "We need more supplies," Oleg said coldly.

"STOLI ONE, STOLI FIVE. Secondary RZ. Coordinates to follow," Aleksandr said into his radio as he punched an inquiry into the Subaru's GPS and quickly texted Viktor.

"STOLI FIVE, STOLI ONE. Copy coordinates," came Viktor's curt reply over the radio. He passed the burner phone to Pavel, who typed the new destination into their vehicle's navigation system.

The air inside both vehicles was thick with tension as they raced to regroup, their focus shifting to the next phase of their mission. The hunt for Brody Hayes and his daughter continued.

Sergey retraced his route to the Preston–Fall City Road and took a right. The small town of Fall City was alive with flashing red lights and blaring sirens as local fire trucks joined those from North Bend and Snoqualmie, racing toward the reported house explosion in Snoqualmie Ridge. To avoid the chaos, Sergey veered onto a side street, bypassing the clutter of emergency vehicles navigating through the snow flurries. He merged west onto Highway 202, and within 20 minutes, they arrived at their rendezvous point at the Redmond Town Center. The weather had shifted; the snow gave way to heavy rain, and the winds, though still present, were less severe in Redmond. Sergey maneuvered the Subaru into a discreet location behind a two-story REI, carefully positioning the vehicle in a blind spot away from the parking lot cameras. Inside the tight, fogging confines of the car, Aleksandr, Oleg, and Sergey changed into fresh clothes. The metallic smell of blood, sweat, and adrenaline lingered, but their new attire offered a thin layer of anonymity for the next phase of their operation.

"Andrei died tonight because he was weak," Aleksandr stated coldly, his words deliberate and aligned with his hardened leadership style.

Sergey's jaw tightened, but he pushed past his boss's harshness, his voice cutting through with urgency. "Andrei didn't make it? What happened?" Sergey's inquiry wasn't just procedural—it was personal. Andrei was more than a comrade; he was someone Sergey had known his entire life, the closest thing he had to family within the brutal world of the KGR. Aleksandr's words landed like a blow, but Sergey needed answers.

"He hesitated, and the American *cyka* shot him," Aleksandr spat, his frustration palpable. "Viktor was also hit, but in the vest. No more mistakes!" His tone made it clear the discussion was over.

In the Subaru's passenger seat, Pavel sat silently, seething with rage at the loss of his brother. His fists clenched, his anger simmering just beneath the surface as the vehicle sped down the back highway toward Redmond. Behind the wheel, Viktor gritted his teeth, wincing with every turn of the steering wheel. The .45 caliber impact to his vest had cracked several ribs, and the curving road sent sharp, excruciating pain radiating through his chest. Yet the physical pain was easier to bear than the emotional toll. The loss of Andrei weighed heavily on him, compounded by a bitter disappointment in himself for being shot. To add insult to injury, he couldn't shake the humiliation—he'd been outmaneuvered by a woman. The thought burned in his mind, feeding a cold, vengeful tenacity as they approached their rendezvous.

After 30 grueling minutes of painful driving, Viktor and Pavel pulled to the side of the street adjacent to the REI parking lot. Spotting the other white Subaru Crosstrek parked discreetly nearby, they did not attempt to communicate. The team had remained radio silent since leaving Snoqualmie, each operative following the secondary plan and designated location without the need for further coordination. Viktor retrieved a roll of duct tape from his duffle bag, tearing off several strips and securing them tightly across his ribs to provide some semblance of support for the pain. Every slight movement was a reminder of the .45 caliber impact that had cracked his bones, but he pushed through with stoic determination. Both men changed out of their bloody tactical gear in the confines of the vehicle, stuffing the stained clothing into garbage bags for later disposal. Exhausted, they reclined their seats, catching a few restless hours of sleep. As soon as REI opened in the morning, they would resupply and head back east. Their mission was far from over, and the operation would not end until Brody Hayes and his daughter were eliminated.

Pavel jerked awake at the sound of the driver's and backseat doors slamming shut. Aleksandr and Viktor had returned with Starbucks coffee and breakfast sandwiches from the nearby shops in Redmond Town Center. At this early hour, most of the outdoor mall's stores were still closed, save for a few popular coffee and breakfast spots. In a few hours, the place would be bustling with wealthy Microsoft spouses indulging in wants over needs, but for now, it remained quiet. With the outdoor supply store not opening until 10 a.m., they had 30 minutes to finish their breakfast and strategize.

Pavel's heart raced from the abrupt awakening, the jolt triggering an overwhelming wave of grief. His mind drifted back to the fog of depression that had settled over him, the reality of Andrei's death flooding his thoughts. The harder he tried to suppress the emotions, the more they clawed at him, threatening to unravel his resolve. In the back seat, Aleksandr unwrapped a steaming egg sandwich. Viktor handed Pavel a Grande latte and a Starbucks paper bag containing his breakfast item. Pavel took a tentative sip from the micro hole in the lid, the warm liquid doing little to calm him. The sausage and egg sandwich remained untouched in the bag—his appetite was gone, devoured by the weight of his loss.

"You can't bring him back, Pavel. He's dead because he hesitated. Use your grief to fuel your revenge," Aleksandr said coldly, choosing words he knew would intensify Pavel's sadness, pain, and ultimately, his rage. Pavel's fists clenched, his face shadowed with a storm of emotion as Aleksandr finished his breakfast and walked back to join Oleg and Sergey in the other car.

Aleksandr had woken after just two hours of sleep to create a list of winter gear they needed for their unanticipated Snow Lake mission. The operatives had to fill gaps in their supplies and replace their blood-soaked clothing to avoid drawing attention. He and Oleg parked near the REI entrance, waiting for the store to open. They waited a few minutes to enter, allowing a handful of early customers to go in first before staggering in behind them. They were fully aware that the store's surveillance cameras would capture them, but they attempted to blend in, donning ballcaps and keeping their heads low to obscure their faces. Splitting up, they navigated the neatly organized racks of REI, efficiently gathering items from their list. After paying in cash, they returned to their cars with their purchases: five sets of snowshoes, gaiters, trekking poles, backpacks, snow shovels, fuel, an additional JetBoil stove, another Garmin GPS unit, upper and lower snow layers, snow jackets, pants, goggles, gloves, and a bag filled with freeze-dried meals and snacks. Each operative collected their allocated gear and loaded it into their respective vehicles. With their supplies secured, the two cars regrouped at a nearby Shell gas station to refuel and prepare for the next phase of their mission.

"You guys heading to the snow?" an extroverted teenage Shell attendant asked as he sorted through the cash Sergey handed him. Handling actual money was rare, causing a slight delay as he carefully counted out the change behind the protective plexiglass wall. Unlike most customers who paid at the pump and drove off without a word, Sergey and his group offered a rare chance for interaction.

"Mount Rainier," Sergey replied curtly, keeping his head low to shield his face. "We're hoping the roads are plowed." The answer was deliberately vague—a location Sergey had overheard in passing but knew little about. He silently hoped the attendant wouldn't press for details, as his knowledge of the area was limited to ensuring their cover remained intact.

"They're pretty good about plowing up there," the teenage attendant offered, trying to extend the conversation. "But still, be safe. There are a lot of dangerous, icy corners on the road to Paradise." Sergey had no interest in continuing the exchange. He grabbed his change without a word and exited the gas station, leaving the attendant behind the plexiglass wall.

The drive to Snoqualmie Pass took over an hour, delayed by the morning commuter traffic on the 520 and 405. Once they merged onto I-90 east, the congestion eased, and the drive became smooth. Snow became visible as they passed North Bend, but the roads were freshly plowed and salted, ensuring safe passage. At exit 52, Sergey and Viktor turned left with their comrades in tow, passing under the freeway overpass. A short mile later, they arrived at the Alpental Ski Resort parking lot, which was bustling with skiers and snowboarders eager to enjoy the fresh early-season powder. As they drove through the upper lot, Sergey's eyes scanned the vehicles and landed on Brody Hayes' black Jeep, partially buried under several feet of snow from the night before. He noted its location but didn't linger, continuing to the lower lot. There, they found a space near the ledge overlooking the South Fork of the Snoqualmie River. The scene was alive with activity, but Sergey's focus remained fixed on the task ahead. The operatives were one step closer to their quarry.

Large snowflakes melted on the Subaru's hot hood but quickly overwhelmed the heat, accumulating in a thickening layer. The five KGR operatives exited their vehicles, unloading their gear and packing their rucksacks with practiced efficiency. They strapped on their brand-new snowshoes, adjusted their trekking poles, and concealed their weapons inside their down jackets. The suppressed AR-15s were slung across their shoulders, the stocks pressing uncomfortably into their chests. For Viktor, every movement sent sharp, agonizing pain radiating from his injured ribs. The black suppressors hung low, protruding slightly from beneath their jackets, but the operatives' attire blended seamlessly into the sea of skiers and snowboarders dressed in similar dark winter gear. While someone deliberately searching for weapons might have spotted the protrusions, no one at the ski resort was looking for Russian operatives. Everyone was focused on their own purpose—carving through fresh powder or enjoying the slopes. The KGR agents planned to keep their weapons concealed until they reached the trail beyond the crowds of hikers and outdoor enthusiasts. Once they were confident they were alone, they would pull them out and prepare for the next phase of their mission.

Sergey powered on his Garmin GPS, clipped to a carabiner on his shoulder strap, and quickly plotted their course to Snow Lake. The operatives moved methodically, crossing the two parking lots through several feet of freshly fallen snow with unsuspicious caution. As they reached the trailhead, they passed by several excited groups, all gearing up for their adventures in the blizzard-like conditions. Laughter and chatter filled the air, blending with the crunch of boots on snow. To onlookers, the five KGR operatives appeared no different from the average Seattleite weekend warriors—a group of recreationists heading out to enjoy a scenic hike in the snowy Cascades. Their shiny new gear and casual demeanor perfectly masked their deadly intent, allowing them to melt into the bustling winter crowd.

CHAPTER 30

Snow Lake

Snoqualmie Pass, Washington

With trembling hands and labored breaths, Brody pulled out his iPhone and switched it off airplane mode. Instantly, the screen flooded with an onslaught of notifications—texts, missed calls, and voicemails from friends, family, and local authorities. His shaking finger dragged across the cold glass, scrolling through the horrific messages. Desperation filled him as he searched for any sign that it wasn't true, silently praying for a miracle. Nearby, Maddy struggled to breathe, her body convulsing in a full-blown panic attack. She was a collapsed heap of down and GORE-TEX in the falling snow, gasping and sobbing uncontrollably. Numb and overwhelmed, Brody sank into the snow beside her. For a long moment, he sat motionless, staring blankly at his phone. Finally, with reluctant resolve, he dialed Bill, their neighbor who lived directly across the street from where their home had once stood.

"Brody! Thank God you're alive! I'm so sorry," Bill's voice answered, thick with emotion. There was a pause, filled with silence and unspoken pain. "There are no words."

"What's going on, Bill? Tell me this is a joke," Brody choked out, his voice cracking as he spoke into the phone's microphone, his heart bracing for an answer he couldn't bear to hear.

"I'm so sorry, Brody. I wish to God it was a joke," Bill said, his voice heavy with grief. "There was a gas explosion. It happened in the middle of the night. Bridget and the kids didn't make it. I'm so sorry."

"What?" Brody's voice cracked with desperation. "Maddy is with me. We're up at Snow Lake. How could we have a gas leak? We have CO2-sensor alarms!" His mind raced, clinging to disbelief as he searched for answers, trying to reconcile the unimaginable.

"Maddy's with you?" Bill's tone shifted to a mixture of confusion and relief. "The news is saying they found three bodies. They assumed it was Bridget and the kids since your Jeep was gone." Brody's heart skipped a beat. Bill's relief that Maddy was alive was palpable, but his words hung heavy in the air.

Then who was the third body?

Brody disconnected the call and wrapped his arms tightly around Maddy. He sat there, numb, unable to cry. The weight of the news felt surreal, as if his mind refused to process the magnitude of the situation. Overwhelmed and paralyzed by shock, he could only hold her as they both shook, their bodies trembling in the cold while snow slowly accumulated on their hunched forms.

"Maddy," Brody finally said, his voice trembling but steady enough to break through the fog. "We need to get up and move. We need to get back to camp, grab our snowshoes and the car keys, and then we need to hike out." His words carried a tone of urgency, grounding them in the present. Despite the unbearable weight of grief hanging over them, survival instincts began to take hold. Slowly, they shifted, forcing their bodies to respond, knowing they couldn't stay frozen in place any longer.

Maddy couldn't speak. Brody gently helped her to her feet, and together they began their slow descent. She followed her dad's lead in silence, unable to think or process anything on her own. Both moved in a zombie-like state, their steps unsteady as they slipped and slid on the snow-covered path. The snow fell harder, swirling around them in relentless flurries. Tears streamed down their faces, blurring their already distorted vision. The crushing weight of grief and the nausea that accompanied it overwhelmed their ability to concentrate. At one point, Maddy stopped abruptly, her body heaving as she vomited the remnants of her breakfast into the snow. Brody knelt beside her, holding her ponytail back until the dry heaving subsided. He placed a steadying hand on her shoulder, silently willing her to continue. It would have been easy to stay there, to collapse into the snow and become a permanent part of the mountain. The thought of freezing to death held a morbid appeal, a numbing escape from their incomprehensible pain. But they had each other. Deep down, they both knew there was still a reason to keep moving, though the thought barely felt real. With sheer determination, Brody found the strength to push forward, guiding Maddy step by agonizing step. One foot in front of the other, they pressed on, clinging to the fragile thread of survival.

What began as a picture-perfect morning had quickly unraveled into a nightmare. Brody and Maddy had never imagined their day could take such a horrific turn. Now, they faced the unthinkable—miles still to hike back to the Jeep and another 30 minutes of driving to confront a grim reality. Worse yet, there was nothing left to return to. Their home, their life as they knew it, was gone. It didn't feel real. As they stumbled into their snow-enveloped camp, the weight of grief bore down on them. For Maddy, that grief suddenly erupted into anger, sharp and raw.

"Why did you make us come early?" she snapped, her voice trembling with rage and sorrow. "If we had waited a day, we'd be with Mom and Mitch!" Her words hung heavy in the frigid air, the accusation stinging even as Brody struggled to process it. He knew her anger wasn't truly aimed at him—it was the pain speaking, lashing out in search of someone to blame. But that didn't make it any easier to hear.

That judging thought had already been haunting Brody's mind, replaying over and over as he imagined scenarios that could have changed what happened. Rationally, he knew there was nothing they could have done, no version of events that would have altered the tragic outcome. But still, he couldn't stop entertaining the impossible "what-ifs," as though clinging to them might rewrite the past. Deep down, he also knew the natural gas explosion would have killed them all if they had been home. And somehow, that thought— being together in death—felt almost preferable to the unbearable weight of surviving. The guilt crushed him, but he swallowed it down, pushing it aside. He didn't respond to Maddy's rhetorical outburst. Instead, he silently validated her feelings, acknowledging the impossible scenario she voiced without argument. He gave her the space to process her grief in her way, even as it burned like an open wound. Right now, Brody needed to focus. They had to get to the Jeep, to Snoqualmie, to find answers—answers he wasn't sure he was ready to face but knew they had to seek.

With minimal supplies packed into their backpacks and snowshoes strapped on, Brody and Maddy prepared for the climb back up to the saddle. It wasn't even noon, but the emotional toll of the morning had left them both drained and dehydrated. Brody gently encouraged his distraught daughter to take a few sips of water before they began. She reluctantly complied, her movements slow and mechanical. They ascended the hill in silence; each lost in their thoughts. Brody's thousand-yard stare reflected a familiarity with trauma, the product of past battles fought and scars carried. For Maddy, the blank, hollow feeling was new and terrible—a weight no one her age should have to bear.

Reaching the saddle, Brody had them pause. The snowfall had intensified into a whiteout, obliterating the tracks they'd made the day before. He scanned the featureless landscape, carefully plotting their descent to the main trail. Any wrong step could be fatal, and he knew they weren't at their sharpest. Both their situational awareness and decision-making ability were dulled by exhaustion and grief. Pulling out his Garmin GPS, Brody retraced their route using the trail map, overlaying their path with care. Taking no chances, they slid on their harnesses and roped up for safety. With gravity on their side, they descended quickly through the series of steep switchbacks. Brody led with diligence, carefully directing their path. A single misstep could send them sliding into a tree well or tumbling down a steep embankment. Each step was deliberate, each decision calculated as they navigated their way down the snowy slope, their survival hinging on focus and resilience.

They reached the main trail, a relatively level path heading east for a couple of miles, which would eventually end at the trailhead in the Alpental parking lot. Despite their exhaustion, they moved efficiently, though cautiously, post-holing through deep, untouched snow. The trail was eerily quiet, with no sign of other climbers or campers for miles. The fresh snow heightened the risk in avalanche-prone areas that they needed to cross. They both knew the dangers, yet neither spoke of the dark thoughts lingering in the back of their minds. The idea of an avalanche burying them—a swift, final escape from the unbearable pain—briefly flickered in their consciousness. But they pushed those thoughts aside. Both Brody and Maddy understood that such a mindset was a dangerous foothold for despair. They were still alive for a reason, even if that reason felt incomprehensible in the moment. They clung to their faith, believing that God had a plan. It made no sense now, and the pain seemed insurmountable, but they resolved to trust in that purpose as they trudged forward through the unrelenting snow.

"Dad, what's that?" Maddy broke the silence, her voice trembling slightly as she pointed ahead.

Brody squinted through the heavy snowfall, trying to focus on what she'd seen. Emerging from the trees about 200 yards up the trail, a group of 4-5 hikers in snowshoes appeared. Their pace was steady, cutting an unfamiliar silhouette against the white backdrop. Between the Hayes and the approaching group lay the large, snow-covered talus field they had observed the day before. The chunky remnants of a recent avalanche were now buried under the fresh snowfall from last night, giving the terrain a deceptively smooth appearance. Above, the massive cornice they had noted yesterday still loomed ominously, an ever-present reminder of the mountain's power and unpredictability. Brody's instincts kicked in as he evaluated the situation. "Let's pause here," he said quietly, his voice calm but firm. The trail was narrowing, the risks heightened by the hazardous terrain and the uncertain intentions of the figures approaching through the storm.

"Looks like some hikers," Brody said, squinting through the snow. "Let's let them cross the avalanche field first. We don't want to get stuck in the middle if that thing gets triggered. Grab some water while we wait."

As Maddy reached for her half-frozen Nalgene bottle, something about the lead hiker's body language caught her attention. Their pace was no longer casual. "Dad?" she said, her voice tinged with unease.

"I see it, Maddy," Brody replied, his eyes narrowing as he watched the group. The snowshoers were accelerating toward them, their pace aggressive and unsettling.

Did they see something we didn't? A bear? An avalanche?

But as the group closed the distance, Brody's chest tightened. What had initially appeared to be trekking poles were now unmistakably assault rifles, slung low and ready.

"MADDY, TURN AND RUN!" Brody shouted, his voice slicing through the storm as adrenaline surged through his body.

PART III

THE RECKONING

CHAPTER 31

Snow Lake Trail

Snoqualmie Pass, Washington

Maddy yanked her right snowshoe free from the snow and pivoted sharply to her right. Her left foot followed in a seamless motion, her backpack remaining steady to avoid throwing her off balance. Confusion, fear, and adrenaline surged through her in an unfamiliar, volatile cocktail, propelling her into a swift stride as she sprinted in the opposite direction. Just inches behind her, her father heard the sharp, unnerving crack of .223 Remington rounds splintering the spruce trees along the snowy trail. A surge of rage blazed through him, his eyes narrowing as his breath quickened. Triggered by the threat, Brody snapped into autopilot—protecting his daughter while his mind burned with the need for vengeance against their attackers.

Branches and bark splintered from the trees above as rogue bullets tore through the canopy, their crack-thump sound betraying their supersonic speed. Instinct took over—Brody lunged toward Maddy, tackling her to the ground and pressing her flat against the snowy forest floor.

* * *

In that moment, he wasn't in the freezing temperatures of the Pacific Northwest. He was back in the dusty, rugged mountains outside Kandahar, Afghanistan, running toward enemy fire to extract the aircrew and Army Rangers from a downed UH-60 Black Hawk. It was October 2001, and the U.S. Army's 75th Ranger Regiment had parachuted into an airfield for a high-stakes reconnaissance mission. The operation—dubbed Operation Rhino—would later become mired in controversy, criticized for prioritizing a White House photo opportunity over meticulous preparation for enemy resistance. Though intelligence reports had indicated no significant Taliban presence, the Ranger Reconnaissance team prepared for the worst. They knew the unforgiving nature of combat rarely conformed to predictions. B-2 Stealth Bombers and AC-130 gunships unleashed devastating aerial strikes, pounding the target with overwhelming firepower before the Rangers' nighttime drop under zero illumination. The bombardment eliminated numerous Taliban fighters, forcing others to retreat into the shadows. Once on the ground, the Rangers swiftly secured the base and airstrip, a critical foothold that would later serve as Camp Rhino. The base would become a launchpad for forward operations conducted by the 15th Marine Expeditionary Unit and the U.S. Army's 101st Airborne Division, solidifying the U.S. presence in Kandahar and intensifying the push into Taliban-controlled territory.

During the extraction, an Army UH-60 Black Hawk's tail rotor was struck by a Taliban rocket-propelled grenade. The aircraft successfully autorotated into the mountains south of Camp Rhino, but its crew quickly found themselves surrounded by enemy forces armed with small arms. Brody Hayes and his U.S. Navy Helicopter Combat Crew, deployed as a detachment in Pakistan, were assisting with combat search and rescue (CSAR) missions in the wake of 9/11 and the launch of the Global War on Terror. Their HH-60H Sikorsky helicopter had been on standby during Operation Rhino and launched immediately upon receiving the call about the downed Army helicopter. Two AH-64 Apache helicopters accompanied the Navy HH-60H, laying down a relentless barrage of aerial firepower as Brody's team approached the landing zone (LZ).

Hayes and another CSAR crewman disembarked as the two door gunners aboard the Sikorsky remained to provide suppressive fire. The deafening 150-decibel roar of the engines and the powerful downdraft from the spinning rotors kicking up debris didn't faze the two NVG-equipped crewmen as they sprinted toward the fight. At the crash site, the UH-60 personnel had established a defensive perimeter, successfully avoiding casualties. The hillside erupted as the Apaches unleashed a devastating onslaught of 70 mm rockets and Hellfire missiles, their explosive detonations blending with the whizzing and popping of small arms fire and tracer rounds cutting through the night sky. Miraculously, all the Army crew and Rangers were extracted with only minor injuries—a testament to their rigorous training and the rapid response of the CSAR team.

* * *

BOOM!

The thunderous roar of an explosion rocked the valley, shaking the earth beneath them. The KGR operatives, moving in a staggered single-file line across the exposed clearing, froze mid-step. Weapons shouldered, they had been firing suppressed semi-automatic bursts, but the unexpected blast stopped them cold. Instantly, they hit the snowy ground, flattening themselves to become smaller targets. Hearts pounding, they scanned the forest for the source of the deafening retaliation, their minds racing to make sense of the sudden turn of events.

On the south side of the I-90 freeway, the Snoqualmie Pass Ski Patrol was carrying out its routine avalanche control operations. After heavy snowfall, they coordinated with the Washington State Department of Transportation to temporarily close eastbound and westbound traffic, ensuring safety as they triggered potential avalanche hazards along the freeway. For decades, the patrol had relied on an M60 tank to fire explosives, but now they used a Howitzer to launch 105 mm artillery shells. These shells were directed at 30 designated avalanche tracks, strategically detonating unstable snowpack to proactively mitigate the risk of devastating natural avalanches that could endanger passing motorists and outdoor enthusiasts.

It took Brody a moment to process his surroundings, to register what was happening, and to snap back to reality. His focus locked onto Maddy, who lay beneath him, frozen in a panicked state of shock. She struggled instinctively, wanting to get up and run, but her father's weight pinned her firmly to the ground, shielding her from danger. Two hundred yards behind them, Aleksandr and his team were similarly thrown into disarray, the deafening explosion disrupting their assault. For a brief moment, confusion reigned, until Oleg, at the front of the formation, bellowed, "RETREAT!"

The shockwave and vibrations from the 105 mm explosions rippled through the mountain valley, triggering a fissure that released the massive cornice hanging precariously above the Russians' vulnerable position. A bus-sized block of ice broke free, crashing 100 feet down onto the 45-degree slope below. The impact instantly fractured the upper layer of the snowpack, unleashing a massive slab avalanche. With each passing second, the torrent of snow and ice gained momentum, fed by the relentless pull of gravity. It roared down the mountainside, tearing apart everything in its path. The deafening sound thundered through the gorge, accompanied by a choking cloud of airborne snow and debris. Across the valley, skiers and snowboarders paused to listen, unable to see the unfolding chaos but feeling the ground tremble beneath them.

The five KGR agents scrambled to react, but panic overtook them. They tripped over their snowshoes and each other, clawing and fumbling as they tried to escape the oncoming devastation. Pavel and Sergey managed to stagger to their feet and dive for cover in the shelter of the tree line. Behind them, Viktor, Aleksandr, and Oleg were caught in the icy tidal wave, swept away by its crushing force. The avalanche roared with unrelenting power, ripping 100-year-old trees from their roots and carrying them down the mountain. Pavel pointed frantically toward Viktor and Aleksandr, their bodies tumbling uncontrollably near the edge of the avalanche's fall line. The valley echoed with destruction as nature claimed its path, leaving no mercy in its wake.

Oleg was nowhere to be seen. The initial force of the avalanche had slammed the air from his lungs as he twisted helplessly in the violent, churning chaos—the deadly "washing machine" of snow and ice. The crushing force entombed his body in suffocating layers, as he tumbled in and out of consciousness. His harrowing ride came to a brutal halt when he collided with a 160-foot Douglas fir. The impact shattered his spine, sending instant shutdown signals through his central nervous system. His lifeless body would remain buried in the snow, undiscovered until the spring thaw.

Meanwhile, Brody and Maddy seized the distraction as their chance to move. Staying low, they crept further down the trail, out of the avalanche's path and away from their armed pursuers. Yet, despite the urgency, they couldn't resist glancing back to witness the breathtaking power of nature's wrath. From their safe vantage point, they watched the massive wave of snow and debris consume everything in its path with unrelenting ferocity. For Brody, the scene struck differently. He had been involved in numerous avalanches throughout his mountain-guiding career—usually on the other side, conducting rescues or recoveries. He was used to employing avalanche beacons, probes, and shovels to locate the buried and save lives. But today, he was forced to leave others behind, to abandon those who might be injured, trapped, or dead. His only mission was to protect Maddy and get her to safety. Nothing else mattered.

CHAPTER 32

Snow Lake Trail

Snoqualmie Pass, Washington

"Aleksandr! Are you okay?" Pavel shouted from the safety of the trees.

The silence that followed the avalanche was as unsettling as the violent chaos that had preceded it. Sergey and Pavel dropped their rucksacks and weapons, moving cautiously toward the broken, unsettled snow in search of survivors.

"There!" Pavel pointed roughly 300 yards down the slope. Both men scrambled to reach their comrades, their snowshoes clogging with snow and sending them sliding and tumbling at times. Aleksandr and Viktor were partially buried but alive, each struggling to free themselves from the icy grip. Pavel reached Aleksandr first, dropping to his knees and feverishly digging with his hands to unearth their leader. Nearby, Sergey worked to free Viktor, who was gasping for breath and coughing up blood that splattered against the pristine white snow. Unbeknownst to him, the sheer force of the avalanche had driven a broken rib shard into his lung, causing a pneumothorax. Though Viktor's breathing was shallow and strained, the fact that he was still able to draw air gave him a sliver of hope. Pain coursed through his chest with every breath, but in his mind, he convinced himself that he could press on. For now, survival was his only option.

"Where's Oleg?" Aleksandr asked, his voice strained as Pavel pulled him to safety.

The mountainside was a scene of utter devastation. It looked as if a nuclear bomb had detonated, obliterating everything in its path. There was no sign of Oleg. Deep down, they all knew there was no chance of finding him alive. Even if he had survived the initial impact, the suffocating weight of the snow would have claimed him long ago. The operatives knew their priority now was survival. They needed to recover their weapons and gear, assess their injuries, and press on with their mission. The deafening sound of the avalanche was likely to attract locals, adding an urgent need to move quickly and discreetly. With two men down and one gravely injured, the KGR operatives found themselves fueled by a growing hunger for revenge.

"Dad, who were those men? Why would they shoot at us?" Maddy asked, her voice trembling as they hurried back toward Snow Lake. Her wide, dazed eyes reflected a mix of fear and confusion, but she kept moving, driven by her father's urgent pace.

"I don't know, honey," Brody said, his voice heavy with emotion as the pieces of the puzzle began to fall into place. "I think they might be the reason my Navy crew is dead or missing—and why Mom and Mitch are gone." He paused, clearing his throat to steady himself. "But I don't know who they are or why they're after us. Right now, we just need to keep moving."

The snow continued to fall, but it was lighter now, and the winds had calmed. Despite the more manageable weather, the freezing temperatures clung to them like a constant reminder of their peril. The only sounds were the crunch of snow beneath their snowshoes and their labored breathing, each step a struggle against exhaustion and fear. Brody's mind raced as he silently assessed their options. The trail behind them was no longer viable, especially if the assault team had survived the avalanche. Moving forward, past the switchbacks to the lake, would leave them exposed in the wide-open cirque—a prime area for backcountry skiers but a tactical nightmare for staying hidden. That path led toward Chair Peak, but the risk of being spotted was far too high. His only feasible choice was to climb back up to the saddle. It was their best shot at gaining enough elevation to get a signal and call for help. Brody's jaw tightened with resolve. The climb wouldn't be easy, especially with Maddy in tow, but it was their only hope.

By the time they reached the sharp turn to the switchback, their leg muscles were screaming with fatigue, and both were desperate for hydration. The relentless series of events had drained their energy reserves, forcing them to pause and take a drink. Brody sat in silence, his eyes scanning the path they had retreated from, his ears straining for any sign of their pursuers. Nothing. No human sounds, no birds, no movement—just the eerie quiet of a gentle snow flurry. It all felt surreal, like a dream. Or rather, a nightmare. Without the aid of a climbing rope, Maddy took the lead up the mountain. She carefully followed the remnants of their earlier trail, now partially obscured by the morning's fresh snowfall. Brody trailed behind, silently praying for heavier snow to cover their tracks and conceal their path. But his prayers went unanswered; if anything, the snowfall was beginning to lighten. The thought of leaving a breadcrumb trail for their pursuers gnawed at him, but he had no choice. They needed to gain elevation and find a signal. Every few minutes, they both stopped to check their phones for a flicker of connectivity, but the screens remained frustratingly empty of bars. With each step up the steep incline, Brody's resolve hardened. They had to keep moving, no matter how exhausted they were—because stopping wasn't an option.

At the final switchback before reaching the top of the saddle, both climbers felt their phones vibrate as new messages filtered in. Determined not to stop short of the summit, they pushed through the last stretch before pulling out their devices. Maddy quickly scrolled through her notifications, seeing the familiar stream of condolences mixed with newfound relief—messages celebrating the news that she was alive. The shift in focus momentarily yanked her mind from the urgency of survival to the crushing reality that her mom and brother were gone forever. She stood in silence, her breath shallow as the gut-wrenching weight of grief hit her like a blow to the stomach. Her body, dehydrated and fatigued, struggled to produce tears, leaving her pain raw and unrelenting. She wiped at her dry eyes, feeling the ache deepen as sobs refused to surface.

Brody raised his iPhone to his face, unlocking the screen with a defeated sigh. He buried his turmoil, forcing it down as he scrolled through his recent calls. His cold, trembling finger hovered over Bridget and Mitch's names, their entries hauntingly fresh in his call log. He hesitated before sliding past them and stopping on the name he knew he could trust: Conrad Jacobia. Conrad, a Senior Chief Aircrewman currently serving with Naval Air Station Whidbey Island Search and Rescue, had been one of Brody's protégés early in his Navy career. Over the years, the two had forged an unbreakable bond, a brotherhood strengthened through shared service. Now, both settled in the Pacific Northwest, their friendship extended beyond their military roots to a shared love of mountaineering, biking, snowboarding, and family barbecues. Brody knew Conrad was his best chance at help—someone he could rely on when it mattered most.

"Hayes, it's good to hear from you. I'm so sorry…" Conrad began.

"Maddy and I need your help!" Brody cut him off, his tone sharp and urgent.

"Wait, what? I thought—"

"I know. I heard from my neighbor," Brody interrupted again. "Maddy is here with me, and we were just shot at by a group of armed men." He fired the information in rapid succession, barely pausing for breath.

"Slow down, Brody. What men? Where are you guys?" Conrad's voice was steady but edged with concern as he tried to process what his friend was saying.

"We're at Snow Lake," Brody answered, his words tumbling out. "Bridget and Mitch were supposed to meet us today. We got the news about them when we climbed up to the saddle this morning.

We tried to hike out, but we ran into four or five men with assault rifles. They shot at us!"

"Someone shot at you?" Conrad's voice sharpened with disbelief.

"Yes! Suppressed fire, too!" Brody replied, his tone urgent. "We ran back toward the lake, and now we're at the saddle. On the way, an avalanche came down near the main trailhead. I don't know if it hit the men or not, but we need an emergency evac!" His plea was laced with desperation as he leaned on his SAR brother.

"Of course!" Conrad answered without hesitation. "My crew just briefed for a training flight up near Baker. I'll change our mission set and brief them in the air. We can be at the lake within the hour."

"I don't know who those guys are or if they made it through the avalanche," Brody continued, "but I'll take Maddy to the north side of the lake and wait for extraction."

"Got it. We'll be there. Stay safe, Brody," Conrad reassured him.

"Thank you, brother. I owe you," Brody said, his emotional voice thick with gratitude.

CHAPTER 33

Snow Lake Trail

Snoqualmie Pass, Washington

Maddy sat slumped over on an outcropping of snow-covered rocks, light flakes gently accumulating on her beanie. Her damp gloves pressed against her face as she wept, her body too exhausted to shield her emotions any longer. She could hear her dad on the phone, making plans for their extraction, but the weight of grief and fatigue had drained her of the energy and purpose to keep going.

"Honey, we need to keep moving," Brody said gently, kneeling in front of her. "There's nothing we can do to change the past, but we can change what happens now. Mom and Mitch would want us to keep going." His voice was soft yet firm, a desperate attempt to coax his emotionally paralyzed daughter forward. He wasn't just trying to convince her—he was trying to convince himself, too. Brody had learned through his years in the military and mountaineering that serving others in moments of despair created a powerful feedback loop. By focusing on helping others survive, it provided the distraction and determination he needed to lead, even when his own hope was running dry. But this moment was unlike anything he'd faced before. The crushing grief and the constant danger made him feel like he had nothing left to live for—except for Maddy.

Keeping her alive was all that mattered now, and that purpose was enough to keep him moving.

Reluctantly, Maddy stood and began moving her feet toward the lakeside of the saddle. They descended along their earlier, partially covered footprints, now sunken into the snow. The storm had eased, with lighter flakes falling and pockets of blue sky breaking through the clouds that shrouded the surrounding peaks. A few miles to the east, hundreds of skiers and snowboarders reveled in the fresh dump of powder at the resort, blissfully unaware of the harrowing events unfolding to their west. Many of them would read about it on social media the following day, embellishing posts for their followers, claiming they were traumatized and narrowly escaped danger—overdramatizing as if they'd been at risk themselves.

Brody paused often during their descent, scanning their six for any signs of pursuit. But the forest was quiet, save for the crunch of snow underfoot. When they reached their campsite, it was barely recognizable under the fresh snowfall, with only glimpses of bright orange nylon peeking through the drifts where their tents were buried. They dropped their packs and spent a few minutes digging out the shelter to crawl inside and retrieve additional gear. For Maddy, it felt like an impossible task. Every movement drained her, and her depleted body was overwhelmed by waves of hunger, nausea, and vertigo. Her vision blurred, and a sense of futility gnawed at her.

Why bother?

She struggled to care about gathering personal items, but Brody insisted, calling out what to take and what to leave. His voice was steady, commanding, and unyielding, driving her to push through her haze of despair, even as every fiber of her being begged her to stop.

Brody planned to wait at the north end of the frozen lake for their helicopter extraction, but kept their options open. He knew they could retreat in a few directions if necessary or, worst-case scenario, dig a snow cave for shelter overnight. They left behind the tents, sleeping pads, and sleeping bags, focusing on what they could carry for survival. They stuffed their backpacks with clothing, the JetBoil, fuel canisters, headlamps, batteries, and the remaining food. Already burdened with ice axes, crampons, harnesses, climbing rope, and pickets from earlier, their loads were heavy, but they couldn't risk being unprepared if the NAS Whidbey SAR helicopter couldn't reach them and they had to hike out or spend another night.

His daughter was a shadow of the witty, capable young woman she'd been just that morning, before her world had been shattered. The devastation of sudden loss tears the soul apart like nothing else. No words or actions could mend such heartbreak—only time could attempt to heal the wound. Grief is a relentless force, striking each person in its own brutal way. It paralyzes, consumes, and lingers. Sometimes, it seems to recede, only to return with a vengeance, sharper than before. It defies logic, yet we keep trying to reason with it. We deny. We bargain. We rail at God in fury, desperate for answers. We can't comprehend His plan, and we don't agree with it—it doesn't align with ours. Yet, the questions persist, and the ache remains.

Brody was grappling with the same grief as Maddy, but had to suppress it to lead them both to safety. Every step forward was a battle against the pain that threatened to overwhelm him. When he urged Maddy to keep moving, her eyes burned with anger and hopelessness, as if blaming him for what had happened—or accusing him of not caring as much as she did. It hurt deeply. Brody had faced trauma his entire life: from childhood abuse, to harrowing war zones, to deadly mountaineering disasters. He had witnessed death beyond what any human should endure. But this—this was different. This was his wife. His son. No amount of past pain could prepare him for the depth of this loss. Yet, he couldn't let himself crumble. He had to harden his mind, bury his grief, and be the strength Maddy needed to survive. Delivering his remaining child from evil was his sole purpose now.

With their heavy packs strapped on, they marched out of the snow-buried camp, carving fresh tracks in the deep snowpack. The trail was barely visible, leading tightly along the eastern edge of the frozen lake, perched ten feet high on the steep hillside. The distance wasn't far, but the snowy conditions would make the trek slow and grueling. Brody's priority was to reach the lake's northern side as early as possible to create a clear landing zone (LZ). If the area proved too hazardous for landing, they could at least find a place to be hoisted through the trees. The weather wasn't ideal—intermittent visibility and gusting winds—but the NAS Whidbey SAR team were professionals, skilled at assessing the risks for a successful extraction. Having a former SAR member on the ground was rare but would undoubtedly expedite the rescue. Stomping out an LZ would be labor-intensive, but the physical effort would provide a welcome distraction for both Brody and Maddy. The rhythmic crunch of snow underfoot would give them something tangible to focus on, pushing their grief momentarily aside. They both knew there would be time to mourn later. For now, survival demanded their full attention. The tasks within their control were the only things keeping them moving forward.

CHAPTER 34

Naval Air Station Whidbey Island
Oak Harbor, Washington

An hour before receiving Brody's call, Senior Chief Conrad Jacobia sat in the NAS Whidbey SAR squadron ready room, briefing with his aircrew. Commander Regina Gladwell was the Helicopter Aircraft Commander (HAC), with Lieutenant Scott Thomas serving as her Co-Pilot. Senior Chief Jacobia, the Crew Chief, was joined by Petty Officer Mike Tofino, the Second Crewman and Rescue Swimmer, and Petty Officer Drew Washburn, the Flight Corpsman. Their planned mission was to conduct overwater rescue qualifications in the Puget Sound before heading east to train in overland rescue techniques and snow mountain landings near Mount Baker in the North Cascade Range. As with any training flight, their operations in the mountains would depend on the on-scene visibility and weather conditions. Each decision would be made carefully, balancing training objectives with safety.

The morning began with less-than-ideal flying weather, low clouds blanketing the area, though forecasts predicted it would burn off in the coming hours. The entire crew was aware of the Hayes house gas explosion, but Conrad Jacobia had been unable to get in touch with Brody. The lingering uncertainty weighed on him, and he briefly considered trying to excuse himself from the training flight to search for answers. However, with a shortage of available crewmen, he decided to complete the mission as planned, resolving to head straight to Snoqualmie once they landed and try again to contact his missing friend.

After the flight crew briefing, they had two hours to grab food before gearing up for their 3.5-hour training operation. Jacobia made his way to the squadron's snack shack, opting for a burger and fries. As he was about to take a bite, his phone buzzed. That's when his screen lit up with an incoming call from Brody Hayes.

"Commander Gladwell, have you seen Tofino?" Senior Chief Jacobia burst into the ready room moments later, his voice sharp with earnestness and his demeanor tense.

"He was prepping the rescue litter down in the PR shop. What's going on, Senior Chief?" Commander Gladwell asked, her tone sharp with concern.

"I just got off the phone with Hayes," Jacobia replied, his urgency evident. "He and his daughter are at Snoqualmie Pass and need an immediate evac! They were hiking out after hearing the news about his wife and son, and they were shot at by some men near the trailhead. They're heading back to Snow Lake and will secure a location for extraction on the north side of the lake."

"Slow down, Senior," Commander Gladwell interjected, trying to process the rapid flow of information. "Hayes was shot at?"

"I have no idea what's going on, but I trust Hayes!" Jacobia said firmly. "If he says he's in trouble, then we owe it to him to investigate."

"Agreed," Gladwell said, her voice steady despite the tension. "Lieutenant Thomas, Petty Officer Washburn, let's gear up and get out to the flight line for pre-flight. I'll inform maintenance of the situation and we'll brief the specifics in the air. Senior Chief Jacobia, get Tofino prepped and let the AOs know to arm the aircraft. I don't want to go in unprepared if Hayes took fire."

"Yes, ma'am!" Jacobia responded, already moving toward the PR shop as the crew sprang into action.

Tofino unknowingly strolled out of the head, oblivious to the urgency in the ready room. He had just finished wreaking havoc on the number two stall, courtesy of a lingering case of long-term IBS he'd picked up after his last deployment to the Persian Gulf.

"Get your gear on! We're launching to extract Hayes!" Jacobia shouted at his second crewman, snapping him out of his post-relief haze. Without waiting for a reply, Jacobia turned and sprinted toward the PR shop. A bewildered Tofino quickly followed.

The pilots and aircrew headed straight to their respective gear cages, grabbing survival vests, helmets, and the necessary equipment for the unexpected mission. Moving on autopilot, they ran through the motions of gearing up, well-practiced from countless overland rescue launches. Meanwhile, Jacobia briefed Tofino in quick, clipped sentences, keeping him up to speed as they prepared for departure.

Across the hangar, the AO (Aviation Ordnance) team worked efficiently, mounting M240 automatic machine guns on the helicopter's port and starboard door mounts. Green metal ammo cans, filled with linked 7.62 mm rounds, were carried over by other

AOs. Since the squadron's primary mission rarely—if ever—involved weapons, the team had retrieved the guns and ammunition from the base's EOD (Explosive Ordnance Disposal) unit. The uncharacteristic preparation underscored the seriousness of the situation. The crew moved like a well-oiled machine, each person focused on their task as the urgency of the moment pressed down on them. The rescue mission was rapidly taking shape, and the stakes were clear: this was no ordinary operation.

After completing a walk-around visual inspection of the aircraft, the pilots powered up the auxiliary power unit to conduct ground checks. Jacobia meticulously inspected the rescue hoist's mechanical controls and rigged the FRIES bar for rappelling, should it be required. Each aircrewman worked through their specific pre-flight checklist, their experience evident in their seamless efficiency. The MH-60S, a versatile combat helicopter, had replaced the legacy HH-60H that Brody Hayes had once flown during CSAR missions. Unlike its predecessor, the MH-60S was designed for a broader range of missions, including anti-surface warfare, combat support, humanitarian disaster relief, Combat Search and Rescue (CSAR), aeromedical evacuation, special warfare (SPECWAR), and airborne mine countermeasures. Equipped with cutting-edge technology, the aircraft featured a digital GPS map, AN/AAS-44 FLIR for enhanced situational awareness, and a robust electronic warfare self-defense suite. Its additional pylon allowed for the carriage of Hellfire air-to-surface missiles and MK54 digital torpedoes, while its cabin supported crew-served weapons, including 7.62 mm and .50-caliber guns mounted on port and starboard windows. The countermeasures suite included the Northrop Grumman AN/APR-39AV(2) radar warning system, the ATK AN/AAR-47V(2) missile warning system, and the BAE Systems IEWS AN/ALQ-144V(6) infrared countermeasures set. Although the MH-60S was mission-capable for this extensive array of operations, its primary role within NAS Whidbey SAR was overwater and overland search and rescue. The ability to reconfigure the cabin for each mission set—stripping it down or equipping it as necessary—was critical for the variety of rescues they routinely launched. This adaptability, combined with the crew's expertise, ensured they were prepared for whatever challenges lay ahead.

"NASWI Tower, FIREWOOD 616," Commander Gladwell radioed as they taxied down the runway.

"FIREWOOD 616, NASWI Tower," the dispatcher responded promptly.

"FIREWOOD 616 is changing mission-set and diverting to investigate possible climbers in distress. Stand by for location." Commander Gladwell glanced at the waypoint Senior Chief Jacobia had already plotted on her digital display. "NASWI Tower, location is 47°28'8.85" N, 121°27'49.91" W. Be advised, reports indicate the extraction may be hot."

"FIREWOOD 616, please repeat last," the dispatcher replied, the confusion in their voice unmistakable.

"The extraction may be *HOT!*" Gladwell repeated firmly. "Please radio JBLM and have a DUSTOFF crew on alert for assistance."

"Roger that, FIREWOOD 616," the dispatcher acknowledged. "Radioing JBLM to have a DUSTOFF alert helo standing by for assistance. Please check in when on scene—and please, be careful."

Gladwell's grip tightened on the cyclic as the MH-60S rolled forward. The weight of responsibility hung heavy in the cockpit, but the crew's focus was unshakable. This wasn't just a mission—it was a rescue of one of their own.

CHAPTER 35

Snow Lake

Snoqualmie Pass, Washington

WHOMP! WHOMP! WHOMP!

"Hear that, Maddy? FIREWOOD is inbound," Brody said, his voice cutting through the still air. He looked toward his distraught daughter, hoping the sound of the approaching NAS Whidbey SAR helicopter, callsign FIREWOOD, would temporarily lift her spirits.

The unmistakable *WHOMPING* of the main rotors echoed through the valley, blending with the high-pitched whine of the twin turbine engines. To Brody's seasoned ears, the distinct volume and tone told him the SAR team was moving fast—pushing hard toward their extraction point. The MH-60S was a sound he knew well, its presence both reassuring and urgent. The powerful noise reverberated off the mountain walls lining Interstate-90, carrying for miles. The thunderous vibrations shook the snow-laden peaks, triggering minor avalanches deep in the surrounding hills. As the sound grew louder, Brody felt a glimmer of hope—a brief reprieve from the relentless grief and fear that had consumed them all day. Help was coming.

"Keep moving! We're almost to the clearing!" Brody urged, his voice filled with a newfound energy. Fueled by hope, he and Maddy moved efficiently to the north side of the frozen, snow-covered lake.

As soon as they arrived, Maddy dropped her pack, ready to signal the pilots on their approach. Brody scanned the area, knowing the crew would likely make a pass to assess the winds and determine the safest SAR approach. He quickly evaluated their surroundings: the tall trees posed a significant risk for rotor strikes, and the ice covering the lake wasn't thick enough to support the 8-ton rescue helicopter. A hoist extraction would be their only option. He briefed Maddy on the plan, explaining what to expect. Together, they arranged their packs and gathered downed branches from under the trees to create visual references for the pilots. Brody knew the hurricane-force winds generated by the MH-60S's main rotors would whip up snow and debris, drastically reducing visibility. They needed to make their position as clear as possible before the aircraft arrived. When the helo approached, Brody would use hand signals to guide the pilots, relying on his years of experience to help effect the rescue. The sound of the approaching rotors two valleys over grew louder, the anticipation and adrenaline building with each passing moment.

"1,000 feet and passing mountains on the left. Clear of mountains and coming left," Lieutenant Thomas communicated, pressing his left foot pedal and gently pulling the cyclic control to angle the helicopter left. The aircrew in the cabin confirmed the clearance of hazards, assisting with navigation through the closed doors. "Transferring controls to HAC."

"HAC has controls. Aft, rig for rescue and ready weapons," Commander Gladwell instructed, her voice calm yet commanding.

The three aircrewmen immediately set to work, executing their well-rehearsed plan. During pre-flight and transit, they had prepared the cabin for both a hoist and a rappel insertion, in case the LZ was compromised. Jacobia and Tofino slid open the port and starboard gunner's windows, securing the mounted M240 machine guns. Both men worked in tandem, charging their weapons by pulling the cocking handle back and locking the bolt in the rear position. They opened the cover and feed assembly, carefully threading the linked belt of 7.62 mm rounds into the feed tray. After securing the ammunition, they closed the cover assembly, switched the safety to the "F" position, and announced their readiness.

"Aft rigged for rescue. Port and starboard weapons locked and loaded," Senior Chief Jacobia confirmed over the intercom, his voice steady despite the rising tension.

Sliding the starboard cabin door open, Jacobia was hit with an icy blast of air that immediately engulfed the cramped space. The frigid wind burned the exposed skin on his cheeks—the small area left vulnerable between his helmet's face shield and facemask. Outside, the stark winter landscape rushed beneath them, and the stakes of the mission became even more palpable.

"Roger that. Dropping to 500 feet ground clearance at 50 knots. Remaining parallel to the starboard-side cliffs. Senior Chief, keep an eye on our rotor clearance," Commander Gladwell instructed, her tone steady.

"Yes, ma'am. Holy crap! We're passing over the avalanche area Hayes mentioned. I don't see how anyone could have survived that!" Jacobia reported, his eyes scanning the debris field below. The entire aircrew leaned forward, their trained eyes sweeping the terrain for any signs of movement or survivors.

WHOMP! WHOMP! WHOMP!

The pounding of the rotors reverberated through the mountains, the sound intensifying as they neared the hidden lake nestled in the high alpine. The MH-60S cut through the frigid air, its tactical landing approach taking it into the northern headwind. On the ground, Brody and Maddy crouched anxiously on the lake's north side, their eyes fixed southward, waiting for the helicopter to emerge from behind the ridgeline. The thunderous roar of the rotors grew closer, a promise of rescue but also a stark reminder of the nightmare they were still living. This part of their ordeal was almost over. Relief flickered at the edges of their fear, yet both dreaded what awaited them back in Snoqualmie. The shattered pieces of their lives were still there, waiting to be faced. For now, they focused on the immediate—the pounding approach of salvation through the snowy peaks.

"Coming up and right. Prepare for approach. Let's take a pass to check the winds and LZ. Keep a lookout for Hayes," Commander Gladwell instructed, her voice calm but focused. She pulled up the collective control, increasing elevation and power to clear the saddle. The helicopter smoothly gained altitude before beginning a gentle descent over the frozen lake, setting up for the final approach.

"Taking fire! Taking fire!" Jacobia's voice erupted through the internal communication system, cutting through the tension like a knife. Without hesitation, he depressed the M240's spade grips, unleashing a storm of 7.62 mm rounds and tracers toward the col's snow-covered rock outcropping and the tree line beyond.

Tofino immediately joined the fight, raking the port side of the mountain with equal ferocity. The sharp crack of machine gun fire filled the cabin as spruce pines splintered into shards, and bullet impacts tore through the deep snow and exposed the jagged igneous rock beneath. The mountainside erupted into chaos as debris sprayed in all directions, the relentless barrage silencing the attackers' position—or forcing them into retreat. Inside the cabin, the crew maintained their composure despite the pandemonium outside, their training taking over as they prepared to continue the approach under fire. The stakes had risen, but the mission remained the same: extract Hayes and Maddy at all costs.

Sparks exploded inside the cabin as a barrage of .223 Remington rounds tore into the exposed helicopter, which was struggling to lift over the saddle. The MH-60S jolted violently, lifting and banking hard to the right, sending the aircrew's stomachs into free fall. Lieutenant Thomas instinctively grabbed the controls as he saw Commander Gladwell slump forward, unconscious in her seat. A single 55-grain bullet had pierced the forward floor window, entering her right thigh and ripping upward through her body. Traveling at 3,000 feet per second, the round tore through vital organs, shattered bone, and exited through the top of her skull, punching through her helmet. She died instantly, and without a second's thought, her co-pilot seamlessly assumed control of the aircraft.

Inside the cabin, bullets ricocheted, shredding the walls and filling the air with a vociferous clamor. Sparks and debris flew as the aircrew held their positions, continuing to fire relentlessly despite the mayhem. The helicopter swayed erratically, its tracers arcing through the sky and cascading back down as it fought to stabilize. Through the madness, Tofino spotted something in the trees. He fought against the counteracting G-forces to angle his mounted M240 toward the enemy's location. Locking onto the general direction of the attackers, he pressed and held the butterfly trigger, unleashing a relentless stream of 7.62 mm rounds. The powerful gunfire chewed through the snow and branches, carving a destructive path toward the hidden assailants. Suddenly, a pink mist erupted from the tree line—a grotesque cloud of vaporized human flesh and blood. The impact obliterated Sergey, ripping his body apart with brutal precision. The pristine white snow was instantly stained bright red, the 98.6-degree heat of his blood and flesh melting the frozen surface beneath him. Tofino maintained his barrage, adrenaline driving him as the rest of the aircrew fought to suppress the attackers and keep the helicopter aloft. The unforgiving reality of combat surged through the scene—death and survival balanced on a knife's edge.

The remaining KGR agents, concealed behind the cover of the dense trees, continued unloading magazine after magazine from their suppressed AR-15s. Aleksandr, with accurate determination, trained his weapon on the helicopter's most vulnerable point: the tail rotor. His rounds found their mark, ripping through the drive shaft and severing the critical Thomas coupling. Without its main source of stability, the rescue helicopter lost all tail rotor authority and began spinning uncontrollably.

"MAYDAY! MAYDAY! MAYDAY!" the remaining pilot called out over the emergency frequency, his voice strained and frantic as he instinctively executed ditching procedures. "Brace for impact!"

On the ground, Brody's heart sank. "Oh my God! NO!!" he screamed, his voice breaking as he and Maddy watched the tragedy unfold before them in agonizing slow motion.

The MH-60S rose above the saddle, thick smoke billowing from its twin turbine engines as it spun violently toward the center of the frozen lake. Its once-powerful rotors now looked helpless as the helicopter spiraled downward. Acting on instinct, Brody grabbed Maddy and forced her behind a large tree stump, shielding her as best he could. The anarchy grew deafening. Weapons fire still erupted from the doomed helicopter as stray 7.62 mm rounds sprayed the lake's surface. The ice exploded in random bursts as bullets ricocheted off the frozen expanse, creating a deadly and unpredictable hail of fire. Inside the cabin, the gunners released their grips on the M240s, abandoning their weapons to brace for the inevitable crash. The aircraft spun wildly, an unstoppable force hurtling toward impact, as Brody clung to Maddy, hoping against hope for a miracle amidst the horror.

The helicopter's main rotors struck the ice 350 yards from the north edge of the lake with a booming crash. The violent impact tore the four blades from the mast hub, sending fragmented shrapnel spinning across the frozen surface, obliterating everything in their path. The force of the collision triggered the aircraft's Emergency Locator Transmitter (ELT), which automatically began broadcasting a distress signal on 406 MHz. The incredible impact ejected Petty Officer Washburn from the starboard cabin door, his lifeless body still tethered to the gunner's belt. The aircraft rolled over violently, crushing him beneath its immense 24,000-pound frame. Inside the cabin, the rest of the aircrew was rendered unconscious as the helicopter broke through the ice and began filling with 38-degree freshwater. The remains of the rotor hub spun furiously, fragments of attached blades whipping through the freezing water as the helicopter sank. Washburn's tethered body was dragged down with it, disappearing into the icy depths. The engines emitted a high-pitched scream, their final defiant noise gradually muffled as the aircraft was consumed by the lake, until complete silence overtook the scene.

"Daddy, NO! They're gone!" Maddy cried, pulling on Brody's arm as he impulsively moved to run toward the crash site. Years of training pushed him to act, to help the victims, but Maddy's desperate plea stopped him. She was right. Even if anyone had survived the crash, they wouldn't have lasted long in the frigid water if they hadn't surfaced already. Brody froze in place, disbelief buckling him to his knees. The horror of what he had just witnessed consumed him. His mind raced, yet he was paralyzed, unable to reconcile the magnitude of the loss. All hope seemed to drain from him as the icy wind howled across the lake, carrying with it a crushing sense of finality.

CHAPTER 36

Snow Lake

Snoqualmie Pass, Washington

"DAD! DAD! We need to keep going!" Maddy's voice cut through the cold air, desperate to snap her father out of his thousand-yard stare.

Brody's mind was a chaotic swirl, racing and frozen all at once. Flashes of his traumatic military past blended with the horrifying scene unfolding before him. The eerie silence that followed the crash was deafening, amplifying the torment in his head. He could almost see the pilots and aircrew sinking into the icy depths, their final moments playing out in his imagination like a nightmare he couldn't escape. Helplessness consumed him. The weight of responsibility pressed down on him like a physical force. He had made the call—the call that sent those men and women to their deaths. The realization crushed him, leaving him numb, his grief and guilt blending into a single unbearable ache.

* * *

In his unyielding gaze, Brody Hayes was transported back 20 years to a routine training flight off the coast of Kuwait. His carrier-based helicopter combat squadron was operating two HH-60Hs carrying a SEAL Team Three platoon. The mission was to test a new deployment method for the Combat Rubber Raiding Craft (CRRC), commonly known as a Zodiac. This technique, referred to as "Tethered Duck," involved attaching a fully inflated Zodiac to the helicopter's underside aboard an aircraft carrier. The helicopters would then fly to a designated insertion point, release the Zodiacs into open water, and deploy the SEALs to board the rafts and conduct a reconnaissance mission along the shore.

As Brody sat frozen on the edge of Snow Lake, watching the aftermath of the Whidbey SAR helo crash, the horrific memory of that fatal flight in the Persian Gulf replayed with haunting clarity. On that day, Brody's aircraft's HAC hovered low over the ocean, holding steady as the Crew Chief prepared to release the Zodiac from the cargo hook. The port side detached cleanly, but the starboard side snagged on the hook. Within seconds, the aircrew sprang into action, kicking at the hook to free the webbing. But the rotor wash's immense force made the task impossible. Milliseconds later, the tethered Zodiac made a powerful pendulum beneath the hovering HH-60H, flipping upward into the helicopter's main rotor blades. The catastrophic impact tore through the rotors, sending the aircraft into chaos. The pilots didn't have time to issue a distress call before instinctively jamming the collective down in an attempt to mitigate the damage. The sudden maneuver pinned the aircrew and SEALs to the cabin ceiling with crushing G-forces. Before they could process what was happening, the aircraft slammed into the ocean surface with brutal force. The memory of the deafening crash, the suffocating saltwater, and the screams of his teammates surged through Brody's mind, merging with the present-day tragedy unfolding before him.

Two SEALs were ejected from the starboard cabin door as the helicopter hit the ocean. They frantically swam away, narrowly avoiding the main rotors, which tilted with the helicopter's momentum and violently chopped into the water before breaking off entirely. The Zodiac, still tethered to the helicopter, ripped free from the cargo hook as the aircraft began flooding with saltwater, tilting precariously and starting to turn over. Brody could still hear his Crew Chief's voice echoing through his mind, even years later: "Stay calm! Grab a point of reference and hold tight until we're fully inverted!" The words had been drilled into him through countless crash simulators and water survival training sessions, but the reality of a crash was far different. Chaos engulfed the cabin. Brody fought to keep his composure, trying to lead by example for the alpha personalities around him.

A few SEALs ignored the Crew Chief's orders, scrambling out through the cabin door, now pointing upward as the helicopter tilted sideways and continued sinking. As the aircraft filled with water, Brody spotted a lone SEAL floating face down near the cockpit, motionless. His training told him to focus on survival, and in that moment, there was nothing he could do to help. Gripping his HEEDS oxygen bottle, which provided 3 minutes of compressed air. He placed it in his mouth, took a deep breath, and braced for submersion. The HH-60H flipped completely and began sinking like a stone. Panic erupted as aircrew and SEALs scrambled to egress through any open door or window. Brody unlatched his gunner's belt, surprised as the force of gravity sucked him out of the cabin door and into the cold, dark water. Breaking the surface, he scanned the waves, seeing his teammates surfacing around him—but not the face-down SEAL.

Against every instinct of self-preservation, Brody broke the cardinal rule of helicopter crashes: never reenter a sinking aircraft. He knew one of his own SAR instructors had died doing the same, but he couldn't live with himself if he didn't try. Stripping off his helmet, he dove back into the freezing water, kicking his Danner boots hard against the crushing drag of the depths. The helicopter loomed in the dark, its sinking frame disappearing into the abyss. Grabbing the welded handle on the doorframe, Brody pulled himself back into the overturned cabin. The scene was disorienting—the ceiling was now the floor, and everything was shrouded in murky darkness. He spotted the unresponsive SEAL pinned to the floor, which was now overhead. Ignoring the crushing pressure in his ears and the searing pain in his chest, Brody used his fading strength to pull the operator toward him. His HEEDS bottle sputtered empty, and he instinctively let it go, the lanyard still tethering it to his survival vest. With his lungs screaming for air, he reached across the SEAL's torso, unlatched his gunner's belt, and pulled him free. The motion sent both men sliding through the cabin door just as the helicopter slipped into the depths, vanishing into the void below. Brody kicked with everything he had, dragging the unconscious SEAL upward toward the surface and praying he wouldn't black out before breaking free of the crushing dark.

The investigation into the crash revealed that the unconscious SEAL, SO2 William Lockette, had broken his neck on impact and likely died instantly. Despite the tragic outcome, Brody Hayes was both reprimanded by his peers for reentering the sinking helicopter and awarded the Navy Cross Medal, the second-highest military decoration for the United States Navy, Coast Guard, and Marine Corps, for his heroic actions. At Lockette's military funeral at the Fort Rosecrans National Cemetery in Point Loma, California, Hayes pinned his medal onto the top of Lockette's casket, surrounded by a multitude of SEAL Tridents, each symbolizing the respect and grief of Lockette's brothers in arms.

* * *

"Dad!!" Maddy's desperate voice finally broke through Brody's frozen state of shock.

"Ok. Ok. Let's move. We need to move. We need to…" Brody trailed off, trying to build a plan as he fought to compartmentalize the overwhelming collision of past and present trauma. Guilt clawed at him, threatening to anchor him down.

Was Bridget's and Mitch's death his fault? Had the Whidbey SAR team died because of him? Had his former aircrew perished because of his decisions?

The questions swirled relentlessly in his mind, but he knew he couldn't afford to dwell on them now. He shook his head, forcing himself to focus. "We need to find a safe route out of here, Maddy," he said, his voice steadying.

"Why are those men after us, Daddy?" Maddy asked, her wide eyes searching for answers.

"I don't know who they are or what they want," Brody admitted, crouching next to her. "But we'll figure that out when we're safely off this mountain. Right now, they're likely following our tracks past the campsite. That gives us a chance to gain some ground." He pointed toward the far side of the lake. "We'll move to the other side and take the higher ground up on the ridge. They don't know this place like we do."

Brody placed a steadying hand on Maddy's shoulder, his resolve strengthening despite the weight of guilt and grief. "Stay close, honey. We'll get through this."

Brody made a command decision with the limited information he had. They didn't have a gun, and staying in one place would make them sitting ducks for men armed with assault rifles. The only way to survive was to stay out of range, keep concealed in the snowy forest, and stay ahead of their pursuers. Their tracks would inevitably lead the assailants straight to them, which meant they needed to move faster than their aggressors could track. As Brody's mind raced, piecing together a plan, a glimmer of hope surfaced—a necessary shift to an open and focused mindset. He pursed his lips, his eyes narrowing with determination as he locked in his attitude. Fear and doubt couldn't have a place now. Not when Maddy's life depended on him. He scanned the horizon, his sharp eyes searching for any sign of movement among the trees. Nothing. The forest remained eerily quiet, the falling snow muffling every sound. Satisfied, he turned to Maddy, giving her a reassuring nod. Without another word, the two stepped toward their escape route, their footprints carving a fresh path in the deep snow. The cold bit at their faces, but Brody's resolve burned stronger. Survival was their only option.

CHAPTER 37

Snow Lake Trail

Snoqualmie Pass, Washington

"Sergey's dead." Viktor surveyed the carnage splattered across the snow—flesh, bone, hair, and blood woven into a grotesque tableau. Their comrade was unrecognizable, his remains violently scattered after being torn apart by the American helicopter door gunner.

"Leave him. Our cover is blown. That downed helicopter will bring the Americans straight to us," Aleksandr said, his voice edged with urgency. He scanned the scene, mind racing to salvage their rapidly disintegrating mission. The situation was spiraling out of control, and a critical course correction was their only hope. In Mother Russia, anything short of absolute success was branded as failure. Loose ends were unacceptable, and Aleksandr knew they would not be welcomed back home if any remained. His worry compounded as he counted the dwindling numbers of his team. KGR operatives were expendable, and their government would certainly disavow all knowledge of their existence, regardless of whether they succeeded or perished in the attempt.

"Aleksandr, their trail leads this way. They dropped down to the east side of the lake," Pavel reported, scanning the terrain with calculated precision. His sharp gaze swept the snow-covered expanse, pinpointing the path of their elusive target.

"We've lost the element of surprise," Aleksandr replied, his voice cold and measured. "Hayes knows we're here. He may know these mountains better than anyone, but he's burdened with his daughter. She'll slow him down." Aleksandr paused, eyes narrowing as he studied the white, frozen expanse below. "We'll follow their trail to the lake and flank them. You two will move left, and I'll take the right. The steep, snowy mountains surrounding the lake leave them only one escape route. We'll choke both paths. This ends here and now—no more mistakes!"

His words carried a simmering anger that barely masked the storm within. Aleksandr's mind drifted momentarily, unbidden, to the memories of his parents' untimely deaths.

What would his life have been like if they had lived? If this last American hadn't been the catalyst for their destruction?

His entire existence had been fueled by a relentless thirst for revenge, and now, he was on the brink of delivering it. Pride swelled within him at the thought of honoring his KGR unit, his nation, and the family he had lost. Heavy flakes began to fall again, a welcome gift for Brody and Maddy as the fresh snow gradually filled in and masked their deep tracks. Snow Lake, sitting at an elevation of 4,000 feet and sprawling over 153 acres, offered little mercy to those traversing its rugged expanse. Positioned on the opposite side of their pursuers, they were forced to carve a new path along the lake's western edge, ascending toward the ridge. To conserve their dwindling energy, they alternated the grueling task of breaking trail through hip-deep snow. Adrenaline and sheer will to survive propelled them forward, but even that would eventually falter. Through the conceal-ment of the trees, Brody scanned the horizon, his sharp eyes search-ing for the slightest anomaly. He knew their hunters would likely flank them on both sides of the lake—it was exactly what he would have done. This assumption powered his decision to guide Maddy to higher ground, where they might gain a tactical advantage.

Every step was calculated. A single misstep on a snowshoe could send spindrift cascading down the slopes or dislodge a tree's burden of snow, creating a telltale disturbance visible from afar. Brody's eyes roved over the terrain, searching for hazards he could use to their benefit. An avalanche-prone slope, a fragile snow bridge, an unstable cornice, or a hidden crevasse could all become traps to turn the tables on their pursuers. As they climbed, Brody's mindset began to shift. The CSAR veteran's protective instincts, sharpened by years of experience downrange, transformed him from prey to predator. His adversaries had weapons, but Brody had resolve—and he wasn't going down without a fight. Thoughts of his family, his crew, and the haunting images of the Whidbey SAR rescuers who had met their end stoked a fire within him. That searing anger charged his every step, turning his desperation into a focused deter-mination to survive—and to protect his daughter to his last breath.

As they climbed toward the ridge encircling the lake, Brody instinctively took the lead, positioning himself between Maddy and any potential threats. He scanned every angle, ensuring his daughter remained shielded. Maddy followed mechanically, her legs moving despite the paralysis of emotion that seemed to engulf her. Her mind was a blank void, numb to everything but the rhythmic crunch of snow beneath her snowshoes. Maddy had grown up embracing adventure with a resilience that far exceeded the norm for kids her age. She had faced multi-day expeditions, endured blindfolded drown-proofing drills, and mastered lifesaving rescue swimmer techniques, tackling each challenge with unwavering confidence. But this—this was something else entirely. She hadn't yet faced the kind of loss that sears itself into the soul. Her life's experiences had prepared her for hardship, but not for the sudden, cruel finality of losing someone you love. Pets and grandparents, yes—but never like this.

Brody knew the hollow ache of grief all too well. He had seen it many times during his military service and in the unforgiving mountains he loved to climb. Yet, for all his experience, he was no closer to finding a way to ease his own pain, let alone guide his daughter through hers. Grief was merciless and untrainable. Every loss was different. Every person's journey through it, unique. Time, reflection, and sometimes counseling could help—but things were never the same afterward. They couldn't be. Maddy's steps were slow and deliberate, each one a small act of courage as she fought her internal battle. She moved like a ghost, her body plowing forward while her mind struggled to comprehend the enormity of it all. Even in her zombie-like state, she pushed through, her strength rooted in the grit and resilience.

"Hold up here, Maddy," Brody instructed, motioning for his daughter to stay put as he climbed 20 yards higher to inspect a clearing on the ridge. Each step was cautious, his instincts sharp. He paused frequently to listen, scanning for any sign of life in the quiet wilderness. Although the snow-covered trees below provided some concealment, he wasn't taking any chances.

As Brody reached the windswept edge, he approached with heightened attention, mindful of the thick cornice crusting the ridge. One wrong step could break it loose, sending him plunging into the ravine. After a careful survey, he made his way back down to Maddy, who was munching on a handful of trail mix, the effort leaving her mouth too dry to swallow easily.

"How's it look?" Maddy asked, her voice cracking as she forced down another dry mouthful of nuts and raisins.

"The cornice is solid," Brody replied, already constructing the plan in his head. "We'll set an anchor and simul-rappel down. Might need to downclimb a bit at the end of the rope, but the bottom angles out, so it should be safe. Once we're down, we'll circle the base of the cliff and connect to the main trail." He calmly spoke despite knowing there were no alternative routes that didn't risk drawing fire.

"How are you holding up? Drinking enough?" he asked, his eyes scanning her for signs of fatigue.

"I'll make it," Maddy replied, a mixture of exhaustion and determination in her voice. "I just want to get out of here."

Brody gave a small nod, his silent agreement conveying everything they both felt. They shared the same hope—to escape this nightmare—but the road to safety was still long and grueling. Without another word, Brody retrieved the pickets strapped to the outside of their packs and retraced his steps to the ridge. Carefully maneuvering beyond the edge of the cornice, he found solid ground away from any potential fractures. The experienced mountain guide swung his ice axe and began digging, every motion focused on ensuring their next move would bring them closer to survival.

CHAPTER 38

Snow Lake

Snoqualmie Pass, Washington

Brody and Maddy swapped their snowshoes for crampons for the rappel, securing the bulkier footwear to the rear of their packs with the attached webbing. Their snowshoes would be essential once they descended the icy cliff and resumed their escape along the main trail over 200 feet below. They also exchanged their trekking poles for ice axes, strapping on their climbing helmets in preparation for the technical descent. Maddy approached her father at the anchor point he was configuring, careful to avoid stepping on the fragile, bulging cornice that jutted precariously from the ridge. She reached into her pack and pulled out their 70-meter, 9.8 mm climbing rope, carefully uncoiling the tightly wound cord. Locating the center, marked with a painted line, she fluently tied a butterfly knot. The symmetrical knot formed a secure loop in the middle of the rope, perfectly suited for equalizing the anchor—a technique widely used in mountaineering for both glacier travel and simul rappelling. They would be employing the latter. The plan was clear: the two 35-meter (114-foot) strands would allow them to descend together, moving in tandem to cover ground quickly and safely. Maddy's hands worked deftly, her training and experience taking over as she prepared for the demanding task ahead.

They had set up similar anchors and belays hundreds of times, working in practiced rhythm without the need for instruction or verbal communication. Both Brody and Maddy had complete confidence in each other's skills, trusting implicitly in the final product. Yet, even with their deep trust, they conducted a quick cross-check—a silent acknowledgment of the ever-present risk of error. In their current situation, the stakes were magnified by harsh conditions, tight timing, heightened stress, and the mental weight of their circumstances. Neither said it aloud, but both felt a fleeting sense of reprieve from their crushing sadness as they focused entirely on the critical task of securing their literal lifeline.

Brody worked efficiently, building the anchor with two pickets. Pickets—long, lightweight aluminum devices with a T-shaped design—are essential tools in mountaineering. They can be hammered vertically into the snow or set horizontally in a deadman position to create a reliable anchor for rappelling, running belays, or crevasse rescue. Each picket is equipped with a series of holes for attaching cables or webbing, secured with a locking carabiner. From his years of Combat Search and Rescue in the Navy—configuring anchors for rappelling during special operations insertions—to guiding climbers on the world's highest peaks, setting anchors had become second nature. Under normal circumstances, he would have hammered the pickets into the snow using the top face of his ice axe. But now, he moved with deliberate silence, avoiding any sound that might betray their position. Instead, he carefully stomped the tops of the pickets with his boot, driving them deep into the compacted snow at a counter-angle to the cliff they were about to rappel down. Every movement was precise, deliberate, and infused with the unspoken understanding that their survival depended on getting this right.

With the two pickets set a few yards apart, Maddy handed her father the butterfly knot at the center of the rope. Brody secured it to the anchor with counter-facing locking aluminum carabiners, ensuring the connection was both redundant and secure. Once the center of the rope was equalized and tensioned, he tossed the coil over the edge, watching it unravel into the void below. Both Brody and Maddy fed their respective lines through their ATC rappelling devices, carefully attaching the devices to their harnesses. Together, they stepped backward toward the edge, leaning their full weight into the buried pickets and webbing to test the anchor's integrity. The system held firm.

Maddy glanced to her right, gave her father a thumbs-up, and received the same gesture in return. From a young age, Maddy had been taught to release her fear in these situations and put her faith in the equipment. Doubting the gear wouldn't change its strength but would undermine her ability to focus on the critical skills needed to survive. She also understood that trust in the anchor didn't eliminate the stakes. The setup relied on two major points of protection—if one failed, the second would take the load. If that failed too, there were no backups. The outcome would be final. Accepting this risk had always been a quiet part of the process.

Rappelling over a cornice was highly dangerous and universally discouraged due to the unpredictable nature of the icy overhang. But this was no ordinary situation, and desperate times called for desperate measures. The entire ridge was laden with windswept ice formations, leaving them no alternative routes. Brody had chosen the shallowest and most solid point he could find, where they would carefully carve a slot in the cornice near the edge. This slot would act as a controlled funnel for the rope, reducing the risk of snagging or failure as they descended, rather than relying on the sheer integrity of six feet of overhanging ice and snow. With gloved hands gripping their ropes as brakes, they moved in unison toward the edge, step by careful step. Each weight shift caused the frozen structure beneath them to creak and shift ominously, a haunting sound like the groans of an old house settling against changes in temperature and humidity. Maddy held her rope steady at the small of her back, her right hand wielding the ice axe. She chipped carefully at the ice, working alongside her father, who mirrored her technique with his left hand. Together, they methodically whittled a slot into the cornice, taking great care not to compromise the integrity of the entire looming ice block.

"Maddy, JUMP!" Brody yelled, releasing his grip on the rope with his right braking hand and forcefully lunging backward over the cornice. Without hesitation, Maddy obeyed, falling back over the frozen edge and letting gravity take hold of her descent. Ice chunks and spindrift cascaded past them, the sharp particles ricocheting off their helmets as they plunged downward.

As their combined weight pulled the rope taut, it crimped against the icy edge before jolting into the slot they had carved, cutting deeper into the partial groove. The sudden disruption caused Maddy's ice axe to slip from her grasp. It dangled precariously, swinging near her knees, secured only by its leash clipped to an equipment carabiner on her harness. The father and daughter slowed their descent, coming to a stop in the shadow of the overhanging cornice. Brody pressed a finger to his lips, signaling for silence as he motioned upward. His sharp eyes darted to the edge above. While carving the ice, he had caught a faint movement just beyond his limited view. He couldn't be certain whether they'd been spotted, but he wasn't about to wait and find out. They hung motionless, suspended 20 feet below the cornice and about four feet away from the sheer, glassy ice cliff. Their anchors were concealed, and their weighted descent had buried the rope deep into the snow slot. Still, the disturbed snow above was a glaring sign of their presence, with stomped-out tracks leading straight to the edge. Though fresh snow continued to fall, it wasn't heavy enough to obscure their trail. If their pursuers saw the disturbed ridge, they'd have no trouble piecing together what had happened—and where they had gone.

Maddy held tight to the rope, but panic began clawing its way into her mind. Brody could see it in her wide, dilated eyes and hear it in her rapid, shallow breathing. She was struggling. Without speaking, he mouthed instructions for her to box breathe—a controlled breathing technique where you inhale for four seconds, hold the breath for four seconds, exhale for four seconds, and hold again for four seconds, forming a steady square of breath cycles. This method was designed to help regain control when panic threatened to overwhelm. Maddy closed her eyes, her lips slightly moving as she silently counted through the rhythm. Her breathing slowed, and her grip steadied as calm gradually replaced her fear. Suddenly, splinters of ice exploded from above, showering them with snow and jagged fragments. A deafening crack rang out, echoing across the cliff face, followed immediately by a sharp, unsettling surge in the rope.

"SWING TO THE SIDE!" Brody shouted, his voice cutting through the chaos.

Maddy's eyes snapped open, her body responding to his command before her mind fully registered it.

Brody twisted his legs, using the torque of his body to swing away from the cliff face. Gravity fueled his momentum, and as he swung back toward the wall, he braced his feet against the slippery surface to push off again. Maddy mimicked her dad as best she could, but as Brody passed her, he caught a fleeting glimpse above—a man leaning over the edge, pulling a knife from his vest. Brody's heart pounded as he slammed the pick of his ice axe into the bulletproof ice coating the cliff. The sharp pick caught, and he immediately kicked in the right front points of his crampon, driving them into the ice, followed by his left. As he stabilized, he saw Maddy swinging toward him, her movements less controlled. With his free hand, Brody lunged and grabbed a fistful of her down jacket, yanking her toward him with a surge of adrenaline-fueled strength. Maddy flailed, her feet scrabbling against the ice, but they both froze in shock as the rope between them suddenly went slack. They watched, horrified, as the severed lines whipped through the cornice slot above, weightlessly feeding through the anchor point. A guttural shout rang out from above—indistinct but sharp, and unmistakably in Russian. Brody didn't look back. He forced himself to block out the sound and focus entirely on his daughter.

"Plant your axe! Get your crampons in!" he barked, his voice low but firm as he pinned Maddy against the ice. She was dead weight in his grasp, her panic threatening to overtake her again. Brody's muscles screamed as he held her steady, adrenaline temporarily granting him the strength to counter gravity.

Maddy's hands trembled, but she swung her axe, chipping into the dense ice. "You've got this," Brody said, steadying her with his tone as much as his grip. She hacked again, the blade finding purchase, and followed his lead, kicking in the front points of her crampons until she felt them bite. The cut rope flapped wildly above them in the wind as the two clung to the unforgiving cliff face, suspended in a precarious fight for survival.

"Up here! They're up here!" Viktor shouted, his voice cutting through the heavy snowfall as he waved down to Pavel, who was 200 yards below. While the two KGR agents had been traversing the west side of the frozen lake, Viktor had climbed to investigate the upper ridge, suspecting their target might attempt a higher path. The footprints in the snow and the freshly set anchors confirmed his hunch. Without a second thought, he severed the ropes.

Pavel stopped in his tracks, turning his attention uphill. He adjusted his footing and began climbing toward Viktor, each step a struggle against the steep, slippery incline, the fresh snow giving way beneath his boots. Meanwhile, Viktor leaned out over the edge of the cornice, scanning the cliff below for any sign of their quarry. Heavy snow swirled around him, obscuring his view. All he could see was an endless expanse of white—the jagged snow-covered trees and the sheer, icy face of the mountain. Frustrated, he inched closer to the edge, craning his neck for a better angle.

A loud, resonant crack echoed through the valley, the sound amplified by the surrounding cliffs. Viktor froze, his eyes widening in horror as the cornice beneath him gave way. A car-sized slab of snow and ice broke free from its tenuous hold on the rocky cliffside. He didn't have time to scream or react. In an instant, he was weight-less, falling along with the massive slab like a passenger trapped in a free-falling elevator. The icy world around him blurred into chaos as he plunged into the void.

"Hold tight!" Brody yelled to Maddy, his voice strained as they pressed themselves against the ice wall. A blur of snow, ice, and a thrashing figure plummeted past them as the cornice gave way, four of its six overhanging feet of ice breaking loose. The thunder-ous cascade of falling ice reverberated through the cliff, shaking loose 2- and 3-foot-long icicles above their heads. Maddy pivoted sharply to her left, narrowly avoiding a frozen dagger that speared the space she had just occupied.

Below, Viktor's uncontrolled freefall accelerated, his trajec-tory steering him toward a dense cluster of evergreen conifers. The jagged, ice-covered tip of a towering Douglas Fir met him mid-fall, piercing through his lower spine and shattering his L1 and L2 discs. The sheer velocity and force of his weight drove the frozen tree's pointed top through his back and out of his chest, pulverizing ribs and vital organs in an instant. The impalement continued until an eight-inch-thick, sap-heavy branch abruptly halted his descent. Viktor's broken body swung grotesquely from the treetop, dislodging snow from the surrounding pine needles as the tree trembled under the impact. His arms and legs dangled lifelessly, his shattered form convulsing involuntarily with the last vestiges of reflexive movement. Within seconds, Viktor succumbed to the brutal injury. His internal body temperature rapidly matched the freezing air, while his blood cascaded down the snow-covered trunk like molten red wax dripping from a burning candle. The contrast against the pristine white snow was visceral, a crimson trail threading through the frost-laden branches. The stench of death permeated the crisp mountain air—a nauseating blend of metallic blood from oxidized hemoglobin mingling with the sweet, sticky aroma of sap. The chaotic violence of the moment gave way to an oppressive silence, a stillness so complete it was almost deafening.

CHAPTER 39

Snow Lake

Snoqualmie Pass, Washington

"Don't look, honey. Get your ice screw and anchor yourself," Brody said, his voice firm but laced with concern. He wanted to distract Maddy, to pull her focus back to the task at hand. But he should have taken his own advice—he couldn't stop himself from glancing at the gruesome scene below.

Maddy, too, ignored his suggestion. Her eyes locked onto the ghastly sight, an unnerving mix of horror and grim satisfaction rising within her. If this man had anything to do with her mom and brother's deaths, then his brutal end felt justified—a twisted form of justice served by the mountain itself. The thought sent a chill through her, but she couldn't turn away. She was both repulsed and transfixed, knowing that this image could haunt her dreams if she managed to survive. And yet, in this fleeting moment, she felt a flicker of triumph amid the turmoil.

Maddy and Brody unclipped their ice screws from the gear loops hanging on the backs of their harnesses. Ice screws are a vital piece of climbing equipment in ice climbing and mountaineering, designed for safety in even the most precarious situations. Lightweight and straightforward to use, they often prove to be literal lifesavers when the stakes are high. Both father and daughter scanned the ice in front of them, searching for solid, reliable spots to place the screws. They carefully avoided any visibly rotten ice, which could shatter under even minimal pressure. They twisted the screws into the dense, stable ice. The integrated metal rings on the screws provided an immediate attachment point for their carabiners, which they clipped into for a moment of desperately needed relief. Their legs and arms shook from the strain of clinging to the vertical, icy cliff, supported only by their crampons and ice axes. Each carried a couple of spare quickdraws—two carabiners connected by 12 centimeters of durable webbing. They clipped one carabiner of the quickdraw to the ice screw and the other to the belay loop on their harnesses, reinforcing their connection to the wall. With their ice screws firmly in place and their harnesses securely clipped in, Maddy and Brody were now safely anchored to the frozen mountain face, their immediate peril momentarily alleviated.

Viktor had severed the rope from the anchors above before falling to his death, leaving the line still threaded through Maddy and Brody's ATC rappelling devices. The excess rope dangled into the snowy chasm below, its ends swaying faintly in the mountain wind. As Maddy tried to pull her line free, she realized it was fouled, snagged on something far below. The collapsed cornice had pancaked into the ice block, compacting and pinning her rope against the frozen surface.

"Pull it through and let it fall. We'll use mine," Brody instructed, his voice steady despite the tension of their predicament. He carefully retrieved his rope, coiled it, and got to work. Tying a figure-eight knot, he secured it to the locking carabiner on his harness. After counting out 10 meters, he tied a butterfly knot in the line and handed it to Maddy, who clipped it to her harness. Now tethered together by the remaining rope, they prepared to ice climb the 20 feet back to the ridge.

Brody scanned the icy cliff face as they secured their gear, knowing the stakes were higher than ever. They didn't know how many attackers remained in pursuit. The horrifying sight of Viktor's fall provided hope that he might have been the last—but there was no certainty. Downclimbing wasn't an option; the fractured ice lower on the cliff wall made it too dangerous. Brody considered the possibility of using the ice screws as anchors to rappel down instead. The thought lingered uncomfortably. If the screws failed under their combined weight, it would be the end for both. After witnessing Viktor's death, the fragility of the ice felt more like a grim certainty than a remote possibility. Brody's mind raced, calculating their next move. "We need to climb," he said firmly. Maddy nodded, adjusting her grip on her ice axe. Both father and daughter understood that their survival depended on every step, every swing of their axes, and every ounce of trust in their skills—and in each other.

"You good?" Brody asked, glancing over at his daughter as he began unwinding his ice screw.

Maddy hesitated, her voice trembling as she replied, "What if there are more men up there? What then?" Her fearful question cut through the air like the cold wind whipping around them. She had no combat experience, and her terror was justified.

Brody paused for a moment, locking eyes with her. He appeared calm and confident, projecting the assurance she desperately needed, but inside, his fear lingered. He had been in life-or-death situations before, but this was different. This was his daughter. And the odds were stacked against them. He clenched his jaw, suppressing the intrusive thoughts threatening to paralyze him. The reality was bleak—he had no weapons, no real way to defend them other than his ice axe, which was hardly a match against a firearm. It felt like bringing a knife to a gunfight, and he knew it.

Still, he couldn't afford to let his doubts show. "Then we keep moving. We stay smart. Stay together," he said firmly, though his mind raced with contingency plans, none of which offered much reassurance. "One step at a time, Maddy. That's all we need to focus on right now."

Maddy nodded. She didn't feel comforted, but her father's tenacity gave her something to cling to. For now, it would have to be enough.

"It's okay to be scared, Maddy. I'm scared too," Brody admitted, his voice steady but tinged with sincerity. He held her gaze, locking eyes with his firstborn. "I'll climb up and set an anchor just below the remaining overhang to get a better look. Hold tight and try to stay calm. We'll get through this."

He tried to sound as convincing as possible, though he wasn't entirely sure himself. Fear gnawed at him, but he buried it beneath the urgency of the moment. Twisting the safety device counterclockwise, Brody freed the ice screw and clipped it securely to a carabiner on his harness. He then kicked his crampon front points into the ice, gaining height one careful step at a time. The sharp teeth of the axe found solid purchase with every strike, but each impact sent fragments of ice raining down onto Maddy. The shards pinged off her helmet and shoulders before plummeting over 100 feet below. Maddy's gaze drifted downward despite herself, her eyes catching the horrific sight of Viktor's impaled body. The blood-splattered snow around him had been dusted with a faint pink hue, a macabre blending of snow and death. Her emotions churned violently—anger, disgust, and a morbid fascination she couldn't fully suppress. She gripped the rope tightly, her mind racing as she tried to process the madness that had become her reality. With every second that passed, she felt pieces of herself slipping away—the parts that once held innocence and security. She knew, even as she clung to the icy cliff, that she would never be the same after this. Even if she survived, she understood she would never truly escape the trauma. It would cling to her like a shadow, a constant reminder of the day her world changed forever.

Brody methodically inched his way up the icy wall until he reached the crux—just inches below a cluster of colossal, sharp overhanging icicles. Each one hung like a frozen dagger poised to strike. Moving with utmost caution, he carefully twisted an ice screw into the dense ice a few feet below the deadly formations, ensuring not to disturb them. Any misstep or vibration could be catastrophic for his vulnerable daughter below. Once the screw was securely set, Brody pulled up slack from his rope and snapped it into a quickdraw, clipping the other end to the ice screw's metal ring. He glanced down at Maddy and gave her a reassuring thumbs-up, signaling her to tighten the rope for a secure belay. Then, with a practiced motion, he lunged backward, testing the integrity of his anchor while arching his body outward to gain better reach. His ice axe swung, embedding firmly into the remaining surface of the cornice. Brody's white climbing helmet blended with the fractured ice bulge as he cautiously peered up and over the edge. With his left hand, he drove the pick of his axe deep into the heavy snow layer above, pulling back hard to confirm a solid hold. Every muscle in his body burned as he held the awkward arched position, his calves cramping painfully from the unnatural angle. He hugged the underside of the ice block, his lower body twisted to avoid snagging or disrupting the precariously hanging icicles below. The stakes couldn't have been higher. If the cornice gave way or the icicles broke free, the cascading ice would carry both him and Maddy to their deaths. Brody's breath was slow as he steadied himself, every motion calculated to preserve their fragile tether to survival.

Brody froze. Every muscle in his body tensed, and he held his breath, not daring to make even the slightest movement. Slowly, almost imperceptibly, he dipped his snow-covered helmet just below the edge of the cornice, glancing back at Maddy to signal with a clenched fist—a silent order to stay still. Her heart pounded in her chest, the rapid rhythm nearly deafening in her ears. She didn't know what her father had seen, but she assumed the worst—more attackers.

Above, Brody had spotted something—a lone figure carrying a suppressed rifle, methodically scanning the area. The man's motions and readiness suggested he was searching for either Brody or his fallen comrade. Brody's heart raced as he realized his precarious position. He slid down the icy surface slightly, praying he hadn't been seen. A single shot would be all it took to end him, and with his ice axe still embedded in the ice and plainly visible, time was running out. His mind raced as he assessed the situation, weighing his options in a split second. If he released his axe, his body would swing and pivot violently on the single ice screw anchor holding him to the wall. Assuming the screw held, the resulting noise and action would immediately reveal his position. He dismissed the thought—it was too risky. Instead, Brody blindly stretched his hand under the cornice, feeling for anything that might give him an edge. His fingers brushed against a foot-long icicle. He gripped it tightly and began wiggling it back and forth, desperation fueling his attempt as he tried to snap it free.

SNAP!

The icicle broke loose with a sharp crack that echoed louder than he had hoped.

"Viktor?" Pavel called out, his voice sharp and wary as he trained his weapon toward the sound. Stepping cautiously further onto the cornice, he scanned the snow-covered expanse below for any sign of his comrade.

When his gaze landed on Viktor's lifeless, impaled body dangling grotesquely from the tree, Pavel's eyes widened with shock, quickly darkening into a furious crimson glare. Rage boiled within him, but his focus shifted sharply as something caught his eye—the pick of Brody's ice axe, embedded in the snow mere inches from his boots. In a single, fluid motion, the seasoned KGR operative lowered his AR-15 from his shoulder and aimed, his finger tightening around the trigger. But before he could fire, Brody exploded upward from beneath the cornice, emerging from what seemed like an impossible position. With accuracy and brute force, Brody drove the icicle straight into Pavel's left eye. The improvised weapon sliced cleanly through the optical nerve, penetrating deep into the prefrontal cortex and hypothalamus before stopping abruptly as its jagged edge crushed into the far corner of Pavel's skull. The Russian's body convulsed violently, his nerve endings firing in chaotic disarray before his central nervous system shut down entirely. Death was instant. His lifeless, 220-pound frame collapsed forward, sliding off the cornice and vanishing into the snowy depth below, where it struck the base of the trees 100 feet beneath with a muted thud.

As Brody's brief burst of upward momentum ceased, gravity reclaimed him. His ice axe slipped free from its hold, and the sharp front points of his crampons released from the ice. Helpless to stop himself, he whipped downward toward Maddy, his fall rapid and uncontrolled. Maddy's eyes widened in terror as she watched her father plummet past her, her mind frozen between the horror of seeing one man fall to his death and the imminent impact of her dad following him. Instinctively, she braced for the shock load. Her knees bent slightly as she pressed tightly against her single anchor point, clinging to her ice axe and footholds with every ounce of strength. The rope went taut with a vicious snap, slashing across her right side. A deep purple friction burn instantly bloomed on her skin, the searing pain barely registering as the weight of her father's fall wrenched the rope downward. She held her position, praying the last ice screw would hold against the incredible force. Metal screeched against the ice like fingernails dragged across a chalkboard. The sound was ear-piercing, each vibration sending a fresh wave of terror through her. The rope stretched to its limit, flexing impossibly tight—then retracted. It held.

Brody slammed into the ice wall during the 50-foot freefall, his right shoulder dislocating with a sickening crunch. His helmet cracked on impact, blood trickling down his face as his body swung limply from the rope. He clenched his jaw, swallowing the scream threatening to escape. *Die silently,* he told himself. *Don't give away your position.* Dangling heavily from the line, Brody's ice axe swung loosely at the end of its wrist-attached leash. His head pounded with the unmistakable symptoms of a concussion. This was another traumatic brain injury to add to a long list accumulated during years of military operations and high-altitude mountaineering. The pain was excruciating, but he knew there was no time to wallow. Fighting through the fog and nausea, he forced his body into position, kicking the front points of his crampons into the ice. Sharp bursts of pain pulsed through his shoulder, but he managed to secure himself against the wall. The tension eased slightly off the single ice screw keeping him and Maddy tethered to life. Brody took a slow, ragged breath, blood dripping from his cracked helmet. He was conscious—but barely. They were still alive, but only just.

"Daddy?" Maddy's voice was trembling, her body visibly shaking. Tears streamed down her face, unchecked, as emotional shock engulfed her. The weight of the moment—of everything that had happened—pressed down on her like the collapsing world around them. She clung to the ice wall, frozen not by the cold, but by the overwhelming chaos that had become her reality.

How could she possibly recover from this?

And then, amid the turmoil, her father's voice broke through. Calm and steady, his words cut straight to her soul. "I'm good, honey," Brody said, his tone soothing despite the pain radiating through his body. "Give me a second to catch my breath. You do the same. Stay calm. Breathe."

The words were simple, but their weight was profound. It wasn't just a command—it was a lifeline. Brody repeated the advice he had clung to countless times before, during those brutal moments in Aviation Rescue Swimmer School. Moments when he had been pushed beyond his physical and mental limits. Moments where others panicked, broke, or quit. Moments when he had to find a reason to keep going.

A reason to live. A reason to take one more step forward. A reason to survive.

"Stay calm. Breathe," he said again, the words like an anchor in the storm.

Maddy closed her eyes, focusing on the steady rhythm of her breath. In and out. Just as her father had taught her.

Stay calm. Breathe.

CHAPTER 40

"Gentlemen, we have a green light. Mr. Talbott, plot our course to Snow Lake. Aft, rig for a possible hot extract," Captain Janet McKenzie ordered, her tone calm and authoritative as she addressed her co-pilot and aircrew. The directive came moments after receiving the call from Joint Base Lewis-McChord (JBLM) air traffic control.

Chief Warrant Officer Alex Talbott quickly entered Snow Lake's longitude and latitude coordinates into the navigation system. The base tower communication officer had relayed homing information picked up from the Emergency Locator Transmitter (ELT) beaconing from the suspected crash site of a NAS Whidbey SAR helicopter. The urgency of the mission was unmistakable. In the cabin, Crew Chief Sergeant Daniel Van Buren and Flight Medic Sergeant Robert Steele moved swiftly, preparing for the possibility of a hot extraction. The port and starboard windows, outfitted with M144 pintle mounts, housed M240 machine guns, each crew-served weapon ready for use. Ordinance personnel had stacked metal canisters of 7.62 mm ammunition belts, and every crew member carried an M4 carbine assault rifle for close-quarter defense if needed.

The MEDEVAC helicopter was fully equipped for search and rescue operations. Onboard were two full-sized medical litters, an MK-III Forest Penetrator, rappelling gear, and an Advanced First Aid Kit. The crew worked efficiently, ensuring every piece of equipment was accounted for and ready for immediate deployment. As they prepared to launch, the crew noted the rapidly dwindling daylight, a challenge exacerbated by the approach of the winter solstice. Fortunately, both the aircraft and its personnel were outfitted with night vision capabilities, ensuring they could operate effectively in the dark. With the coordinates locked in and preparations complete, the aircraft was ready to head toward Snow Lake and whatever awaited them there.

The aircrew belonged to Yakima DUSTOFF, a U.S. Army Air Ambulance Detachment under the 16th Combat Aviation Brigade's 2-158 Assault Helicopter Battalion. Similar to NAS Whidbey SAR, the DUSTOFF team regularly undertook search and rescue missions across the Pacific Northwest, responding to emergencies in the region's rugged and often unforgiving terrain.

Just a few hours earlier, the crew had been dispatched to recover the body of a deceased climber, discovered by a husband and wife snowshoeing near the base of Mount St. Helens. However, the mission quickly became too dangerous. Strong winds and heavy snow created hazardous flying conditions, and Captain McKenzie made the prudent decision to abort the operation. Before returning to base, she radioed in the coordinates of the body and requested that local ground authorities take over the recovery effort. As the team flew back to Joint Base Lewis-McChord (JBLM), news broke of NAS Whidbey SAR's launch to Snow Lake for a critical rescue. DUSTOFF was immediately placed on high alert. They were ordered to return to base, refuel, and stand by as a backup search and rescue asset.

The DUSTOFF crew followed their orders and promptly returned to base. The dark, overcast sky hung low, with constant rain showers making it appear later in the day than it truly was. After topping off the helicopter's fuel tanks, they taxied to their assigned flight line and shut down the aircraft. With the immediate tasks completed, the crew seized the opportunity for a quick bio break and some food. As seasoned military personnel, they were well accustomed to the "hurry up and wait" mindset. Though they remained on standby, they knew the odds of launching again that day were slim. Still, readiness was paramount. Sergeant Van Buren and Sergeant Steele ensured the helicopter was fully prepped for takeoff, double-checking the fuel levels, equipment, and the unusual armament configured for a potential hot extraction. With the helo squared away, the two enlisted crew members headed to the rec room to unwind. There, they immersed themselves in battling Covenant aliens in their pursuit of the mysterious *Halo*. Their laughter and playful banter echoed faintly through the hangar, a brief reprieve from the high-stakes reality of their job.

In the officer's lounge, Captain McKenzie took advantage of the downtime to chip away at administrative tasks on her laptop, while Chief Warrant Officer Talbott leaned back in his chair, mindlessly scrolling through his Instagram feed. The air was calm, but the underlying tension of being on alert status lingered—a silent reminder that the call to action could come at any moment.

LAUNCH THE ALERT SAR ASSET!

At 1452, the DUSTOFF crew received the launch order. The urgency in the command left no room for delay. By 1512, the U.S. Army UH-60M Black Hawk helicopter lifted off from Gray Army Airfield, its rotors slicing through the misty, overcast sky. The aircraft surged northward at 150 knots, covering the 80-mile journey toward Snow Lake with relentless purpose. With the green light to deploy to Snow Lake, the crew was ready to assist in what was shaping up to be another challenging mission. Rigged for rescue, the Black Hawk carried its full complement of search and rescue gear, while its M240 machine guns stood locked and loaded, ready for a potential hot extraction.

The crew was focused, each member prepared for whatever challenges lay ahead in the rugged, snow-covered wilderness.

CHAPTER 41

Snow Lake

Snoqualmie Pass, Washington

Aleksandr brushed the snow off the top of his jacket hood and removed his fogged goggles. With his suppressed AR-15 shouldered, he moved with acute awareness, swiveling steadily from side to side as he scanned the dense forest on the north side of the lake. Moments earlier, he had inspected the Hayes campsite and the surrounding woods. The KGR operative had fired a couple of silenced rounds through each tent before unzipping their vinyl doors. He doubted the American would be foolish enough to hide in such an exposed spot, but Aleksandr wasn't one to take chances. Once he was satisfied the area was clear, he discovered lightly snow-covered tracks leading out of camp toward the north. The trail ended at a large, stomped-out area of flattened snow, clearly the result of excessive foot traffic.

To Aleksandr, the design of the area was unmistakable—an obvious manmade extraction point. The flattened snow provided the perfect approach zone for a helicopter extraction. A faint smirk tugged at the corner of his lips. *Fools.* Their escape plan had been well thought out, but Aleksandr and his team had ensured its failure. Circling the exfil point, his semi-automatic weapon's safety remained disengaged, his gloved finger hovering lightly over the trigger. His sharp eyes flicked over the terrain, every shadow and snow-laden tree a potential threat. He knew Pavel and Viktor were supposed to be flanking the target from the opposite side of the lake, but Aleksandr took no chances. He avoided engaging where his men might be positioned, but his resolve was absolute—he would fire on the slightest movement. If it turned out to be one of his own? So be it. Aleksandr could live with that.

At the far edge of the lake, Aleksandr's sharp eyes caught an outcropping of decaying, moss-covered tree stumps. Following a set of existing snowshoe imprints, he approached a sizeable snow-covered stump, its weathered bulk a natural hiding spot. Aleksandr widened his arc around the massive tree base, his weapon centered and ready to engage. With swift, concentrated actions, he spun around the wooden mass, eager to eliminate any threat concealed behind it. But there was nothing.

Frustration flashed across Aleksandr's face as he stood momentarily exposed, feeling the vulnerability of having directed his focus on a single point. He spun around to check his surroundings, scanning for signs of an ambush. Still nothing. Then, his gaze locked onto fresh tracks leading around the opposite side of the lake. They were heading directly toward the paths of Pavel and Viktor, his two flanking operatives. Aleksandr's mouth curled into a cold smile. *Perfect.*

Brody grimaced with every lunge up the ice wall. His right arm hung nearly useless at his side, the dislocated shoulder radiating excruciating pain. He concentrated on driving his crampon's front points into the frozen surface, using his legs to propel himself upward. His nondominant left hand gripped the ice axe, pounding it into the wall with deliberate effort. Every strike sent shards of ice raining down, but he pushed through, ignoring the screaming protests of his body. When Brody finally reached the height of his daughter, he paused, breathing heavily. Without hesitation, he wrapped his arms around Maddy, holding her tightly against him. They clung to each other in silence, their shared embrace a brief refuge from the storm raging around them. Tears streamed down Maddy's red, frozen cheeks, her sobs muffled against her father's chest. Brody's own eyes welled up, but he quickly shut it down, forcing the emotion deep inside. There wasn't room for anger or sadness—not now. He had to compartmentalize, to channel every ounce of himself toward survival. For Maddy. For both of them.

It doesn't take much to fall into the victim role, but once you're there, it's hard to recover.

Brody refused to let himself fall into that mindset. He remained focused, inching steadily up the ice wall until he reached the final spot to anchor his ice screw—the same location where it had torn free earlier during his harrowing fall. Balancing entirely on the sharp front points of his crampons, his legs bore the brunt of the effort, the metal spikes gripping the ice beneath his steaming mountaineering boots. His calves screamed in agony, the unrelenting flexion making them feel as though they might burst. Every muscle burned with fiery cramps, a stark and painful reminder of how dehydrated he was. His body begged for water, but time was not a luxury he could afford. Stopping now, even for a moment, was too risky. Gritting his teeth, Brody ignored his needs and focused solely on the task at hand. With his left hand, he twisted the ice screw into the solid ice, turning it round and round until the threads bit deeply and the screw felt secure. He tugged on it once, testing its hold. Satisfied, he pulled the rope slack up to his mouth, clenching it between his teeth to free his left hand. He then connected the slack to the safety device anchored in the wall. Brody looked down at Maddy and gave her a reassuring thumbs-up, signaling that he was moving over the top of the cornice to investigate. Her response was subtle—a hesitant thumbs-up followed by tightly closed eyes. She clasped her hands together and silently prayed. Brody took a deep breath and steeled himself, knowing the stakes hadn't changed. Every action mattered, and failure wasn't an option.

Brody's right arm hung useless at his side as he hammered his ice axe into the upper edge of the ice bulge with his nondominant left hand. Each deliberate act sent surges of pain radiating through his body—agony so intense it bordered on excruciating and, in some twisted way, euphoric. Pain was familiar territory for the decorated veteran. His high tolerance didn't mean he felt less of it, but rather that he had learned to rewire his brain's response. It was a mental toughness forged through years of hardship, much like the mindfulness required during ice baths. You don't just resist the torture—you embrace it, transform it, let it become fuel for your will to endure.

As Brody lunged higher, he muttered a silent prayer, exposing himself more than he had previously dared. He knew the risk—another attacker waiting at the top would leave him with little chance of survival. But the alternatives were no better. His body trembled with exhaustion, muscles shaking under the strain. He paused briefly to assess his surroundings, his breath shallow and meditative. Wind gusts howled around him, carrying larger snowflakes that clung to his contorted frame, sapping warmth and testing his determination. Seeing no signs of life above, he committed to the climb. With his ice axe secured, Brody pulled with every ounce of strength his left arm could summon. His crampon front points released their hold as he swung his legs vertically, hanging unprotected beneath the cracking edge of the cornice. Pain shot through his body, but he dragged himself upward using sheer upper-body strength. Twisting his torso, he flung his right side onto the cornice, slamming his dislocated shoulder against the surface to gain leverage. The momentum allowed him to pull his ice axe free from its hold, plunging it further into the flat snow above. The axe bit deeply into the frozen crust, giving him just enough stability to avoid sliding backward off the ledge. For a moment, the sound of his rapidly beating heart seemed to echo against the ice, amplified by the fresh snow smothering everything around him. Wasting no time, Brody pulled his legs up and scrambled forward, crawling across the frozen earth until he was completely clear of the ledge. He collapsed briefly on solid ground, his breaths ragged but steady. He wasn't safe yet, but for now, he had survived.

Brody lay low on the ridge, scanning the horizon and forest below for any signs of movement or sound. Nothing. The eerie stillness pressed down around him, but he stayed alert, his senses keen. Using the aluminum picket anchors still set in the ice, he clipped in the rope with a Munter hitch, a versatile knot used by climbers and rescuers to control friction in a belay system. He gave the rope a couple of firm tugs, the signal for Maddy to start climbing.

As she began ascending the same route he had taken, Brody maintained a running belay, carefully feeding slack through the hitch to keep the rope tight. This ensured that any slip or fall on her part would be safely arrested. Maddy moved quickly and confidently, her climbing efficient despite the icy conditions. As she passed the two ice screws, she unclipped from them but left them in place. She didn't want to waste precious time unscrewing them. Breaking the "leave no trace" rule felt like a small price to pay under the circumstances. Fortunately, she didn't need to test her dad's belay. Maddy reached the top without issue, surfacing over the icy edge in a burst of energy. Brody extended a hand, helping her up the final few feet. For a moment, father and daughter embraced tightly, celebrating their minor victory in the face of overwhelming odds. They quickly chugged their water, savoring the brief respite before turning their attention to the next challenge.

"It looks like they came up from our right," Brody said, scanning the snow-covered ridge for tracks. "Let's follow their path to the saddle." His tone was firm, a command decision made with daylight rapidly dwindling.

Maddy hesitated, glancing at the terrain ahead. "What if there are more of them?" she asked, voicing the question that had been lingering unspoken.

Her dad nodded, his expression grim. "Keep your head on a swivel. We have to assume there may be more."

After swapping their crampons for snowshoes, the two began their descent down the steep, snowy path, carefully following the footsteps recently punched into the powder by the two dead men. The steady wind picked up, carrying heavy snow flurries that swirled around them and plastered the east sides of tree trunks. The icy flakes stuck to their faces and gear, chilling them further despite their exertion. Both wore Oakley snow goggles, but the sharp contrast between the cold outside air and the heat from their labored breathing caused the lenses to fog repeatedly. They paused often, scraping away accumulating snowflakes and wiping the interior with gloved fingers to clear the fog. The repetitive task felt both frustrating and futile, but was necessary to maintain any visibility in the storm. Physical and emotional exhaustion clawed at them. Their legs felt like lead, every step a monumental effort. The biting wind and freezing temperatures drained what little energy they had left. But there was no option to stop. They both knew the only way out was to keep moving, to dig deeper than they ever had before.

Find a reason to take one more step forward. Find a reason to live.

The mantra pulsed in their minds, driving them onward through the relentless storm. Within minutes, they descended to the edge of the frozen lake. The downhill hike, though treacherous, was a welcome reprieve from the brutal ice climb beneath the cornice. Visibility remained poor as encased cloud cover and worsening blizzard conditions reduced their view to a blurred whiteout. Through the swirling snow, they could just barely make out the massive hole in the center of the lake. Its dark, jagged edges stood as a grim monument to the trauma Brody and Maddy were living. A bleak reminder of what had been lost.

The NAS Whidbey SAR helicopter and its five crew members lay silently entombed beneath the freezing water. Snow had continued to fall since the crash, building up a slushy film over the shattered ice and open water. By nightfall, the lake would freeze completely, erasing all signs of the tragedy and restoring Snow Lake to its tranquil, majestic facade—the way it had appeared only 24 hours earlier. But Brody and Maddy couldn't look at it the same. The lake would never again represent peace. For them, it was a graveyard.

CHAPTER 42

Snow Lake

Snoqualmie Pass, Washington

Maddy froze, paralyzed in her tracks. Her mind refused to process what was unfolding before her. One moment, her dad was leading her watchfully through the snowy trees lining the side of the frozen lake. The next, he collapsed silently into the fresh powder, a plume of pink mist hanging in the air like a horrifying specter. Shades of red spilled across the pristine white ground as Brody groaned, clutching his left thigh. Blood poured from the wound, staining the snow beneath him as the torment coursed through his body. His teeth clenched, his breaths shallow and ragged as he fought to remain conscious.

"RUN, MADDY! RUN!" Brody forced the words out, each syllable strained against the immense pain shooting through his leg.

"Daddy? Daddy?" Maddy's voice was faint, trembling as her mind blurred in and out of shock. Her vision swam, her chest tightening as panic stole the air from her lungs. She felt like she was drowning, her body frozen, unable to respond. She couldn't move. She couldn't think. Her world was collapsing, and she was powerless to stop it.

"RUN!" Brody shouted, his voice cutting through her shock. He wasn't waiting for her to process—her survival depended on her moving now.

Maddy took a step forward, then another, and another. Her body seemed to move on its own, instinct overriding thought as she stumbled into motion. Her mind felt detached, as though she were outside herself, watching the scene unfold in slow motion. Above and around her, spruce branches erupted in splinters as bullets tore through the forest. Debris rained down, dusting her hair and shoulders, but she barely registered it. In her petrified state, she was oblivious to the fact that additional rounds were being fired at her from 150 yards away. She just kept moving forward, weaving clumsily through the snow-covered trees, following her dad's desperate command.

"AHHH!" Her dad's agonized scream pierced the air behind her, freezing Maddy mid-step. She turned, her mind racing.

What should I do? Go back? Keep running?

Every fiber of her being screamed to help him, but she had seen what the attackers were capable of. She knew she'd be as good as dead if she tried to save him. And then she remembered: he had told her to run. He had given her direct orders. Her dad knew what he was doing. He always knew what to do. She trusted him with her life. Tears blurred her vision as she forced herself to stop overthinking. She clenched her fists, turned away from the sound of his pain, and ran. She ran as if her life depended on it—because it did.

"Call to your daughter!" Aleksandr barked, his assault rifle aimed squarely at Brody's head. The wounded American lay face down in the snow, blood seeping from the bullet wound in his thigh. Brody refused to respond, his body trembling from pain and cold, but his will unbroken.

Aleksandr's face twisted in frustration. He knelt down, driving his left knee deep into the bleeding wound in Brody's leg. A guttural groan escaped Brody's lips, but he bit down hard, refusing to give Aleksandr the satisfaction of a scream. From his vantage point on the far side of the lake, Aleksandr had watched the father and daughter descend from the ridge through the dense forest and heavy snowfall. Camouflaged in the whiteout conditions, he had tracked them with the patience of a predator. When Brody stepped into a small clearing where the trail hugged the lake's shore, Aleksandr seized the opportunity.

At nearly 400 yards, a single suppressed shot from his AR-15 found its mark. The .223 Remington round tore into Brody's left thigh, dropping him instantly in a cloud of crimson haze. Seeing the American collapse brought a surge of triumph to Aleksandr—a bitter, long-awaited sense of redemption for his fallen comrades. But he didn't allow himself to revel in his victory. There was still the daughter, the last witness. Aleksandr hurried forward, his sights set on eliminating her before finishing off Brody Hayes.

"Go to hell!" Brody spat, his voice defiant despite the agony coursing through his body. "She's gone! I killed your rookie comrades, too!"

Aleksandr's eyes flared with rage. He pressed his knee harder into the wound, drawing a pained scream from Brody, "AHHHH!"

The Russian operative, triggered by Brody's deceptive words, pressed his left thumb into the warm, blood-spattered entry wound. Aleksandr's expression was cold, but his mind briefly processed a grim realization: he was the last living KGR operative on the mission. Determined to extract something—anything—from his defiant target, Aleksandr dug deeper, his thumb probing the raw wound, pressing hard on exposed nerve endings. A shockwave of near-blackout pain surged through Brody's body, momentarily blinding him with its intensity.

Brody had endured pain and torture before, having survived the brutal demands of Survival, Evasion, Resistance, and Escape (SERE) training during his time served in the U.S. Navy. In training, they could hurt you, but they couldn't kill you. Here, death was a very real possibility. Still, Brody clung to the one lesson ingrained in him during those grueling sessions:

Find a reason to live. Never give up hope.

And Brody's reason was clear—his daughter. The love he had for Maddy far outweighed any amount of pain Aleksandr could inflict. He would die before giving her up.

"Who are you? Why are you doing this?" Brody asked, his voice strained and trembling with pain. It wasn't just a plea—it was a tactic. A small, feeble attempt to distract his captor, to sow confusion and buy even a shred of time, just as he'd been trained.

Aleksandr's lips curled into a sneer. "Does the name Kapitan Yaroslav Vasiliev help answer your question?" he snarled. Hatred burned in Aleksandr's eyes—a hatred born of deep, unrelenting pain. The name alone radiated with the weight of history, of vengeance rooted in bloodlines and grudges. Aleksandr's family had been nearly wiped from existence by American hands, and his mission was more than duty—it was personal.

"Vasiliev?" Brody's voice wavered as he fought to stay conscious, his mind struggling to process the unbearable pain. The warmth of his blood leaving his leg was replaced by a creeping cold, and his body's core temperature dropped rapidly. Uncontrollable shivers wracked his body—a trauma response he couldn't suppress. "The Russian captain from the *Medved*?"

In that moment, the pieces fell into place. Something buried in the past, something he had sworn to secrecy decades ago, had come back to haunt him. He turned his head, forcing his gaze to meet the piercing gray eyes of the man torturing him. A young man.

"Are you his son?" Brody croaked.

Aleksandr's lips curled into a wicked grin. "As you Americans would say, BINGO!" he spat, his voice dripping with venom. Without hesitation, he plunged his entire left hand into the blood-lubricated wound, twisting cruelly. The searing pain sent Brody over the edge, his vision tunneling until he momentarily passed out.

Aleksandr leaned closer, his voice rising with unrestrained rage. "Your military comrades have been eliminated. Your wife and son are dead. And I will give you the pleasure of watching me put your daughter in the grave!" Spittle flew from Aleksandr's mouth as he delivered his tirade, his words fueled by years of seething hatred. For Aleksandr, this was justice. This was vengeance. He would finally avenge his family's untimely death, and nothing would stop him now.

"AHHH! I'm sorry about your father! But we didn't blow up the *Medved!* We never heard an explosion. We were called off the scene. You have it wrong!" Brody Hayes pleaded through gritted teeth, his words laced with sincerity. He wasn't just trying to reach Aleksandr—he was stalling, desperate to buy more time for Maddy to escape.

"You lie! All Americans lie!" Aleksandr's fury erupted like a storm. His KGR command and the Russian government had warned him: the Americans would lie. They would do anything to save their skin. To Aleksandr, they were cowards. He sneered down at the gory, incapacitated former soldier, his hatred boiling over.

"You aren't going anywhere," he hissed. "I'll drag your daughter back by her hair so you can watch me slowly end her life."

With that, Aleksandr stood and turned, briskly following the trail of snowshoe prints leading toward the mountain saddle, his weapon at the ready. Brody reached out in desperation, his trembling hand clawing at the snow, but it was no use. The attacker disappeared into the forest, leaving Hayes alone in the silence of the storm.

"RUN, MADDY! RUN!" Brody bellowed, pouring every ounce of energy into his echoing words. His voice carried through the trees, willing his daughter to find the strength to outrun the armed Russian aggressor.

Maddy was no ordinary teenager. Her fitness far exceeded that of her peers—and most adults. Years of club soccer, swimming, snowboarding, and mountaineering had honed her body and endurance. Brody knew she could likely outrun her pursuer, but she couldn't outrun his weapon. He had to do something. He had to help her.

Brody painfully rolled to his right side, using his hands to lift and reposition his deadened left leg. The limb dropped into the snow with a heavy *thud*, sending a flash of searing agony through his body. He forced himself to ignore it, focusing instead on his next move. With trembling fingers, he unclipped the plastic waist buckle of his backpack and shrugged his arms free of the shoulder straps. Unzipping the top lid, he pulled out a small red pouch marked with a white cross—a mountaineering medical kit. His hands worked quickly but deliberately as he retrieved the scissors and began cutting away the shredded fabric of his Gore-Tex pants to assess the wound. The bullet had entered cleanly through the back of his thigh and exited through the front, leaving torn muscle, veins, and flesh in its wake. Bright red blood flowed steadily, pooling around him in the snow, but it wasn't spurting in sync with his heartbeat. That gave Brody a glimmer of hope—the bullet had likely missed his femoral artery. He clung to that possibility, knowing it was the difference between life and imminent death. Reaching into the kit, Brody found a couple of battle dressings, which he tightly applied to both the entry and exit wounds. Then he pulled out a tourniquet, wrapping it high on his upper left thigh. He torqued the strap down with all the strength he could muster, cutting off blood flow and buying himself precious time. The pressure sent a fresh wave of excruciating pain through his body, but Brody didn't make a sound. The throbbing numbness threatened to overwhelm him, but he forced his focus outward. Pain was secondary. His daughter needed him. And he couldn't protect her if he were dead.

CHAPTER 43

Snow Lake

Snoqualmie Pass, Washington

"MADDY, RUN!"

Her father's voice echoed through the forest, cutting through the storm like a beaconing lifeline. Maddy felt a fleeting wave of relief wash over her—he was still alive. The sound renewed her determination, even as her legs burned with exhaustion. Each step sent a fresh surge of pain through her cramped muscles as her snowshoes pressed deep into the powder, leaving heavy waffle prints in the trail behind her. Her tongue clung dryly to the roof of her mouth, each labored gasp pulling more precious moisture from her already dehydrated body. Maddy could never have imagined the intensity of an adrenaline-fueled flight like this—her body pushed beyond its limits, drained of every ounce of fluid it needed to function. But there was no time to stop, no chance to hydrate. Stopping would mean death.

During warmer seasons, Maddy always carried a rubber bladder hydration system, equipped with a long tube for easy access. Brands like Osprey designed these systems specifically for athletes and adventurers, allowing them to hydrate on the go without the hassle of digging through a backpack for a water bottle. But in the frigid winter temperatures, the tube often froze, rendering the system useless. It simply hadn't made sense to bring it this time. The absence of such a convenience now felt like a cruel irony. With every passing second, her body begged for hydration, but she knew stopping was not an option. She forced her mind to push through the discomfort, driving her exhausted legs forward. The only thing that mattered was creating more distance between herself and the armed Russian chasing her.

Maddy Hayes fell into a disciplined trance of survival: one step at a time. She forced herself to focus on the immediate—each snowshoe pressing through the thick powder—and not on the unknowns that loomed over her like a storm cloud. She didn't know how many men were hunting them or how far behind they were. She didn't know if others were waiting at the saddle, ready to ambush her, or even lying in wait near the parking lot—if she could make it that far. The possibilities spun through her throbbing head, each more terrifying than the last. But none of it mattered if she stopped moving.

Keep moving forward.

After what felt like an eternity, Maddy reached the far side of the frozen lake where the trails merged. Her familiarity with this section brought a small flicker of confidence. She knew the path climbed steadily, switching back and forth to gain altitude before mirroring the same zigzag descent on the other side. It was the most efficient route to the saddle. But efficiency wouldn't save her life. Maddy's heart pounded as she weighed her options. Taking the defined switchbacks would be easier, but they were exposed—she would be visible to anyone approaching from the east or west. The higher elevation of the saddle would provide a strategic advantage, but against firearms, that wouldn't mean much. She needed to think smart, to stay ahead of her pursuer and minimize her vulnerability. Scanning the snow-covered terrain, she made her decision. A direct route—straight up the side of the mountain. It would be taxing, but it offered more concealment among the trees and less predictability. Her mind raced, but her body acted decisively. She tightened the straps on her snowshoes and plunged into the steep slope, her survival instincts leading the way.

The vertical, snow-covered mountain terrain was dense with towering conifer trees, their tops swaying rhythmically in the gusting wind. Among them lay scattered fallen giants, victims of the harsh elements that defined the Mount Baker-Snoqualmie National Forest. Through the colder seasons, it wasn't uncommon for these ancient 100-year-old trees to succumb to the relentless 100 mph winds that swept the valley. Maddy bounded up the 60-degree hillside, her legs burning with every step as she pushed forward into the unknown. The thick blanket of snow concealed everything beneath it—fallen trees, jagged rocks, and unseen hazards. Several times, her snowshoes punched through the crust, sending her waist-deep into hidden gaps. Each time, she quickly fought to free herself, dislodging her snowshoe from between the buried obstacles. The jagged metal teeth of her snowshoes struggled for traction on the slick, icy incline, forcing her into a relentless battle against gravity. She slid backward more than once, scrambling to regain her footing with a desperate, gloved bear crawl. Her hands clawed at the snow and ice, fingers digging for purchase as she inched her way upward.

"Maddy Hayes!" Aleksandr called from a distance below.

The sound of her name cut through the forest like a blade. The deep, unmistakable Russian accent shattered the rhythm of her climbing efforts. Maddy froze momentarily, her pulse pounding in her ears. The attacker stood at the edge of the frozen lake, back at the trail crossroads where she had chosen to divert from the exposed switchbacks. He stood still, watching her from below like a predator eyeing its prey. She couldn't stop. She wouldn't. After a fleeting pause, Maddy surged upward, her limbs trembling with exertion. She ignored the Russian's voice, the weight of his presence, and focused solely on reaching the top. Her breath came in labored gasps as she lunged higher and faster, desperate to reach the safety of the saddle.

As Maddy pushed off with her dominant right leg, her left snowshoe suddenly plunged into a hidden gap created by the decomposed trunk of a fallen Douglas Fir. Her forward momentum, already committed, betrayed her as the false sense of security gave way beneath her. The unexpected collapse knocked her off balance, and a gasp escaped her lips as she felt the air leave her lungs. Weightless for a terrifying instant, she was yanked backward by the pull of her backpack. She landed hard on the steep slope, her body flipping completely head over heels. Momentum took over, and Maddy's small frame accelerated down the fresh snowshoe trail she had painstakingly climbed. She slid headfirst, her body twisted and contorted on top of her pack, the slope turning her into an unstoppable projectile. Her ice axe, securely stowed on her pack, left her with no means to self-arrest or control her descent. Snow and ice sprayed around her as she rocketed downhill, the incline growing steeper with every second. The world spun as Maddy gained speed, barreling straight toward Aleksandr, who stood at the bottom of the slope. The Russian operative had no time to react—his attention fixed on the ridge above, oblivious to the teenager hurtling toward him. In a collision that was as sudden as it was violent, Maddy's 110-pound frame struck Aleksandr squarely, sending both sprawling in a chaotic spray of snow and limbs.

The crash felt like a sledgehammer striking Aleksandr, cutting him down with the sheer force of Maddy's uncontrollable tumble. The impact knocked the wind out of both, their bodies tangling and spinning across the snow-covered surface of the frozen lake. Aleksandr's AR-15 slipped from his grasp, disappearing into the snow and sliding out of sight on the ice. Maddy hit the surface hard, sliding on her chest. Automatically, she dug the fronts of her snowshoes into the snow, creating a makeshift self-arrest. Snow and shaved ice piled behind her as she gradually slowed to a stop 20 yards from the shore. Aleksandr slid about 10 yards before rolling onto his back, using his rucksack to break his momentum.

Maddy lay face down, her body limp and trembling with exhaustion. The warmth of her flushed face melted into the fresh powder, only to chill in an instant as the snow froze against her skin. Motionless, she let the pulsing plumes of her breath form a small cloud of steam, momentarily concealing her. In that brief pause, her thoughts churned, grasping for options. They were grim. She was completely exposed on the frozen expanse of Snow Lake. Behind her, the massive hole from the helicopter wreck loomed a few hundred yards away. Ahead of her lay an armed man, blocking any hope of escape. An overwhelming sense of defeat washed over her. Maddy pushed herself up with trembling arms, twisting her body to roll over. As she adjusted her snowshoes and began the effort to stand, a sudden, unnerving sound pierced the stillness—a sharp *creak* followed by a low *crack*. The ice beneath her groaned ominously, shifting with a sound that sent terror surging through her chest. She froze, heart pounding, as the disconcerting noise of settling ice grew louder, its cadenced groans building. Then came the sound that shattered all others—a thunderous, almost laser-like *snap* as the frozen earth beneath her began to fracture. It was an unnatural disturbance—a fierce rupture in the ice, its deafening roar overtaking the wilderness.

Stunned, Maddy was ripped into the air by the sheer, unrelenting strength of the KGR operative. Aleksandr had closed the distance from the shoreline in moments, his immense physique crashing across the frozen lake like a force of nature. Each heavy footstep reverberated through the ice, sending fractures splintering outward. The thick ice creaked and split beneath him, the fissures spreading like a web across the lake's surface.

The breaking ice followed the same rule as a shattered windshield: the cracks raced toward their weakest point. And that point was the combined weight of Aleksandr and Maddy. As the Russian hoisted the teenager into the air, the frozen ground beneath them gave way with a thunderous *crack*. The sound echoed across the lake as the ice shattered beneath their feet. In an instant, both Aleksandr and Maddy disappeared into the frigid, 40-degree water.

From the shoreline trail 100 yards to the west, Brody watched in horror. His breath caught in his throat as he witnessed the frozen lake swallow his daughter. His life had been a relentless test of endurance, but this was a torment beyond anything he had ever faced. The ghosts of his past rose to taunt him: his wife and son were gone, his combat crew gone, the Whidbey SAR helicopter crew gone. And now, Maddy—his last living child—was in grave danger, and he was powerless to stop it.

Brody closed his eyes, his body trembling with anguish. He surrendered the moment to the only power he had left.

Lord, please help. Give Maddy strength. She can't do this alone.

CHAPTER 44

Snow Lake

Snoqualmie Pass, Washington

The shock of the icy water was immediate, cutting through both victims with brutal agony. Shards of broken ice sliced through their winter clothing and tore into exposed skin, leaving jagged cuts across the right side of Maddy's face. As a reflex honed by years of training, she instinctively gasped for air before submerging, though she inhaled a small amount of the frigid water in the process. The freezing liquid burned her throat and lungs as she coughed violently, forcing herself to the surface through the maze of floating ice. Spluttering and gasping, Maddy managed to expel the water, her breath coming in ragged, shallow bursts.

Aleksandr, meanwhile, flailed wildly, his survival instincts overriding all else. In his panicked state, he latched onto Maddy's head, gripping it with desperate force as if she were a life preserver. The weight of his attack nearly pushed her back under. Maddy felt the Russian's thrashing grip tighten and recognized the life-threatening danger in an instant. Her mind clicked into focus, pivoting to the years of rescue training she'd undergone with her dad. Confidence replaced panic as she calmed her thoughts and executed what she had practiced so many times before. With two powerful arm strokes, she disappeared beneath the frigid surface, slipping away from Aleksandr's grasp. The sudden loss of his makeshift flotation left him floundering as he redirected his panicked attention to the jagged edges of the shattered ice. His thrashing activities turned frantic as he clawed at the frozen rim, searching for a way out. Maddy, now free, let muscle memory and training take over. She forced herself to ignore the searing cold that threatened to paralyze her body, focusing instead on survival. The Russian had lost interest in her for the moment, consumed by his desperate fight against the icy grip of the lake.

The frigid water sent sharp bursts of pain shooting through Maddy's head and extremities, the cold seizing her muscles with every passing second. She could feel the onset of hyperventilation creeping in, but years of training with her dad kicked in. She forced her mind to remain calm as she sank deeper into the freezing depths. Realizing her backpack was dragging her down, she quickly released it, but her snowshoes became the next deadly anchors. The metal frames, designed to aid her escape across the snow, now threatened to pull her to the lake's bottom. Fighting the panic that threatened to take hold, Maddy bent at the hip, reaching down to unbuckle the back rubber strap from her left heel, then her right. The straps released with a satisfying snap. A couple of flutter kicks freed her legs completely, and the snowshoes sank 30 feet to the lake's bottom, disappearing into the icy darkness.

Maddy surged upward, breaking through the shattered surface with an exhaled gasp. A fog of steam emitted from her still-warm body, a fleeting reminder of the heat her system was rapidly losing. Her dad's lessons, repeated to the point of exhaustion during training, echoed in her mind.

Don't panic. Stay calm. Move with purpose.

The frigid water had already triggered vasoconstriction, her arteries narrowing in response to the cold. She could feel her heart pounding harder, working overtime to send blood to her core. Her extremities began to lose sensation as the blood flow shifted to protect her vital organs. Maddy knew the brutal truth: this was the first stage of hypothermia. If she didn't act quickly, her body would soon begin to shut down. It was a race against time—a fight against the unforgiving cold and her failing physiology.

Through the haze of her steaming breath and the sharp, floating debris around her, Maddy saw her attacker struggling to escape the icy lake. Each time Aleksandr clawed at the fractured edges of the ice, the surrounding slabs broke away, sending him crashing back into the freezing water. Waves of icy slush radiated outward with each failed attempt, splashing against Maddy's trembling body. But something shifted inside Maddy Hayes. The helplessness and fear that had consumed her moments earlier dissolved. She was no longer a fragile teenage girl, outweighed and outmatched by an aggressive assassin. She was in her element now, the cold and the water no longer liabilities but tools to equalize the playing field. Her hazel eyes, once wide with innocence, hardened into a look of predatory determination. Her breathing slowed as she focused on her objective. Maddy took a deep, composed breath and sank silently below the frigid water's surface. In the dark, numbing depths, she glided toward the unsuspecting KGR operative from behind with committed determination.

Aleksandr kicked frantically, his snowshoes still strapped to his feet, as he made another desperate attempt to lunge out of the icy pool. His trembling body surged upward, but just as he neared the edge, his progress was violently halted. An arm wrapped across his neck and chest with unrelenting force, dragging him backward. Aleksandr's grip on the ice slipped, and he toppled helplessly back into the freezing water, headfirst into the black abyss. Maddy had surfaced from behind him, her right arm stretching up and over his right shoulder to secure a powerful hold. She locked her hands tightly together in a controlled cross-chest carry—a diagonal bearhug designed to dominate and subdue. Using her body weight, momentum, and the surprise of her attack, she yanked them both backward into the ice bath. As Aleksandr thrashed and sputtered, trying to process the sudden reversal, Maddy kicked ferociously, pulling them both deeper. The water, once a death sentence, was now her weapon.

Panicked and out of control, Aleksandr thrashed wildly, desperate to break free of Maddy's hold. His initial shocked response caused him to swallow a mouthful of freezing water, sending him into a fit of coughing and sputtering. He twisted his body back and forth, using his superior strength to claw his way out of her grip. Maddy held him tightly, maintaining control as best she could, but Aleksandr's relentless struggle eventually allowed him to spin free. He clawed upward with all his might, breaking through the surface just enough to steal a small, desperate gasp of air before Maddy yanked him back under.

Facing her now, Aleksandr flailed his arms wildly, his hands clawing toward her head and throat in a blind, furious attempt to regain dominance. But Maddy was ready. Years of training had prepared her for this exact moment. With calm precision, she executed a move drilled into her muscle memory—a technique commonly called the front head hold release. Her right thumb jabbed into a pressure point on the right side of his jaw, sending a sharp shock of pain through his face. Simultaneously, she shoved his right arm, which had locked around her neck, up and over her left shoulder. In one fluid motion, she twisted his body in the opposite direction, using his strength and momentum against him. Before Aleksandr could react, Maddy had regained control. She secured him once again in a powerful cross-chest carry, locking his flailing body into a vise-like grip. Her legs scissored with forceful kicks, propelling them both deeper into the icy void. The frozen landscape above disappeared as she dragged him below, the dark water becoming her ally in the fight for survival.

Maddy, desperate for air, fought to remain calm even as her heart and body struggled against the creeping inevitability of hypothermia. Her muscles screamed for oxygen, her lungs burned, but her unwavering courage kept her anchored. Aleksandr thrashed violently, his powerful frame twisting and jerking in a desperate attempt to break free. Yet, Maddy's grip held firm—an unrelenting show of strength born from a determination far greater than fear. An overwhelming sense of peace washed over her in that moment. Despite the chaos, she clung to the Russian murderer with a quiet resolve that felt almost otherworldly. Time blurred as the seconds stretched into an eternity. Nearly two minutes submerged, Maddy's vision began to fade, and she felt herself slipping into the edges of unconsciousness. The blackness crept closer, her body nearing its limit. Then, something unexplainable happened.

Maddy, teetering on the brink of collapse, released her left hand from Aleksandr's chest while still maintaining a powerful hold with her right arm wrapped around his shoulder and torso. In the absolute darkness of the icy water, she reached up with her left hand, finding his forehead. With a sudden, forceful motion, she jerked his head backward, opening his airway. Freezing water rushed down the Russian's throat, flooding his lungs with an unstoppable torrent of icy liquid. His chest heaved reflexively, convulsing in Maddy's iron grip as hypoxia claimed him. His powerful thrashing slowed to weak spasms before stopping altogether. Maddy loosened her hold, releasing Aleksandr's lifeless body into the depths of Snow Lake. She watched, her mind and body detached from the moment, as he sank slowly out of sight. Then, as her strength ebbed away completely, her world faded to black.

CHAPTER 45

Snow Lake

Snoqualmie Pass, Washington

An overwhelming sense of peace consumed Maddy's mind as she drifted deeper into the freezing lake. The biting cold faded away, replaced by a strange, numbing warmth. Her body no longer shivered, her fierce emotions evaporated, leaving only a dead calm of nothingness. The world around her went dark. Suddenly, she was hiking with her family on one of her favorite mountains. It was a perfect spring day, the kind she loved for beating the weekend crowds of hikers clogging the local trails. The four of them marched single file, navigating the switchbacks that wound their way to the summit of McClellan Butte.

The towering 5,162-foot Cascade Range peak loomed majestically over Interstate 90, a vertical mile above the millions of drivers who admired its beauty from afar but seldom found the courage to attempt its rocky spire. Maddy felt light, almost weightless, as she moved forward, watching tender green leaves unfurl from their March buds. Patches of snow clung stubbornly to shaded crevices, destined to melt away with the growing warmth of spring. The air was perfectly still, save for the occasional 4 mph breeze, which carried a gentle warmth. Ahead, her brother Mitch and her mom chatted about the blooming mountain flora and how it would inevitably wreak havoc on their allergies. The comforting sound of their voices made her smile. Her dad followed behind, saying something she couldn't quite make out. His voice was muffled, distant, but comforting. Maddy's steps felt effortless as she closed the gap between herself and her mom and Mitch. She couldn't remember the last time she felt so happy, so at peace. It was as if nothing else mattered in this perfect moment. She was truly in heaven. Her mom and Mitch turned sharply at a switchback ahead, their steps purposeful yet relaxed. Maddy followed them, rounding the corner with ease. Then, she stopped abruptly, jolted as if hitting an invisible wall. Her mom and Mitch were suddenly right in front of her, only inches away, their forms startlingly close.

"Goodbye."

The single word, spoken in unison, startled Maddy. She felt a sudden, jarring force from behind, as though she had been whiplashed out of her serene moment. Bright light pierced her senses, followed by the biting cold, and splintering pain surged through her body. She gasped as her fragile form scraped across breaking ice and snow.

"Maddy! Breathe, honey! Come on!" Her dad's desperate voice cut through the confusion. Brody dragged her out of the freezing water, inching them closer to the shore. Maddy convulsed, coughing violently as she vomited up the icy water that had invaded her lungs. Life sputtered back into her trembling body, her heart struggling at a dangerously low rate of fewer than 20 beats per minute. It worked overtime, frail but determined, to push blood to her extremities. Her body shook uncontrollably as hypothermia gripped her like a vice.

Brody knew he had to get her off the lake and to safety, fast. Moments earlier, Brody had watched in helpless horror as Maddy and the Russian attacker broke through the ice. Lying helpless in a pool of warm blood, he had surrendered himself to prayer, pleading for divine intervention. Then, as though guided by an unseen force, he felt an undeniable urge to move. Despite his injuries—a dislocated right shoulder and a .223 Remington bullet wound in his left thigh—he summoned the strength to drag himself 100 yards across the fragile ice. Using a modified army crawl, Brody clawed his way forward with his left arm and pushed with his right leg, gritting his teeth against the searing pain. His thigh tourniquet held firm but couldn't completely stop the trail of bright red blood seeping behind him, streaking across the snow-covered lake.

Brody distributed his weight carefully, lying flat instead of standing, to prevent the ice from breaking further. The technique was second nature, one he had used countless times crossing fragile snow bridges on glaciated peaks around the world. Each agonizing effort sent cracks and squeals through the ice beneath him, the sound an ominous reminder of the razor-thin margin between survival and catastrophe. But the ice held, just enough, allowing him to inch closer to his daughter. Now, with Maddy in his grasp, Brody fought through the pain, dragging her fragile, freezing body toward the shore. The battle was far from over, but he wasn't giving up. Not now. Not ever.

Within minutes, Brody reached the edge of the ten-by-ten-foot crushed ice pool where Maddy had fallen through. Without a second thought, the former Aviation Rescue Swimmer slid into the freezing water, the frigid temperature delivering a brutal shock to his body. But Brody had spent a lifetime enduring cold water—his mind overpowered his body's instinctive reaction, focusing instead on the mission at hand. Through the icy darkness, his lifeless daughter came into view, her body drifting facedown just beneath the ice shelf. Below her, the deceased Russian assassin hovered in the depths, his form eerily still, 10 feet below. Brody ignored the shadowy figure and locked his gaze on Maddy. Reaching forward, he grabbed her by the collar of her soaked down jacket, twisting his body to orient himself. With a modified frog kick using only his right leg, Brody powered backward toward the surface. The freezing water numbed his injuries, dulling the searing pain from his dislocated shoulder and bullet wound, though every desperate kick reminded him of his physical limitations. He pushed through, summoning every ounce of strength he had left.

As he kicked, Maddy's body shifted upright, her face and torso scraping along the underside of the solid ice shelf. Brody maneuvered her carefully, guiding her toward the relief of the broken ice section. His body shrieked in dispute, but his determination was unshakable. Shards of ice and water cascaded from Brody's head as he breached the surface, gasping for air. With a quick, practiced motion, he pulled Maddy's head above the water. Her face was pale, her lips tinged blue, her body lifeless in his arms. Brody tilted her head back and delivered two long rescue breaths, watching as her chest rose slightly beneath her sodden jacket. His lips trembled from the cold as he repeated the breaths, his mind racing. Her body remained still, unresponsive, as he held her close.

"Come on, Maddy," he whispered hoarsely, desperation laced in his voice. "Breathe."

Pushing through the searing pain in his shoulder and leg, Brody towed Maddy through the labyrinth of frozen debris toward the far side where he had previously entered. "Maddy! Breathe, honey! Come on!" he called to her over and over, his voice desperate yet determined.

Lightheaded and dizzy from extreme blood loss, he struggled to lift her limp body onto the fragile ice edge. Her back pivoted on the jagged rim, but as her weight shifted out of the water, a three-foot section of ice cracked and gave way. The sudden collapse sent both plunging backward into the freezing water. Brody scrambled, his body objecting with every movement as he fought to keep Maddy's head above water. He spoke to her continuously, his words steady despite the hopelessness threatening to consume him. He delivered more rescue breaths, his own oxygen running thin as he assessed the dire situation.

Dying is not an option. Not for him. Not for Maddy.

Realizing the ice would be thicker closer to shore, Brody made a grim decision. He would deliberately break the edges of the ice from within the water, carving a path until they reached more solid ground. It was their only chance. Holding Maddy tightly with his right hand to ensure her head stayed above water, Brody lunged upward with his left side, pressing down hard on the ice to break it.

The fragile surface cracked under the weight and momentum of his push, sending him back into the icy depths. He spun underwater, using his left arm to stabilize Maddy and ensure she remained afloat. Over and over, Brody repeated the process, transitioning between icebreaker and first responder. His body screamed for rest, the freezing water leeching what little strength he had left, but he pressed on. The laborious effort kept his blood circulating, keeping him alive for now, but he knew with every passing second, Maddy was freezing to death.

"Hold on, Maddy," he whispered, his voice trembling with exhaustion. "Just hold on."

As Brody continued chiseling his way closer to shore, he noticed a promising change—the ice was growing thicker. He could lunge further without breaking through as easily, a sign of progress. Summoning what remained of his strength, he pressed onward. After an unsuccessful attempt to create another fissure, Brody lunged upward, sliding his body forward across the icy surface. Like a seal breaching a floating glacial iceberg, he dragged himself forward while maintaining a firm hold on his floating daughter.

Inching carefully away from the water opening, he switched arms, relying on his left upper body to crawl and pull. His right hand, attached to his dislocated shoulder, clung impossibly tight to Maddy's jacket collar, refusing to let go. As he painstakingly dragged her toward him, her dead weight caused another section of ice to collapse. Unfazed, Brody adjusted his leverage and used momentum to pull her closer, refusing to stop. Inch by inch, he shifted her body until her weight finally equalized onto the solid, flat surface. He didn't relent until Maddy was completely clear of the water. Only then did he collapse momentarily from sheer exhaustion, his body trembling with fatigue. But Brody wasn't done. In an instant, he sprang back to life.

"Maddy! Breathe, honey! Come on!" he shouted, his voice raw with fear. He knelt by her side, his hands trembling as he delivered more rescue breaths. When she remained unresponsive, he began chest compressions, pushing down on her small frame with his right hand. Then, a sputter. Maddy coughed convulsively, water spraying from her lips as her body struggled to inhale the frigid air. Brody swiftly turned her onto her side, helping her cough and expel the water trapped in her lungs and stomach. Tears streamed down Brody's face as he cradled his daughter in his arms, holding her tightly against his own trembling body. He rocked her gently, his warmth surrounding her as life gradually returned to her fragile form.

"You're okay, Maddy," he whispered, his voice breaking. "You're okay."

CHAPTER 46

Snoqualmie Pass, Washington

WHOMP! WHOMP! WHOMP!

The mountains lining the Snoqualmie Pass valley reverberated with the rhythmic thumping of the approaching Yakima DUSTOFF UH-60M Black Hawk helicopter. The sound grew incrementally louder, cutting through the stillness of the snowy wilderness.

Brody Hayes cradled his daughter tightly in his arms, his body trembling with exhaustion and pain as he fought to share what little warmth he had left with her hypothermic form. The familiar sound of the helicopter blades triggered a mix of hope and desperation in his chest. Hours earlier, that same sound had heralded tragedy—the death of his Whidbey SAR brothers. But now, it represented salvation, a fragile thread of safety and rescue. The snowfall had diminished to a light flurry, the winds easing to a gentle whisper. As the sun dipped lower, the fading light revealed a broader view of the rugged valley, the sky painted with hues of orange and gray. Brody turned his face upward toward the approaching helicopter, his raw determination mingling with an unspoken prayer.

They must make it in time.

The thrum of the Black Hawk grew closer, the sound carrying the weight of hope as it descended toward them. Brody inched across the frozen lake toward his backpack. Digging into its contents, he fished out two ChemLights to signal the helicopter as the shadows of nightfall crept over the valley. He shoved them into his left jacket pocket before retracing his path back to Maddy. The thundering rotor blades and engine noise of the approaching UH-60M Black Hawk grew louder, the vibrations rippling through the frozen surface beneath him. Brody reached his daughter, who sat huddled in shock, shaking uncontrollably from the cold and trauma.

"Help is here, honey," Brody said softly, his voice steady despite his exhaustion. He pulled the ChemLights from his pocket, bent them sharply in his left hand, and snapped the plastic tubes. Shaking them vigorously, he activated the internal compounds, creating two glowing green lights that pierced the encroaching darkness.

Above, the spotlights of the Yakima DUSTOFF helicopter appeared through a swirling artificial snowstorm kicked up over the saddle by its powerful rotors. The pilots quickly spotted the two glowing ChemLights being waved on the west side of the frozen alpine lake. Captain McKenzie skillfully maneuvered the aircraft into an approach, while the door gunner's M240 machine guns remained trained on the signaling survivor. The aircrew, equipped with night vision goggles, scanned the area using the Black Hawk's infrared instruments, searching for any potential threats. The limited details of the mission demanded caution—there was always the possibility of being drawn into an ambush. The crew moved with proficiency, balancing their focus on the survivors below with the vigilance required for an uncertain extraction.

As the Black Hawk descended closer, the wind and snow intensified around them, but Brody stood his ground, the glowing green ChemLights cutting through the dark, a beacon of hope in the frozen wilderness.

"Oh my God," CWO Talbott muttered solemnly as the Black Hawk flew directly over the wreckage of the Whidbey SAR MH-60S. From above, the sunken aircraft was unnervingly visible through the massive hole in the frozen lake. The sight hit the crew like a punch to the gut, a stark reminder of the mission's stakes. But they pushed aside their emotions and stayed focused.

On an initial pass, with weapons trained, SGT Van Buren visually confirmed the survivors' location. The Yakima DUSTOFF helicopter flew a high circular pattern around the lake, scanning for threats before transitioning into a steady hover facing the wind. SGT Van Buren lowered SGT Steele 60 feet down the hoist, landing him near the Hayes. Brody cradled Maddy tightly against his chest, shielding her face from the powerful rotor wash and debris kicked up by the hovering aircraft. The sound was deafening, but SGT Steele interrogated Brody over the noise, confirming his identity. Satisfied, he used hand signals to direct the Crew Chief to lower the rescue basket.

With the basket in position, Steele guided Maddy inside, securing her carefully before giving the signal. It rose steadily toward the cabin. Moments later, Brody and Sergeant Steele were hoisted up behind her. Once inside, the cabin door was slid shut, sealing out the bitter cold as the pilots plotted a direct course to Harborview Medical Center. SGT Steele and SGT Van Buren immediately began treating the Hayes. Maddy and Brody were placed into rescue litters, securely strapped in as SGT Steele administered IV fluids and treated them both for hypothermia. Meanwhile, SGT Van Buren attended to Brody's tourniquet and bullet wound, working efficiently under the roar of the UH-60M's powerful rotors. The helicopter banked upward, climbing over the mountains to follow Interstate 90 westward for 50 miles toward Seattle.

Inside the cabin, father and daughter lay flat in their litters, unable to unlock their gaze from one another. The intense vibration of the aircraft and the constant thrum of the rotors seemed distant, oddly muted. A surreal calm settled over them, the adrenaline of survival ebbing into an emotional emptiness. The two remaining members of the Hayes family stared at one another, emotionless but bound by an unspoken connection. The shock coursing through their bodies etched indelible memories into their souls—memories that would forever alter the purpose and direction of their lives.

EPILOGUE

Harbor View Medical Center
Seattle, Washington

"Good morning, Dad. Well, it's not exactly morning." Maddy sat beside Brody's hospital bed, her voice soft and fragile. The dark, sunken circles beneath her hazel eyes told a story of trauma and exhaustion, a silent testament to what they had endured.

After the DUSTOFF UH-60M Black Hawk helicopter delivered them to the capable staff at Harborview Medical Center, both were rushed to the ICU. Maddy had been treated for severe hypothermia. Two IV bags and a heated blanket stabilized her condition, and she'd passed out for over 12 hours, her body finally succumbing to much-needed rest.

Brody's situation had been more critical. He had lost over 40% of his blood to the gunshot wound in his leg. Paradoxically, the freezing cold and his submersion in Snow Lake had saved his life, slowing his heartbeat and reducing blood loss. He was taken directly to the operating room, where the entry and exit wounds were meticulously cleaned and stitched. Though the injury left permanent muscle and nerve damage, the doctors confirmed he wouldn't lose the leg. Now, groggy but alive, Brody turned his attention to his daughter, the only thing that mattered.

"Hey, honey," he murmured, his voice rasping from fatigue. "How are you feeling?" He ignored his own pain and condition, his concern solely for her.

The lingering effects of the propofol sedative coursing through Brody's veins caused his reality to flicker in and out. Each heavy blink of his eyelids created a strobe-like effect as he watched his daughter approach, closer with every fleeting moment. Then, they were in a tight embrace, their warmth cutting through the sterile chill of the hospital room. Tears flowed freely down their faces, their unspoken bond palpable. It was a connection forged through unimaginable adversity. Thoughts of shock, loss, survival, confusion, fear, and murder twisted through their minds, tangling into an emotional storm neither could fully process. The trauma of the past 48 hours loomed large, a burden that would take a lifetime to unravel.

Their tender moment was abruptly interrupted. "Mr. Hayes, I'm Special Agent Reynolds with the Central Intelligence Agency," a voice said firmly, breaking the fragile silence. "We need to talk."

* * *

Gulf of Maine
12 miles east of Gloucester, Massachusetts

"Pedro, come up here! Bring the binoculars!" Captain Derek called out over the sound of the boat's engine. His voice carried across the deck to one of his crewmembers, who was celebrating a successful day's catch with the charter clients.

"What's up, Skipper?" Pedro asked, climbing up to the helm and handing over the binoculars. He took a swig from his bottle of Ipswich Summer Ale, his casual demeanor in stark contrast to the captain's focused expression.

"There!" Captain Derek said, raising the binoculars and pointing toward the one o'clock position. After a moment of study, he handed them back to Pedro and adjusted the wheel slightly to the starboard, setting a new heading.

The low rumble of the 36-foot Phoenix tuna fishing charter boat's engine rose as it accelerated, cutting through the calm waters. The sudden change in direction drew the attention of the fishing clients on the deck. Curious, they leaned around the superstructure, craning their necks to see what had piqued the captain's interest.

"It's a body!" Pedro shouted, his voice sharp as he struggled to steady the binoculars against the bounce of the 2-foot swells. "It's definitely a body!"

Captain Derek pushed the throttle forward, racing across the ocean toward the floating figure. As they neared, he slowed the boat and carefully maneuvered it alongside the face-up body before cutting the engine. Pedro and another crew member grabbed a 15-foot telescoping boat hook pole and leaned over the edge, trying to snag the unnerving figure adrift in the water.

After a few failed attempts, the pole caught the waistband of the man's pants. With a coordinated pull, they brought the body closer to the boat. That's when they noticed the man's hands and feet were bound. A chill ran through the crew as they realized the implications. Moving quickly, Pedro and the crew dragged the lifeless body toward the aft deck and hauled him onboard. Joe, one of the three fishing clients, pale and trembling, doubled over and vomited the beer he had just downed. The other two stared in disbelief, frozen by the horrific scene unfolding before them.

Captain Derek knelt beside the bound, swollen figure, his hands trembling as he began an initial assessment of the man's condition. Running through the first aid ABCs—airway, breathing, and circulation—he pressed two fingers against the carotid artery on the man's neck. He held his breath, watching intently for any sign of life.

The usually composed skipper suddenly jerked backward, his face drained of color. "Oh my God!" he gasped, his voice barely above a whisper. Turning to Pedro, he shouted, "Radio the Coast Guard dispatcher. *He's alive!*"

ACKNOWLEDGEMENTS

Writing a military thriller turned out to be more of an undertaking than I imagined. Nonfiction is challenging because every detail is real—you strive for total accuracy, and reliving the experience can be emotionally draining. Fiction, on the other hand—especially in the military thriller space—can be just as intense. Tapping into real-world operations, scenarios that may or may not have occurred, and weaving them into a complex web of characters and storylines requires a different kind of depth. It stretched my creativity in new ways, and at times, reopened wounds I thought had long healed.

Bloodline of Redemption is rooted in real experiences—those of warriors and mountaineers I've had the honor of knowing. I'm forever grateful for those relationships and continue to mourn the loss of brothers who never made it home.

To **JoAnna Dickinson**—thank you for reading through a military thriller you wouldn't normally pick up, and for pushing through the moments that made you uncomfortable. Your unique perspective and honest feedback helped shape this book into what it is today.

To **Emily Dickinson**—you were the first to hold a printed copy in your hands and offer the fine-tuning it needed. Your timely input eased the pressure of my release deadline while I was traveling, and I'm deeply grateful.

To **Joe Sutherland**—thank you for taking an early look at my draft and offering the blunt but honest feedback that it needed more work. You helped me get out of my head and ensure the story made sense on the page. Also, thank you for being such a good sport as I subtly incorporate cameos of you into everything I produce.

To **Cory Merritt, Jonathan Showerman, Larry Grossman, Drew Worth, and Erica Gibson**—your early reads and feedback on the ASW and SAR sections were invaluable. Thank you for keeping it real.

Brian Dickinson

To **Jack Carr, Chad Robichaux, Eric Blehm, Marcus Luttrell, Jason Redman, Don Mann, Brandon Webb, and Rodney Magallan**— thank you for taking the time to read the manuscript and offer guidance, endorsements, and encouragement. Your work, your stories, and your lives have inspired me more than you know. I'm honored to walk among you.

Brian Mitchell and **Dave Schroeder**—you've been with me since day one. Thank you for believing in me and supporting this journey from the very beginning.

Jeff and **Jacki Jones** for an early read, feedback, and your infectious positive energy and friendship.

To **Eric Lupfer** at United Talent Agency—your insight and guidance during the publishing process helped shape the direction of this book, even though we ultimately took a different path. I appreciate your mentorship more than you realize.

JoAnna, Emily, and Jordan—your unwavering support means everything. You inspire me daily, and I love you with all my heart.

And most of all, I thank **God** for the platform, the opportunity, and the ability to share my experiences with others. None of this would be possible without Him.

— Brian Dickinson

AUTHOR'S NOTE

Bloodline of Redemption is my first novel in the fiction, military thriller genre. My previous books—*Blind Descent* and *Calm in the Chaos*—are nonfiction accounts of real-life events I experienced on Mount Everest and during my time as a U.S. Navy Aviation Rescue Swimmer. *Calm in the Chaos* also shares the untold stories of more than forty other Rescue Swimmers—acts of heroism that deserve far more recognition than they've ever received.

That's exactly why I launched the *Calm in the Chaos Podcast*—to continue sharing these powerful stories from humble heroes who live by the motto: **"So Others May Live."**

So, why fiction?

There are a few reasons. My nonfiction writing has focused on traumatic events—experiences I'm incredibly grateful to have survived but have no desire to relive. While I have plenty of material to write more in that genre, I wanted to try my hand at something different—something that allowed me to channel those experiences in a new way.

Fiction became a powerful outlet, offering a means to process real-life moments while exploring alternate outcomes. During my six years in the Navy, I had the opportunity to conduct several unforgettable mission sets during two deployments to the Persian Gulf in support of Operation Southern Watch. My squadron, HS-2, logged thousands of flight hours conducting SAR/CSAR operations, ASW missions, medical evacuations, and nearly every other task our H-60 helicopters could handle. *Bloodline of Redemption* draws from that experience. Several missions in the novel are inspired by actual operations—presented at a high level to protect identities and operational security. The same is true for the mountaineering scenes; while rooted in reality, they've been woven into the fabric of a fictional narrative.

This story contains intense content and may stir deep emotions—especially for veterans navigating the aftereffects of war and trauma. If that's you: thank you for your service. And please know that healing is possible. The path to recovery from post-traumatic stress is steep, but like any challenging ascent, it begins with the courage to take one more step. I know this firsthand. I spent years compartmentalizing emotions I didn't want to face before finally seeking help. It felt impossible at times—but there is always hope.

Researching and writing *Bloodline of Redemption* also brought me to many of the real-world locations featured in the book. I wanted to breathe the air, hear the sounds, and experience the energy of each place firsthand. That occasionally meant crossing a few literal and legal lines—what I'll call "borderline trespassing," though there wasn't much "borderline" about it. Combine that with a browser history packed with tactical, legal, and possibly criminal topics, and I'm probably flagged on at least one FBI cybersecurity watchlist.

Ultimately, my goal was to craft an entertaining military thriller grounded in authenticity—true to history without breaching classified territory. It's also one of the rare thrillers to feature a U.S. Navy Aviation Rescue Swimmer as the protagonist—a role that showcases the adaptability, capability, and mindset we consistently see in this small but elite community.

This novel is also dedicated to **Brian Gurr**, a gifted Navy helicopter pilot who lost his life in a tragic training accident, and **Tony Dicenso**, a Master Chief Aviation Rescue Swimmer and ASW operator, whose life was cut short in a motorcycle accident. Both served with honor as part of my combat crew during deployment. Their legacy lives on in every mission, every story, and every moment of silence we hold in their honor.

From the beginning, it was important to me that this story stayed engaging from start to finish. I worked hard to ensure there was never a dull moment. Writing this book has been fun, challenging, and ultimately therapeutic—and I'm proud of what it's become. I hope you enjoy *Bloodline of Redemption* and are as excited for future installments in the series as I am.

— Brian Dickinson

GLOSSARY

MILITARY & AVIATION TERMS

ABC (Airway, Breathing, Circulation) — The foundational sequence used during emergency medical assessment and trauma care.

ADCAP (Advanced Capability Torpedo) — Upgraded variant of the MK-48 heavyweight torpedo used by U.S. Navy submarines.

AO (Aviation Ordnanceman) — Navy aviation rate responsible for aircraft weapons systems, ammunition handling, and ordnance loading.

ASMOD (Anti-Submarine Warfare Module) — Specialized operations center aboard an aircraft carrier used to coordinate ASW missions and tactical tracking.

ASW (Anti-Submarine Warfare) — Military operations focused on detecting, tracking, and engaging enemy submarines.

Auxiliary Power Unit (APU) — Independent onboard power system used to start aircraft systems and provide electrical power while on deck or on the ground.

AW / Aviation Warfare Operator — Naval Aircrewman designation for enlisted aviation warfare specialists operating sensors, rescue systems, and mission equipment.

AWC (Aviation Warfare Operator Chief) — Senior enlisted Naval Aircrewman specializing in airborne warfare systems and mission operations.

AWRCS (Naval Aircrewman Tactical Helicopter Senior Chief) — Senior enlisted Aviation Rescue Swimmer and Naval Aircrewman responsible for rescue operations and crew coordination.

Battle Group — Naval strike formation centered around an aircraft carrier and protected by cruisers, destroyers, submarines, and support ships.

CIC (Combat Information Center) — Tactical nerve center aboard a warship where radar, sonar, intelligence, and combat operations are coordinated.

CMDR (Commander) — U.S. Navy officer rank equivalent to Lieutenant Colonel.

Countermeasures — Defensive systems or decoys designed to confuse, evade, or defeat incoming weapons.

CSAR (Combat Search and Rescue) — Military rescue missions conducted in hostile or combat environments.

Cyclic — Primary helicopter flight control used to direct aircraft pitch and movement.

DUSTOFF — Military medevac helicopter mission designation originally associated with Army medical evacuation operations.

ELF (Extremely Low Frequency) — Specialized radio transmission frequency capable of communicating with submerged submarines.

ELT (Emergency Locator Transmitter) — Emergency distress beacon carried aboard aircraft that automatically transmits a location signal after a crash or severe impact to assist search-and-rescue personnel in locating survivors.

EOD (Explosive Ordnance Disposal) — Military specialists trained to disarm and dispose of explosives and hazardous munitions.

FLIR (Forward Looking Infrared) — Thermal imaging system used for night operations, targeting, navigation, and search-and-rescue missions.

FRIES Bar (Fast Rope Insertion and Extraction System) — Helicopter-mounted system allowing personnel to rapidly rappel or fast-rope from hovering aircraft.

GPS (Global Positioning System) — Satellite-based navigation and positioning system.

HAC (Helicopter Aircraft Commander) — Pilot in command of a Navy helicopter mission.

Hellfire Missile — Precision-guided air-to-surface missile commonly deployed from helicopters and drones.

HH-60H — Legacy U.S. Navy combat search-and-rescue and special warfare helicopter.

HS-2 — Helicopter Anti-Submarine Squadron TWO, Golden Falcons, a U.S. Navy helicopter squadron specializing in ASW, SAR, and combat support missions. Redesignated to HSC-12 in 2009.

IEWS (Integrated Electronic Warfare System) — Defensive electronic warfare suite used to detect and counter incoming threats.

JBLM (Joint Base Lewis-McChord) — Major U.S. military installation in Washington State.

LCDR (Lieutenant Commander) — Mid-level U.S. Navy officer rank equivalent to Major.

M240 — Belt-fed 7.62 mm medium machine gun widely used by U.S. military forces.

MH-60S Seahawk — Multi-mission U.S. Navy helicopter used for SAR, CSAR, logistics, special warfare support, and combat operations.

MK-46 Torpedo — Lightweight anti-submarine torpedo launched from ships and aircraft.

MK-48 ADCAP — Advanced heavyweight submarine-launched torpedo used against enemy submarines and surface vessels.

MK54 Torpedo — Advanced lightweight digital torpedo used in anti-submarine warfare operations.

NASWI (Naval Air Station Whidbey Island) — Major U.S. Navy aviation base in Washington State.

Passive Sonar — Sonar mode that listens without transmitting acoustic signals, allowing stealth tracking.

P-3 Orion — Long-range maritime patrol and anti-submarine warfare aircraft.

PR Shop (Parachute Rigger Shop) — Naval aviation workspace responsible for survival gear, harnesses, parachutes, and rescue equipment.

SAR (Search and Rescue) — Missions focused on locating and recovering individuals in distress.

SATCOM (Satellite Communications) — Secure communications transmitted through satellite systems.

SEAL (Sea, Air, and Land (SEAL) Teams) — Elite U.S. Navy special operations force.

SH-60F Seahawk — Carrier-based anti-submarine warfare helicopter used extensively by the U.S. Navy.

Situation Room — Highly secure White House command center used during military and national security crises.

Sonobuoy — Deployable sonar sensor used to detect submarine activity underwater.

SPECWAR (Special Warfare) — Military special operations missions involving direct action, reconnaissance, or unconventional warfare.

SSN (Nuclear-Powered Attack Submarine) — Hull classification for fast attack submarines powered by nuclear reactors.

TAO (Tactical Action Officer) — Officer responsible for directing tactical combat operations aboard a warship.

Tiger Cruise — Navy tradition allowing family members to sail aboard a ship during part of a homecoming transit.

TSO (Tactical Sensor Operator) — Aircrewman responsible for sonar, radar, and tactical sensor systems during airborne operations.

VHF (Very High Frequency) — Radio frequency range commonly used for aviation and maritime communications.

VLF (Very Low Frequency) — Long-range radio transmission capable of communicating with submerged submarines.

SHIPS & SUBMARINES

K-151 Medved — Fictional Russian Oscar II-class nuclear submarine central to the story's conflict.

USS Chosin (CG-65) — U.S. Navy Ticonderoga-class guided missile cruiser.

USS Cimarron (AO-177) — Fleet replenishment oiler supporting naval operations at sea.
USS Constellation (CV-64) — Kitty Hawk-class aircraft carrier serving as the primary carrier in the story.
USS John Paul Jones (DDG-53) — Arleigh Burke-class guided missile destroyer.
USS Kitty Hawk (CV-63) — U.S. Navy aircraft carrier referenced during Pacific operations.
USS Lake Erie (CG-70) — Ticonderoga-class guided missile cruiser.
USS Merrill (DD-976) — Spruance-class destroyer.
USS Mount Hood (AE-29) — Ammunition supply ship supporting fleet logistics.
USS Santa Fe (SSN-763) — Los Angeles-class nuclear-powered attack submarine tasked with tracking the Medved.
USS Topeka (SSN-754) — Los Angeles-class attack submarine operating with the battle group.

MOUNTAINEERING TERMS

Avalanche — Rapid downslope movement of snow, ice, and debris capable of overwhelming climbers.
Carabiner — Metal safety connector used in climbing systems to attach ropes, anchors, and gear.
Crampons — Metal traction devices attached to mountaineering boots for travel on snow and ice.
Crevasse — Deep crack or fracture in a glacier, often hidden beneath snow bridges.
Fisher Chimneys — Technical alpine climbing route on Mount Shuksan in Washington State.
Fixed Rope — Anchored climbing rope used to assist ascent or descent on steep terrain.
Glacier Travel — Technical mountaineering movement across glaciated terrain while managing crevasse and avalanche hazards.
Ice Axe — Mountaineering tool used for balance, climbing, and self-arrest during falls on snow or ice.
Ice Screw — Metal climbing anchor drilled into ice for protection and securing ropes or shelters.
Rope Team — Group of climbers connected by rope while traveling across hazardous terrain.
Self-Arrest — Emergency climbing technique using an ice axe to stop a fall on steep snow or ice.

Serac — Large unstable tower or block of glacier ice capable of collapsing without warning.
Snow Bridge — Thin layer of snow concealing a crevasse opening.
South Col — High-altitude saddle between Mount Everest and Lhotse, commonly used as a staging area for summit attempts.
Sulphide Glacier — Glacier route on Mount Shuksan used in alpine mountaineering ascents.
Upper Curtis Glacier — Glacier located on Mount Shuksan in the North Cascades.

ALSO BY BRIAN DICKINSON

Bestselling Author • Everest Survivor • U.S. Navy Aviation Rescue Swimmer

Blind Descent

Surviving Alone and Blind on Mount Everest
An unforgettable true story of survival, courage, and faith after losing vision near the summit of the world's highest peak.
[Available in hardcover, paperback, ebook, and audiobook]

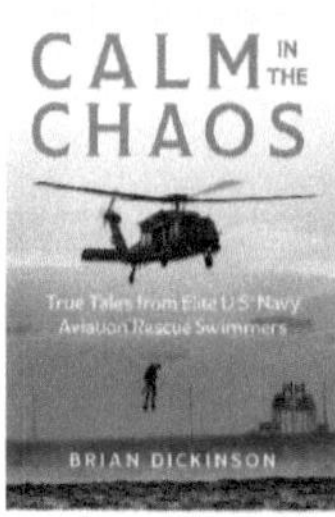

Calm in the Chaos

True Tales from Elite U.S. Navy Aviation Rescue Swimmers
A powerful, real-life look at rescue swimmer missions, leadership, and how to find peace amid chaos.
Includes true stories from over 40 elite U.S. Navy Aviation Rescue Swimmers.
[Available in hardcover, ebook, and audiobook]

Calm in the Chaos Podcast

Untold Stories from America's Military Heroes
Host Brian Dickinson interviews fellow veterans, rescue swimmers, and first responders—exploring grit, resilience, and real-life survival.
→ Listen on Spotify, Apple Podcasts, and YouTube

Learn more at www.briandickinson.net